THE
MONSTROUS
KIND

THE
MONSTROUS
KIND

LYDIA GREGOVIC

DELACORTE PRESS

Text copyright © 2024 by Lydia Gregovic, LLC
Jacket art copyright © 2024 by Christin Engelberth
Map art copyright © 2024 by artist

All rights reserved. Published in the United States by Delacorte Press, an imprint of Random House Children's Books, a division of Penguin Random House LLC, New York.

Delacorte Press is a registered trademark and the colophon is a trademark of Penguin Random House LLC.

Visit us on the Web! GetUnderlined.com

Educators and librarians, for a variety of teaching tools, visit us at RHTeachersLibrarians.com

Library of Congress Cataloging-in-Publication Data is available upon request.
ISBN 978-0-593-57237-5 (trade) — ISBN 978-0-593-57238-2 (ebook) —
ISBN 978-0-593-90266-0 (international ed.)

The text of this book is set in 11-point Mrs Eaves XL.

Printed in the United States of America
10 9 8 7 6 5 4 3 2 1
First Edition

For Nevenka and Geneva,

who believed in me first,

and for Milan and Merlin,

who gave me my history

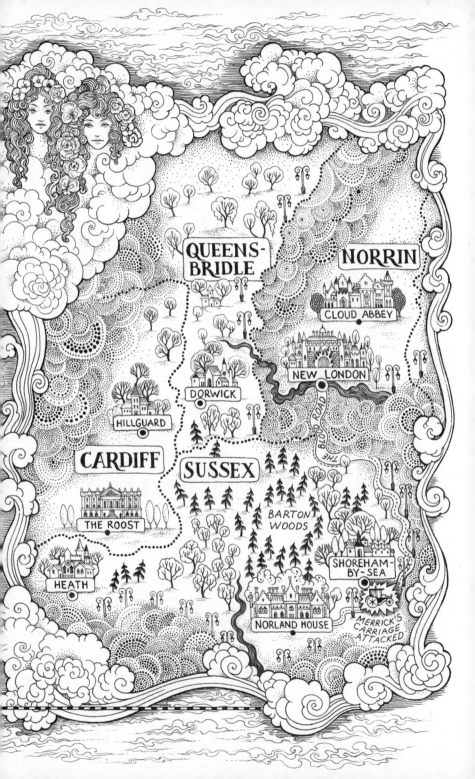

A GUIDE TO THE
MANORS OF THE SMOKE

SAVAGER

Reigning over the untamed North, the Savagers are foes best left uncrossed: wild as the land on which they dwell, with memories as deep as the famed archives they keep beneath their gloomy estate of Castle Mount.

Manor Lord: Warden Savager

Rule over: Cael

BALLANTINE

Caught between the mercurial Savagers and the bloodthirsty Warchilds, Manorborn of the Ballantine lineage are born looking over their shoulders—but beware, for like all cornered beasts, they bite quickly when threatened.

Manor Lord: Hyacinth Ballantine

Rule over: Umberland

WARCHILD

Unmatched in combat, the Warchilds are true to their name, guarding their province ferociously. Yet under young Lord Percival, they have exchanged their swords for satins and their battles for balls.

Manor Lord: Percival Warchild

Rule over: Rochester

VANNETT

The Vannetts are a steadfast and loyal Manor, regarded highly by all. But in their haste to aid their many friends' ascents up the social ladder, they often find themselves left at the bottom.

Manor Lord: Corinth Vannett

Rule over: Heatherton

SAINT

Presiding over the rural province of Cardiff, the parochial Saints have long been overlooked by their cosmopolitan colleagues. Leave a Manor in the shadows for too long, though, and one risks losing track of what it is doing in the dark.

Manor Lord: Ianthe Saint

Rule over: Cardiff

CACHEMAR

A common saying in Levath advises, "Cachemars and birds travel in flocks." Members of this Manor are rarely seen without at least one of their relations—and when they strike, they do so together.

Manor Lord: Lavinia Cachemar

Rule over: Levath

CARRINGTON

Cast to the far corner of the Smoke, the Carringtons are used to watching the political games of their fellow Manorborn from afar. If they do choose to enter the fray, take caution—they are keen-eyed, and do not miss a trick.

Manor Lord: Florabelle Carrington

Rule over: Southhook

DARLING

The Darling Manor's proud family tree has suffered its fair share of blows in recent years—the latest, the death of Manor Lord Silas Darling himself. Which of his two daughters will ascend to carry on his legacy?

Manor Lord: Silas Darling (deceased)

Rule over: Sussex

IRELAND

Critics of this Manor often say that the Irelands' love of luxury keeps half the nation's dressmakers employed. Their supporters, however, would argue that more wars have been fought and won on the dance floors of Lord Clare Ireland's balls than any other place in the nation.

Manor Lord: Clare Ireland

Rule over: Queensbridle

FAULK

The five granddaughters of Manor Lord Elodie Faulk have been praised across the provinces for their beauty. But tread carefully around these diamonds, for they have been known to cut.

Manor Lord: Elodie Faulk

Rule over: Norrin

IBE

Masters of propriety, Manorborn of the Ibe family have been known to treat a mislaid dinner invitation as an offense as great as an attack on their borders. Yet to earn the friendship of this Manor is to make an ally for generations.

Manor Lord: Reginald Ibe

Rule over: Ridewell

TUDOR

A vicious and formidable Manor, Tudor sharpens its young like daggers from their infancy. These unfortunate children's first opponents? Commonly, members of their own family.

Manor Lord: Albion Tudor

Rule over: Kyrie

The New London Toast

Saturday, September 13, Year 211 of the Turning

There is nary a heart in all the Smoke that will not hang low upon hearing today's sorrowful news—His Eminence, the esteemed Manor Lord Silas Darling, died early yesterday in his home, the Darling Manor seat of Norland House. Fall's approach shall now certainly be hastened, as even the trees shall shed their leaves at the loss of this great man, who did nobly shepherd the province of Sussex for over two decades, safeguarding those who dwelled within against the wicked hunger of the Phantom horde. With his passing, every Saxon has lost their father.

Slayer of beasts and protector of borders, Lord Silas is preceded in death by his wife, the beloved Manor Lady Artemis Darling, and is survived by his two daughters, Archdaughters Estella and Merrick Darling.

PART ONE

Ghost Stories

Who is the maid who knocks at night?
Her arms are bare, her eyes, pure white.
Her face is one you knew before,
the bride you lost to mist and moor.
But though she cries, trust not your flesh.
She is a stranger; she is your death.

"THE MAID WHO KNOCKS AT NIGHT,"
CHILDREN'S SKIPPING RHYME, CIRCA
THE SMOKE, YEAR 32 OF THE TURNING

CHAPTER ONE

In the end, it is death that calls me home again.

I rest my forehead against the cool glass of the carriage window, attempting to lose myself in the crisp evening chill of it on my skin, its smoothness like an unbroken crust of ice atop a pond. When I fled Norland House last May, spring was unfurling; now the beginnings of autumn have perfumed the air with decay. Somewhere beneath the wheels of my vehicle, worms slide through the summer-dark earth, waiting for nature to shed its past season like a snakeskin for them to feast on.

The route I'm traveling should be familiar to me. After all, it is the same path I took when I left home—only the direction is different, heading toward our province rather than away from it. Yet gazing through the window at the stretch of rugged landscape beyond, the scenery seems utterly foreign to my eyes, any recollection of it tossed forcibly from my mind months prior like a glove I'd outgrown.

What was there to remember? Up until a week ago, I'd believed I was never coming back.

Merrick—Papa is gone. If you've no more pressing social obligations, I urge you to return to Sussex at once.

My sister's words have burned themselves onto the backs of my eyelids like a brand, searing me anew every time I blink.

Even before I'd read the letter, I'd been suspicious when the Eaveses' footman handed me a letter bearing the Darling seal—my Manor's seal—on it at breakfast two mornings ago. I hadn't heard from my sister since my hasty departure from Norland House just over four months past. My leaving was the second blow to our proud family tree in a little over a fortnight: three weeks prior to it, the beloved Lady Artemis Darling's coach had been found overturned at the edge of the Graylands, what was left of her remains a few yards beyond her vessel, cast aside like a napkin tossed from the table. The tragedy quickly consumed our province, though it was not, exactly, unexpected. Even in a place as well-guarded as Sussex, we all knew the risks of traveling so close to the border. Knew what dwelled on the other side of the fiery lamps, hidden in the mists—had seen the bones of the victims they left behind, shards of ivory picked clean, pure and white as sacrificial lambs.

At the thought of my family, guilt presses at my chest, a balled fist against my sternum. After Mama's death, I should have stayed with my sister and my father. I should have mourned. Instead, I remained by their side for less than a month before running as fast and as far as I could like a rabbit sprinting from its burrow.

Do not leave me here alone. My sister's voice is a whisper in my mind, her plea one that has trailed behind me like a heavy train with each mile I've traveled, threaded its way through every crowd at all the gilded parties I've attended while in New London. Even before Mama's death, Essie and I had been drifting apart for some time—as we aged, it became harder and harder to deny that beyond any blood ties, we were chiefly one another's competition—but still, the distance between us hadn't lessened the sting I felt when I'd denied her. She'd asked me for help that day, and I'd abandoned her without any, without so much as a backward glance before I had the maids whisk the rest of my luggage out the door.

The truth was, I left because I couldn't stand to be in the same province with her, much less the same house. Not when the memory of what my father had told me was angled like a knife to my neck, hindering my every breath.

A shiver runs down my spine as from his bench up front, the driver guides the horses around a bend, bringing Sussex's coastline fully into view. Bathed in the vicious tangerine glow of the sunset, jagged seaside cliffs gnash limestone fangs at the darkening sky, while from far below I can hear the hushed crash of frothing waves lapping at the pebbled strip of shore like dogs begging for scraps. A line of iron lampposts extends along the cliff edge for as far as I can see in either direction, fires burning steadily in the lanterns that hang from each of their boughs, blazing against the approaching night.

Beyond that lies the fog.

It has long since swallowed the beach whole, twining, ivylike, up the cliffside before cresting over its top like ocean spray. Banks of mist the color of dripping candle wax fill my vision, undulating gently just outside the fire's reach like a nest of eels. Where the weak evening sun hits it, the fog gleams with a metallic gray sheen, like coins catching the light.

The Graylands. That's what we call them—the mist-choked, uninhabitable swaths of our nation, the Smoke, contained only by legions of fiery border lamps like the ones in front of me. My ancestors erected the first of the barriers almost two centuries ago, and in the years since they've become our primary line of defense in our fight against the fog that otherwise would seep onto our land like pus from a wound.

That would bring its monsters with it.

Unease settles over me like a coat of damp morning dew. When I was a girl, the Graylands only licked the base of the cliffs in this area. Now, despite my family's best efforts, the mist lurks a couple meters away from the road, hovering in the corner of my eye like an unwelcome guest. A few more years—a few more breaches—and we'll likely have to remap this route entirely.

I force my thoughts away from the subject. Those of us born in the centuries after the fog's arrival have grown used to living like holidaymakers at low tide. We eat and drink, we even laugh on occasion, but we know that regardless of any defenses we raise, one day the water will come and sweep us all away.

Just as it swept away my parents, I think. Frustratingly, the obituary the papers ran about Father's passing was as scarce on details as my sister's letter had been. But as Manor Lord of Sussex, Silas Darling had more contact with the Graylands than most in our land. Part of our sacred bargain, is how Father always described it to me—the hundreds-of-years-old pact made between my ancestors, the original twelve Manor Lords, and those they governed. Manorborn, like my family, use the immunity we've been gifted against the mist's transformative touch to protect our respective provinces: repairing damaged border lamps, overseeing patrols, and, when necessary, slaying the beasts that slip through the cracks in our armor. In return, a portion of each province's income is reserved for the ruling Manor. It is a system that has been honed through the turning of the generations, a birthright that passes from Manorborn to Manorborn like a lit torch—unfaltering, unfailing.

I remember the first time I followed my father into the fog. I was thirteen, barely past my first blood, when it happened: a

Phantom spotted along the cliffy southern ridge of Sussex, apparently having evaded our patrols. Father and I tracked it together, following it along the seaside before plunging after it into the Graylands, snaring the creature just as it tried to escape into the milky obscurity of its home. I can still see it—the way the mist parted in plumes around my father's back as he rode like enormous feathered wings. As if he were some divine warrior sent from the heavens, untouchable to us mere mortals.

Yet looking at the mist now, I can't help but wonder if it has inched closer in the time I've been away. Whether one of the creatures Father hunted finally bit him back.

Leaning against my seat, I fish in my handbag for a distraction—and am rewarded when my fingers brush the pulpy skin of a folded newsprint. Carefully, I pull the paper out and flatten it in my lap. The Eaveses, long-time family friends as well as pillars of New London's social scene, are devoted subscribers of *The New London Toast,* our capital's most notorious scandal sheet and required reading for any young lady attempting to navigate the treacherous waters of its season. I managed to snag the latest edition just before I left, intending to save it for whenever I needed a touch of drama to disrupt the stillness of my journey.

I glance again at the banks of mist outside my window, the empty miles of countryside stretching out before me like an unfinished canvas. Now, I think, seems like exactly that time.

The *Toast* is easy to skim. I breeze through the first couple paragraphs before the sight of my own name catches my attention, making me hunch over in a distinctly unladylike fashion to better make out the inky words:

Readers will delight to hear that our jewel of the season, the beguiling Archdaughter Merrick Darling, continued her shining reign at Lady Fairfax's ball on Friday last. Though the Archdaughter's card was filled with admirers attempting to capture her heart, our watchful eye noted that she gave two dances to only one gentleman: Sir Fitzgerald Vannett of the Vannett Manor. Could it be that New London's most treasured dove has at last found a nest in which to roost? Our sources tell us an offer has not yet been made, but if we have learned anything from observing last year's hunt, it is that a prized stag is sure to attract a chase.

Relief spills through me, and I flutter my eyes closed. So they were watching—just as I'd hoped they'd be. Good. Fitz was a pleasant enough companion at Fairfax's ball, though not pleasant enough to justify the grueling hours in front of my vanity that I'd been forced to endure prior to dancing with him. More important, though, as a member of one of the Smoke's twelve ruling families—even if he is the son of a lower-ranking Rouge rather than a powerful Red Duke or a Marquess of the Blood—his attention should stoke the interest of other suitors.

Interest I'll need when I return to New London after Father's funeral. Desperately, if I'm honest. As the past months have taught me, the only thing Manorborn love more than a society darling is a girl scorned. The *Toast* may be singing my praises for the moment, but my aforementioned shine would tarnish fast if they knew the truth.

The reason that unlike my ancestors, the only hunting I'm currently doing is for a husband.

The piercing shriek of the horse's whinny is a blade through my thoughts. My eyes fly open as the carriage judders, its wooden skeleton rattling and making my teeth clack together on impact. Steadying myself, I grip the padded bench beneath me with both hands and turn my gaze to the window, my heart a thrashing bird.

I suck in a breath. Not ten yards ahead of our carriage, the air is clouded and opaque with fog—a mass of it, glowing with a silvery spectral aura that seems to flare brighter the longer I watch. And somehow, directly in our path.

Panicked, I glance toward the line of lampposts, searching for protection in the form of a pinprick of orange light. Ice cracks through my chest when I make out a gap in the lamps' ranks, a shadowed spot like an abscess—one of the lanterns up ahead is dark, creating a passageway for the mist to leak through. Now milky tendrils of it wind their way up the iron post affectionately, caressing the metal. Squeezing it tightly.

A breach. In Sussex. My breath catches. While far from impossible, for as long as I've been alive, a downed border lantern has been an event rare enough that a person could almost forget the last one before the next arrived. In other provinces, governed by weaker Manors, breaches are a daily concern—but not here. At least, not under my father's rule. The fire should be holding the Graylands back.

For a fevered moment, the world stills, time catching and holding as if it, too, is hesitant to plunge ahead. Then the snap of the driver's whip breaks me free again, and I am back in my body, hurtling toward the fog.

I lurch forward, pounding on the glass divider that separates the passenger compartment from the driver's seat so hard I half expect it to shatter.

"Are you mad?" The words rip from me, rough with terror; on his bench in front of me, the driver wrestles with his reins, yanking them left, then right, to no avail. The horse charges onward. I raise my voice. "Stop your beast, now, before we—"

A white wall swallows us.

I watch, stricken silent, as ahead of me, the mist wraps its maw around the driver, plunging him into its depths. Blood roars in my ears. My limbs feel waterlogged, heavy and bloated; I stare, motionless, as if from the bottom of a lake, as cottony plumes of fog web across the carriage windows, blinding me to anything beyond.

Outside, all is quiet, muffled as if by a thick quilt as I feel the carriage grind to a creaky halt.

Bile rises in my throat. *The driver.* Where is he? I strain my eyes, struggling to make out anything other than the ivory curtain that hangs over my surroundings. Manorborn or not, all children of the Smoke are taught what to do in the event of a breach as soon as they can walk. First, cover your nose and mouth. For everyone except the Manorborn, breathing in the mist means a death more certain than any bullet.

And, the almost-as-essential second rule: keep moving. It is when you stop—during that thin pause between one inhale and the next, when you think the danger is finally at your back—that they find you.

I'm still squinting into the blind white when I hear it: a wet, organic noise, like an untidy dinner companion gnawing at a leg of lamb. Chewing; the meaty grind of teeth against flesh.

My nausea swirls, solidifies into a fear leaden and hot. No matter how many times I've followed my father and his men into the Graylands before, this terror never fails to surprise me. A nightmare-panic, a swift descent into those realms of bent reality where monsters are real—where they can wander off the pages of a storybook, sit at your breakfast table.

Eat you up.

A Phantom. It's here.

As if in response, a sickening crack resounds from somewhere in the mist beyond the carriage, the crisp snap of a bone. A spatter of crimson sprays across the window to my right, droplets of blood hitting the glass like a sudden fall of rain. My instincts finally kicking in, I reach slowly toward my ankle, lifting my skirts to retrieve the knife strapped to my calf. I'd prefer the familiar weight of my Ghostslayer, but I'd been forced to give up my favored pistol when I arrived in New London—the Eaveses having deemed weapons unseemly accessories for the society crowd, and rather unsuitable for tea.

Luckily for me, Mr. Eaves is a gentleman and didn't bother to check my person for blades after my arrival, or my current predicament would be much more dire.

Outside, the chewing stops.

What little breath I had left leaves my lungs as a shadow falls across my lap—at first barely brushing the edge of my skirt, then spreading farther as its owner advances steadily nearer. I keep my stare fixed on the wavering charcoal stain, clutching the hilt of the knife tightly in my fist, my father's voice echoing in my mind.

Strike first, and strike hard. Target its weak points: base of spine, groin, knees. Remember, the creatures were men once. They may die as a man may.

Tap, tap. Like a meek houseguest, something raps tentatively at the glass. A second later, it comes again: *tap, tap, tap.*

I say a quick, wordless prayer to the Divine Three—the Burning King, the Lightkeeper, and the Bloodletter, the triumvirate of gods believed to watch over the Smoke, who legend tells were the ones to bless the original Manor Lords with their immunity. Then I look up.

For a moment, I almost believe the creature on the other side of the window is human. It was, once, before the mist crept into its veins and made them flow ivory instead of red, burrowed deep into its mind and ate and ate and ate until there was nothing left. Now the Phantom's eyes are pure white, bulbous spider's eggs set into its bony face. The little skin that still clings to its skull is shrunken and tough, like its head is a dried apple, most of the peel fallen away. Wiry strips of sinew and muscle bind its bones together, and from its mouth, chipped, yellowed teeth sprout from blackened gums, gnashing and chittering against one another as if in depraved song.

At the sight of it, something in me shutters, sealing away the soft parts of myself until I am nothing but a hard shell, resolute and ready for a fight. *This.* Though I've refused to admit it, this is what I've missed the past months, while I've been busy letting the Eaveses polish me into the season's most precious jewel, pretty and sparkling and light. This challenge—this ephemeral boundary between life and death, when survival is nothing but a gamble, a bet you make with yourself.

This is who I've trained to be. Not the girl Father forced me to become when he—

The Phantom throws itself against the carriage door—locked, though that won't last long—violently, its ragged-nailed hands scraping down the vehicle's sides. With nowhere to go, I raise the knife higher, steel myself, and wait.

The window shatters beneath the Phantom's claws. I leap forward to meet it, wincing as a sliver of flying glass bites into my cheek. Just before my knife connects with its chest, a burst of sound like a clap of thunder rips through the fog, and I fall back. An agonized howl emits from the Phantom's throat, a horrible droning shriek like a swarm of bees—inhuman, unearthly. Stupefied, I can only look on as the creature slumps forward, thudding against the window frame before falling out of sight to the ground.

Around me, the mist pulses noiselessly, the echo of the shot trembling through the air like the lingering hum of a violin. I clutch at my chest, which is burning painfully, as if it had expected to fall out of use and now isn't sure how to function again.

You're fine, Merrick. You're alive, you're—

The carriage door wrenches open with a splintering of wood.

I barely have time to register the man's face, half-hidden behind a knotted handkerchief, emerging from the mist like a ghost. A hand wraps around my head, pushing a cotton rag over my nose and lips, and then the man is lifting me from my seat, pulling me up, out—

Into the fog.

CHAPTER TWO

F ire fills my vision: a torch, held aloft like a beacon in the man's other hand. The flame is a scythe, cutting through the smothering haze, which hisses like a snuffed-out candle at the heat's kiss.

I'm dragged forward through the narrow corridor of fresh air, the mist knitting seamlessly back together in my wake. More of it slides over my slippers—inky satin, and entirely inconvenient—as I walk, watery and pale-bellied as a dead fish. It seems to tug at me with each step, clinging, vinelike, to my skin.

My stomach turns at its slick caress, the wet, oily feel of it as it twines up my leg. I've ventured into the Graylands before, but I've never quite managed to get used to the experience of traveling within them. How close up, the mist has a presence, pervasive as pond damp through a wool cloak.

The fog climbs higher, brushing the back of my knee. Its touch is almost familiar, as if it remembers me—has been patiently waiting for the day I returned to it. Resisting the urge to gag, I scan the area around me for movement, the lurch of a body hurtling toward us. The blank whiteness is oppressive, its empty stare impossible to parse, but that in itself says nothing. Unlike their unturned, human brethren, Phantoms are able to easily navigate the fog by way of their heightened hearing, an unfortunate gift from their pale maker. And they rarely stalk alone.

In the distance to my left, I think I see the haze waver, part, as if around a hunched form—

Then the man gives me a hard yank and we're through it—out into the clear evening. Immediately, I pull away from him, ripping the cloth from my face. The taste of the surrounding countryside floods into my mouth, sweet on my tongue: the humid brine of the ocean, the musky tang of seabirds nesting at its fringes. I've always preferred the smoke-and-sweat aroma of the city to the wild, pungent scent of nature, but now I heave in deep gulps of it as if it were holy water, as if it alone can cleanse me of the Graylands' touch.

Next to me, my savior—captor?—swipes at the banks of fog with his torch, burning away their furred edges. The effect won't last long, but graciously, the mist is as slow-moving as it is deadly. We should have a few minutes, at least, before it makes up the lost ground and wraps us in its arms again.

Once he's finished, the man pulls down his own handkerchief, exposing the lower half of his face, before staking his torch in the ground and reaching for something at his side. I catch the flash of a sleek silver pistol—a Ghostslayer, I note, its compact size designed specifically for easy portability in instances like this—holstered at his right hip and tense reflexively, but he passes over it, pushing something cool and metal into my hands instead.

"You should drink."

His voice is soft, not quiet so much as carefully, precisely measured, as though if he expends too much of it at once, it will run out. Despite it, and despite his aid, a rush of irritation boils through me at his brusque address. Throughout our childhood years, Essie frequently chastised me for my hotheadedness—I prickle easily at any perceived affront, whereas she is like the sea that stretches out to my side, slow to churn but deadly when it does so.

Father preferred my sister's style of anger—calculated and controlled—over my tempestuous emotions, which he always said were detrimental to a ruler. But then again, he preferred almost everything Essie did.

Biting back my annoyance, I turn the object—a flask, simple and unadorned—over in my grasp before lifting it to my lips, letting the cool water within slide down my throat. It leaves behind a bitter aftertaste, like greening copper.

Slightly steadied, I pass the flask back and lift my gaze to examine the man standing in front of me. At second glance, I'm surprised to find he's barely more than a boy—likely only a couple years past my own seventeen. The fading sunlight glances off a collection of raised ridges that cut haphazardly across his skin. Scars, I realize with a start, gone vining and white with age. One streaks like a bolt of lightning through his right eyebrow, just missing the corner of his eye as it cuts its way toward his cheek; farther down his face, a savage cleft splices his upper lip like a chunk of skin has been bitten off. I trail my gaze over a particularly knotted mark along his neck and question if a Phantom gave it to him—if, perhaps, I am not the first girl he's pulled from a mist-choked carriage with a monster beating down her door.

If so, I wonder what he's doing here, roaming the shores of my province like a rogue searching for a damsel to whisk away from distress.

The boy watches me as I observe him, silent and calculating, his eyes ticking over my face like he's marking off the seconds as they pass. One of his eyes is brown; the other is pale blue, the pure, crystalline color of January ice. His stare is intense—it's disconcerting, itching at me the longer I look.

I glance away.

"Thank you for the rescue, back there," I say, feeling slightly as though I've lost a contest of some kind. "Though," I add, flipping my knife around in my grasp and thrusting it toward him, hilt first, "I had the situation under control."

"Did you now?" the boy asks. There's no mockery in his tone—just that same, steady tenor—but when I snap my gaze up, I catch the flicker of a smirk pulling at his lips. "Well, in that case, there is no need to thank me. I suppose it was not a rescue at all."

Our eyes meet again; before I can react, his hand is darting out and slipping the blade from my grip with the practiced ease of a pickpocket.

"This is a fine weapon." The boy cuts off my cry of protest, rotating the knife one way, then the other, so that it bleeds in the orange-red dusk. Then he lowers it, offering it back to me. "To where are you traveling, if I may ask?"

I snatch the knife back, clutching it like a lifeline. "To home," I snap.

The boy raises a brow, unruffled. "Home?"

"Yes." *Calm, Merrick. Whoever this boy is, he is your inferior in rank. Do not cede your control.*

I bite down on the inside of my cheek, forcing my tone flatter. "If you must know, my father has just passed. I've been called back for his funeral."

"Your father . . ." For the first time, uncertainty carves furrows into the boy's brow. His gaze rakes over me again, lingering on my hair—blond curls, now come loose from their neat bun and wisping around my face—my unfashionably thick eyebrows, and my sharp Darling nose, before he bends at the waist in a bow. I can almost feel the moment his eyes leave me—my skin pricks as if his gaze is a tangible thing, leaving behind a tacky residue.

"Forgive me, Archdaughter Merrick," he says, two spots of pink blooming high on his cheeks. "I—I did not recognize you."

Any sense of victory at his apology is rapidly usurped by discomfort at his supplication. The sound of my title pinches at me like a too-tight corset—a false crown. While all descendants of a Manor receive the gift of its immunity, we are divided according to rank and duties: at the top of the system of peerage is the Manor Lord, the Manor's head, who governs the province and helms its defenses, followed closely in power by a handful of Red Dukes and Duchesses—usually direct relations of a Lord, such as his siblings or married children. Beyond that, in descending order of influence, follow the ranks of Marquess and Marquioness of the Blood, Sanguin and Sanguine, Rouge and Rougess, and lastly the simple Sir and Lady. Archdaughter, my own title, is a rare one, used only for the unmarried daughters of a Manor Lord.

But my Lord is dead.

"And you are?" I ask quickly—too quickly, likely, though the boy doesn't seem to notice. The fact that he entered the mist at all, earlier, tells me he must be Manorborn, too, though he doesn't bear a resemblance to any Darling relation that I know. Has he traveled from one of the other provinces, perhaps, to pay his respects to Father? I squint at him. Not a Ballantine, certainly—the hair is all wrong, his a muted blond like dried wheat rather than their characteristic auburn. Perhaps a Warchild, or a Carrington?

"Brandon, my lady," he replies, straightening, before I can consider him further. "Killian Brandon. At your service, of course."

He turns, shifting his attention back toward the fog that rises like a swell of surf behind us. "We'll need to move soon," the boy—Killian—says. "The others won't be far behind me—I sent up a flare soon as I saw your coach go into the mist. They'll want to perform a burning before any more territory is lost."

My nose wrinkles with confusion. "The others?" I echo.

The boy angles his chin my way at my comment, and at once, I pick out the details in his wardrobe I missed before: the red epaulets that glint from the shoulders of his dove-gray coat, the crisp white breeches they're paired with, and stockings beneath. The single ruby brooch in the shape of a rose gleaming on his breast.

The Darling crest.

Understanding wings through me like the swoop of a bird. "You're one of my father's sentries," I say as Killian dips his head in confirmation. Easier now that I've placed him, I offer him a conciliatory smile. So he *isn't* a foreign well-wisher, then. Though . . .

"Brandon—I don't believe I'm familiar with that branch of the family." I turn his surname over in my mind. "To which great-aunt do I owe a thank-you for my safety?"

I search his face again, hunting for some hint of my relatives in his mauled features. It is strange to think that somewhere, deep in our veins, he and I share the same blood—that he is technically my kin. Another piece of the Manors' bargain: while guardianship of a province is a responsibility primarily carried by its Lord, additional bodies are needed to assist in the executing of patrols, the maintenance of our borders. As only Manorborn can safely risk working in such close proximity to the Graylands—without immunity to protect them, exposure to a potential breach would mean disaster for all others—it is not uncommon for the children of lower-ranking members of the Darling Manor to enter into a year or two of militia service in the hopes of gaining the favor of their Lord once their term is completed.

To serve as a sentry is considered a role of utmost valiance, not only because of the physical risks posed by the Phantoms, but also because those on the fringes of a Manor are more likely to secure less advantageous matches—matches that fall outside the twelve noble houses—resulting in descendants of mixed lineage. Growing up a young Manorborn lady, I was treated to no shortage of cautionary tales: stories about doomed branches of a Manor whose bloodlines became too diluted, to the point that their offspring no longer inherited their ancestors' gifts. My father's own marriage to my mother—a commoner—created a scandal unlike anything Sussex had seen for generations, one that died only when my and my sister's immunity was proven, years later.

Some sentries stay on even after their service has ended and rise through the ranks, but most are content to accept a parcel of land somewhere in the north of Sussex, away from the mist's reaching grasp, and let the memories of their past battles waste away in the backs of their minds like a pair of moth-eaten trousers. Let them become soft and easy to the touch, until they can almost believe that the monsters they once fought were nothing more than legend.

As for those of us left behind—we do not have the same luxury.

But Killian is shaking his head.

"I'm not a Darling, Archdaughter. My mother hails from Kyrie—her father was a Rouge of the Tudor Manor, but he gave his title and the accompanying land to her brother, my uncle, leaving us unfortunately bereft after my own father's passing last year. I only arrived in Sussex a little less than a month ago, in response to Archdaughter Estella's call offering territory in exchange for more men."

His comment sends a jab of alarm through my gut. It isn't that recruiting sentries from other provinces is unheard of—several times during my childhood, in fact, Father was asked to lend troops to some ailing Lord or another—but most Manors avoid doing so if they can, the corresponding implication being that one's own blood is no longer enough to defend one's people. And my own province, Sussex, has certainly never needed any help.

I picture again the single dead lantern lost somewhere in the mist behind me, a black, rotten tooth in the curved smile of the border. Have there been more incidents like the one I've just experienced while I've been away? No gossip of the sort reached me in New London, but if there have, how many people were not lucky enough to have a sentry nearby them when the Phantoms came calling—and how many monsters escaped unscathed, left to prowl the misty coastline?

Did one of them kill Father?

Stop it, I chastise myself. *You're getting ahead of yourself, Merrick.*

But then there is the other piece of Killian's remark—the one that digs at me for reasons all the more personal. "You say my sister employed you?" I ask Killian, forcing my mind to clear. "I should think that would have been a Manor Lord's responsibility, no? Was my father aware of these recruitment efforts of Essie's?"

He promised me that he would wait . . .

Killian grimaces, shifting his weight from one leg to the other as if my question unsettles him. "I do not wish to speak out of turn, Archdaughter, but I believe Manor Lord Silas was . . . unwell in the months before his passing," he replies, his eyes skittering away from mine. "I know nothing in detail—only that since my enlistment, I have taken orders from your sister."

"Papa was sick? Is that why he passed—because of an illness?" The stone in my gut grows heavier, the vitriol in Essie's note calling me home suddenly feeling more justified than ever—if in leaving Norland House when I did, I abandoned her not only to the memories of a vanished mother but to the reality of a father ambling slowly toward death himself.

"I believe his condition was more mental in nature," Killian replies haltingly. "As I said, I cannot supply you with details, but word among the sentries' barracks was that he was sick with grief over the loss of your mother."

Oh. Shame floods me, thick as tar. "I . . . I did not realize he was suffering so. I have been away for the past months, residing with family friends in New London. If Papa had written to me—"

"I am not passing judgment on your absence, Archdaughter Merrick," Killian says, cutting me off.

The directness of his words draws me back to him. Despite his blunt manner, his tone is surprisingly mild, accommodating in a way that I might otherwise attribute to a priest, a person used to the hearing and absolving of sins. His gaze is open, sincere; I can sense how easily, if I were to confess my guilt over my departure to him, he would forgive me. The idea is as tempting as a warm bath.

The thought of it makes me bristle. "And whatever do you mean by that?" I challenge.

His wintry eye pins me, a needle through my center. "Only that I, too, am far from home. And I have learned that most of our kind do not leave without good reason."

A beat of silence passes between us then. My lips part in response just as, high and piercing, a whinny crests over the horizon, the quiet breaking like a twig underfoot. Killian twists toward the noise, a relieved exhale escaping from his mouth.

"They're here," he sighs before turning back to me. "Allow me to escort you home, Archdaughter."

The screams of Phantoms follow us as we ride away.

True to Killian's word, the rest of his regiment arrived shortly after he did, on horseback and with Ghostslayers at their sides. They cordoned off the mist-covered section of the cliffside first, creating a makeshift border with fiery stakes shoved into the ground, then slipped between them to disappear into the white haze, weapons in hand. We left before their hunt was complete, but I knew from experience that after they'd finished searching the breached ground for bodies—Phantom or human, dead or alive, though few of the latter category were ever recovered—the sentries would then set fire to the affected area, razing it utterly in the hopes of burning the fog back.

I'd pictured the border lamps again, how the fog had clung so closely to them when only years prior, it had been forced to prowl along the rocky beach below. Even if our men managed to reclaim most of the lost land today, how much more territory would we cede to the Graylands? A centimeter? Two?

How many did we have left to spare?

When the first shot rang out at our backs, I'd been caught off guard by the rush of pity that had pulsed momentarily through me. Not a half hour earlier, a Phantom had almost taken my life—nevertheless, I couldn't deny the whisper that told me their deaths were no triumph.

Whether one of the monsters killed me, or I them, we were always just eating our own.

Killian and I pass the return journey in silence atop the horse he commandeered from one of his fellow sentries, my arms slung uncomfortably around his waist. The position is one of practicality, yet the warmth of him seeping into my bones is excruciatingly intimate after the rigid rules of New London courtship. There, every flirtation was a game of chess, something to be strategized and precisely planned, each side working diligently toward their desired end: money, most often, or status. Sex, for some, though I was always too frightened of the consequences to engage in any trysts.

Love, I learned early on during my stay, could result in

mistakes, sloppiness—both of which could damage a girl's reputation irrevocably, Manorborn or no. And I'd worked tirelessly to keep mine spotless, to abstain from any activities that might warrant me a closer look, lest the secrets I was keeping seep like stains through my dress.

To distract myself, I watch the countryside as it rolls past: the cottages glowing yellow from the inside with candlelight, the neatly tended pastures dotted with wide-eyed cows. This is the Sussex of my memories—a portrait of pastoral innocence, safe and simple and *boring*. But try as I might to forget it, the image of the Phantom's fangs bearing down on me has firmly etched itself into the grooves of my mind, overhanging my thoughts like a coal-bellied rain cloud.

My eyelids droop with weariness, lower closed. *The fog, rushing toward me like a leaping cat, wrapping around the driver—*

My shoulders tense. I force my eyes open.

Killian's chin angles in my direction, just a hair. "Are you all right, Archdaughter?"

I wish I'd never mentioned my father, my title. Though I know he doesn't mean it, Killian's address sounds too much like a mockery—a reminder of that which I've lost. "Fine," I reply tightly. Placated, the sentry dips his head in a nod of acceptance, his attention ahead of himself once again.

"Mr. Brandon." The sound of my own voice surprises me; I hadn't realized I intended to call out to him until his name was on my lips. "If you don't mind—may I ask you a question?"

From his position in front of me, Killian nods his assent. "Of course, Archdaughter."

Keeping my hands fastened around his waist, I lean back in the saddle, following the line of my thoughts in reverse until I find the snarl in the thread that's been needling at me. "Well, it's only that I've been pondering what you said earlier—about my sister putting out a call for more sentries. I am surprised that no news of her decision reached me in New London." I shrug nonchalantly, the gesture lost to the countryside and the flat landscape of the sentry's unseeing shoulders. "Gossip tends to travel fast in the capital, is all."

Though it may be my imagination, I think I feel Killian tense in my hold. "Archdaughter Estella preferred that the recruitment be carried out with as much discretion as possible," he answers slowly. "She had concerns about how the province would react to such news, I believe."

"Yes, but what led her to take such drastic measures in the first place?" I push, emboldened. Killian says nothing, only curls his knuckles around his horse's reins, flicking them to drive the beast onward. He seems defensive—I can make out his profile, and his jaw is taut, like a cornered fox's.

By contrast, I am a hound that has caught a scent. "Please, sir," I urge. "You must understand how upsetting this entire situation is for me. I wish only to understand."

Killian's shoulders bunch together. For a long moment, he is quiet, and I think I've lost him, but then his voice comes again. It's softer this time.

"There may have been other . . . incidents . . . recently," he says, glancing back at me. "Similar to the one you just experienced."

My pulse thrums faster, my breath catching. "Other breaches, you mean?"

Jerkily, Killian inclines his head in confirmation. The air trapped in my lungs turns rancid, tickles at me like smoke.

"How many?" I press—possibly too far, any question could be too far, but now that the chase has begun I find myself unwilling to relent.

Killian hesitates, his silence heavy with an emotion I can't place. By the way it slides over my skin, though, I'd almost call it fear.

A shiver trips along my spine as he clears his throat. "Forgive me, Archdaughter, I cannot say more," he says, and there is the line—I've found it, and I've crossed it. "You must speak with your sister—she has forbidden us from discussing the topic."

"Yes, but—" I begin a rebuttal only to let it die away as, just as the sun is about to dip beneath the horizon, we crest a hill and I see it: the angular body of Norland House looming like a stone leviathan in the distance. Its craggy structure, centuries older than I am, has been designed for intimidation. Rambling wings, erected in the Georgian style by some pre-Smoke noble-man, blot out the setting sunlight; arched windows stand half in shadow, like hooded, sleepy eyes. The entirety of the estate, from the weathered brick to the roof shingles, is a deep, violent red. It drips crimson in the dusk, even the shadows a slow bleed of scar-let, syrupy and viscous as they seep into the ground.

I can feel the house's presence pulsing through the atmo-sphere like the beat of a living organ. Along with the sensation, a bitter nostalgia rises within me. There was a time when I believed I would never leave this place—that it was an extension of my very being, the same way every Darling is an extension of one singular line, forever growing from the same roots. Now, seeing Norland feels like standing in a foreign land and dreaming of home. As soon as Father's funeral is over, I will bid it farewell again—and the next time I return, it will be with a new name.

In front of me, Killian winces, the movement so slight I might have missed it, were I not clinging so closely to him. I flush when I notice my nails, digging nervously into his torso like talons. Forc-ing my hands to unclench, I shift as far away from him as I dare, keeping my vision trained on the estate while we approach.

Our horse has barely come to a stop at the end of the wind-ing gravel drive when the front doors of Norland House fly open. A young woman strides out from between them, tendrils of her long black hair whipping free from her bun and waving in the breeze like dark ribbons, and even at this distance, I feel the weight of her attention strike me like a front of cold air. *Beautiful* has never been the right word for my sister. Even in her simple black mourning dress, Estella is formidable, her angles left rough and harsh, her thin lips and slate gray eyes somehow both imposing and elegant, in the way a rainstorm is just at its peak.

"So," my sister says when we near her, raising a brow in my direction. Her voice is low and grating, the kind of voice that runs a finger down your spine and demands you stand at attention. "You came back."

Her gaze drips over me slowly, taking in my disheveled state, my obvious lack of carriage. "I must say, I thought you would have managed to wrangle a ring off someone by now."

Unruffled, I catch her eyes as they rise back to mine. "I'm weighing my options."

Killian lets out a shallow cough at that. Remembering him, my cheeks redden and I hurriedly dismount, muttering a few words of gratitude as he readies his horse and departs—slightly more quickly than is necessary, in my opinion.

Left alone, my sister and I regard one another awkwardly. If this reunion were occurring only a few years ago, I would have run into her arms by now—and she would have caught me, I know it. But seeing her again after four months apart, I can't deny that it feels strange, the two of us together. Ill-fitting, like a childhood dress I've grown out of.

Or, more accurately, like a dress I tossed away when I fled Norland, leaving my sister alone with a mourning father, a province-worth of responsibilities, and an empty estate stuffed to the brim with our family's ghosts.

Word . . . was that he was sick with grief over the loss of your mother.

"Is it up to me to say hello, then?" Essie's remark cracks

through my guilt, and I sweep the remnants away like shards of glass. She's standing with her arms crossed, looking not unlike one of the Lightkeeper's avenging angels with her furrowed brows and her pale skin.

"I thought you might lead us off, seeing as you did such a wonderful job with your goodbye," she continues. Pausing, she purses her lips in mock concentration. "Or did you—funny, now that I consider it, I can't seem to recall one at all."

I smile in spite of myself. "Hello, Essie," I reply, moving toward her. "I've missed you."

It is true; I *have* missed her, even if thinking of her while in New London felt like staring too deeply into my own shadow. Every recollection, no matter how innocent, seemed to bring me back to the darkest part of myself—the moment I left her—so eventually, I stopped looking. Like my shadow, though, that didn't stop her from trailing after me wherever I went. It didn't prevent me from glimpsing her every couple days, her twisted shape thrown upon a wall at a party: flashes of her withering stare, her wry smile. Snatches of her laugh.

Taking Essie's arm, I steer her back toward Norland's entrance, dropping my voice so as not to be overheard by any servants waiting inside.

"I must tell you something," I murmur. "There was an . . . accident, on my drive here." I pause, my next words gumming in my throat. "A—a breach in the border. My carriage went right into the mist."

—*Like a leaping cat, wrapping around him*—

I swallow hard. "The driver was killed, Essie. There was a Phantom—it would have gotten me, too, only one of your sentries shot it before it could. Killian Brandon, he said his name was—he was just with me now."

Beside me, Essie stiffens. "*Shit*," she hisses.

28

I snap my head toward her, certain I've misheard—my sister, the perfect diplomat, the perfect lady, would never curse—but she repeats the swear. "Shit. That makes three this month. I thought the additional forces . . ." She falls off, pinching the bridge of her nose. Her eyes are bright as a fever patient's, desperation burning in their centers. I'm not sure what I expected from her—horror? sympathy?—but this reaction, her *knowledge,* curdles something deep within me.

Killian's words float through my mind, a haunting litany: *There may have been other incidents . . . she has forbidden us from discussing the topic.*

"Essie," I ask, "what's happened since I left for New London? Your sentry, he said—"

She hushes me abruptly, her glare shriveling any resolve I had to press forward. "We can't talk about this now. They're waiting for us inside—the footman came and told us when your carriage was approaching. I'm only meant to fetch you."

The deference in her tone gives me pause. My sister's pride having been my constant companion since childhood, I am well aware that there are very few people before whom Estella Darling will kneel—and not one of them do I want waiting to meet with me. "*They?*" I repeat slowly. "Who are *they,* exactly?"

Essie's mouth drops open in reply just as a figure bursts through Norland's front door—a man, his black-clad body instantly recognizable to me. His lanky arms are outstretched, his broad smile the easy, untroubled grin of an experienced host, as if we are his guests and not the other way around.

At the sight of him, ice water sluices through my veins.

"There she is!" my cousin says as he descends toward me. "The lovely Merrick, returned home at last."

CHAPTER THREE

The last time I saw the Red Duke of Sussex, Thomas Darling, it was his wedding day, and my family was still whole.

I remember the event well. In the time since, the images have taken on an oversaturated quality in my mind, like the lush red of an apple just before rot sets in. The ceremony had taken place last summer, just after the solstice, on a long yellow evening that seemed to go on forever, the hours spreading lazily around us like the petals of a buttercup. All of the Smoke appeared to have gathered at Norland House for the occasion, even New London shuttering its ballrooms for what was certain to be the party of the season: the union of Darling and Faulk, two of the most powerful Manors in the nation, now joining themselves together in holy matrimony. There was wine and dancing and general celebration of the couple's great love, their whirlwind courtship: all the pieces needed to construct a fairy tale.

And beneath the trappings and trimmings, there were rumors. Talk that the former society darling Cressida Faulk, grand-daughter of Manor Lord Elodie Faulk and my cousin's blushing bride, was aging—nearing thirty prior to her engagement and with no husband or children to show for it. Whispers of her involvement with a married man, a minor Rouge of the Ballantine Manor far below her station; of her family's desire for increased access to Sussex's timber forests and an advantageous marriage to repair the damage to their own reputation done by the affair.

None of this was discussed outright, of course—at least, not with me. But I saw the way Cressida's spine stiffened under her gossamer gown as she neared the altar that day, as if she were parading herself into a cage and had just heard the door swing shut behind her.

Gravel gnaws at the thin soles of my slippers as I stand watching Tom's approach. With his polished shell of brunet hair and warm brown-black eyes, he resembles my father far more than I do—though my features still cluster closer to the family tree than Essie's ink-black locks, the color of a bad omen. But whereas Father cut an intimidating figure even in just a nightshirt, Tom's wife's money and the relative safety of Norrin, the Faulk province, where he and Cressida have made their home since the wedding, have rubbed away my cousin's edges. I eye his crisp charcoal jacket and polished shoes, both a vast improvement from the shabby, oversized garments he favored up until his wedding, and wonder, briefly, whether anyone's warned Cressida to keep a tight grip on her purse strings since their union.

For both of their sakes, I hope so. Though I've barely spent a minute in his presence, this Tom seems far happier than the one I knew when I left for New London—jovial and laughing like the boy I recall from my childhood. As he grew, I'd seen that boy fade like an aging painting, his careless façade peeling away bit by bit until the parts left of him were brittle and wan as an eggshell. After his last encounter with Father, I thought he was dead for good.

Yet now he stands before me again, resurrected and whole—and *here.*

How is it possible he arrived ahead of me? Norrin is at least two days' ride from Sussex; even if we received news of Father's passing at the exact same time, Tom should still be several nights away from this place.

As if sensing my skepticism of him, Tom steps around Essie and pulls me in for a tight hug, his movements loose with the confidence of a man who has never had to make a decision for himself in his entire life.

"What a delight it is to see you," he says. Despite the grim circumstances surrounding our reunion, it almost sounds like the truth.

I give myself over to his embrace for a few moments before pulling gently away. "And you, too," I tell him. "Though I must admit, I wasn't expecting for our reunion to occur quite so soon."

Tom chuckles. "Oh, Cress and I arrived yesterday," he says cheerfully. "Lucky your sister wrote us when she did—we were already on our way to Sussex when the news about Silas reached us. Otherwise, she would have been stranded here alone, without another soul for company."

He claps Essie heavily on the shoulder. "Perfect timing, eh?"

My nose wrinkles—*perfect timing* seems an odd word choice to me when discussing my father's death—but rather than correct himself, Tom turns back toward the front doors.

"Come, now," he urges, beckoning me forward. "Cress is waiting for you in the dining room. She guessed you'd want a hot supper after your long journey—she's considerate like that, you know."

Cress. Hearing her nickname repeated makes my jaw clench harder. It's a mild endearment for such a formidable woman, and though past her bloom New London may have deemed her, Cressida Faulk-Darling is nothing if not formidable. It is one of the many reasons I found her and my cousin's coupling so strange when it was initially announced. While Cressida has long been a favorite to be named her grandmother's Vessel—or at least she was before scandal put her prospects in danger—Tom's greatest achievement, prior to his marriage, was his ability to ride a horse after downing an entire bottle of wine. An only child, he spent most of his twenties gambling away his deceased father's—my uncle's—fortune in New London, making brief appearances at Norland House whenever he needed my father to get him out of one financial scrape or another.

I dip briefly into a memory: Tom and my father during Tom's last visit to Norland House, a few months prior to his engagement to Cressida. A rainstorm had plunged the estate into false night, dusk's pink shadows ripening to a full violet. I'd been passing by Father's study when the hum of low voices had drawn me in, their conversation too muffled to be decipherable but clipped with agitation. Curious, I'd sidled nearer, glancing once down the corridor to ensure that Essie wasn't nearby to chastise me for eavesdropping.

Then: a slam like a crack of thunder. The study door swung open, Tom framed behind it like a villain sprung free of one of the gothic novels I hid beneath my mattress for reading in secret. His brown curls were ruffled, not in the rakish, mischievous way he usually preferred, but truly askew, as if he'd been tugging on them in frustration. Behind him, I saw my father rising from his desk, his call of protest choked halfway when Tom yanked the door closed again.

"Tom," I'd stammered unsteadily. "What—"

My cousin cut me off. "He thinks I'll bow to him," he'd hissed, his expression at once lit by fury and oddly vacant, so that even though he was facing me, I couldn't be sure whether I was the one he was addressing at all—or if his mind was elsewhere, in a far-off place full of devils. "Well, I won't. I *won't*. Not while he parades that commoner wife of his around and auctions me—his own blood—off like some sheep to be slaughtered." He'd growled, the sound filled with such violent desperation that it made all my hairs stand on end. "If my father were here . . ."

He'd twisted abruptly as my *own* father had burst into the hallway, shooing me sternly away and speaking to Tom in a hushed tone I couldn't make out. I'd known better than to ask Father what they'd been discussing that had upset Tom so, but the next time I saw my cousin, his hair was slicked back and neat, and he was standing at the end of an aisle, grinning as his new wife strode toward him.

It wasn't difficult, then, to parse out the truth layered underneath the couple's wedding vows: that my cousin's union had likely been closed by a handshake in some dusty drawing room long before it was sealed with a kiss. And that my father's unconditional support of his nephew had, in fact, not been the safety net Tom believed it to be, so much as a web formed of invisible strings, designed to ensnare.

On the latter point at least, I could empathize.

The progression from the drive to the dining room is a blur. Inside, Norland House is cool and damp, its hallways a collection of wood paneling and evening gloom. Like most Manor estates in the Smoke, Norland was abandoned by its aristocratic owners after the arrival of the mist, and subsequently repurposed for my family's use when my ancestors came to power. Darlings have dwelled here for two centuries now, but sometimes, when the light filters into the corridors just so, I could swear that I've seen the shadows of its past inhabitants lingering in the air like a handful of thrown dust. Have felt the eerie sense of intrusion that comes with dwelling in an ancient place, of discovering nooks and crannies that were not built by my hands—like the house is a mystery I've never quite been able to solve.

I've scarcely stepped foot across the threshold of the dining room when I'm distracted from my reflection by a shift in the atmosphere, as if everything in our vicinity is being tugged slightly toward a new center of gravity. Or, more accurately, toward the woman sitting primly at the head of the table with a cup of tea in hand, lithe and dark in her mourning gown like a cat stalking its prey.

Though I hate to admit it, Cressida Faulk-Darling wears death well. Her black dress clings to her shoulders and falls in a low scoop at her chest, then billows into waves of midnight satin below the bodice. Her thick sheaf of umber curls has been piled gracefully atop her head, her skin glowing and dewy in the waning evening light. Two red ribbons encircle her wrists, a common trend among Manorborn ladies. Even the elite know that here, your status is only as good as your blood.

As I take her in, my heart stutters. The seat she's occupying is—*was*—my mother's, for the entirety of her life. No one, not even my sister, has used it since her passing; though we haven't discussed it, I assumed we all felt that to do otherwise would be sacrilegious, akin to putting on one of Mama's old dresses or powdering our cheeks with her rouge. Seeing it filled now, I feel immediately dirty, my skin hot and itchy as if caked with mud. How *dare* she—

"Merrick, there you are. Estella told us you would be arriving soon." My cousin-in-law's brown eyes flick over me before rising to my face, the intensity in them a dare—to meet her stare, to look away, or perhaps both in equal measure. "You are coming from New London, are you not?" she asks. "I have only just finished the latest edition of the *Toast* myself. It seems you are having quite the successful run this season." She smirks. "I am ever so sorry you've had to disrupt your . . . efforts . . . for a matter as somber as this."

Beside me, my sister fidgets with her dress, her eyes cast unhelpfully downward. Her complacence sends a fresh surge of indignation through me. Why has she not put a stop to Cressida's behavior—this willful shrugging off of our parents' legacy? I want to shout at her, demand that she quit standing limp as a rag doll and *act*. More than that, I want her to explain why she invited our cousin and his wife to Norland at all, when it took Father dying for her to pen me a single letter.

Instead, I clear my throat. "Mourning my father is more than a worthy reason for a disruption, I should think. Though I'm afraid my journey was troubled. There was a breach at the border, along the coastline. The Graylands overtook my carriage." I pause, then add for effect, "I would have died, had one of our sentries not been riding nearby."

A tad melodramatic, but it sparks the desired reaction. Cressida's expression darkens at my comment, her forehead creasing with concern.

"Oh dear," she murmurs soberly. "How terrible. Please, sit, eat—I am sure you need to regain your strength after such an ordeal."

Absent-mindedly, she waves toward the edges of the dining room. I flinch as a trio of maids peels off from their positions against the wall at her command, solemn and nearly invisible in their muted gray dresses, and rush forward to pull out our chairs. The girl attending me is doughy-faced and utterly unfamiliar, her eyes turned demurely toward the ground as she works.

My neck prickles with discomfort as I slide into my seat. Since when, I wonder, do our servants take their orders from my cousin-in-law? Out of the corner of my eye, I watch Essie fold herself into her chair, her hands positioned primly in her lap like an obedient child awaiting her mother's inspection, and my stomach turns.

"A cup of tea for the Archdaughter, Delilah," Cressida instructs, oblivious to my unease. "And then, perhaps the soup?"

With an anxious bob of her head, the maid behind me rushes to lift the hefty porcelain teapot—patterned with curving foxes' tails—from the center of the table and fill my cup. A bead of hot liquid splashes over the brim as she pours, landing on my wrist. I hiss involuntarily at the sudden sear of pain, which only causes the maid to startle further, half of my drink sloshing out of its cup and puddling in the saucer. The tea itself is a familiar pink-red, like drowned rose petals, or blood thinned with water.

I draw it carefully toward me, raising the cup to my lips and taking a delicate sip. Moorflower tea is a favorite of the Manors for its rarity and steep price, its odd coloring derived from the crimson moorflower leaves of its namesake. The taste itself is bitter, tart, and slightly acidic like fresh lemon juice squeezed on my tongue, and though I've been drinking it since I was a child, the flavoring hits me with a fresh sourness now. Father adored moorflower tea—would tease Mother for her commoner palate when she turned it down in favor of sweeter blends like brushberry. *You are a Manorborn now, dear,* he'd tell her. *You must drink like a Manorborn.*

It is an effort to swallow.

Once we're all settled, Cressida shoos the remaining maids back to their stations and turns back to us. The way her gaze roves over the room reminds me of my old governess—always searching for something to reprimand, an anxious look or a flicker of unpreparedness to latch on to like a spider.

It comes as no surprise, then, when her attention lands on me.

"Are you quite all right, Merrick?" she asks, her fingers delicately toying with her napkin. "You look pale—were you injured in the attack at all?"

Collecting myself, I straighten. "No, not at all," I answer quickly. "I am perfectly well." I hesitate, and then, sensing an opportunity, I plunge ahead. "It is only that the breach left me a bit shaken. The sentry who came to my aid—he suggested the incident may not have been the first in recent months. A Tudor-born sentry, under *your* employ," I say, turning reproachfully toward Essie. "Care to explain?"

But it is Cressida who answers me, the clink of her nails against the slender handle of her own teacup drawing me back to her.

"It is true that there have been troubles along the Sussex border recently," she says, holding up a hand when I lean forward, another question already leaping to my tongue. "Let me finish, please. The *incidents* you speak of were the initial reason for Tom's and my visit, in fact. Fortunately, the majority of the breaches have occurred in unpopulated areas, which have allowed us to keep the commoners mostly ignorant of the situation, though rumors are already springing up in some villages. As for the foreign sentries," she continues with a nod toward Essie, "I applaud your sister for her judgment there. Certainly, recent events prove that your Darling forces cannot be trusted to maintain the border on their own, even without taking into account the turnings of late. We feel—"

"*We*, you say. *Us.* Was everyone included in this conversation but myself?" I cut my cousin-in-law off, my rage a hot thread unspooling in my core. Shoulders tensed, I shift to face my sister again. "I've been in New London for the past few months, Essie, not dining with the Far Prince in Cael. You could have written me at any time. Why have I not heard anything about this?"

"Because you left, Merrick." Essie's reply is soft but immediate. Unwavering. Finally leveled with mine, her gray eyes are steely; I forgot, while I was away, this look of hers, how her judgment can burn through a person, sit in their chest like a blazing coal until they mistake it for their own. "Without a word of explanation to me, if you'd care to remember that bit," she goes on. "Why would I write to you when it was clear that you had no desire to be a part of this family—"

"I *had* to leave," I interject. "You'd have known why, if you bothered to ask, but you just shut yourself off the way you always do. A locked chest would be a more forthcoming sister than you."

"You could have at least finished mourning our *mother* before you ran off in search of a husband—"

"Girls, enough."

Cressida's clipped interruption breaks through Essie's rebuttal, quieting us both. She sighs, a ladylike noise dainty as a cat's mew, and takes a sip of her tea. The long column of her throat is still for two counts before it bobs with a swallow; I get the sense that she is playing time like a hand of cards, waiting to lay down her next one until the room's attention is firmly back on her.

It is a relief when her lips finally part again. "Estella, sweetheart, I fear we are losing track of this discussion. I assume you have brought Merrick up to speed on the news regarding your father?" Cressida arcs a brow. "It is imperative that our messaging remain consistent across the family, lest the gossip grow . . . out of hand."

Essie's lips part, her cheeks visibly paling. "I . . . I did not have time," she murmurs. "I thought it imprudent to put anything in writing, in case the Eaveses asked to see my letter when it arrived."

Her demeanor is hesitant, her eyes darting guiltily toward me and then away again. Immediately, it makes the hairs on my arms rise. There is only one subject I can think of that could produce such a reaction in my sister: the same one that caused me to flee from her four months ago.

She is scared to tell you the truth. A low murmur in my mind, an oily caress. *She pities you—pities you for the title Father awarded her over you.*

"If you are referring to the matter of Father's Vessel," I say crisply to the room, "I have known his position for months. Father as good as told me he intended to Nominate Essie as his heir before I departed for New London. It is part of why I decided to debut this year."

My phrasing is harsh but honest. Manor seats aren't awarded by sex or birth order; rather, all children of a Manor Lord are eligible to receive their parent's title. As one might guess, this can result in multiple siblings vying for the position of head of the family, so to make the process less bloody, most Manor Lords Nominate a descendant—who then adopts the title of heir, or Vessel—to take their place once they pass.

Instead, Father had let me hope. Had trained Essie and me alongside one another; had done nothing as resentment began to fester between us, spoiling the friendship we'd had as children. He'd offered us both the world, and then, over the span of a single conversation, he'd stolen it away from me.

You will never be Manor Lord, Merrick.

I dig my nails into my palms, focusing on the bite of pain rather than the tears threatening to well in the corners of my eyes. Even after the months I've spent away from home, the potency of Father's words refuses to be diluted by time or space. I still feel his admission like a slap across my cheek, red and searing. Can still see him hunched in his favorite armchair, his palms flattened against his desk, his expression somber even when I cried, even when I begged him to explain.

Never, Merrick. Never.

Pushing the memory away, I stare around the silent dining table. "Well?" I demand, leaning forward in my stiff chair. "Am I correct, or aren't I? Please, do not attempt to spare my feelings—Father certainly did not."

"You are." Essie answers quietly, her long, graceful fingers intertwined in her lap. Her gaze slips past mine when I try to catch it. "I am the Darling Vessel. Father informed me of his decision a few days prior to his passing," she says. "Cressida and I sent notice to the Mortal Council last night."

An ache spreads through my chest at her confirmation, the dull, purple agony of an old bruise newly pressed on. *So he wasn't lying, then.* I never believed he was, but the more weeks I passed in New London without an announcement of my father's heir reaching me, the harder it was to keep from wishing it. From wondering if perhaps he'd changed his mind.

"Good." I swallow, blink away the unshed tears blurring the edges of my vision. "I am glad he was able to notify you of his choice before his death. It will make the transition much cleaner."

Essie's chin wobbles. "Merrick, I . . ."

I squeeze my eyes shut, inhaling deeply. I can tell she's going to say she's sorry, can hear it in the quiver in her speech, and if she does, I think I may just fall apart. My bones feel curiously fragile, as if all of me is paper and string, my demise as imminent as the next rainstorm.

"And how did he die, exactly?" I ask abruptly. Opening my eyes again, I meet Essie's startled gaze, my heart thumping against my lungs. "Father—was he killed in one of the breaches you spoke of earlier? Your note did not say."

"Manor Lord Silas took his own life on Friday morning last." Cressida speaks tonelessly from the head of the table, her teacup still in hand. "He was visiting your mother's grave, as he often did, when he crossed the border at the edge of Norland's grounds and entered the mist without a Ghostslayer. Your sister saw him and gave pursuit, but by the time she entered the Graylands, a Phantom had beaten her to him."

Took his own life. Your sister saw him . . . a Phantom.

Cressida's proclamation cuts its way through me slowly: understanding blooms first in my mind, then my body, and last, with a vicious stab, it drives into my heart. To my left, I'm vaguely aware of Essie pounding a reply into my ear, the thump of her voice like a drumbeat, but I can't make out a single word.

In her own seat, Cressida *ahem*s. Even the gentle sound is grating against my flesh, as if my nerves have been stripped raw.

"It would be beneficial to the remaining members of your Manor if you would handle this information with care," she says mildly, and it is only then that I see the socialite in her—that way she wields power like a lace handkerchief, an object of grace and refinement. "As I mentioned earlier, the messaging here will be all-important in minimizing unrest among the commoners."

I watch on, silent, as her attention flicks past my shoulder, as her mouth curls into a polite smile and her head dips in recognition of someone approaching at my back.

"Now," she continues, "I believe dinner is served."

CHAPTER FOUR

H ere is what I know of how the Manors came to be:

They began with the change, and the change began as a fog off the ocean. Not uncommon for an island nation such as Great Britain, but this white lingered, spread across the harbors and over the hills and valleys, settled into the towns. As days passed and the mist crept farther inland, a few went in to investigate—to try to retrieve the land that had been lost.

When they came out, they were different.

In the centuries since, we have learned that the mist consumes its prey slowly, festering in the bodies of its victims for several weeks before claiming them, mind and soul. The symptoms, though, have remained the same from generation to generation, taking a little over a fortnight from start to finish. First comes the rot: filmy lines like pale, furry mold that bloom under the corrupted individual's skin, tracing lacy patterns along their veins. Next, the mist takes their minds—twisting their dreams into strange, unholy shapes. Their eyes go last, their irises swelling with a full white emptiness, a presence at once internal and wholly alien. It is at this point, too, that their hunger for food and drink is usurped by a crueler desire for the flesh of humankind—those they previously claimed as their brethren.

Resistance, as every child of the Smoke is assured over and over again in their youth, is futile. For all whom the mist calls, they must eventually obey, running into the white like children toward their mother's breast. Emerging again as something different than they were before.

Something monstrous.

Phantoms, my ancestors called the changed creatures, for that was what they seemed to be—as if their corpses were nothing more than a shell for some vaporous force, a ghost puppeting their bodies from within.

My ancestors killed as many as they could. They thought it would be enough.

They realized quickly, however, that their efforts were futile. For as many monsters as they put in the ground, the mist had only to advance an inch and birth a new brood of children, turning all that came within reach of its hungry arms. Its appetite was insatiable, its capacity to hunt boundless as a jealous god's. It called us all to its folds. Those who did not obey, it pursued.

How it loved us so. How it does, still.

And then, in the midst of the chaos, rose the Manors. Twelve families gifted with immunity to the Graylands' touch, who alone could enter the mist and leave it again, unchanged. It was the Manors who initially observed that Phantoms, once transformed, could not roam apart from the mist for more than a quarter of an hour without needing to plunge back into its pale belly, as fish leaping from a river must soon return. The Manors who took that knowledge and sharpened it, who weaponized fire to drive back the fogs before they could swallow the country whole. Together with the small portion of the population that had fled inland enough to avoid the Graylands' touch, my forefathers built the first border lanterns, designed to keep the mist contained and the Phantoms at bay—and then, later, towns, cities.

From our ancestors' bravery, each following generation of Manorborn reaped their reward—certainty, not only in the purity of our blood but in our name, our place in the world. No matter its Lord, the Darling Manor is a living thing, an establishment carried in the very bodies of its members. A Manor child cannot lose their claim to the legacy they bear any more than they can lose themselves.

Ireland. Faulk. Cachemar. Vannett. Carrington. Savager. Tudor. Ibe. Ballantine. Warchild. Saint. Eleven lines, eleven families tasked with protecting their people against the mist.

And the twelfth Manor, my own—*Darling.* The Manor that fed itself to the beasts it was sworn to kill.

Manor Lord Silas took his own life on Friday morning last . . .

. . . he was sick with grief over the loss of your mother.

I open my eyes.

Night has painted my bedroom indigo. By the way the silence hangs like a wool curtain around me, I know instinctively it is late—sometime in that early-morning space when the darkness is so complete it catches you like a fly in a spider's web, where time melts and the concept of day feels impossible.

I've been drifting in and out of consciousness for hours now, lurking in a dreamlike state that leaves me more exhausted every time I resurface from it. After a stiff, disastrous dinner during which no one ate, much less spoke, Cressida scattered Essie, Tom, and me like a horde of roaches under a lit spill, demanding that we all reconvene in the morning to discuss "next steps."

I'd attempted to tail Essie back to her room, desperate for some explanation—some reason to justify our father's final, fatal act—but she'd shut her door before I could get more than a word in, a cup of cooling moorflower tea in her hand: the only companion she'd been willing to admit.

A lump forms in my throat. Giving up on sleep for now, I slip out from under my sheets and pad, barefoot, past the unopened traveling trunk at the foot of my bed, pulled from my abandoned carriage by our sentries and delivered to my room while I was at dinner, to the garden-facing wall. Three picture windows overlook Norland's back grounds, the moonlight washing the winding hedges and rose gardens in a blue-silver glow that makes me think of damp grass on my neck and dew on my tongue, of secrets too delicate to see the morning. Farther back, where our land drops away to a stretch of steep seaside cliffs, a barricade of lampposts burns diligently, warding off the tendrils of mist that dance around the flames like moths.

Beyond that is only fog.

I rub my tired eyes, my head swimming. With every blink, the Graylands seem to press nearer, crowding me like a flock of woolly sheep around their shepherd. My bare arms prickle with the sense memory of the fog—how damp it was against my skin, when Killian Brandon pulled me from the carriage earlier this evening. How, if I'd lowered my mask for even a second, it would have swept inside me, filling my throat and nostrils like plugs of cotton.

My lungs constrict, the loneliness of my room suddenly unbearable. I need someone to smooth away my fears, to assure me that when the sun rises, I will be all right, and the world will look hopeful and new again.

I need my sister.

Without giving myself time to reconsider, I find a flimsy shawl discarded on the floor and wrap it around myself, grateful for its warmth. Crossing to the door, I open it slowly and slip into the predawn quiet of the hallway.

The windowless corridor is almost cavelike without a candle to light my way, the blackness an open mouth in front of me. In the dimness, I can just make out the muted hues of the tapestries hanging on the opposite wall: Phantoms, their skin like sour milk, their already gruesome features further contorted in pain as hungry flames devour their limbs. Sagging jaws yowl at me while my ancestors stand proudly to the side, watching, their smiles almost wicked.

Above them, leaping from the oak molding along the ceilings, carved foxes prowl the hall. Their bared fangs are dark as pitch, like teeth formed by the night itself.

I shiver. The art has a hysterical quality to it, as if it could turn a viewer mad, should they gaze at it long enough.

Luckily, Essie's room is farther along the same hall as mine, and my feet have traversed the route enough to guide me there easily. After a few moments, her door leaps out of the shadows, its gilded knob winking with a dull golden sheen.

Raising my hand, I knock gently on the wood. "Essie?" I call, feeling slightly foolish—like I am a child again, running to my older sister's room to escape the claws of a nightmare. A moment passes without any sound of movement from behind the door, so I try again, slightly more forcefully this time. "Essie, are you awake?"

Nothing. A chilly draft groans through the estate's old bones, snaking down the hallway and making me pull my shawl tighter around me. Never one to be easily dissuaded, I knock once more, a third time, but only silence answers me. *Can she not hear me?*

I step back, squinting at the door. The part of myself that is already growing snappish from lack of sleep urges the rest of me to go back to bed, leave my questions until the morning, but perhaps I am still scared of bad dreams, because when I try to move I find I cannot.

Helplessly, I stretch my arm out and grip the doorknob. Turn it.

It holds fast, refusing to twist past a quarter of an inch. Jammed? I rattle it harder, as hard as I can, to no avail.

Not jammed, then. Locked.

My pulse ticks faster, apprehension making me jittery. Why would Essie lock her door? Did she guess I would try to wake her, and take measures to avoid me? Stooping, I peer through the keyhole but glimpse only a sliver of a lumpy form buried under a mound of blankets.

Frustrated, I lurch back. It is only then that I catch sight of it.

Down the hall, a white face emerges from the darkness, its eyes large and moonlike as it makes its way forward—growing closer, so quickly closer, to me.

CHAPTER FIVE

The figure's pale mouth is twisted in a scowl, leering at me as they approach. Petals of sour orange light stroke the planes of their face, emanating from the lantern they're holding out in front of them. The flicker of the candle flame within makes the illumination dance wildly over their features, exaggerating the figure's frown, glowing like stars in their white eyes.

I stumble back in surprise, my bare foot banging painfully against the wall as I do so.

"You'll wake the whole house like that."

The voice that calls out to me is male, subdued and steady, like the brush of a gentle hand in the dark. Still jittery, I swallow a cry as they move nearer still, raising their lantern to better illuminate their face.

Candlelight washes over them, rendering them in more detail. Killian Brandon stands watching me in the same uniform that he wore when he pulled me from the mist-drowned carriage, his brown eye solemn, the other winking in the lamp's glow, a chilly blue like sea ice.

"*You.*" It is almost a whisper, tinged with disbelief. In the past twelve hours, my life has taken on a quality of unreality—I did not realize, until this moment, how much I want this boy to reappear, to prove that the attack we underwent was more than just another wild flight of fancy on my part.

Killian's expression is impassive—he does not seem similarly moved by *my* reappearance, I note. "What are you doing out of bed, Archdaughter?"

The thick scar trailing down his neck pulls tighter when he speaks. All at once, humiliation warms my blood, reddening my cheeks. How ridiculous must I look, just now—stumbling away from him like he's some monster come to stalk me.

"I—I couldn't sleep," I reply, gesturing to the nightgown I'm wearing as feeble evidence. My flush intensifies when I notice Killian's gaze catch on it, flicking quickly up and down my figure. Defensively, I clutch at the fabric, pulling the folds of the gown in front of me like they're a robe I can draw closed, and am rewarded when Killian glances away immediately, blinking rapidly.

"What are *you* doing here?" I press, narrowing my eyes. "Perhaps things have changed while I've been away, but last I checked, the sentries' barracks were nowhere near my sister's bedroom." Though it's difficult to tell in the dimness, I think the sentry's neck might tinge with pink at my remark, and the notion fills me with a mean sort of self-satisfaction. *See?* I want to say. *I can unsettle you, too.*

"I patrol this wing of your estate, along with a few other men who rotate shifts with me," he answers after a moment, nodding toward Essie's door. "Archdaughter Estella believed that the extra security would give her peace of mind, with all the breaches. And after what's happened since . . ."

He falls silent, his gaze flicking back to me. All it takes is a glimpse of the guilt pooling in his expression, leaking into his eyes, for me to be certain—he knows. Perhaps everyone at Norland has this whole time, except for me.

I swallow hard, biting back the swell of emotions that rolls roughly through me: embarrassment at my ignorance, anger at Essie for shutting me out. And beneath them both, a deep, pulsing ache like a second heartbeat.

"Did you see it? See him . . . go in?" I whisper. My voice is thick, as if my throat is packed with mud.

Killian's mouth softens, briefly parting with sympathy, but his eyes hold mine. "I did not," he offers simply in reply. "No one did, save for your sister. Lord Silas insisted on privacy when he visited your mother's grave, despite the fact that the cemetery plot abuts the border. Even if I or another sentry had seen him walking alone that morning, no one would have thought it odd."

He pauses, shaking his head as if chastising himself. "I do not mean to make excuses, Archdaughter," he says more firmly. "My fellow men and I were negligent, and because of it, your father . . ." He clears his throat, then swallows down the sound. "Please know that it is a mistake I will never forgive myself for."

I nod dully, dropping my gaze to the floor. Part of me wonders if Killian expects me to cry at his admission. I cried for Mama, after all—but when I try to summon tears now, none come. Instead, a painful, swollen sensation fills my chest, like a pocket of hot air straining against my rib cage.

Resentment, I think with a flash of shame. I resent Father—and not just for choosing Essie over me as his heir. I resent the way he raised us as soldiers rather than daughters, tied our worth so closely to our duties as Manorborn that when he took mine away, I barely had anything left to hold on to. For the hard-crusted nature of his love, its conditions always clear: to fail him, to fail Sussex, was to lose both.

"He did it early—when he knew the night and dawn shifts would be rotating, and our guard down," Killian says, evidently interpreting my silence as a desire for more information. "We believe he had been planning it for some time. I am so sorry, Archdaughter."

The kindness in his tone loosens something in me, a wet emotion that slides queasily in my stomach—sorrow or anger, I can't tell. "But why?" I ask. The word cracks in half as I speak it. "Why would he do it at all?"

Killian's brows draw together, their dirty-blond color bronzed by the candlelight. "That, I am afraid, I can't tell you. Perhaps he did not know, himself—as I said before, he was deep in mourning for your mother. And with the province in the state that it is—the breaches and turnings . . ." Killian sighs. "He may have thought it easier to just . . . let go."

I go still. "The turnings—Cressida mentioned that, too. What do you mean by them?"

As if realizing his mistake, Killian takes a step back, the lamp dipping so that his face is shrouded briefly in shadow. "I—" He coughs shallowly. "Forgive me, Archdaughter, I did not mean to speak of matters beyond my station. I only assumed . . ."

He drifts off as I move closer, stepping forward so that the warmth of his lantern sinks into me like body heat. The scent of him catches in my nostrils: sea air and smoke, a trace of gunpowder.

"This is my house, too, Mr. Brandon," I tell him, pleased when my voice doesn't shake. "I am a Darling, just like my sister. You took an oath to serve me.

"What turnings?" I repeat. "Have we lost men to the mist?"

Killian tenses, then lets out a long exhale. I'm close enough that I can see the muscles of his shoulders sinking in resignation, feel the damp humidity of his sighed breath, and am surprised when something twinges in my gut—a spill of hot water.

"It is to be expected," Killian says, and at once, all other thoughts fade. "Every sentry knows the risk they take when they agree to enter service—that there is a chance, however slight, their blood may not be strong enough to save them." He shrugs, but the movement is too stiff, the effort in it too obvious to provide any comfort. "Only a couple men have succumbed thus far. With the new recruits coming in, there are plenty of bodies to replace them."

I remain silent, taking in his words. Breaches are one matter, but, to my knowledge at least, a sentry has not turned in Sussex since before I was born. The possibility has always existed, of course—that a soldier whose lineage is too diluted may not inherit the immunity of their ancestors—but it has always seemed a distant danger, far-off as a rainstorm during a sunny day. A problem for other lands, unnamed strangers.

My gaze drifts toward Essie's door, the golden knob glinting invitingly. *Locked.* What kind of home, exactly, did I abandon my sister to when I left four months ago? And why does it feel like though physically I've come back, the rest of me is still out in the cold, waiting to be let in?

"I'm sure your sister was only frightened of overwhelming you. The past few months have not been easy on her."

Killian's voice catches me off guard. I glance back, nearly flinching when I find him watching me, his eyes bright and reflective. There is a depth to them, I think—a knowledge that makes me feel as though he could peer inside my mind as easily as gazing through a glass.

It is a few seconds before I can gather my response. "I never assumed they had."

He doesn't falter. "I only meant it was evident that she missed you, no matter the front she put on when you arrived. Give her some time. She has been alone for a while, even before your father died. That sort of isolation . . ." His gaze fogs over. "It has a way of making one feel like a ghost—like no one can touch you. Like you might curse them if they tried."

Now it is my turn to stare. "You speak very directly, for a sentry," I say slowly. "Who did you say your mother was, again?"

Killian stiffens, his lantern guttering dangerously for a moment. Blackness presses in around us, velvety and cool, and I realize, suddenly, how narrow the sliver of space between us has grown. How alone we are here, trapped deep in the bowels of Norland House.

Then Killian breaks the quiet. "No one of importance to a lady such as yourself," he replies. Abruptly, he bows in farewell, his jaw tense. "I should be taking my leave. You're right; it is inappropriate, my conversing with you like this. My apologies." He clears his throat. "Do you need me to escort you back to your room?"

I blink, thrown by the change in topic. "I can find my own way." I dip my head in a return of his gesture. "Good night, Mr. Brandon."

"Good night, Archdaughter," he returns. He casts me one last, lingering look before he turns, taking his lantern with him and leaving me in the dark.

CHAPTER SIX

The troubles of the night follow me into the next day, a gray cast atop my vision.

The sun is lifting over the horizon by the time I abandon any final, stubborn notions I had about getting an hour of rest in and rise. I let my maid dress me in an oppressive, broad-hemmed bombazine gown—black, of course, lest I forget we are still in mourning—before dismissing her and examining myself in my vanity mirror.

Despite steeling myself, I can't stop my heart from sinking at the reflection that stares back at me. While Tom takes after our father's side of the family, I have always resembled my mother—a woman who, despite her un-Manored status, managed to claim the attentions of her province's Lord over two decades ago.

Though not unprecedented, her feat was noteworthy—and not only because she grew up, as Mama frequently liked to remind Essie and me whenever we whined about new ribbons or silken-haired dolls as children, *poor*. Raised in an orphanage in the coastal village of Shoreham-by-Sea, Mama stayed on at the institution when she came of age, tending fussy infants and mending little boys' clothes while other girls were practicing their pianofortes. Her and my father's meeting was something pulled from a fairy tale: him, the dashing new Lord of the Darling Manor, on an introductory tour of his province following his swearing-in; her, a sugar-spun waif trapped in a poorhouse, so pure it seemed impossible that her graceful hands had ever scrubbed away a baby's vomit, or that her cheeks had felt the salty bite of tears. My father loved my mother instantly, the papers quicker still. *Artemis Darling,* the headlines read the day of their wedding, *Lady of the People.*

My father's fellow Manorborn, though, were not won over so quickly. As a rule, the Manors tend to encourage matches within the twelve ruling families to ensure the continued strength of their respective lines—and, more importantly, to preserve our collective immunity. I remember the bitter fear that clogged my airways the first time Father took me with him into the mist, my heart screaming not only at the ugly form of the Phantom scuttling ahead of us but at the possibility that it was my future, that my lineage might be too diluted to offer me protection.

It wasn't. Though, looking back, that fate might have been easier in some ways. To slip into monstrosity like a loophole, to grow wild and never have to worry about sisters or fathers or suitors.

With her cascade of flaxen curls and her wide, doelike green eyes, my mother had beauty on her side, but many have had similar advantages and allowed them to waste away. Artemis Darling's talent was in her cunning, the ability she had to make herself seem desired; she was a commoner, and yet she glittered like the Manorborn, a counterfeit coin among their ranks.

I inherited my mother's looks—a blessing that felt more like a curse after her death, when her echo lurked in every mirror. Yet as I look at myself now, my white-blond ringlets hang lank around my head, and bruise-colored bags carve crescents beneath my eyes—the same clover green as hers. My cheeks are absent of their usual rosy blush; even my skin seems clammy, as if I would melt beneath a candle's heat.

I pinch the apples of my cheeks in a halfhearted attempt to bring some color into them, then turn away. Not even one full day, and already, being back at Norland is draining me. I knew it would, but the collective tug of all that I've learned since I returned—the truth of my father's death, the breaches at the borders—is more depleting than I ever could have expected. Even now, my anxieties have clasped onto me like dozens of leeches, greedily sipping away at my remaining energy.

This morning, I promise myself, I'll speak to Essie about Father's funeral—make sure all the arrangements have been sorted. Mourning periods are brief in the Smoke, relatively informal—a vestige left behind from the time after the mist's arrival, when the deaths were too numerous, and the danger too near, to waste time crying over them all. Once the burial has been carried out, I'll be free to return to New London. Waiting any longer would be imprudent, anyhow. The season was already winding down when I departed, and while I left the capital in good standing, Mama always said that the memories of men are short. I'll need to return soon or risk my potential suitors becoming distracted by more readily available offerings.

And leave Essie to clean up Father's mess alone, just like you did last time, a voice hisses. With some effort, I swat it away. My sister is Father's Vessel now—will soon be a Manor Lord, after the Mortal Council votes to confirm Father's Nomination. Caring for our province is her responsibility, not mine.

Goose bumps erupt on my arms as I make my way downstairs

for breakfast. The tapestries in the hallway are somehow even more disconcerting when viewed in daylight—their colors jarring and overly bright, the glee on my ancestors' faces almost manic as they delight in the Phantoms' demise. I duck my head as I continue walking, fixing my gaze to the ground.

Has our estate truly always felt this way, I wonder—corrupted to the point of unhealthiness, like the stagnant, dead air beside a sickbed? It's true that I have been gone for some time, but Norland House seems different. As if a bad seed has been planted at its core, rotting it from the inside out.

"Merrick—there you are." Cressida glances up at me as I enter the dining room. She's seated near the far end of the dining table, Tom lounging in a chair next to her, a newspaper spread open in front of him. Someone, presumably a maid, has overlaid the table with a gauzy white cloth, upon which a lavish breakfast spread has been laid out.

My sister is nowhere to be seen.

Cressida nods to the full plate in front of her, triangles of toast with dainty bites already taken out of them, as I make my way to an empty seat. "I hope you don't mind that we've started without you."

I assess the state of the table as I slide into my chair—the half-depleted porcelain tureens of food, the damp ruby stain seeping out from beneath the teapot. This is not the careful, hesitant meal of a guest. Rather, the morning's offerings are arranged on the tablecloth in a lazy sprawl, napkins crumpled alongside them, spoons still dripping jam balanced haphazardly on the lips of their pots. I imagine my cousin-in-law ordering all of this, calling for our servants as if they were her own, and my fingers tighten around the edge of my seat.

I most certainly do mind, I think.

"Not at all, thank you," I reply aloud. Ignoring the dishes in front of me, I scour the dining room for any sign of Essie. There isn't a place laid out for her—did she eat already?

"Has Essie come down yet?" I ask, curious.

Cressida's butter knife clinks against her plate as she sets it down, her mouth pursing at my question. Already, she's expertly made up, clad in a deceivingly simple ebony day dress, her glossy hair pulled into a tight bun. Several coiled ringlets have been pulled free and frame her cheeks, bouncing with her every movement.

"Your sister requested that her breakfast be delivered to her room," she replies smoothly. "She has taken most of her meals alone since Tom and I arrived, poor girl. I believe the stress of Silas's passing has been particularly difficult for her to bear."

That sort of isolation . . . it has a way of making one feel like a ghost. Killian's words echo in my ears, bringing with them a rush of memories: his skin slick with candlelight, the thinness of the dark air between us, as if night had bled away some of its weight. What he told me about Father's death—the turnings.

To my cousin-in-law, I say, "Will she be better soon, do you suppose?"

With a small sigh, Cressida scrapes a dollop of jam over her toast. "I am not sure. Why do you ask? Is there something you wish to speak with Estella about?"

Reaching forward, I lift my steaming teacup—filled without incident, this time, by a uniformed maid who scuttles hurriedly away. "Only Father's funeral arrangements," I say to Cressida as I bring the cup to my lips. "I am sure my sister will want to begin planning shortly, and she'll certainly need assistance. Father handled most of the details for Mama's service, and it nearly overwhelmed him."

I take a sip of tea, then draw back as an unexpectedly sweet taste fills my mouth—floral, almost perfumelike, in comparison to the bitter tang of the moorflower leaves I was expecting. Lowering my cup, I gaze into it. Now that I'm paying attention, I notice the liquid is a darker red than usual, bits of delicate-looking plant matter swirling at the bottom of the drink. *Rose petals?*

"What is this?" I ask Cressida, looking up. "We always take moorflower tea with breakfast—it was Father's favorite. Have the kitchens run out?"

Next to his wife, Tom glances abruptly up from his newspaper at my question, the forkful of eggs he was in the process of shoveling into his mouth forgotten. His eyes dart to Cressida's, some wordless communication passing fluidly between them, too quickly for me to catch, before my cousin sets his paper aside and turns toward me.

"Ah—Merrick, I'm afraid we hadn't the chance to bring you up to speed at dinner last night," he says in the tone I've long since come to recognize as his gambling voice—glib, with the wicked smoothness of a shot of liquor. "Your sister didn't want to deny you anything on your first evening back, but unfortunately, it seems that Uncle Silas was rather . . ." He drifts off, searching for a word. "*Generous* in the weeks before his passing. He'd given nearly half the estate's pantries away to various charities by the time Estella caught on, and Lightkeeper knows what else. We believe he was attempting to clean house, so to speak, before he . . ."

Another pause, this one heavier than the first. With it, the swallow of tea in my stomach turns sour, threatening to rise back up my throat. *Before he . . .*

Mist creeps across my mind's eye, my father's form in the midst of it, hung with white. Killian mentioned his belief to me last night that Father had been planning his trek into the Graylands for a while prior to his passing; still, Tom's words chill me. If Essie hadn't put a stop to him, would Father have given our entire lives away before he died? Have sold Norland itself out from under us?

He was . . . sick with grief over the loss of your mother, Killian said. But this sounds like something beyond sickness to me. This . . . it sounds like insanity.

Tom clears his throat, continuing. "Along with the added expenses related to border maintenance . . . well, the Norland coffers are a bit lighter than usual at the moment," he goes on, with a forced lightness that only makes the spike of alarm in my center stab at me harder. "Not to worry—they'll fill back up after taxes come due later this month—but for now we all may need to go without certain luxuries. Besides." He pivots, taking his wife's hand. "Cress feels it's best to save the remaining tea for the party, right, dear?"

I blink, momentarily distracted by his last statement. "I'm sorry. What party?"

In response, Cressida smiles at me. "Merrick, sweetheart," she coos, "the people of Sussex are in mourning. You are too young to have yet witnessed the unrest that comes with a transfer of power, but trust me when I tell you that commoners are like deer. If they detect the slightest hint of danger, they will grow reckless, trample over one another in their haste to flee. And with the border in the state that it is—not to mention the nature of your father's passing—I fear your situation has the potential to grow quite . . . messy." She wrinkles her nose at the word.

"No," she continues, "what the Manor needs right now is a figurehead—someone for the people to anchor their hopes to, not a dead monarch for them to weep over. Which is *why,* instead of a funeral, I have decided that the Darling Manor will host a ball."

She takes a triumphant sip of her tea, sitting back in her chair as if pleased with herself. Beside her, Tom nods guilelessly along.

"A ball?" I scoff, disbelieving, but Cressida's expression remains unchanged, her lips kissed with red from the rose.

"At the end of the week," she confirms. "Invitations went out this morning. The entirety of the Mortal Council has been invited, naturally, as well as most of the Manorborn . . . a few commoners as well, as an act of goodwill." Her fingers flutter dismissively. "Only the rich ones, not to worry."

"Yes, because the cheery mood would be spoiled by the presence of anyone with less than a thousand marks a year," I mock. Shifting to face my cousin, I challenge him. "Tom, this is absurd. You wish people to celebrate Father's death?"

His neck flushes above the white collar of his shirt. "Merrick, of course not—"

"I want them focused on the future of the Darling Manor, not the present—and Estella is that future," Cressida interjects. With visible effort, she lets out a controlled exhale, lowers her voice to a purr. "I apprenticed under my grandmother for many years before Tom and I married, and if Elodie Faulk has taught me anything, it is that people wish for their ruler to make them feel safe above all else. Secure. It is imperative that we convince the citizens of Sussex that your sister can protect them the way your father did, at least until the Nomination Hearing is through." She tilts her head, her ringlets bobbing. "We don't want to give the Council any reason to doubt Estella's competency, do we?"

I tense at the mention of the Mortal Council—the interprovince governing body composed of all twelve reigning Manor Lords, whose sessions Father used to often travel to New London to attend. Along with managing disputes between provinces, the Council's duties include confirming all incoming Lords through a swearing-in ceremony known as a Nomination Hearing. Father's Hearing took place before I was born, but I've attended others in my life—I remember the murmur of the Councilors' chatter, the flash of the ceremonial knife through the air, and the lick of crimson liquid slipping across the Nominee's skin like a dog's tongue after they'd been confirmed.

My mouth dry, I take another swallow of my tea. "And the breaches?" I hedge. "What of them? We cannot simply hand the Phantoms a glass of wine and spirit them away."

Cressida shrugs. "A product of Lord Silas's deteriorating mental state, and nothing more. With Estella in power, and Tom and me here to assist her, they will soon be rectified." She brings a hand to press against her breast, her eyes wide and reassuring. "I promise it, Merrick."

I sit back, observing her. Though it gives me no pleasure to admit, Cressida's plan, laid out like this, makes a certain amount of sense. Dazzle the province with a show of wealth, splendor—even if that show is only a façade. Keep them looking forward, toward the promise of a bright tomorrow, rather than back at our dreary past.

Bury our skeletons and enchant them with the flowers that grow over the gravesite. Bury Father, his memory—and his mistakes.

I cross my arms. "Fine. What is my role in this scheme of yours?"

Cressida's mouth curves in a victorious smile. "You need do nothing except attend the ball," she replies. "Support your sister—through your presence *and* words, if at all possible. I want it known that the Darlings are a united front in this matter. We stand by our Nominee, no division."

A united front. I almost flinch at that, my fists balling in my lap. Where was that front when the mist was about to swallow me whole yesterday afternoon? I am certain my driver did not feel my family's support when he was pulled from our carriage, when the Phantom's teeth sank into his neck.

"I will consider it," I reply in a level tone. "If another breach like the one I experienced occurs, though, I should feel obligated to alert the Council—consequences notwithstanding. Our duty is to our people above our own reputation."

Cressida's grin falters. "Of course," she concedes demurely. Her eyes flick up to me as she lifts her knife to cut another bite of her breakfast, her full lashes like a ruff of black satin around them. "Though I must say, my dear, the *Toast* has been raving about your early success this season. I'd hate for potential matches to be dissuaded by any . . . unsavory news coming out about Sussex."

My shoulders stiffen. So this is my cousin-in-law's strategy—to frighten me with talk of lost Nominations, then use my own marriage prospects against me to ensure my cooperation. I'd despise her if I didn't admire her cleverness. If I didn't already know, on some deep level, that she's right.

Without my name—without the influence of my Manor supporting me—my beauty, my charm, would mean nothing in New London. I'd be like a cut flower, traded for a coin and then stuck in some man's bedroom until I wilt, dried up and forgotten.

"I understand you completely," I say, rising. "Now, if you'll excuse me, I seem to have lost my appetite."

Curtsying briefly to Tom, I make my way swiftly to the door and then out into the hallway. Without a destination in mind, I let my feet wander of their own accord, my attention drifting. *Balls, reputations.* I thought I'd left these games behind in New London, but it seems they've followed me here. And I am not nearly as good a player as I believed.

Eventually, my vision clears and I find myself outside, seated on a bench in Norland's back gardens, facing the cliffs and the sea beyond. It's drizzling—a fine mist falls past my shoulders, clinging dustlike to my curls and dampening the somber black fabric of my dress—but I make no move to head back inside. Instead, I let my skirts grow heavy with moisture as I watch the Graylands pulse on the other side of our fiery border, the mist rising and falling like the flank of a slumbering beast.

I imagine Father walking into the white, tears on his face. I imagine him alone.

"Excuse me. Are you all right?"

Instinctively, my hand flies to my side—reaching for my knife, or a Ghostslayer—only to come up empty. Muscles tensed, I turn.

Standing in the garden behind me is the lanky figure of a boy about my age, droplets of rain pattering off his shoulders and ringing his blond hair like a halo. Where it's broken through the clouds, the weak morning sunlight dapples his features, revealing long-lashed blue eyes and high cheekbones, a curved, frowning mouth.

My thoughts fuzz. Though I don't think we've met, this boy seems familiar in the same vague, hazy way that makes you recognize certain phenomena—snow, the ocean—even the first time you see them, just by their descriptions. *Blond hair. Blue eyes.* Where have I heard tell of someone like that before?

"I'm sorry," the boy says, taking a hesitant step back at my silence. He's clutching a bouquet of flowers in one hand: I spot wild daisies and red campion among the cheerful clash of colors, all tied together with a simple periwinkle ribbon. "I don't mean to intrude," he continues, "it's just, I noticed you out here without any cover, and with the weather as it is . . ."

His gaze sweeps over my mussed hair and sodden dress before darting toward my face again. When I meet his eyes, he pauses, his posture loosening as if with a realization.

"Ah," the boy murmurs. "Wait a moment. I know you."

I'm struck by the flash of genuine delight that crosses his expression—as if we are old friends who have unexpectedly been reunited. "Archdaughter Merrick Darling," he declares happily. "You've come home."

His smile is warm, his voice rich, with a husky smokiness to it that reminds me of an expensive cigar. Taken together, the qualities disarm me more than they should. "I have," I say cautiously, rising from the bench. "Though I seem to be at a disadvantage, sir, for I am not sure I can recall your name as easily as you have mine. Pray tell, have we met before?"

The boy flushes, a pink tinge creeping over his cheeks.

"Forgive me—my mother is forever reprimanding me for my lack of propriety, and here I've managed to bring shame on her again," he says, shaking his head in bashful self-castigation. "My name is Saint—Archson Ames Saint."

Closing the distance between us, he dips into a bow, his free hand finding mine and bringing it to his lips. His mouth is cool and dry against my ungloved wrist, his touch unexpectedly tender, like the press of a cloth against my rain-damp skin. At it, I feel myself quiet, my thoughts dispersing like clouds blown across the sky.

Ames Saint. The name calls forth an image: the crawling wings of a sun-washed, sprawling estate, nestled in the rolling green countryside like a slumbering dragon. A blue flag whipping in the breeze, a golden hawk stitched on its fabric.

The Roost—home of the Saint Manor, rulers of our neighboring province, Cardiff. The grand house is just visible from the top of the hills along the northern edge of our territory, its yellow stone like a buttery pearl among the surrounding fields. I should know; as a child, I made the climb whenever I could, observing the estate and searching for evidence of the boy that I knew dwelled within, elusive and fascinating as a storybook prince.

The only son of Manor Lord Ianthe Saint, Ames should have been an ideal playmate for Essie and me, yet my family rarely interacted with the Saints while I was growing up. The distance was partially due to the fact that Ames spent much of our youth living with his father in New London, but I know, too, it wasn't only that—know that on some level, the choice was one my parents intentionally made. Despite sharing a border, Father looked down on the Saints' quaint farmlands, the respectively smaller size of their province compared to ours. As a result, Ames remained more an imaginary friend than anything else, an intriguing rumor I'd never managed to confirm.

And yet, here he is, finally in front of me.

A fizz of desire trickles through me. Looking at this boy, I feel more myself than I have in a while.

"Of course," I say, my neck heating. "Archson Ames—it is wonderful to meet you at last. What brings you to Norland House?"

"I'm afraid my mission is a rather somber one—I've been sent by my mother to offer our condolences on your loss," Ames replies, his expression dimming. Releasing my hand, he holds the bouquet of wildflowers out toward me. "We were deeply saddened to hear about Lord Silas's passing, Archdaughter. The nation will feel his absence most keenly."

For some reason, the show of sympathy from him—a boy who, in the New London circles in which I traveled, was as famous for his tawdry affairs as for his looks—makes me feel shy. Ames was not present for this year's season, but I've heard tell of the extensive trail of broken hearts he left in his wake at past ones. A willoughby, he's been called. A bachelor, just a bit too charming to earn the title of full-fledged rake. Among eligible ladies of my age, he's become something of a romantic holy grail, his elusiveness an allure that glows brighter even than his title. I myself passed several restless nights under the Eaveses' roof constructing elaborate fantasies of our nonexistent courtship.

In none of those scenarios did I envision encountering him like this, unkempt and wild-haired, standing escortless by a bench in the rain.

I accept the proffered flowers gingerly, suddenly self-conscious. "Thank you, sir," I reply. "My sister and I are grateful to you—and to Lord Ianthe for her consideration. It has been a . . . trying week, to say the least."

Ames's mouth twists in a sympathetic smile. "I'm sure. My own father passed only a couple years ago. You should have heard the talk among the servants—something about the girlish timbre of my sobs." Throwing me a wink, he adds, "I'm disappointed to find you so sober-faced, by comparison."

Surprising myself, I laugh. "So you understand."

"As much as one can ever understand another's pain," he replies with a shrug. "Power complicates grief. To lose a parent is one thing—but to lose a Lord and a father at once . . ." His eyes mist over, his gaze turning thoughtful. "The confusion lies in which to mourn, and how."

My skin pricks, the hairs on my arms rising. "Exactly," I breathe. "I—"

"Merrick."

From behind Ames, a voice calls my name—its intonation weary more than anything else. Letting my eyes slide silently over Ames's shoulder, I settle my gaze on my sister, who's lingering farther down the garden path. She's dressed in plain black, a spencer jacket of the same color fastened over her dress, and a raven cloak pulled around her shoulders to keep off the rain. The hood has fallen back, exposing her face; her hair hangs in a neat ebony braid, moisture coating the strands with a wet, glistening sheen.

"Essie," I answer, by way of greeting. Without moving to meet her, I motion to Ames, who's standing, seemingly paralyzed, beside me. "The Saints send their condolences."

My sister's flat gaze travels sideways, landing without interest on Ames. "Ah, Archson Ames," she says, dropping into a shallow curtsy. "How nice to see you again."

Again? I cast a suspicious glance Ames's way. His playful, relaxed demeanor has hardened like a shell; he seems formal, stiff even, like a schoolboy called to face the headmaster.

Do they know one another?

"Archdaughter Estella," Ames says levelly, bowing. "My mother and I—"

Essie cuts him off with a wave of her hand. "Thank you for the flowers," she says, gesturing to the bouquet I'm still clutching in my grasp. "My cousins are inside—if you are weary, they can have Cook make you a cup of tea for your journey."

Turning her attention to me, she raises an appraising brow. "Merrick, I should like a moment to speak with you. Alone."

It's a brusque dismissal, but if Ames is offended, he hides it well. Throwing me a parting smile, he bows once more to Essie and then makes his way past her, back up the path toward Norland. My sister watches him go, her gray owl eyes tracking his receding figure. Once he's a suitable distance away, she sighs, crossing to the stone bench and sinking down onto it.

She smooths out her skirt, the dark fabric crinkling under her touch. "Cressida said you were asking after me."

I tear my gaze from Ames. "Yes," I say, sitting next to her—but I can't keep my attention from drifting unconsciously back to the Saint Vessel, his blond hair like a slant of sun breaking through the rainy murk. Lower, I add, "Are you and he acquainted?"

Essie follows my stare, her mouth twitching with a grimace. "He called once or twice while you were gone," she says evenly. "Put up to it by his mother, I'd bet. You know how Lord Ianthe was with Father—always pestering him about improved relations, the importance of being a good neighbor, all that drivel." My sister picks at a crescent of dirt that's wedged its way under her thumbnail. "Once I bored him to tears, he stopped visiting."

I hate the prick of jealously that stabs at me. "Ah."

Evidently interpreting my succinctness as criticism, Essie scowls at me. "They weren't *those* kind of calls, Merrick," she snips. "Ames is his mother's Vessel; it is important that he develop political relationships early. Not all of us had the luxury of attending balls for the past four months."

Her comment hits me like the flick of a switch. "I've told you already, I had no choice but to go to New London. Without the hope of becoming Lord, there was nothing for me here—you know that," I say, my voice terse. "If I'd been informed of the border situation earlier, perhaps I could have helped—organized patrols while Father was grieving, ensured that the lanterns were maintained."

My sister's lips part, a rebuttal flaring in her eyes—and then, sudden as a passing summer storm, her rage departs. Her shoulders sag forward, bony beneath her dress. With a start, I realize how much weight she's lost since I saw her last, how frail she seems—like a straw doll, one hard pinch away from snapping.

"There was nothing you could have done," she says. Her voice is hollow, knocking dully against me.

"But we could have tried," I reply, scooting closer to her. "You and I, together. Instead, I've had to hunt down snippets of the truth like breadcrumbs—to beg it out of sentries. Men who've devoted themselves to *serving* us, Essie. Do you realize how humiliating that is?" My tone is pitching upward without my meaning to, the accusation in it breaking free. I bite my lip, forcing my nerves to settle before I start again. "You needn't to hide Father's sins from me any longer. Cressida and Tom told me how he drained our supplies *and* our treasury before he died. And . . . I spoke with Killian Brandon last night."

Essie's head snaps up. "About what?"

I blink, taken aback. In the instant between one second and the next, my sister has changed again, a nervous energy pushing her upright. She watches me warily, like a feral cat, as if she's waiting for me to strike her.

"About the turnings," I answer unsteadily. "The sentries who changed?"

"Oh." My answer seems to calm Essie; frowning, she picks at her nails again, absent-mindedly. "Yes, that's—that's under control," she says. "Brandon shouldn't have worried you with it."

I wait for her to go on, to explain her reaction just now, but my sister's expression is curiously blank—as empty as if I were not present at all. The back of my neck prickles with trepidation.

"Is there something else bothering you, Essie?" I prod, trying again.

Is it a trick of the light, or do I see her eyes flicker away for a half second before returning to me? Adrenaline clenches like a fist in my chest as she blinks, her gaze vacant and doll-like.

I can barely breathe when she exhales.

"I was so angry at you, when you left," Essie murmurs haltingly, and my heart lurches at the shift in topic. "You can't imagine what it was like while you were gone—what Father was like. It wasn't only his neglect of the borders, his failure to assign patrols." She rubs at her temples, as if trying to blot out a memory. "There was this hopelessness to him—this malice—it was almost as if he *wanted* to ruin us, as if he thought our whole Manor should die along with Mother. You say Cressida and Tom told you about his so-called charitable efforts?" She scoffs. "He was giving away our food, Merrick. I had to start rationing staff portions because he was sending all their bread to peasants, like by tending to them, he could bring his own commoner wife back from the dead. And then, that morning"—her voice drops almost to a whisper, trembles—"I heard him in the corridor, early, and I swear, his footsteps shook me to my bones. They were so heavy, it was almost like a warning, or an omen of some kind, and I *know*

71

how I sound, I know, but something just told me to follow him. So, I . . . I did."

She averts her eyes, her mouth quivering slightly. Even now, attempting to rein herself in. To people who are not intimately acquainted with her, Estella Darling is untouchable—unruffled by the passing of the seasons, by the trials that come with them. By death.

But I have swum in still waters before. I know that under their surface, there is movement. A current.

Conflict.

I reach out, brushing her shoulder. "Essie, I—"

Abruptly, Essie pushes herself up, swipes at her face to brush away the moisture rimming her eyes. When she turns back to me, she is composed again, all her fears slotted neatly back in place.

"This place . . . Norland House . . . there's something wrong with it," she says urgently. "There are things happening here . . ." She trails off, bites down on her cheek. "You made the right choice, leaving it behind—even if I didn't see that at the time. And I believe it will be in the best interests of all of us if after the week is through, you return to New London at once."

CHAPTER SEVEN

I *believe it will be in the best interests of all of us if after the week is through, you return to New London at once.*

Essie's words haunt me for the next few days. Every night, I toss for hours before I can finally shuck them off and tumble into an uneasy sleep; still, they always crawl back to me with the dawn, lingering like a dark spot in the corner of my mirror.

For three mornings following our conversation in the gardens, I barely see my sister. Though the rest of Norland House is caught in a swirl of party preparations, Essie herself rarely leaves her room aside from at mealtimes. On the few occasions that she does join Tom, Cressida, and me at the dining table, I find myself startled by the exhaustion that seems to radiate from her every pore, her eyes like dull tin spoons set into her ashen face.

Whether it's Father's death that's upset her so or something else, I don't get the chance to ask, nor am I able to question her further about her previous remarks. In the solitude of my room, though, I turn them over and over in my mind, revisiting them until their edges are as worn as a well-rubbed coin.

There are things happening here . . . in the best interests of all of us if . . . you return to New London at once.

Paranoia, I assure myself, *it must be.* There is nothing *happening* at Norland House—my sister has merely been alone for too long, as Killian said. She has started to see monsters where there are none, to read her own doom in every crack in the wall. With time, the borders will heal, and so will she.

During the day, I almost convince myself of this. But at night, when I wake to the bleak darkness surrounding me and the mist a white line beyond my window . . . then, in the seam between waking and dreaming, I think I can feel it.

A force, watching me. Collecting Darlings, one by one.

My fifth morning at Norland House—the day before Father's Memorial Ball—I rise early and make my way to the stables after breakfast. I tuck a letter for Fitz Vannett in the pocket of my cloak before I go, along with a couple more addressed to fellow debutantes I'd befriended in New London, leaving word with the stable boy to tell Cressida if she inquires that I've gone into town to post them.

In truth, though, more than crossing a chore off my list, I need an escape. A couple hours away from the endless ivory flank of the Graylands and my sister's empty gaze—just enough to remind myself that the world does not stop at the end of Norland's front drive.

That though I've come home, I can leave it again, if I wish.

The velvet fabric of my riding habit clings to my legs, whipping in the wind as I ride. Beneath me, my horse, a dove-gray mare named Pegasus, huffs with exertion as I drive her onward, plunging toward the horizon that hovers in the distance, a blue seam between heaven and earth.

I inhale a lungful of briny air, the salty sting of it in my nostrils rousing me as I push Pegasus faster, faster. The Sussex coastline is a blur to my left: green hills bleeding into an overcast sky, the thin line of the coast beyond it, chalky cliffs like powdered bone. Along their edge, lanterns burn steadily. The Graylands linger just past the reach of the flames like a murky, leaden cloud, contained enough that a more naïve person could almost be fooled into believing they pose no threat.

I squint at them warily. Is it my imagination, or has the fog crept closer over the past few days? Drawing nearer inch by careful inch, like water rising with the tide.

Giving Pegasus's reins a tug, I direct her away from the cliffs, following a fork in the dirt road toward a copse of trees farther inland. Shoreham-by-Sea, the nearest town to Norland House, is accessible by the coast, but cutting through Barton Woods is quicker—and besides, there's something about our timber forests I've always found soothing. It is their nobility, I think. Passing under the regal green crown of the treetops, over the ancient stretch of knotted roots, is enough to make even Manorborn feel mouselike by comparison.

The temperature drops once I enter the trees' cover, the atmosphere heavy with the rich smell of soil, of growth and decay. Shadows coat the forest floor, thick as moss, patches of sunlight scattered here and there like a spill of gold coins upon the ground. Aside from the occasional whistle of birdsong above my head, the area is quiet, peaceful.

"Traveling all alone, Archdaughter?"

The call comes from behind me—gruff and rumbling like the scrape of stone on stone. Heart pounding, I yank on Pegasus's reins, easing her to a halt, then twist around in my saddle.

About twenty paces away stands a man, broad-shouldered and roughly clad in a patched coat and trousers. A beard covers the lower half of his ruddy face, the hair wiry and unkempt; above it, cunning blue eyes twinkle in the dimness. He's smiling; the emotion is too sharp at the edges, like the glittering curve of a scythe.

"You ought to be careful," the man says, taking a step forward. "Sussex isn't as safe as it used to be—or haven't you heard the rumors?"

He passes underneath a break in the branching canopy overhead, and light bathes him. My pulse slows as it carves out his features, bringing him into better view. *I know this man.*

"Mr. Birks," I say with a sigh of relief. "I—I didn't recognize you. What are you doing out here—why have I not seen you at Norland House?"

Despite the fact that I've placed him, it's still a struggle to reconcile my image of my father's well-coiffed butler with the wild-haired, snarling man in front of me. If I look closely, I can almost make out the strong cut of his jaw underneath the choking bramble patch of his beard, but it's the difference in his demeanor that disturbs me the most. Gone is his composed manner, the gentle wisdom that always made our guests feel so at ease, back at Norland. Now he looks at me like I'm a fish he'd like to gut.

Birks chuckles, drawing another step closer to me. Instinctively, I tug on Pegasus's reins, urging her back. "You should ask your sister," he tells me. "She's the one who fired me."

"Essie fired you?" I flinch, at both the harshness of his expletive and the poison with which he hurled it. "But why would she . . ."

I fall silent as he shifts, dipping his chin so that the left side of his profile is angled toward me. Creeping up his neck like a vine is a grayish-white pattern, a shadow under his skin as if his veins have been filled with ash. A thin tendril stretches out from his beard toward his left eye, like an arrow aimed at his iris.

Grayrot. The first stage of the turning—and one of the Graylands' most visible love marks. My throat constricts, my hands clenching the strips of leather in my fists harder.

The former butler's grin spreads wider at my reaction. "Frightened, are you?" he taunts. "Your sister was, too. Silly girls—don't you know it won't kill you until it's through with me?" He traces the moldy line of the grayrot, following it to where it disappears under the collar of his shirt, then lets his hand drop to his side. "Though perhaps you are right to be scared. After all, Phantoms aren't the only creatures who can take a life."

I see the flash of the knife at his side just as the bushes rustle ahead of me, a branch cracking like a bone snapped clean. Whirling around, I gasp as I catch sight of another man—this one unfamiliar and taller than Birks, with a hungry, feverish air like a starved fox—emerging from in between the trees. He's armed with an identical blade, the metal gleaming liquid gold where it catches the light.

Blood pounds in my ears. "What do you want?" I spit the question through gritted teeth, glancing back toward Birks.

He gives another low, dry laugh, as if my words amuse him. "Only what I'm owed," he says, sliding the knife out from his coat and tapping the flat of it against his palm. "What your father owed me."

His shoulders tense, as he's readying to dart forward. The motion is just the push I need. Fury breaks through my shock like the snap of a whip, focusing my mind. In a single, fluid motion, I slip one hand beneath my cloak, my fingers closing over the handle of my Ghostslayer. The solid weight of it in my grasp bolsters me, like the steady arm of a friend.

Smoothly, I pull it out, level it at the bearded man's skull. "He owed you nothing," I reply, cocking the gun for emphasis. "And neither do I."

I expect Birks to shrink at the sight of my gun, stumble back toward the safety of whatever cave he crawled out from. Instead, the threat of a bullet only seems to rile him. His smile twists into a grimace, all bared teeth and swollen, ruined gums.

"*Liar*," he hisses, his eyes blazing, "You Darlings . . . you sit in your pretty clothes in your pretty house and you play at being gods, while the Graylands grow fat off the rest of us." *Tap, tap, tap* goes the knife, faster and faster as it slaps the palm of his hand. "Well, I won't let it take me, no," he mutters. "Silas promised to help us. But now he's gone, so you'll have to help instead."

I hear leaves crunch beneath the boots of my second attacker just as Birks lunges toward me, his features contorted in a howl. My bullet finds him midleap, tearing cleanly through his chest and bringing him to the ground. Heart a battle drum in my ears, I leave him there, broken, as I steady Pegasus, whipping her in the direction of his companion.

The sound of a second shot roots me in place. For a terrible moment, I fear it's been fired by the other man—wait for the fleshy rupture of the bullet as it tears through my skin—but no pain comes to sink its fangs into me. It is only then that I see the smoking bit of metal buried in a nearby tree, take in my remaining attacker standing slack-jawed next to it, his knife clasped in a shaking hand.

"I would advise you to consider your next move very carefully. Sentries are trained to shoot first, repent later."

A familiar voice echoes through the trees, terse and controlled like a drawn bowstring. Hooves clomp over the forest floor, moving steadily nearer.

I briefly abandon my watch over the remaining attacker to look in the direction of their approach. A figure on horseback breaks from the indigo shadows of the woods, the scattered light draping over him in pieces: hair the saturated color of wet sand, a pale, smirking mouth, mismatched eyes set into a scarred face.

"As you can clearly see," Killian says, motioning with his Ghost-slayer toward the first man's corpse, "Archdaughter Merrick is a far better shot than I am." He cocks his head to the side, his blue eye burning in the dimness. "That first bullet was a warning. I may miss you the second time, but I promise you, she will not."

Waxen-skinned, the taller attacker gives me only a parting sneer before dropping his blade and racing deeper into the forest. As soon as he does, Killian spurs his horse into motion, sidling the animal closer to me until I can almost taste the musty heat emanating from its body. Flustered, I move to flick my own reins and guide Pegasus away, but Killian covers my gloved hand with his own before I can, taking my reins in his fist.

"Are you hurt?" His gaze is locked on mine, interrogating—intense.

A soft noise of protest catches in the back of my throat. He is holding me fast, but when I try to break from his grasp, I find that my muscles are frozen. It is as though there is a thread stretched between us, binding us both together; if I so much as flinch, the connection might tear and break us apart.

"No," I finally manage, my voice strangled. Immediately, Killian nods, releasing me.

"Shall I give pursuit?" he asks, inclining his head in the direction my surviving attacker fled.

The tall man's eyes—black with loathing, two polished bits of obsidian—flash across my vision. I shift in my saddle to take in Birks's prone corpse, the grayrot cobwebbed over his neck, frozen in its conquest of him, and guilt burns the back of my throat like a swallow of alcohol.

"No," I say again. "Let him go."

Killian raises a brow, but he doesn't question my decision,

leaning over to rub his horse's heaving flank. His nearness has left me unsteady; I feel fuzzy-headed, buzzing with nervous energy.

"You don't need to keep doing this, you know," I say.

Killian halfway lifts his head, giving his horse a final, solid pat. His mouth twitches as if he's restraining a smile, sandy stubble glinting around his jaw.

"Do what?"

I glance away, suddenly flustered. "Keep . . . swooping in, whenever I'm in trouble. Playing hero."

He exhales—a single, hushed breath of laughter. "Trouble seems to have a habit of finding you along my patrol routes. I'm not playing at anything," he parries. His expression shifts, turning reflective. "And I'm under no illusions about you needing a hero."

My skin prickles; I can feel his gaze on me, and it is like the press of a blade, or the brush of a moth's wings. If I move, it may cut me. If I move, I may frighten him away.

Finally, he clears his throat, gesturing at Birks's body. "So. Robbers?"

Grateful to him for changing the subject, I shake my head. "The other man was a stranger, but I know—knew—him. Mr. Birks. He was my father's butler, though I suppose Essie dismissed him while I was away. He was . . . he'd been exposed to the mist." Anxiety, a dark, slippery eel, coils its way around my lungs. I close my eyes and see Birks darting across the backs of my eyelids, see his tormented expression. "He wanted something," I say, blinking my eyelids open again. "Something he felt my father owed him, apparently."

Killian hums, observing the figure on the ground curiously. "Ah."

I glance at him sidelong, my awareness prickling at the recognition I hear in his tone. "What?"

"I thought he looked familiar, is all." The sentry lifts his shoulders in a shrug, still focused on the corpse splayed before us. "There was talk around the house after your sister severed his employment—that he didn't take the news well. I haven't heard mention of him being owed anything, though in truth, your sister was being merciful by letting him live at all. Procedure would have dictated she have him slain as soon as he showed signs of turning."

His attention flicks to me. "Could it be wages he was after?"

"Most likely," I respond. "Or food, perhaps. Essie mentioned Father had started giving some of our supply away in the weeks before he died. Birks might have wanted in on his charity."

You sit in your pretty clothes . . . while the Graylands grow fat off the rest of us. I shiver at the ghost of the butler's voice in my ear. Avert my eyes from his limp body cooling in the dirt nearby. *He was dying,* I tell myself. *You brought him no end that was not already coming to him. In some ways, it is a mercy.*

Next to me, Killian rubs at his jaw, his chest heaving with a sigh. "Your father was a good man," he says, bringing me back to the present. "I wish I'd had the chance to become better acquainted with him."

I can't help the bitter scoff that slips from my throat. "He was generous with his subjects. Not so much with his daughters."

Killian stares at me, watchful and silent in a way that reminds me of a graveyard crow. Then, abruptly, his gaze pulls away, his face clouding over.

"Do you see that?" he asks. I twist to look over my shoulder, stiffening when I make out the column of red smoke spiraling above the treetops. *A distress call.* The color is distinctive: created using a special beetroot dye, which is then mixed with powder and burned as a signal to nearby sentries. The kind that only means one thing.

Phantoms. Nearby, judging by the distance of the smoke signal. There's been another breach.

CHAPTER EIGHT

The house is half-drowned when we arrive, its front door flung wide as if in a groan. Banks of mist the wan color of tallow have engulfed it on all sides, swallowing the first floor whole and stretching toward the second like an open maw, hungry for more. A few wisps of pinkish-red smoke from the signal fire we glimpsed drift from the building's chimney—a dwindling echo of the steady plume that drew us here.

Though I can't make out the source of the breach, the fog seems to be coming from a forested area behind the house, the land in front of it still relatively clear. I'd bet if I followed the white back through the trees, I'd find another blackened lantern, just like the one I spotted on my drive to Norland. Another of our fires gone out.

Aside from myself and Killian, the area is quiet, the gentle rhythm of our horses' hooves like the soft patter of rain against the earth.

It is the silence that tells me: we have already lost.

"Archdaughter."

The forceful way Killian says my title tells me it isn't the first time he's repeated it. I hum a low note in response, my eyes hooking on the house's shadowed, open doorway, barely more than a thumbprint of darkness against the cottony plumes of mist.

What waits for us within?

Killian coughs. His shoulders are bunched together under the gray fabric of his uniform, his attention half on me, half on the scene in front of us—as if the house is a predator, poised to leap at him any second. "We should wait for your sister to arrive before attempting any further action," he says. "Or the other sentries, at least—they'll have seen the signal, too. The house is too dangerous to approach without backup."

Deep inside me, a rebellious muscle flexes at the implication buried in his words. Weak—despite what he just witnessed me do, back in the forest, he thinks I am too weak, too dainty to withstand the brutality of the task ahead. My sister, with her sharp wits and regimented way of conducting herself, he would trust, but me—the girl who ran to New London at the first sign of trouble, drowned her troubles in the sweet words of suitors and left her family to bear the burdens she shrugged off? I am the china doll to Essie's tin soldier, built of glass rather than metal. Beautiful, breakable. Made to marry a man and then sit on his shelf, far away from harm.

My father always said that of Essie and me, I was the romantic. I used to wonder if that simply meant he thought I was a fool.

I smooth my features into a neutral mask as I answer Killian. "That may be so," I reply evenly. "But what of the people who made the distress call? They could still be inside. Dangerous or no, we can't abandon them without at least attempting to help."

Killian hesitates. "They are not Manorborn, Archdaughter," he says cautiously. "The mist has already entered the house—if they have not escaped already, there is no saving them."

They will turn—become the monsters they now fear. Though he does not speak it aloud, his meaning is apparent. Shame chews at my organs. Father always spoke of our immunity as a duty—something to be wielded like a shield, to protect those who depend on us from the fog and its monsters. Yet looking at the scene before me, I can't stop Birks's earlier accusations from tolling through my head once more.

The breaches—I don't think I've felt the weight of them fully until today, staring their consequences in the face. Haven't understood the truth: that when my family fails, we patch over the problem, get back up. But our people die.

"They lit a signal fire, Mr. Brandon," I say firmly, raising a challenging brow at Killian. "They called for aid. Hopeless or not, it is my duty as a member of their ruling Manor to provide it to them."

Without waiting for Killian's reply, I dig my heels into Pegasus's sides, urging her into motion. Part of me hopes she'll allow me to lead her all the way to the door, but we've barely made it a few paces when she whinnies nervously, spooking at the fog that's snaking its way up her legs. Steadying her, I dismount, swinging myself to the ground, my Ghostslayer already in hand.

My feet sink into fog, thick and deep as a bank of fresh snow. It worms its way beneath the hem of my riding habit, weaving itself over my legs like a swarm of bugs. I wrinkle my nose in disgust, force myself onward.

Though I don't admit it, I'm grateful when Killian follows me.

"Here," he says, pulling gently on my elbow. "I brought extra. They'll be of more use to you than me."

In his palm, five bullets sit winking in the hazy light, a deadly sort of peace offering. I debate only for a second before accepting them, scooping the metal bits from his hand. When my fingertips brush Killian's, a sudden jolt—sharp and sweet like a kiss of lightning—zips through the second skin of my riding glove, coursing with a honeyed buzz up my veins.

He inhales—once, sharply—and looks away, gesturing toward the mist ahead of us.

"After you," he says.

The house is empty, dust hanging heavy in the air and clogging my nose. Remnants of its occupants—a husband, wife, and son, judging by the charcoal portrait hanging in the front vestibule—cling to the space, evident in the careful arrangement of flowers displayed on a table near the door, the bag of ribbons discarded by the stairway. The place feels peaceful, as if awaiting its owners' return.

"Divine Three."

Killian's voice is choked, his attention fixed on something halfway up the wooden stairs. Acting on impulse, I step toward it, reeling back as a sour, coppery tang like rusted metal fills my mouth, sticking unpleasantly to the back of my throat.

Blood.

It drips down the steps, pooling in shallow puddles the rich red hue of spilled wine. My ears ring with a piercing, high-pitched noise as I trace the flow back to its source: an ashen hand dangling over the top step, fingers reaching out as if for help.

Despite my training, my knees go weak at the sight of it, leaving me feeling childlike. I have seen plenty of dead Phantoms—even a few sentries slain during hunts—but never like this. Surrounded by domesticity, the grisly slaughter seems sacrilegious in a way that battlefield casualties do not. As if something evil has invaded this place, a sinister presence pulsing through the mist itself.

Killian trailing close behind me, I race up the stairs toward the body. My stomach rolls as more of its form comes into view— it's the husband, the corpse's features the same as those I just glimpsed in the charcoal drawing. His eyes are open, wide and petrified like a deer's as they stare sightlessly at the ceiling above them; his mouth lolls in an unvoiced cry.

Keeping a tight hold on my Ghostslayer, I squat down. The blood is coming from a gash on the man's neck, about five inches long from one end to the other. The violence of the wound— piercing through muscle to cartilage, bone—is disturbing, but it isn't what catches my attention. Furrowing my brow, I lean closer, observing the man more carefully.

"Mr. Brandon." I shift, making space for Killian to stoop alongside me. "Do you see this?"

I trace the cut, underlining the easy way the flesh is peeled back like a pair of parted lips. I've witnessed sentries wounded by Phantoms before. The marks they bear are like Killian's scars: messy, made by teeth and nails, organic weapons.

But this . . . this injury is neat, almost clinical. Made by a thin, sharp object, designed to kill and nothing more.

A blade? I shake my head. *It can't be.*

Killian releases a breath, leaning closer. "What . . ."

He goes still as, deeper within the house, a muffled thud echoes, like the sound of a chair being turned over. In unison, Killian and I turn toward one another, the corpse in front of us momentarily forgotten. Clutching my weapon close, I raise my free hand to my mouth, press a finger to my lips in warning.

Killian nods, noiselessly drawing his own gun from the holster at his hip. Motioning for him to follow, I creep back down the stairs.

I've barely set foot on the ground floor when, on the right side of the entry hall, a door flies open. I catch a glimpse of a sitting room behind it—sofa overturned and spattered with red, stuffing leaking from it like entrails—before fixing my attention back on the form currently hurtling toward me.

The Phantom runs on all fours like a dog, its stringy blond hair whipping about its face. Its mouth is open in a howl, its thin arms, purple with bruises, reaching for me as it pushes itself off from the floor and leaps.

I bring it down with one shot, its nails swiping futilely through the air in front of my throat as the bullet pierces its chest. Its skull clacks against my boot as it falls, and I kick the still-warm body away, embarrassed when I feel myself start to tremble. The walls of the house throb in my vision, heaving in and out like a pair of lungs.

"It's all right, Archdaughter." Killian's hand on my shoulder steadies me, a reassuring weight. "Your shot was good," he murmurs. "The creature is dead."

I angle my chin to glance back at him, breathing hard. "Do you think there are others?"

As if in answer, another thud judders my bones—followed by a dragging sound this time, like a body being hauled across the floor. Releasing me, Killian gestures to the sitting room with his weapon. The door has drifted mostly closed again, and as we watch, a shadow shifts behind it, painting the fog webbed across the floor with a strip of darkness. The shape moves erratically, darting to the left, then to the right, like a buzzing gnat.

As soundlessly as possible, I move closer, clenching my Ghost-slayer. Once I'm in position, I nod to Killian and wrap my hand around the doorknob, pulling it swiftly open.

It swings outward, emitting a half-sighed creak.

Inside: a horde of them, gathered like flies around a piece of rotting fruit. Three Phantoms are crouched over a body: the first two at the head and foot, respectively; the largest hovering, spiderlike, astride the corpse. From the blood-soaked cotton dress the figure wears, I can tell it is the wife, though large chunks of her neck and face have been bitten away to expose the raw muscle beneath, the color vicious as a ripe plum. Blood is everywhere—on the floor, streaked over the sofa I saw earlier—and farther back in the room, near the windows, I can make out the lump of another, smaller corpse. The son, no doubt.

Bile burns against the back of my throat. My nostrils flare, filled with the scent of copper and stale body odor, but I force myself to remain upright as I face down the monsters that now stare directly at me.

Their eyes are soulless white pits, their flesh lumpy and misshapen like congealed lard. Milky, moldlike veins crawl over their faces, branching across their wasted cheeks like burst blood vessels: grayrot, far more advanced than that which I witnessed on Birks. Protruding from the sore-covered gums of their open mouths are dozens of needle-like teeth, some still squat and rectangular at their roots, reminiscent of the human features the creature once possessed.

Upon observing us, the Phantoms sit back on their haunches, chittering to one another in a discordant song. Their mouths and necks are painted with fresh blood like berry juice, as if we have interrupted a macabre picnic. Cocking its head to the side, the largest Phantom leers at me from across the room, its cracked lips widening into something that almost resembles a smile.

I swallow and raise my gun, cursing at the sweat that's slickened my palm. In unison, the Phantoms spread out, their yellowed nails clicking against the floor as they scuttle away from the corpse of their victim.

A hiss slips from the leader's torn throat, rattling and deadly. I root my feet more firmly to the floor, my father's voice a ghostly murmur in my ear. *Steady. Focus your aim, that's it—*

My heart skips as the biggest Phantom lets out a droning shriek and sprints at me. I fire at it, but my shot only clips its side, causing it to swerve to the left, yowling. Panting, I whirl around in horror as I watch the two other beasts race toward the entryway, where Killian stands.

Bang. Bang. A pair of shots; a flurry of corresponding screams as the Phantoms collapse to the floor, inches from his feet. Past them, Killian slumps heavily against the doorframe, bent over his thigh. He's groaning—his leg, something about his leg.

Then: silence, the slow, ragged shuffle of the final monster pulling itself across the room. Back toward me.

Killian's voice is desperate. "Archdaughter, *shoot!*"

The Phantom's withered face stares at me, its unseeing eyes locked onto my own. As I watch, it crawls forward another few inches, mist pouring from a wound in its side, intermingling with the white that already swamps the room.

Its fangs part in a rictus grin. Gathering its strength, the creature leaps again—

I aim the barrel at its head and pull the trigger.

CHAPTER NINE

Later, I wake to a timid *rap rap rap* at my door, and I lurch upright with a start, drawing my sheets tighter around me. Night
has Norland in its palm again, purple-black shadows draped le-
thargically over the furniture. Rubbing at my eyes, I blink away
stray bits of dreams that cling to my vision like loose threads: the
Phantom's yellow teeth, bared as it leapt for me; Killian's mangled cry as he bent over his leg; a woman's body on the floor, half
of her face bitten away.

Even after several cups of tea, it had not been easy to coax my
body into slumber earlier. The trip back to Norland House had
been a blur, my panic at the attack lessened only by the fact that
Killian himself, by some miracle, was fine—uninjured except for
a shallow gouge on his left calf, which he tightly bandaged with
rough white strips of cotton after the rest of his regiment arrived
at the scene, shortly after we did. We passed the journey home
mostly in silence, each of us understanding that even the menial
effort of conversation might be enough to unravel the other.

The best I can guess at it, the residents of the house must have seen the mist as it approached the back of their property. Likely, they lit the signal fire Killian and I witnessed in an attempt to alert any nearby sentries, but failed to flee before the fog and the monsters that accompanied it overtook their dwelling. With the help of the additional guards, we'd discovered the source of the mist, afterward: a dead lantern in the woods behind the house, just as I'd supposed. Another breach.

Yet despite the supporting evidence, even that explanation feels thin, unstable. I hadn't had the chance to examine the corpse we'd found again before the sentries initiated the burning, but the memory of the cut—the viciousness of the slash, the poppy red bloom of the blood—lingers in my head all the same. It isn't so much the preciseness of the wound that bothers me; more so that it was the only *one*. I've witnessed enough Phantom attacks in my life to know that they don't hunt to kill but to eat—like the creatures that were feasting on the bodies of the wife and son in the sitting room. Why bring down a full-sized man and then just leave him there, untouched, to rot?

Tap tap.

I shift beneath my covers, twist toward the front of my room. The noise is so faint that at first I question whether I've imagined it—nightmares running into reality, nothing more. A few silent moments pass and then I roll back over, submitting to the sleep-fuzz that wells around my mind like a warm bath.

Tap. Tap tap.

It's louder this time, the unmistakable rap of knuckles against wood. Someone is knocking at my door.

"Hello?" I sit back up, heart pounding. "Who's there?"

Only the suffocating, midnight quiet answers me. The back of my neck turns clammy with nervous sweat as I fumble for the tinder box resting on my bedside table. It takes several attempts for me to coax a spark from the flint, but eventually, I'm able to light a spill and bring it to the wick of the brass candlestick waiting nearby. My pulse slows as the orange flame leaps into being, its warm glow a feeble defense against the blackness, but a defense nonetheless.

Barefoot, I cross to my bedroom door with the candlestick in hand, and, after a second's hesitation, twist the knob. My breath catches in my chest as on noisy hinges it swings wide, revealing the hooded corridor beyond—and the figure hovering just on the other side of the threshold, watching me with tired gray eyes.

I flinch. Silhouetted in the doorframe is a ghost.

My sister's ebony hair hangs in lank, unwashed strands around her shoulders, its usual glossy shine dulled to a greasy black. Illuminated by the candle flame, her complexion is sallow, like cream that has been left in the sun and gone sour. Sleepless nights are evident in the purple crescents beneath each eye, like thumb swipes of blackberry juice; restless days in the bitten, chapped skin of her lower lip. Clad in a plain cotton nightgown and with darkness billowing around her, she is spectral—a creature crawled out from the grave.

My shock manifests in a choked cough. "Essie?" I whisper, glancing up and down the hallway. No sentry's lantern parts the gloom—I wonder if Killian is on bed rest tonight, recovering. "What are you doing here?"

The barest sliver of emotion stirs in my sister's expression, like a breeze spinning dust into the air. "I came to check on you," she replies tonelessly.

Without another word, she slips past my shoulder into my bedroom, unbalancing me. The candle flame flickers, threatens to gutter out entirely; I clutch at the base of the candlestick to steady it, some ancient instinct insisting that if I allow the light to fail, the Phantoms from earlier will return, poured out of my head and into reality by some malignant trick of the night. "*Careful*," I hiss.

Once she's safely past the door, Essie seems to relax slightly—the cold shell of her face cracks a little more, a touch of warmth leaking out like groundwater pushing up through a dry riverbed. "I'm sorry," she apologizes, less rigidly. "And I'm sorry to call so late. I should have come earlier, as soon as you and Brandon returned. I don't know why I delayed."

She tugs at a strand of hair as she speaks, wrapping it around her finger and then unwinding it again, like a sable ribbon. Though she's standing still, all of her is in movement: her eyes dart to the corners of the room as if seeking out hidden eavesdroppers, her bare feet shift over the floorboards. *Agitated.* That's the word for it—my sister is agitated, and at the realization, apprehension pools in my stomach, leaden and cold. The Essie I know—the Essie I grew up with—changes like the seasons, gradually. She is not rash; she does not jitter, jump from one place to the next. *Where has she gone?* I think. *And who is this girl standing in her place?*

"It's fine," I tell her, moving to set my candle down so that I will not grab her hands instead, force her to stay still. "*We* are fine, both Mr. Brandon and I." I pause, debating whether to say more, to tell her about the body we found at the site of the breach and the odd wound I noticed on it. Or, perhaps I'd go further back, even—describe my encounter with Mr. Birks, how he blamed Essie for his firing. The hate I saw festering in his gaze as he looked at me, as if he wished to skin me alive just for the pleasure of it.

You sit in your pretty clothes in your pretty house and you play at being gods.

In the end, though, I keep quiet. Whatever the reason for her visit, my sister is upset enough without my adding more burdens to her load. After tomorrow is through, I decide, after the ball is over, we can talk. I'll tell her about Birks, and the strange corpse, and then . . .

What? a voice sneers in my head. *You'll leave? How very like you.*

"Are *you* all right?" I ask Essie, to distract myself.

She sighs, her arms wrapping around her rib cage—every part of her thinner than before I left for New London. "I'm not sure," she admits, her eyes lowered. "I couldn't sleep. And . . . it sounds ridiculous, but I was frightened of being alone."

With a sigh, she crosses to my bed, sinking down on the edge of the mattress without asking my permission. Her nails dig into the plush material of my duvet, leaving behind imprints like crescent moons.

"I know I've not been a good sister to you since you returned," she goes on, biting her lip. "And I'm sure you think it's because I resent you. I've already admitted to you that I did, back when you first left. But I . . ."

Without warning she tenses. "What was that?"

I whirl around, my frayed nerves like dried hay, easily catching fire. My room, though, appears unchanged—the shadows in the same positions they were a moment ago. "What?" I ask, baffled. Turning back toward my bed, I repeat, "Essie, what did you s—"

The sound of my sister's heavy breathing—a terrified wheeze, as if the air is being wrenched from her lungs—stops me short. A stillness takes hold of me when I see that her eyes are glassy with tears, moisture clinging to their rims; her hands have risen to cover her mouth, trembling against her cheeks.

"Essie." I move to kneel before her, taking her shaking hands in mine. "Essie, calm yourself," I say, squeezing her fingers. "You are safe, do you hear me? No one else is here. You're safe."

My reassurances stick in my throat on their way out. It feels awkward, comforting Essie this way—and not because of the distance that's yawned between us. But before I left for New London, the task of managing my constantly shifting sensitivities usually fell to my sister. When placed under pressure, Essie was like a thick sheet of ice—smooth and unbreakable—whereas my emotions were the choppy waters of a lake, alternatively lifting me up and dragging me into their embrace.

Your sister is her own master, Father had told me once, years ago. *But you are still a mystery to yourself, and that makes you reckless. Unreliable.*

How had I not read his denial then, pulled his rejection from the space between his syllables? Why did it take him spelling it out for me to understand what he'd been telling me my whole life?

You will never be Manor Lord.

"What is the matter with you, Essie?" I continue, swallowing my regrets and rising, tilting my sister's bowed chin down to meet my gaze. She's calmed a bit under my touch, though her eyes are still watery. "What are you so frightened of? If someone has given you reason to feel distressed, we can speak with Tom and Cressida—"

"*No.*" Briskly, she stands, pushing my hands away. "No," she repeats, less violently. "I don't trust them."

Dread swoops in, a bird on velvet wings, at her reaction. "Don't trust them?" I repeat, incredulous. While it's true that I've had my own reservations about my cousin and his wife since I returned, *I* am not the one who called on them for aid in the first place. What could possibly have triggered such a swift reversal of loyalty in my sister?

The creak of floorboards from the hallway interrupts us. Immediately, Essie twitches in the direction of the door, shadows spilling like ink across her face. Painted in monochrome, her emotions are starker—the flash of her fear a pure, dark ribbon against her porcelain skin.

"It is only one of the sentries. Killian Brandon, most likely." I try to placate her again as she glances back at me, her terror evident in the pinch of her mouth, her stiff frame. Unexpected remorse floods me, potent and thick, at the visible evidence of her strain—how accustomed she seems to the tug of it.

You left her to hold this alone.

You left her.

"I—I have to go," she murmurs, already only half-present, her gaze drifting under the crack in the door and away. "I'm sorry. I shouldn't have woken you."

A protest is on my tongue, ready to be spoken, but I take another look at her hollow expression—her wan face an eggshell, so thin and breakable—and relent. "You can always come see me," I say slowly reaching gingerly out to grasp her fingers again. "I'm glad that you did."

Essie rubs her thumb over the back of my hand, a brisk swipe of affection, then steps away. She's almost to the door when she turns, her expression stern.

"After the ball," she says, her voice the firmest I've heard it tonight. "I'll tell you everything. I promise, Merrick."

With that, she opens the door and slips into the corridor, shutting me back into solitude.

CHAPTER TEN

The morning of Cressida's Memorial Ball passes at a dreary, drawn-out pace, each hour welling atop the previous one like dew on a leaf. The building sense of anticipation around Norland fills the house with a buzzing tension like a held breath; time hisses slowly through my teeth, the clock creeping forward at a sluggish pace like a stretching cat.

In between her wardrobe preparations and various other duties, I barely see Essie, but she offers me a reassuring smile when I catch her speaking with our housekeeper after breakfast. Aside from her thinness, she looks mostly recovered from her frayed state last night—her hair is glossy and neat, and her face is freshly powdered. Her composure, too, has returned, evident in the graceful way she moves, the smoothness with which she addresses Cressida when my cousin-in-law corners her. The elder woman's hand on my sister's arm makes me flinch, stirring up images of Essie's stricken expression, the way she started at my very mention of our relatives.

I don't trust them.

Why? I still want to ask. But Essie said we'd speak after the ball, so for now, I wait.

According to Cressida, the response to our gathering has been generally favorable, if not tinged with a hint of scandal. I snuck her edition of the *Toast* when she'd finished with it earlier; as I read it over a steaming cup of tea, the neat black-and-white text sent dual shivers of anticipation and dread through me:

> Among the social creatures of the season, a great migration is under way this weekend as Manorborn fair and fickle alike make their way to the seaside estate of Norland House for a grand gala in honor of the late Manor Lord Silas Darling. Those seeking fresh country air will find Sussex's atmosphere most refreshing—though their revelries may be disturbed by the restless spirits of the still recently dead. Yet fear not, dear readers—our watchful gaze is far-reaching, and we are most eager to observe whether this event proves to be a resurrection for Darling Manor or the hammered nail in its coffin.

The day drags, heaves onward.

Evening comes, and I wear red.

Norland House is resplendent tonight, a glittering jewel underneath the liquid ivory paintbrush of the moon.

Rather than attempt to cram the entire population of Sussex into the grand ballroom of our estate, Cressida opted to make the majority of the Memorial Ball an outdoor affair. In the span of a few hours, Norland House's grounds have been transformed into a swirl of color and movement, the evening preternaturally bright with the glow of a dozen new fiery lampposts burning throughout the grounds. Darkness has been banished altogether tonight—Cressida's invitations specifically instructed guests to forgo all mourning attire in favor of Darling red as a means of honoring my father. The decision was debated fiercely in the *Toast*—exactly, I'd imagine, as Cressida hoped it would be. Say what one will, but I do not know a single politician or poet with a better grasp of language than my cousin-in-law, or a defter ability to twist the public discourse in the direction she desires it.

Her mission is clear: Cressida wants every Manorborn in the Smoke watching the Darling Manor tonight. And, for better or for worse, they are.

Guests attired in every shade of red from vermilion to the faintest rose weave between the lanterns, goblets of wine clutched in their hands. As they move, their expressions are thrown suddenly into view before fading into the night again: a radiant grin, a gleeful laugh, a wide-mouthed scream of ecstasy. Multiple times, I find myself about to reach out and brush someone's arm, if only to prove that they will not flit out of existence the second I get too close.

I have been rooted to the same patch of earth for the past ten minutes, looking for all the world like a potted flower in my garnet empire-waist gown. It's a gorgeous creation—yards of tulle the color of ripe cherries overlaying the skirt, with a darker burgundy ribbon along the bustline—not to mention, I'm sure, obscenely expensive.

Along with feasting on our population, the mist cut our ocean-locked island off from the rest of the world with its arrival, severing centuries-old trade routes as easily as snipping a thread. Rebuilding a national economy took nearly a century; today, most textile production is based out of the Cachemar Manor's province, Levath, to the west of us, and Ridewell, ruled by the Ibe Manor farther north, but resources are limited. Some former delicacies now exist only in the fiction of bygone eras, shelved alongside other figments of myth such as dragons and woodland sprites. Others, like moorflower tea, and certain scarce fabrics, are reserved for the Manors' use only—tokens of wealth for families like mine to collect and display as a peacock spreads its feathers.

Yet whatever its cost, my dress feels like damp wool against my skin, the pressure of the night causing sweat to pool beneath my arms and in the space between my breasts. Cressida made me recite the order of tonight's events so many times earlier that I can still hear the echo of my own voice in my ears. First, my sister and I have been instructed to mingle with the guests, let them see us united in the face of my father's death. Then, when the party is in full swing, we will pause the festivities to formally present Essie as the new Darling Vessel to the public. If all goes as my cousin-in-law has planned, our guests will enter the evening celebrating my father's legacy, and leave ushering in his successor. But my usually punctual sister is nowhere to be seen; though I turn left, then right, in search of her, she doesn't appear.

I worry at the fabric of my gown uneasily. Over the course of the day, Essie's midnight visit—and her haggard demeanor—festered in my mind like fruit left out, becoming more bitter and more potent with every passing hour. Now returning to the memory is as dizzying as a glass of red wine. Though I want to mark it down to nerves, or grief at my father's passing, deep down I know my sister's behavior last night wasn't that of an anxious woman . . . but a frightened one. It was evident in the way she clutched herself close throughout our entire conversation, as if all the while we were talking, she was pressed up against a corner, steeling herself to look around it. As if she was terrified by the prospect of what lay in wait on the other side.

The only question is: *What is she so afraid of?*

A beacon of gold flares beneath one lantern, catching my attention. I follow it to its source, my heart squeezing when my gaze lands on a tall, apple-cheeked girl, her willowy frame wrapped in an elaborate concoction of blush organza and vibrant crimson ribbons. Her blond hair is piled gracefully atop her head, pinned in silken loops that shine in the firelight as she laughs at her companion—and the true source of my distress.

Absence has suited Fitz Vannett well. This evening, he looks more polished than ever in a maroon tailcoat and lighter waistcoat beneath it, his top hat clutched loosely in his hands. At the sight of his familiar dark hair and rich russet skin my chest feels notably tighter, as if a rope has been tied around my breastbone and pulled taut.

I wasn't certain if he would be here tonight. Back in New London, even before the *Toast* sighting of us, Fitz and I had formed something of an attachment during the season: his name routinely filled at least one slot on my dance card, and he'd frequently call on me at the Eaveses'. Despite his outward interest, though, I'd always gotten the feeling that he viewed me as more of a game piece than a girl—a notion to which I took no offense, as it mirrored my own motives almost exactly. After all, if I was going to secure a suitor who wouldn't mind my lack of Lordship, I needed to find someone who was searching for a trophy. And men's favorite prizes were always those they could steal out of their companions' arms.

Yes, Fitz was titled, but as the son of a Rouge of the Vannett Manor, rather than an Archson himself, he was lower in the peerage than the kind of match I aspired to obtain. Still, I believed we could be of use to one another. His interest would invariably attract the interest of others, just as my association with him would raise his prospects. We were mutually beneficial to one another; nothing more.

That, however, was then. Now, I start toward him, suddenly viciously, deeply grateful for his presence.

"Fitz!" His first name flies out of my mouth before I can stop it, so relieved am I to see his face. At my cry, Fitz perks up, his neck swiveling as he searches the crowd. He flushes when he locates me, his eyes darting briefly to the girl beside him before bowing his head in my direction.

"Archdaughter," he says in greeting as I approach, smiling widely—*too* widely, I note, and quickly press my lips together. Mama always said never to show one's teeth or affection to a man before a proposal, and even then, only on very special occasions. I believe I witnessed her truly grin at Father twice in all their years of marriage.

"My family offers our condolences," Fitz continues, bowing his head. His voice is stiff, formal, as if he rehearsed the words during the ride over. My steps hitch with unease for a moment at his tone, my gaze flickering uneasily toward his companion, who's now glaring at me through slitted eyes. I remember her from the capital, too—Annabeth or Annabelle or something, her name is. One of those girls who was forever drifting at the edges of our parties, waving their families' money around like we were starving wolves, trying to lure away the weakest of our herd. Among the Manorborn, there is a name for women like her: bloodgrubbers, we call them. Un-Manored social climbers who use their parents' fortunes to buy their way into our lines, to buy their future children a chance at the immunity that runs through our veins.

What is Fitz doing with the likes of *her*?

Pushing aside my doubts, I laugh breathily, taking Fitz's free arm. "I have told you already, Fitz, you must call me Merrick. The arbitrators of good society have long since deemed me a hopeless case—no further damage can be done to my reputation, I assure you. Now"—I glance around us, at the party spreading outward in a swirl of dresses and liquor—"shall we find you a refreshment? You *must* tell me all the gossip you've heard since I saw you last—it will be a welcome diversion from my mourning."

But Fitz resists my tug toward the bar, standing firm. "I am afraid I promised Miss Crowe's father I would remain by her side until he finished making his rounds," he says. His jaw flexes, his attention frustratingly darting again to the girl—*Amelia,* that's her name, Amelia Crowe—as if ensuring that she's still there. Leaning closer to me, he lowers his voice to a murmur. "We should speak later, Merrick. There are—there is a conversation I must have with you."

A flood of dark water drenches my insides as I take in the stern line of Fitz's mouth, the solid way his feet are rooted next to his companion's. As if they are *more* than just companions—as if they are *together,* in every sense of the word—

Impossible. The Vannetts would never let one of their own become entangled with a girl like the one before me—a *bloodgrubber.* And even if his family permitted such a match, why would Fitz choose to pursue it? The Crowes have no title, no legacy.

Careful to keep my expression steady, I nod. "Of course," I say to him. "Perhaps you wish to reserve me for a dance? Then we may speak all we want."

I lean closer, but abruptly, Fitz jerks back, pulling his arm from my grip. "I—forgive me, Archdaughter, I am not sure that would be entirely appropriate. You see, I am engaged to Miss Amelia Crowe. We are to be wed this fall."

My stomach plunges to my feet. "Excuse me?"

"I thought it best to tell you myself," Fitz rambles on, staring fixedly down at the ground. Next to him, Amelia Crowe's smirk is like the twist of a dagger, digging into my intestines. "I am aware the news may come as a disappointment to you, seeing as how some may have assumed you and I had formed an—an attachment of sorts—before your father's passing."

"*Some* may have assumed?" I can't keep the spite from my tone, nor can I prevent my voice from spiking. "How interesting. Did *some* promenade with me last month, in full view of New London's good society, or was that only you?"

Fitz's neck flares red—if he looks at Amelia *once more,* I swear I shall scream. *Stay calm, Merrick.* The familiar refrain floats through my mind. *If you berate him now, you shall lose your chance forever.*

Gathering myself, I close my errant emotions in a mental fist. "Fitz, please," I say softly. "Let us speak privately. I am certain this is not the kind of match you desire. You and I—I believe we can help one another, if you will only listen to me—"

The muscles in his neck strain, as if my very presence is aggravating to him. "Forgive me, I cannot conceive of a delicate way to put this," he says, cutting me swiftly off. "One of my family's sentries abandoned his post last week. Specifically, he left my great-uncle Lord Corinth Vannett's side to come *here,* to pursue some kind of offer he'd heard your sister had made—additional troops in exchange for land?" Fitz rubs a frustrated hand over his face. "I am my father's only son, Merrick. I have a responsibility to my Manor that is far greater than whatever duty you feel I owe to you—and speaking plainly, my family is concerned about what Archdaughter Estella's decision implies about her leadership capabilities. Father fears it is a sign of . . . deterioration in your Manor, following Manor Lord Silas's passing. And though I will treasure what we shared always, I must now say goodbye."

A chill settles over me as he takes Amelia's hand more tightly in his own, still avoiding my eyes. So *here* is the truth—the reason he would choose a girl of no lineage to wed over me. Better a parasite, feeding where you can see it, I suppose, than a fox in the henhouse. I feel dirty, humiliated, as if my gown has been ripped away. Through all that I've witnessed since returning to Norland, I've kept the possibility of my escape like an ace in my pocket, ready to play when I needed. But if the rest of the Manors believe what Fitz's family clearly does, will I have anywhere to run away to?

I watch Fitz turn his back on me, leading Amelia away. At the last moment, I call after him. "You criticize my family," I hiss, low enough that only he and Amelia can hear. "Yet you attend our ball, drink our wine. If I were your fiancée, I should question the kind of man who would bring me into the halls of a *deteriorating* Manor and feast off their carcass in the same evening."

Fitz pauses, his shoulders drawing together. I remain still, waiting pathetically for him to accept the bait and launch into an argument—anything to keep him here, keep him talking—but he only twists his head slightly over his shoulder. His expression is sympathetic, almost sad.

"Wit will not keep your fires burning forever, Merrick," he remarks. Then he leaves, Amelia Crowe's self-satisfied huff of victory echoing in my ears.

Around me, the party chatter has gone quiet. Without a target to direct it, my anger departs swiftly as a flock of birds scattering across the sky, replaced by shame. I feel excessive and out of control beneath the judging gaze of so many witnesses; I feel like I am spilling out of my own body. *You have no moderation.* Essie's favorite criticism of me—I can almost hear her saying it.

Like a shift in the wind, I sense a presence approaching behind me. A gust of warm breath tickles the back of my neck, making my stomach flip.

"What a bore," the person says. "Fitz and I used to play cards together. He never won. Doesn't know a good hand when it's dealt to him, that one."

I turn. Ames Saint is staring down at me, lamplight spilling over his shoulders like melted butter. He's dressed in a cutaway coat in a rich claret shade and tailored breeches, a blood-red cravat cinched around his neck. The clean, simple lines fit him far better than anything else could; he smirks and the cut of his grin above his dark jacket is a crescent moon, hiding so much more behind it.

I swallow. My confrontation with Fitz notwithstanding, I can't deny that there was a part of my mind that had drifted to the Saint Vessel as I was dressing earlier tonight—that had perhaps urged my maid to yank my stays just a *bit* tighter than normal at the prospect of his attendance. It isn't so much that I've been pining after him—more that since our encounter in the gardens, certain traces of him have worked themselves beneath my fingernails like river dirt. I go to pick up my knife or tuck my hair behind my ears and suddenly there he is, in the middle of my thoughts again.

"I was hoping I'd see you here tonight, Archdaughter." Ames holds his right arm out, offering me one of the two drinks he's carrying. He must see my eyes dart after Fitz, now lost in the crowd—must sense my anxiety at the idea of being overheard—because he winks jauntily, his teeth flashing. "Not to worry—my mother raised me better than to eavesdrop," he assures me. "But I recall reading your name next to Vannett's in the *Toast* a few weeks ago. What happened—lover's spat?"

There's a vulpine glint to his expression, and it makes me bolder simply because of my proximity to him.

"Hardly," I counter, accepting the outstretched drink and lifting it to my lips. The wine is tart as it slides down my throat, like underripe berries. "I was simply congratulating him on his engagement."

Ames raises a golden brow, surprise washing some of the slyness from his face. "Were you?" he asks, his eyes sweeping quickly over me as if in reappraisal. "I'm sorry to hear that."

I lift my shoulders, my skin prickling under the searing force of his stare. "Your pity is appreciated, Archson Ames, but unnecessary," I reply. "I am fine."

He clicks his tongue against the roof of his mouth. "Oh, but it is not you I pity," Ames says solemnly. "I, too, have suffered the attentions of Miss Amelia Crowe. Vannett will be sorely disappointed when he realizes her father's money cannot polish away the personality of a dead fish." He takes a long sip of his wine. "I've always preferred a girl who had her wits about her."

The blush overtakes me quickly, my forehead warming as if with the beginnings of a fever. I fight down the sudden heat, forcing myself to remember the talk I heard while in New London: Ames's many flirtations, the charm he was known for exuding like sweat—naturally, without a second thought.

If I had the ability to do so, I might indulge him tonight, fire another compliment back his way. But Fitz's words still ring clearly in my head, his rejection one I cannot ignore. I need to focus on finding Essie, on getting through this evening without any more disruptions. Supporting her—like Cressida asked me to.

More than ever, it seems as though the future of my Manor depends on it.

"And you have been gifted a kind heart," I say after a moment, looking up at Ames with a smile steadier than that which I feel. "I thank you for your words of consolation—they are a great balm to my ego."

I expect him to back down, am caught off guard when he does not. Instead, Ames only laughs, the sound like fingernails trailing gently down my back. "Kindness is one virtue my friends do not often accuse me of possessing," he answers, stepping closer. "But perhaps you bring out a charitable side of me."

His blue eyes are sharp, all cutting intelligence and hunger. I feel like I could get lost in them; I feel like if I *were* to play his game, he might beat me, might slip my heart from my rib cage before I was even aware it was his to take.

I feel strangely enticed by that possibility.

The high-pitched shriek of a woman's drunken giggle tears through the night, dissolving the tension that has stretched between us. As if coming out of a trance, Ames blinks, his expression clearing. I down the rest of my wine and glance away, my head fuzzy with a vague sense of guilt—the uneasy feeling that I have given up something, shown my hand preemptively. Flustered, I eye my now-empty glass, an excuse to leave rising to my lips, but Ames beats me to it.

"Would you like to dance?" he asks abruptly, nodding toward the far end of the gardens, where I can hear strains of music drifting through the air. He flags down a passing servant, placing his finished drink on the man's tray.

I deposit my glass next to his but pause before answering him, hesitant. Sensing my reluctance, Ames clears his throat. "I am no Vannett, but my mother is a Lord in her own right. Consider me a sacrificial lamb—an offering to show Fitz how terribly he's missing out."

He extends his arm toward me conspiratorially. The gesture loosens the tangle of nerves inside me, and for the first time tonight, I feel myself relax a fraction.

"Let's dance," I agree. "Please."

Ames smiles, pleased. Placing his hand over mine, he leads me to where the sea of guests parts around Norland's newly erected dance pavilion, a behemoth of gleaming tile and a billowing, tented roof hung with colored-glass lanterns. A string quartet plays from a raised platform in one corner of the pavilion, refracted light washing the violinist in pink, the bass player in a solemn blue.

The opening notes of a new melody—playful and airy—drift from the musicians, prompting a chorus of cheers from the assembled couples. I'm an adequate dancer, no more, no less, but this song is so familiar to me that I launch into the steps without thinking. Gathering skirts in one hand, I step back and to the right, surprised when Ames keeps pace with me.

"You know this dance?" I ask, curious. It's a local favorite, jaunty to the point of rowdiness—perfect for country balls such as this one, but generally considered too uncouth for New London's stiff dance halls.

Ames dips his chin in a nod. "The Sussex Reel, isn't it?" he replies. I hum in confirmation, moving through the next sequence—*together apart together*—before coming back to him. "We have a similar version of it in Cardiff," Ames explains. "You forget we are neighbors, you and I."

A stab of embarrassment pierces my side, making me momentarily clumsy. "I forget nothing," I reply airily, meeting his gaze. "Yet you did not spend much time in this area when we were young—at least, not if my memory serves me correctly?" I duck underneath Ames's raised arm and press my palm to his, one pair in a line of repeats. He watches me as I go, shrugging slightly.

"No," he concedes. "My mother believes that children develop best in the city—exposed to the arts, the sciences, so on and so forth. I was raised primarily in New London, by my father, while Mother remained at the Roost to carry out her duties as Manor Lord." He shakes his head, his lips curving in a half smirk. "It is strange, but in many ways, I feel as though I've only gotten to know her—my mother, that is—recently. For so long, she was like this distant queen to me, ruling over a foreign land. It was my father who was my true caregiver."

As he speaks, I search his face for fragments of his mother. I have never met her, but by all accounts, Lord Ianthe Saint is plain, small in stature and frail-looking; from what I've heard, she was a sickly girl, and as a woman her body never recovered from the frequent bouts of illness she endured as a youth. "The Child Saint" they called her, the day of her own Nomination Hearing. The vote was close—several among the Mortal Council considered her too weak to rule.

But rule she has, for almost two decades now, and under her thumb Cardiff has prospered. I wonder if Ames has a bit of her hardness in him—or if he is like his father, handsome and accommodating, the guiding hand to her iron fist.

"I am sorry that he passed," I say finally. "Your father." We dance in silence for a few beats before Ames replies.

"Well," he answers quietly. "Everyone does, eventually."

His gaze returns to me, already brightening. "And I am glad, at least, that his death brought me back here," he says. "I wondered about you, when I was younger. You and your sister both— the girls beyond the hills." He puts a dreamy emphasis on the last words, as if reciting the title of a favorite story, one he's long since learned by heart. "I could never quite convince myself you were real."

My limbs flush with a dewy heat, like hot water has been poured through my veins. "I felt the same way about you."

Abruptly, the music pauses, the interruption making me glance up. At the opposite side of the pavilion, two figures are making their way toward the musicians' platform, the crowd parting before them like softened butter under a knife. The first is Cressida, bedecked in crimson taffeta, the hue so vivid it would look garish if not for the elegance with which she wears it. With her is a dark-haired girl, her bony limbs like twigs protruding out from the cloud of her dress.

Unlike everyone around her, my sister is wearing white. Her ivory gown is a delicate silk creation with puffed translucent sleeves and dozens of seed pearls embroidered along the bust, emphasizing her breasts and her pale-as-milk skin. Her hair is studded with black versions of the same gems, glossy as ink and glittering like dark stars. In an instant, all thoughts of Ames disappear, renewed clarity spilling over me like cool water. *She's here.* The second stage of Cressida's plan is spinning into motion.

Without slowing, my sister cuts her gaze to where Ames and I stand, her mouth curving in the shadow of a smile. My heart squeezes within me as I mirror the gesture.

The crowd falls silent as Cressida and my sister approach the stage, where I see that Tom is already waiting to help them up. Now that I'm paying attention, it's easy to pick out my fellow Manorborn from among the guests—I spot a pair of the Ballantine cousins, shrewd-faced and auburn-haired, as well as a freckled Marquess of the Warchild Manor, a man who famously seems to forget he's twice my age every time we meet at a ball. All members of the eleven families who will decide the fate of my own.

Positioned farther off, toward the gardens, another figure catches my attention. Killian Brandon is a solemn gray statue in his sentry uniform amid the ruby burst of the party, his form almost hidden in the pavilion's shadows. He stands in a line of similar somber-looking men arranged every ten meters or so around the edge of the tent, diligently surveying the guests like hawk-eyed chaperones presiding over their charges. Though I'm sure the display is intended to set the partygoers' minds at ease, the sheer number of guards unnerves me—the way they've blocked us off on all sides, like a pack of wolves closing in.

As if sensing my unease, Killian's eyes flick to mine. His expression is blank, the emotionless mask of a soldier, but his head dips in a shallow nod when he sees me, as if assuring me of his presence.

I face straightforward again as, ahead of me, my cousin extends a gloved hand toward Essie, aiding her as she steps onto the platform. Despite her elegant attire, I can't help but notice how unsteady my sister looks—how her hand shakes nervously in Tom's, as if any moment, her limbs might give way entirely, send her swooning into his arms.

Ames stoops closer to me, his breath damp and humid on my neck. "Is Archdaughter Estella all right? She does not look well."

A trickle of trepidation courses through me. Glancing toward the stage again, I see that my sister's eyes are locked on me—anxious and wide and decidedly not all right. Her gaze draws a line between Ames and me, a question in the arch of her brow. My neck heats at the prickle of judgment I feel emanating from her, even at this distance.

"She is fine," I murmur back to Ames, willing the words to be true. "Nervous, is all."

Ames's brow creases, but his response fades away as, from her platform, Cressida begins to speak.

"Ladies and gentlemen," she begins, her velvety purr just low enough to draw listeners in. "Your Graces, Your Eminences, Your . . ." She pauses, fanning her face in mock exhaustion. "My, we Manorborn do love our titles, don't we?"

A generous laugh rolls through the crowd, and my cousin-in-law brightens—clearly, the veritable river of alcohol she's been serving has done its work. "Thank you for gathering at our humble family home tonight," she continues to the audience. "Together with my husband and my dear cousins, I could not be more honored to welcome you to Norland House—not only to celebrate the life of my husband's beloved uncle, Lord Silas Darling, but to usher in a new season of growth for this, the Darling Manor . . ."

The remainder of her speech is lost as, from deep within my ears, a wave of sound roars. My gaze has caught on a figure hovering just behind the platform Essie and Cressida are standing on, in the shrouded grounds beyond the dance pavilion—not the portion of the gardens that have been cleared for the ball, but the untidy wilderness extending down to the mist-swathed cliffs that make up the sea-facing edge of our border.

The person's skin is a pure spill of moonlight, glowing ethereally against the dimness like something snipped from a dream. Without lanterns to cut through the night, the gardens around them almost appear like a two-dimensional tableau—as if the person is positioned in the center of a canvas over which a tin of black, wet paint has been poured. Their long, ebony hair and dark dress melt into the surrounding atmosphere, giving off the disconcerting impression that they are no more than a collection of parts—two curled hands, a flash of ivory ankle, and a stoic face.

I flinch, then stifle a gasp as I notice their eyes—two identical ovals staring unblinkingly at me. Even from this distance, I can tell that their centers are completely white, smooth eggshells without the usual interruptions of irises or pupils. It is as if a blanket of fresh snow has smothered the person entirely, blurring their features beneath a layer of frost.

Not a person, I realize, just as the first scream pierces through the evening, a warbling, terrible, descant.

A Phantom.

CHAPTER ELEVEN

Cries—first of curiosity, then, increasingly, of fear—swirl around me as one by one, the partygoers begin to notice the creature lingering behind my sister. Instinctively, I reach for my absent Ghostslayer as another face, then a third—a fifth, a seventh—emerges from the tar-thick darkness on either side of the foremost beast, the shadows parting around the pack like a curtain being pulled back.

Some of the Phantoms spider forward on all fours, creeping over the earth with the hunched backs of cats preparing to pounce. Others, like the front-runner, walk upright, the jerky snap of their legs like the drunken lurch of a child's doll—a being out of its own control. Dried blood crusts over the jaws of several; several more bear injuries, their waxy flesh split as if by raking nails. The parting gifts of their previous victims, no doubt.

All of the Phantoms are smiling—the lunatic grins of madmen, those left to fester in dark cells for years with no food or warmth or kindness, their minds turning small and ratlike in their solitude. Who have been finally, unexpectedly, turned loose.

"Hell and the devil," Ames whispers from beside me. Beneath the fabric of his jacket, his muscles have gone taut. Twisting around, I find Killian again, his weapon already in hand, a grayish pallor settling over his skin. We have gone into the mists twice together now, but gazing over at him, I realize that this is the first time I have seen him look scared.

The memory of our earlier encounters stirs something in me. Turning back toward the stage, I parse the murk beyond for a hint of orange—something to indicate that our defenses are still burning. This near to Norland, border maintenance shouldn't be an issue, not even with the many excuses my family has doled out to me since my return. A breach should be impossible.

So how have the Phantoms gotten through?

As if spurred onward by my thought, the monsters amble forward, leering at us through the night.

Their movement seems to break the crowd out of a trance. Screams tear through the pavilion as guests shove against one another, abandoning their partners to run for safety in the lit part of the gardens. Several of the more inventive partygoers pause to hurl their glasses at the delicate colored lanterns dangling from the tent ceiling in an attempt to shatter them and free the flames within. They burst in crystalline explosions of pink and blue, sending fiery missives raining down toward the floor. One man staggers back as flames erupt on the sleeve of his tuxedo; next to him, a woman clutches at her eye, her lips rounded in a howl of agony.

It isn't enough. With snake-like quickness, one of the Phantoms toward the rear of the group darts forward, wrapping its arms around a stunned violinist as if embracing the man. My eyes widen, transfixed, as the beast lowers its mouth to the musician's neck, the sweep of its lips over his skin tender, caressing.

The man is already sobbing when the Phantom bares its teeth, plunges them into his flesh. Crimson sprays the air like thrown coins at a wedding.

"Archdaughter, get down!" Before I can react, Ames is on me, pulling me roughly to the ground. His body is a hard shell curved atop mine, smothering me, preventing me from rising.

Astonishment, then a surge of frustration, rolls over me. "What are you—"

He claps a hand over my mouth, pulling me backward into a kind of protective embrace. I choke back a cry as a stampede of feet pummels the ground around me, headed for the platform where my sister and Cressida still stand, Tom now having joined them, his arms wrapped around his wife's middle.

The sentries. They race past us, shouting commands at one another. Four of them section off once they reach the musicians' stage, taking hold of Essie, Cressida, and my cousin, and leading them away, as the rest continue forward, toward the Phantoms. I make out Killian among the former group, his hand on my sister's arm, his head bent to whisper something in her ear. At their feet, nubs of flame stretch and flicker like budding plants craning toward the sun.

"It's all right. I have you—you're safe." Ames hisses the assurance against my neck, stubble I didn't realize he had grazing my skin. His heart thumps against my back, steady and sure, but his arms are constricting—a bony cage.

I bat his hands aside, slip out of his hold. "Forget about me. Do you have a *weapon*?"

Uncomprehending, Ames blinks at me in response. Shock has dilated his pupils to the size of small stones, the blue rings around them barely visible.

I grit my teeth. "A Ghostslayer," I repeat more firmly. "Did you bring one?"

"No—I . . ." Ames shakes his head, gathering himself. "No."

I don't get the chance to ask anything else before a boom like a thunderclap splits the air. One of the sentries has fired—but the shot goes wide, arcing into the darkness. Bile burns the back of my throat as I watch a soldier, then another, get taken down, pinned flies beneath the Phantoms' grasping hands. A musky, animal scent fills my nostrils: urine and sweat, the mammalian stench of panic.

Sounds tangle, web over me. A sentry's cry. The tear of muscle ripped fresh from a body. The haunting farewell of a scream cut chillingly, abruptly short.

"Archdaughter . . ." Ames calls my title like a warning, and my surroundings snap back into focus. Barely five yards away from us, firelight from the shattered tent lanterns flickers across the body of the Phantom leader, painting it in devilish shades of red and orange. Its feet are bare; its body is clad in a faded party gown, yellow crescents showing through at its armpits where sweat has stained it. The entirety of the left side of its face is covered in patchy gray-rot, pale veins webbing over its skin like cracks in a vase.

Bang. Another shot flares from the end of a sentry's gun, this one meeting its target with a dull *thwack*. The Phantom clutches at its abdomen, where the bullet has broken through its flesh. Its face contorts in pain, a chillingly humanlike sob emitting from its throat as it crumples to the ground.

The tide turns in an instant. As I watch, the sentries fire on the remaining Phantoms, bringing one, then the rest, swiftly down. I wince when the final monster is bested with a boot to its spine as it attempts to crawl away. It flails desperately on the ground, its shrieks gradually weakening to a low, wounded whine that turns my blood to ice.

At last, a single sentry advances forward—one step, then two. A swing of his arm, a final shot tearing through the night, and the Phantom goes silent. In its place, the still night rushes in, plugging my ears like wax.

With its death, the atmosphere loosens, as if the air is heaving out an exhale. In the safety of the gardens, the group guarding Cressida, Tom, and my sister steps back, lowering their weapons, their necks swiveling in search of additional monsters. The few surviving guests who didn't manage to flee the pavilion rise shakily from where they'd fallen to the ground, their eyes wide.

Standing, too, I search Essie out, my view of her partially blocked by the bodies of two sentries. Beneath the stars, her skin is only a shade or two darker than that of the Phantoms; her cheeks are just as hollow. As if sensing me looking at her, she twists in my direction.

A bladed emotion stabs at my breastbone when she meets my gaze. There is no fear in her slate eyes, no hint of surprise or wonder.

Only a grim resignation, like that of someone who spotted storm clouds gathering on the horizon long ago, while all her peers were blinded by the noonday sun. Who has been waiting, ever since, for the rain to fall.

CHAPTER TWELVE

When I was young, my father would spin fairy tales for me.

If he was in one of his rare good moods, the story would be bright, layered and sweet like a rich caramel. I savored those, ran my tongue over the words until my teeth grew sticky.

A girl. A palace. A prince.

If Father was in a bad mood, however—which was much more common an occurrence—the tale would turn tempestuous. Full of hairpin twists that left me feeling claustrophobic and dizzy, trapped in his arms rather than held by them.

A girl. A forest. A wolf.

Once when I was very young, he scared me so horribly with one of these stories that I burst into tears. I remember him stroking my hair, leaning down to whisper: *Are you frightened?* His gray eyes flashed; it was like looking into a cruel mirror.

Yes, I told him, back then. *Was the story true?*

He considered my question for a long time. Finally, he sat back, met my gaze.

The fear is true, he said.

When the veil lifts again I am lying in my room. White flickers at the edges of my vision, coalescing into ghostly masks the color of dripping candle wax: a row of faces, their eyes empty pits, their oblong mouths stretched into screams. They hover above me, soundless and leering, like a line of destroying angels.

Then I blink, and the thread of the dream snaps clean. The faces disappear—the images of their real counterparts, however, remain firmly etched in my mind.

Phantoms. In the gardens.

I surge upward, taken aback when the surface beneath me shifts unsteadily at the movement. I'm splayed on top of my bed, still clad in my dress from the party, the feather-stuffed mattress sinking like river mud beneath me to accommodate my shifting weight. My tongue is sleep-heavy and dry, sticking to the roof of my mouth.

Like the gradual trickle of rainwater, the evening comes back to me. After the ball's disastrous ending, my family and I barely spoke—Cressida and Tom leading the trembling guests out to the front drive to pack them up in carriages, while Essie conferred with the sentries, who were immediately dispatched to perform a thorough border check. I'd lingered at the fringes of the ruined dance pavilion until they returned, remaining just long enough to hear the beginning of their findings before Essie noticed my presence and shooed me away. It appeared that the cause of the breach had been identified easily: another dead lantern, its flame inexplicably gone out despite having been tended to only hours before. That the sentries insisted that the damage had been repaired and our perimeter secured did nothing to lessen my distress over the fact that the incident had occurred at all.

Again.

And still, nobody could say why.

Part of me longed to seek Essie out, after I was back in my room—there was so much we needed to discuss, not only the Phantom's appearance but the overwhelming impression my sister had given off in the wake of it, her gaze doom-laden like she'd expected death to arrive on our doorstep—but I resisted. Instead, I pulled my traveling trunk out from where it had been shoved in the corner and began to pack.

The guilt was instantaneous, deeper the second time around, like sinking one's feet into snow already loose from treading. Was I really going to do this—abandon my family the minute trouble came knocking, the way I had only months ago? Abandon my sister, again?

But the rebuttal was swifter. Essie herself had told me I was better off away from Norland—and after the events of the ball, I couldn't disagree with her. Couldn't count, in fact, on safety anywhere within Sussex's borders. Since my return from the capital, my life had become one long tumble, as if Killian had pulled me from that mist-wreathed carriage and after that initial yank I'd never stopped falling. Father's suicide, the breaches, the fear that seemed to have descended upon my own sister—I couldn't decipher any of the individual events, but I could hear their collective warning, and they screamed *danger.*

No, I needed to return to New London, and fast. If Fitz wouldn't marry me, I'd find someone who would—even if that meant becoming a creaky widower's new toy. Miserable in bed, after all, was better than miserable in the grave, dead.

My brain still foggy with sleep and latent fear, I glance at the half-full chest, lurking forebodingly at the foot of my bed like a

dog waiting to pounce. I must have fallen asleep sometime during my packing. Head throbbing, I pull my knees to my chest, cradling myself as a soft, arrhythmic beat echoes through the room:
one-two, one, one, one-two.

I pause. My heartbeat?

Thump.

The noise—not my pulse at all, but something external—
comes again, startling me. It's muffled, echoing from the hallway
outside my chambers, but clear—a loud thud followed by a quick,
rainlike patter, like someone running down the corridor.

I go still, a vein of ice piercing the center of my rib cage. Cressida and Tom are installed in guest quarters along the east wing,
where they've been staying ever since I arrived. The west wing is
primarily family rooms, mine and Essie's along with those formerly belonging to our parents. My father is dead and my mother
is, too, so that leaves just two occupants in this area of the house:
me, and the person who, last I checked, was safely tucked away
behind a locked door. *Is Killian out there, making his rounds?*

Emboldened by the thought—maybe he can expand on what
he and the other sentries found at the border—I swing my bare
feet to the floor. Feeling slightly ridiculous in my gown, I smooth
out the crumpled skirts as well as I'm able and slip into the corridor.

Almost immediately, goose bumps rise on my arms as I pick
up on a scuttling sound from the hall behind me. My breath coming quick, I whirl around just in time to see something silver glint
near the end of the hallway, where the corridor bends and turns
farther into Norland's west wing. Dust—falling lazily through the
air, glimmering like a puff of frozen breath in the moonlight. But
who disturbed it?

"Who's there? Mr. Brandon?" I call out experimentally. No
one answers, but I think I hear another thump from deeper

within the house, and then a long drag like someone pulling a door closed. *Is Killian hiding from me? Or . . .*

If not him, who is? Trepidation pricking at the back of my neck like cold sweat, I hurry down the hallway and round the corner at the end of it.

Emptiness—a vacant corridor yawns before me like an innocent, widened eye. Nothing stirs in the midnight silence, but even still, I can't shake the strange feeling that has settled over me—the notion that beneath the sleeping bodies of its occupants, Norland House is wide awake. A warm draft brushes past my ankles and it feels hot, ripe and milky and organic as if the house is a living thing, panting at my heels as I walk.

I swallow. If I listen closely, I can almost make out a faint hum in the air, like the murmur of a hushed exhale.

Mine? Or, perhaps . . . a part of me goes cold.

Perhaps is it Norland's?

Stop, Merrick. Enough with your ghost stories.

Steeling myself, I pad forward, searching for signs of Killian's presence. This section of the estate is a smidgen brighter than the area I just left, thanks to a single window positioned at the end of the corridor. Through the glass, the full moon hangs like a ripe fruit against the sky, dusting the floor and the walls with a pale cast. My anxiety lessens slightly as I quickly scan the line of doors, confirming that they're all shut tight, no shadows moving beneath them to indicate someone inside.

I let out a long sigh. The stress of the past day, combined with a restless night, has evidently weakened my hold on reality more than I'd like to admit—there's no one here, and likely, there never was. Resolving to try to at least get a few hours of sleep before breakfast, I turn and begin back the way I came, rubbing at my aching forehead.

Thump.

Somewhere in the bowels of the house, a door slams shut—the sound jolting and aggressive, like the snap of teeth over my ankle. I whirl around, a scream rising to my lips as my eyes parse the thick, interior darkness of the corridor, searching for a face—for the hysterical, leering grins of the Phantoms from earlier, now risen from the dead, or their brethren.

"Mr. Brandon?" I repeat hesitantly. My voice is thick with nerves, my syllables fumbled as a drunk's. "Essie?"

Once again, I am answered only by the house's bones, creaking like a ship in the wind. The silence is watchful, heavy as a coat as it drapes over me, and with it, the last of my reserved strength flees. Suddenly, I have no desire to speak to Killian any longer, no desire to do anything other than run, as fast and as far as I can until I find a place that the night does not reach. Where I can wrap myself in lace and thoughts of suitors and forget all else, forget sisters and death and cold, forget that there is a world past my drawing room window at all.

The sound of my own breathing lopes through the empty corridor as I hurry back the way I came. To keep myself calm, I count the doors as they race past my vision, marking off the number left until I reach my own: *six, five, four . . .*

I stop. To my side, my sister's door stands proud and sturdy like a night watchman, the shadows a slick of oil atop the gleaming wood.

It's open.

Questioning my limited vision, I creep closer, waiting for what I think I see to reveal itself as a trick of the dark. It doesn't. Where Essie's door should meet its frame, an inch-wide crack separates the two, the room inside inky and obscured. Dual shivers race over my arms as I take another step forward, give the door an experimental prod.

With a moan, it lolls inward.

My stomach plummets. "Essie?" I whisper. When there's no reply, I push the door open farther, stepping over the threshold. "Ess—"

A freezing burst of air, winter-sharp, makes my throat seal over. I'm momentarily confused by the billowing swaths of fabric that stretch toward me from the opposite wall of Essie's bedroom, until I realize: the windows have been thrown open, leaving the curtains to twist in the wind. Instinctively, I hiss as a strong gust rattles the window frames, shaking them like a prisoner his cell bars.

Rubbing my shoulders to ward off the icy sting, I rush forward, closing one window, then the other, and latching them for good measure. Once they're secured, I turn to examine the rest of my sister's quarters.

Upon initial glance, everything looks in order: Essie's bed is made, her sheets drawn tight, the way she prefers them; hanging from her dresser, the gown she wore to the ball floats. It's only when I peer closer that I notice the flaws. Like the ivory candle on her bedstand, tipped on its side, a pool of still-hardening wax melting out from beneath it. Or the washbasin in the corner, its accompanying pitcher absent, reduced to a scatter of porcelain fragments on the ground.

And there is a larger absence, too, of course. My sister is gone.

A crush of foreboding weighs me down, an ache spreading outward from my very core. There is a horrible wrongness to this space, aside from the overturned objects, the thrown-open windows. Standing in it, gazing at it, is like looking into a mirror and seeing someone else—a stranger—staring back at you, like sleepwalking, like water in your lungs. A terrible wickedness permeates every seam of the bedroom, every edge. A sense of intrusion.

Of possession.

It is then that I see it: the cream-colored slip of paper on my sister's pillow. Unlike the candle and the pitcher, this has been arranged just so, presented like a gift. Blood roars in my ears as I move to it, pick it up delicately, pinching it between my middle finger and thumb.

A note—about the size of my hand and hard to read in the dimness, the penmanship unfamiliar. The message on it is short, a single line written across the middle the only ink on the page aside from a curiously shaped smudge in the top corner. My gaze is briefly drawn to the marking: a pair of connected arches, like a jagged, upside-down *M*. Most likely the writer testing out their quill, or else part of another message, ripped away.

Whatever it is, I don't dwell on it for long, my attention pulled back to the letters on the page. The sentence they spell out.

Darling Manor will fall.

PART TWO

Empty House

To the Divine Three we offer this triple prayer:
To the Burning King, for fires ever-blazing,
To the Bloodletter, for a line most pure,
And to the Lightkeeper, for safe passage through the Gray
And a sword to battle those that hunger within.

             "A MARRIAGE PRAYER," EXCERPTED FROM
             A COMPENDIUM OF MODERN BLESSINGS, **YEAR 74**
             OF THE TURNING

My darling, your monstrous shape stalks my halls.
I breathe and draw in your own feral breath,
Feel the devouring press of your blood-sweet lips.
If you are a beast, I shall let you consume me.
O come out of the mist and make me whole again!

             "ODE TO MY BELOVED," EXCERPTED FROM
             A COLLECTION OF HUNGERS, **BY SIR ALISTAIR**
             LAMPFORD, YEAR 189 OF THE TURNING

CHAPTER THIRTEEN

S he's gone.

Illusion and memory tangle like sticky threads against my skin as I wake, reality and nightmare twining together: Norland's empty halls, winding pathways of slippery darkness like the twisting belly of a snake; the drapes in Essie's room, wavering arms stretched toward me; the worn rasp of my own voice as I called out, again and again, for my sister.

Essie is gone.

I sit up and am met with the thump of a blanket sliding to the floor. I'm back in my bed; with a surge of humiliation, I vaguely remember Cressida ordering me to my room sometime near dawn, stripping me out of my dress herself and pulling a nightgown over my head, though my recollection of everything else that occurred after seeing the note on my sister's bed is foggy. Aside from myself, my bedroom is empty, early-morning light streaming through the windows. An unoccupied wooden chair is stationed by my bedside as if playing watchman, a melted candle stump on the floor beside it.

Following my discovery last night, I roused Cressida and Tom, who quickly gathered the sentries to search the house from top to bottom, but to no avail. My sister was nowhere to be found—not within our estate, nor among the half-cleaned debris of the ball. I drifted through Norland's corridors numbly, only half-present as I trailed after my cousin, most of me caught in the past: the moment I saw Essie's empty room, her bedsheets crisp and un-rumpled by sleep. The candle turned over atop her bedstand, wax still hot as if she'd only run to the kitchens for a cup of water and would return any moment to stub it out. The note on her pillow.

Darling Manor will fall.

Who could have left it? And for what purpose? Over a hundred people had been in attendance at the ball earlier, and while most of the event had taken place outdoors, plenty of guests had wandered inside our estate, too, cooing over Norland's haunting architecture and extensive collection of art. Had my sister been frightened by one of them, and fled our house when she glimpsed their message? But then, where would she have gone?

Even as I try to cling to that theory, though, I know it is false. I think back on the placement of the note, how the threat had been arranged neatly on her bed like a mousetrap set to spring. If my sister had seen it, wouldn't she have disturbed its positioning?

No, the more I dwell on it, the more certain I become that the message had not been left for her, but for the rest of us. Like a warning.

Like she'd been taken.

Last night, my sister was supposed to have been presented as the new Darling Vessel, our family's resurrection after my father's death. If someone wished to ensure that our Manor perished along with my parents . . . there would not have been a better time to strike.

After the ball. I'll tell you everything.

A rap on the bedroom door interrupts my thoughts. For a moment, a dizzying sense of release, like waking up from a bad dream, spreads in my chest like a moth beating its wings. "Essie?" I call out hopefully, as if I believe hard enough that she'll appear, I can unspool the events of the past day into nonreality. *Maybe she just went away for the night. Maybe she needed time to clear her head, after the ball.*

Maybe none of it ever happened at all.

But when the door creaks open, it isn't my sister's dark head that pokes through. Instead, a maid peers in at me with a worried frown, carrying a tray laden with food and a steaming teapot.

"Excuse me, my lady," she says. She dips into an unsteady curtsy, her gaze demurely trained on her feet. "The Duchess thought you might prefer taking breakfast in your quarters today."

My heart sinks. Cressida is not what one might term a sympathetic woman. If she is showing me pity, it must mean that Essie's absence is not some fleeting thing, spun by my sleeping mind—but serious. Real.

I accept the maid's offering and eat quickly and in solitude, afterward dressing myself in the first article of clothing I pull from my armoire, a plain blue frock with lace trimming. Cressida as good as declared our mourning period over at the ball last night, anyway. I'm careful to ignore the half-packed trunk still lying open in the middle of my floor, picking my way around it as one would a dead rat. The idea of leaving Norland House—so tempting only hours ago—now feels unforgivable in light of Essie's absence, an intrinsic, animal impulse insisting to me that if I move from this spot before she returns, I may lose her forever.

What happened to her? The question resonates through every part of my being. The Phantoms' appearance at the ball seems distant now, fuzzy as a childhood memory, but I recall the chaos, the frenzied rush of the crowd as they raced away from the creatures. What if the sentries missed one of the monsters in the commotion last night? I imagine a Phantom slipping into Norland, creeping into Essie's quarters and . . .

My thoughts refuse to travel further than that—the possibility of my sister injured, or worse, a room I cannot yet make myself look into. Besides, Phantoms do not leave notes, and though dangerous, they are not stealthy. If one had been in our estate, we surely would have heard it.

No, the monster that penned the message in her room was human, of that much I am sure. And if they did take my sister, I can't shake the horrible feeling that I might be next.

Darling Manor will fall.

Eventually, I find Tom in the billiards room, a corner of the house so rarely used by my sister and me that I'd almost forgotten it existed. When I enter, my cousin is leaning against the large green billiards table that dominates the center of the space, sipping from a crystal tumbler filled with a clear liquid that I strongly suspect is not water. From the way his fingers shake against the glass, I gather that he's been here for a while—he has the ragged air of someone who's held on to the night until it's snapped clean.

Tom turns abruptly at the sound of my footsteps, his drink sloshing out of the glass and dotting his white shirt with damp spots. Before he married Cressida, it wasn't uncommon to run across him in a state like this—I met many similar Manor-born men in New London, who, without any responsibilities to ground them, favored drink as their hobby of choice—but becoming a husband has seemed to sober my cousin, both literally and mentally. As I eye the new stain on his shirt, a lick of hot anger swipes at my gut. Is this what he's been doing since he and Cressida sent me to bed? Where are the sentries, the messengers racing back and forth, letters clutched in hand to alert the Council—the papers—the nation—about my sister's disappearance? Where are the constables, ready to sniff out a culprit and make an arrest?

Has he told *anyone* what happened last night, aside from those already dwelling on the grounds of our estate?

"Oh, Merrick, you're up. Did you get the breakfast tray Cressida sent to you?" Tom asks when he sees me. His walnut eyes have the exhausted quality of a snuffed-out match. It makes him look like a different person.

"I did," I respond, my aggravation momentarily displaced by the somber slant of my cousin's expression. Whereas Essie is iron, Tom has always seemed to be crafted from something lighter—as if his bones are knitted together by gossamer strands, a man made for laughter and ease. Heavy emotions do not suit him; his features crumble under their weight, like spring buds crushed by a late winter snow.

I cross closer to my cousin, running my fingers absently along the lacquered rim of the billiards table. "So, I take it there's been no sign of Essie this morning?" I say to Tom. "I was hoping her absence would turn out to be just some terrible nightmare. Still, I assume the Council has been alerted—how long, do you think, until word reaches all of them?"

Tom grimaces, a muscle jumping in his cheek. Raising his glass to his lips, he takes a long sip, then rests the tumbler on the table by his jacket.

"Ah—no," he answers. His consonants are a bit clumsier than normal, slurring into one another as he shrugs. "That is, no, Essie hasn't turned up, yet. We will find her, though, Merrick," he adds, his expression placating. "I swear it."

Alarm pricks, thornlike, at me. "And the Council?" I repeat more emphatically.

"Sweetheart, there you are."

Cressida's voice is resonant, clear as ringing bells. My cousin-in-law is poised in the room's entryway in a plain satin dress the color of rich coffee, her skin dewy, her cheeks pink and bright as if she's just risen from a long, refreshing sleep. When her gaze flicks over mine, nothing moves behind her eyes.

"Did your maid not visit you this morning?" she questions me tonelessly. "That dress is horribly wrinkled—you look as though you haven't slept in a month. It is more important than ever that we present a strong front to society, Merrick, now that your sister is gone."

Her impassive expression—the direct way she lays out her words before me, as if she is reciting a dinner order—jolts me. *Now that your sister is gone.* How buttoned up her phrasing is, as if Estella is only away for the day. As is her disappearance is a crease to be smoothed out, and nothing more.

"Excuse me if I find myself unconcerned with appearances right now," I reply shortly. "Should we not be focused on finding Essie, rather than ensuring the public perceives her absence correctly? In case you've forgotten, we may all be in danger—my sister could be—"

Dead.

I bite the word back, but not too late to feel its barb. It resounds in my skull, tinny and harsh: *dead, dead, dead.*

To my side, Tom's attention is fixed on the trickle of liquid remaining at the bottom of his glass. Cressida's brow crinkles with concern—no, something softer than that—*pity*, steepling her forehead like a folded napkin. Slowly, she approaches me, the click of her heeled slippers muffled by the emerald carpet underfoot.

"I assure you, dear, I have not forgotten Estella," she begins, and at the unspoken *but* I hear in her tone, any remaining hope I had of being listened to sours. "That terrible note you found . . . it is understandable that you would be frightened." She shakes her head. "Unfortunately, those of us who must bear the burden of power must, too, suffer the petty jealousies of others who wish to take it."

I blanch. "*Jealousies?*" I repeat, disbelieving. "Whoever wrote that note did not sound jealous to me. They said our Manor would fall, Cressida. Like Essie was only their first victim—like they wished to see us unseated, or worse—"

"Merrick, my darling." Cressida pauses, near enough now that I can smell the floral notes of her perfume—roses and something else, an earthy, almost masculine aroma like freshly turned loam. "Please be assured that Tom and I will do everything in our power to find your sister, and keep you and all other residents of Norland House safe in the meantime. Yet Estella is no simple peasant girl. The potential political ramifications of her absence could shake your Manor to its core if we do not tread lightly. Which is why," she hedges, "we must choose our next step as carefully as possible."

Her hand extends toward mine—an attempt to soothe me, or perhaps silence me lest I try to protest further. I'm not sure; I twist away before she can make contact, my neck whipping toward my cousin.

"And you support this approach?" I hiss to him. "My sister is not a teapot to be handled, Tom. She is our blood—mine and yours. Am I to assume that you mean to do nothing to find her?"

Something flares in Tom's eyes at my challenge—distinct from both his usual mirth and the dour mask he's donned today. It is fierce, alert, and defensive, and it sets me on edge as though he has dropped into a fighting stance.

"Listen here," he growls, setting his glass on the billiards table with a *clink*. "I will never stop searching for Estella. *Never.* Just because your father couldn't comprehend the meaning of family—" He breaks off, his jaw cutting to the right as if he's physically preventing himself from speaking further. Unsettled, I shrink back.

"*We* will never stop searching, Merrick." Cressida interjects, coolly repeating her husband's reassurance. "If the sentries do not turn up any signs of her by tomorrow, we will of course alert the Council—I will see it done myself. But you must understand"—her tone sharpens, the flick of a razor—"though the other Manor Lords may be our allies in name, they are *not* our friends. If they read Estella's disappearance as a sign of weakness in the Darling Manor, they will not hesitate to bare their teeth. Nor will the threat to your family's reign be a solely external one, should the narrative get out of hand," she adds. "You do not have many close relations, but every Manor has a few distant branches who wish to see themselves anchored closer to the roots, and they will not be content to wait around endlessly for your sister to be restored to her throne. Propriety will keep them from pushing for a new Vessel for a few weeks, at least, but after that . . . No." Her eyes catch on mine, emotions veiled and inscrutable. "I would caution you not to trust anyone who claims to have Estella's best intentions at heart, aside from yourself, Tom, and me."

I don't trust them.

My sister's whisper comes quick as a sparrow, darting through my mind. At it, I take an involuntary step backward. Was Essie only being cautious the night she visited me in my room—driven by a worry that if she confessed whatever she was frightened of to our cousin and his wife, they would see her as immature, incapable of leading our Manor?

Or is it possible the shadow my sister kept looking over her shoulder for was them?

In my periphery, Tom tenses, his scowl like edged glass.

"Cress," he says tersely. "Stop—she is hurting, and you are being harsh."

"I am being *realistic*." Cressida's composure shatters in a burst of anger, startling me. She glares at her husband, hands clenched, elbows bent at sharp, defiant angles. "Think of what we have endured already, Tom! First one daughter flees to New London, then a father takes his own life, and now a second sister has vanished and you want to believe that we should coddle the girl that remains?" Low and humorless, she laughs. "To speak frankly, we do not have the time for kindness. Grandmother made it clear to me that if I ever wished to be named her Vessel, I needed to find a respectable match, and so I did—for the good of my Manor. Just as I am *attempting* to help your cousins for the sake of the Faulks, as much as the Darlings." Her fingers skim nervously over the waistline of her gown, as if tracing an invisible wound. "I cannot afford to be tied to a disgraced line," she murmurs, almost to herself. "Not now."

Her rage is almost intimate, speaking of closed doors and dead arguments, of fights carried on for so long they become familiar. I resist the urge to look away—my own rage stuttering like a candle flame in the wind under the force of her fury. To my horror, Cressida seems to register my discomfort. She steps back, a hint of something like remorse glancing over her features.

"Merrick, I . . ." she begins, then shakes her head, cutting herself off. "Never mind. I have pressed you too soon, on far too much. You need time to mourn—we all do," she says, and I hate how much I feel like a little girl under her stare, in need of protection and swaddling. I bite down on the inside of my cheek, letting the flowering pain distract me from the sting prickling at the corners of my eyes.

Cressida places a comforting hand on my shoulder. "Go rest, Merrick," she tells me. "We will discuss next steps tomorrow. Who knows—Estella may yet be back with us before the day ends."

And if the sentries don't find her? If they discover a body in her place? The protests rise to my mind unbidden, but my already shallow reserves of fight have been depleted entirely by this conversation, leaving only exhaustion in their place. Weariness glazing my bones with lead, I acquiesce to Cressida's suggestion with a weak nod. I have not even reached the hallway before her and Tom's bickering rises up to follow after me again.

Shutting the door firmly on them, I allow Norland's silence to descend over me like a quilt. The quiet clears my mind, my thoughts at last falling into some semblance of order.

There are three of them, precisely:

One: Essie is gone, and Cressida and Tom seem more disturbed by the social implications of this fact than the fact itself.

Two: Where she went, or if she is alive, I do not know. But—

Three: I aim to find out.

CHAPTER FOURTEEN

I move through Norland House with sweaty palms and an un-quiet mind, crossing through the entrance hall, up the principal staircase with its balustrades carved to resemble twisting plumes of mist and onto the second floor. Past the landing, the corridor at the top is throatlike—wide at the top, then quickly narrowing as it leads deeper into the estate. Much of this floor is windowless, so that despite the early hour, sunlight here is little more than a rumor; dimness lingers like a mold, staining the chestnut floors the deep mahogany of wilting roses. Still, I navigate to the house's west wing with ease, bypassing my room and continuing ahead toward my sister's, my feet reading the route almost instinctively.

Darling Manor will fall.

The note from Essie's room stabs at me as I walk, hastening my pace. I attempt to refocus myself on the corridor in front of me; try as I might, though, I cannot seem to push the image of the letters—their malevolent, gleeful scrawl—out of my head. Can't keep myself from picking at them, like a scab I've been forbidden to touch.

You failed her. The words cycle through me, unceasing, in a hushed, spiteful whisper. *Someone was chasing Essie, and you were too focused on keeping your own feet steady beneath you to catch them. Too obsessed with the breaches, with Fitz Vannett, with the coolness of a boy's hand in yours when he asked you to dance.*

Too angry with Father, with Father, with Father—

FALL WILL FALL.

The sight of Essie's bedroom door, sturdy and foreboding, jolts me out of my internal spiral and back into myself—back to the task at hand. *Essie.* I am here to learn what happened to my sister—where she went, how I can bring her back.

And if it is too late for that? A voice pries. I ignore it.

Essie's door is unlocked, swinging open when I turn the knob. Beyond the threshold, the space in front of me has transformed from when I last viewed it, plumed in darkness during the night. Evidence of the sentries' search is clearly visible in the frothy mess of clothes littering the floor, the duvet half drooping off the stately four-poster bed as if kicked away by now-absent feet. Standing against the wall across from it, my sister's lacquered black armoire hangs open like a gutted animal, clothes tumbling from within it.

Cautiously, I step across the threshold, pulling the door shut behind me. I was too distraught to lend much of an investigative eye when the sentries tore through this place mere hours ago, but Cressida's mention of their continued search in the billiards room sparked an idea. Certainly our men have the sheer numbers to execute a thorough hunt, but perhaps the key to discovering what happened to my sister lies in precision, rather than force—a trail of breadcrumbs visible only to those who know Essie best. A red string that I can follow until I find my way back to her and bring her home again.

I slip my shoes off as I venture farther into the bedroom and cross to Essie's writing desk, which is pushed against the wall closest to me. Here, too, the sentries' recent presence is clear: my sister's beloved books, plucked from my father's library and once neatly lined up against the back of the desk, are now strewn across its pocked brown surface, and her slim blue vase is tipped on its side, a few wilting yellow daisies protruding from the vessel's open neck.

Steadily at first, then more hurriedly as the minutes tick on, I sift through the debris mounded on her desk, my hope hardening like a callus with each second that passes discoveryless. When my search yields nothing, I move on, methodically working my way through the rest of my sister's quarters. Yet again and again, I come up empty-handed, the cluttered space around me proving to be just that: a messy room, one that bares its contents willingly, without any secrets to hide.

I turn to Essie's armoire last. Right away, I spot several empty hangers dangling from the closet rod, their corresponding gowns splayed on the floor. An unexpected, shooting pain needles through my chest at the sight. It is one thing to speak of my sister's absence to Cressida and Tom—another to see the proof of it directly in front of me, close enough that I could reach out and touch it if I wanted to, feel the new emptiness that has grown where pieces of her used to be.

Is this how Essie felt, I wonder, when I left for New London—as if a seam of her had torn open, her insides spilling out? I thought she was too steadfast, too reliable, to subject herself to the galloping heave of emotions in the way I always have, but considering her state since I returned, who knows—maybe she was never like that at all. Maybe it was all just a deception.

Reaching out, I pinch the satin sleeve of an undiscarded dress and rub it between my fingers. *How could I have ever believed that I knew you?*

I freeze, my gaze suddenly catching on a garment tucked behind the gown I'm clutching: a green silk pelisse, shoved to the very back of the armoire. Compared to the rest of my sister's wardrobe, the ankle-length overcoat is shabby, out-of-date—its hem fraying, worn patches showing where the fabric has rubbed thin from use. More like an item of clothing one might find buried at the bottom of a charity heap than hanging in the bedroom of a daughter of a Manor Lord.

My heart thumps excitedly in my chest. How could I have forgotten? I know this coat—I'd happened upon it two years ago, when I was snooping in Essie's closet for a dress to steal and instead found something else entirely: her hiding spot. I haven't been back since, assuming she'd moved her secrets to a new location once she realized what I'd done, but if she didn't . . .

I reach for the cloak and draw it toward me, my fingers traversing the threadbare lining inside. The fabric is cool to the touch, the air musty and dust-clogged, itching at my nose as I search for—

There. My pulse quickens further as I find what I'm searching for. Near the bottom of the garment, I can feel the outline of something rectangular and blocky—an object about the size of my hand, sewn into the cloak itself. A swell of victory spreads in my chest as I trace its edges, touch the row of clumsy stitches above it.

My sister has always been a private person, guarding her weaknesses fiercely; I saw it often when we were growing up, the way she only let herself care for things when no one else could see. Like the dog-eared book of sonnets that she used to hide under her pillow, their pages yellowed from exposure and frequent rereading. Or the love letters I found stuffed here, from a round-faced stable boy who'd started on at Norland a few months prior. I made the mistake of hinting at Essie's romance to her a couple weeks after I uncovered the notes, thinking it might prompt her to open up to me.

Instead, Essie had Father dismiss the boy the next day. The servant cried when he left, but my sister did not.

Apparently, though, while she may have cast aside the stable boy, she kept this.

Carefully, I dig my nails into the untidy seam, popping free the loose stitches with ease. Then I slide my hand into the narrow opening until the tips of my fingers brush against something cool and flat. Gritting my teeth, I stretch my arm an inch farther and pull the object toward me, tugging it out and into the light.

In my hands is a book—a journal, made of buttery red leather that glows with an almost liquid sheen in the sunlight. Its cover is plain but for a pair of silver letters engraved in its center. My breath catches at the sight of them: *E.D.*

Estella Darling.

My blood pounds in my veins, a river bursting its banks. Adrenaline roaring in my ears, I flip open the cover, thumbing through the pages inside. The journal is about halfway full, the pages covered in my sister's cramped, neat handwriting. Forcing my hands to remain steady, I lower myself to the floor and turn back to the beginning of the book—the first entry.

16 June, Year 211 of the Turning

Merrick has been gone a month now, Mother about twice that. Though one is lost and the other simply away, I mourn for them both, for I am not sure that either of them will ever return.

I do not know why, exactly, I have decided to begin keeping a diary of this kind. Perhaps it is because I miss having someone to talk to, even if that "someone" is only a blank page; perhaps, though, for reasons I cannot fully comprehend, I feel compelled

to keep a written record of the past few weeks. Maybe then I can
understand the change that has recently come over my family—
and my province.

Father has been behaving strangely as of late. At first, I
simply put it down to grief, but he doesn't seem like a husband in
the throes of despair—more like a man obsessed. When he is not
out on patrol, he sequesters himself in his quarters for hours at
a time, refusing to emerge except for the occasional meal. I can
hear him sometimes when I walk past his room, pacing about
and muttering like a madman. Last night when he didn't come
down for dinner, I resolved to extract him myself—only to find
upon trying his door that it was firmly locked.

I wish Merrick were here. She has mastered the ability to find
the levity in heavy times, as though life's trials are nothing but
a jest that she is always let in on. It is one of the many reasons,
I think, that people prefer her to me. I cannot seem to enter a
room without reminding those within of the various obligations
that they have left unfulfilled, or the petty sins they have
committed and secreted away from their wives and children.
Merrick brings pleasure and joy, and beauty, of course.

But now she has left me, and though summer is blooming
all around us, I fear that winter has settled too deep in Norland
House's bones for us ever to escape the chill.

I pause, unsettled. By now, I've heard multiple accounts of my
father's odd behavior before his passing, but it is not the description of his mental state that disturbs me, so much as the fact that
I recognize it. I, too, have been on the other side of a locked door
recently. Since my mother's passing, it seems that's all my family
has been reduced to—a series of closed rooms, each person turning to shut out the one who attempts to extract them.

Throat constricting, I read on, flipping through entries until I find another that catches my eye.

20 July, Year 211 of the Turning

There has been a breach at the border—the first in almost three years. Fortunately, the downed lanterns were repaired without any casualties, though that fact is of little comfort. Since Mother's passing, the townsfolk have been like a flock of sheep, ready to bolt at a moment's notice. Lanterns hung from the window of almost every home I passed last time I rode into Shoreham-by-Sea, and in the village square, a bonfire spit red sparks into the sky.

Father still all but refuses to leave his room, even after I informed him of the recent attack. In his absence, I have been forced to start taking on duties that should rightfully be his: assigning patrol routes, commanding the sentries. I have gone so far as to begin discreetly advertising for additional forces to help supplement ours until I am confident the border situation is back in hand. Primarily, I have been relying on word of mouth—planting rumors where I know they will not spread to Manorborn ears—but already several men have arrived on Sussex's soil. Interestingly, I have found that these new recruits, never having trained under Father, are more receptive to my orders, less likely to see me as a pretender.

I wish I did not have to resort to such measures at all, but I remain unsure as to what may be disturbing Father so, aside from Mother's passing. Though . . .

I cannot confess these thoughts anywhere outside this journal, but in recent days I've experienced an odd sensation—I feel constantly as though I am being watched. I know I am being foolish, for every time I turn around, there is no one behind me, yet the instinct remains. The other night, I swore I saw a figure standing on the lawn just below my window, only to discover when I looked again that it had vanished.

Of course it had. It was never there in the first place. Father's paranoia is rubbing off on me, I fear.

I have had not a single piece of correspondence from Merrick since she left. I know I should not disturb her—she is doing what she is meant to, after all, finding herself a good match that will elevate the family—but with every day that passes without word from her, I find myself hating her just a little bit more. Most of the time, I think I am angry at her for leaving me behind, for abandoning Father and me when we needed her most.

Occasionally, though, I suspect that I am simply jealous she got away.

8 September

Two more breaches, one after the other. Morale has plunged lower still in the past weeks, both among the men and the local people. Now more than ever before, I know the commoners will be looking to their Lord for support—but Father can barely support himself, and lately, I have been no better.

There was another incident yesterday evening—I know not how else to refer to them besides "incidents." I was riding alone in Barton Woods when, from within the trees to my left, I heard the sound of hooves moving in time with my horse and me. Assuming another rider was nearby, I called out but was answered only by silence. It was past dusk, and I could not see deeply into the forest around me; when I urged my horse onward, though, the noise resumed. Almost as if someone was keeping pace with me, hidden in the gloom.

I made good time through the woods after that.

In better news, at least, the incoming sentries continue to show promise—all the more necessary now that a pair of the old have turned. One, a young man from the Tudor line, has particularly impressed me; I must think of additional uses for him in the future.

12 September
Father is dead.

My hand is shaking as I write these words. He perished early this morning, and in the hours since, I have seen my world wither and fade along with him.

Suicide—that was the cause of his passing, though no one will say as much yet, out of respect for him. I watched him walk into the mists myself just after dawn, dressed far too lightly for the chill. The sentries insist I could have done nothing to save him, but I am not so sure. After all, it was only a couple days ago that he called me into his study and told me, at last, that he was ready to proclaim me as his Vessel. For the first time in months, he seemed clearheaded, sober, and I'd rejoiced in it all—in his presence, and in the news. I thought that finally he'd recognized my efforts, my recent labor. I thought I was being rewarded for good work.

What a foolish girl I am, for not seeing the signs then, when I was looking them in the face.

I shall have to write Merrick of this development, though I do not know yet what I will say. How does one speak to a ghost?

17 September
My sister is due home today, and it is my fiercest wish that she should never arrive. I fear that by calling her back, I am bringing her into a danger I do not understand.

Despite our best efforts, Brandon's and my investigation into
the recent strange occurrences has thus far turned up no leads.
He has promised to keep searching, but—

Behind me, a sudden gust of wind judders the window frames, making me drop the journal in surprise. I whirl around, muscles tensed, only to flush when I take in the vacant room, the lonely furniture arranged within it like a collection of awkward party guests. The windows and their glass windowpanes—solemn, unblinking eyes exposing me to the gardens beyond.

Feeling suddenly watched, I examine the view beyond them. From here, I can just make out the clouded haze of the Graylands pacing the cliffs like a mangy white wolf in the distance, where our grounds abut the seaside. Encased as I am by solitude, the mist's presence is all-pervasive, at once the predator and the forest it dwells in.

With a shiver, I pick my sister's book up again. Her final entry stops at the sentence I last read, cutting itself off midway through a thought as if she'd been interrupted. Still, my heart pounds faster as I look the lines over one more time, taking in the name inscribed there.

Brandon's and my investigation into the recent strange
occurrences . . .

I need to speak with Killian.

CHAPTER FIFTEEN

The sentries' barracks are located to the back and left of Norland House, positioned beneath a canopy of hazel and ash trees. In the summer, the greenery forms a rich emerald roof over the lodgings, but here at the knife edge of autumn, color is already leaching from their leaves like a blush fading from the cheeks of a young girl. Beneath them, the barracks themselves comprise two rough-hewn stone buildings slung low to the ground, their rocky bellies scraping the earth in a way that has always reminded me of a pair of gray cats, slinking across the earth.

I shift on my feet, eyeing the twin buildings with trepidation. After I'd finished reading Essie's journal, I'd debated bringing it to Tom and Cressida, but the memory of their earlier inaction was still fresh in my mind, and it made me hesitant. If Cressida had been willing to dismiss a note calling for the fall of our Manor as petty jealousy, how little would she think of my sister's half-hysterical writings about noises in the woods and shadows outside a window? Most likely, she'd take what I gave her and send me off with empty reassurances, wasting yet more time as she and Tom continued to debate "next steps." Not to mention, I hadn't forgotten my sister's reaction the last time I'd suggested going to our cousin and his wife: *I don't trust them.*

Well, in that case, perhaps I shouldn't, either.

Judging by Essie's journal, there was only one person my sister *did* trust enough to disclose her fears to before my father's ball—one person with whom she claimed to be conducting an "investigation." And if I want to piece together what's happened to her, I'm certain he is where the trail starts.

My palms are slick by the time I reach the barracks entrance. Drawing an exhale, I grip the brass knocker with my free hand, praying the paper hasn't yet turned to pulp in my other.

"—surely don't expect our loyalty, after this? The family are dropping like flies, and as always, we'll be the ones left to bear the brunt of it. Godwin nearly lost his leg last night, you know, and I don't fancy being next."

I freeze at the sound of a rumbling male voice drifting through the cracked window to the right of the door. Behind the dingy glass, a blurry gray form is moving, their features too obscured by grime to be distinguishable—but though I can't identify who is speaking, the flesh of my arm tingles at the subject of the conversation. *The family.* There is only one family he could be talking about: my own.

Curiosity overtaking me, I release the door knocker and duck beneath the narrow windowsill, out of sight of anyone within.

"We took an oath, Mandel—service in exchange for land," a second voice responds—this one easily recognizable, with the cool gray smoothness of a river stone. *Killian.* His shadow is thrown next to the first speaker's against the windowpanes, and despite the fact that I can't see him, I swear I can feel the sting of his blue eye even from here.

"A bargain you were plenty happy to make when you felt it was in your favor, if you'd care to remember," Killian continues, inside the barracks. "And the Red Duke and Duchess have requested that we not speak about the Archdaughter until the public has been alerted—you know that."

The first speaker—Mandel, judging by what Killian called him—laughs, mean and grating. "Divine Three, Brandon, you're among friends. It wouldn't kill you to share a bloody opinion once in a while—I promise I won't tell the Duchess," he mocks. "Besides, if we're speaking of oaths and honor, I'd tell you to take another look at our esteemed rulers. They've got their own citizens believing Lord Silas died of a heart condition, for Lightkeeper's sake. The old man was probably desperate to get away from them." I hear him work up a gob of saliva, then the meaty *thwack* of his spit as it lands on the floor. "Bloody fucking rats' nest, this Manor is."

Rage simmers in my stomach. Based on what I've overheard so far, Mandel is clearly a sentry. Where is his sense of duty, his devotion to the Manor he's bound to protect?

Is he wrong, though? a snide voice murmurs in my ear. *We have done nothing but lie to him since Father died. You know he speaks the truth.*

"You've got an impressive moral compass for a man who was willing to abandon his own province for this one the minute Archdaughter Estella dangled the promise of wealth before you," Killian deadpans. "It's not our duty to pass judgment on the ruling house's decisions. Now more than ever with the Archdaughter gone, Sussex's borders will need patrolling, else we'll continue to suffer attacks like the one last night. You speak of the people—help me keep them safe."

There's the squeal of a wooden chair, presumably as Mandel lowers himself down into it. "And what of our own safety?" he questions, the sour derision in his tone like vinegar on my tongue.

"These breaches—you know as well as I do that there's something odd about them. James told me about the man you found at the site of the last one, with his throat slashed clean through? That doesn't sound like the work of a Phantom to me. And it isn't only that," he continues, his voice turning hushed—almost too low for me to make out. "We've had two of our own turn already, and who knows how many others' immunity might fail in the future? The Darlings don't give a damn about us, they've made that much clear—Estella even less so than Silas. You know we used to get tea with our dinner, and wine on holidays? Now it's just hot water and endless patrols, and if a man dies in action, they bring another one in before he's even settled in his grave. No," Mandel says, "this place is a death trap. I say we leave now—before we're the ones getting replaced."

There's a beat of silence; I strain to make out Killian's response, my nails carving crescent moons into my palms. So it wasn't just me who noticed the odd wound on the corpse Killian and I discovered—the other sentries must have seen it, too, when they swept the house after we'd left. But what else could have killed him, and for what reason? Had the family been dead already when the lanterns went out, perhaps—the victims of robbers, passing through the countryside?

If that is the case, a sly voice argues, *then who lit the distress signal?*

The note I found on Essie's pillow drifts through my mind again. If I let my thoughts blur, I can almost see a string reaching from the attacks at the borders to Essie's vanishing, ephemeral as a strand of spider's silk catching the light, but reaching for it makes the thread snap and dissolve in my hands.

I don't realize how far my mind has wandered until Killian speaks again. "You can go if you like," he counters. "But I gave my word, for better or worse. I won't rescind it just because *worse* has come along."

"We gave it to a girl whose corpse is likely baking in the sun by now!" The form in the window flickers as the other sentry stands, a smoky blur against the glass. "Estella was the only one of the Darlings left with half a brain, anyway. The Duke is an idiot who can barely write his own name without his wife spelling it out for him, and as for the other Archdaughter"—he scoffs, and somehow, the judgment in the noise alone withers me—"she's fine to look at, I'll admit that, but shallow as anything. It's like the whole world is her mirror—like whenever she looks at you, she can't see anything beyond herself. I pity the man who takes her to bed."

My stomach plummets, the ground falling away beneath me. *It's like the whole world is her mirror.* The sentry's jab hits me deep in my bones, making me ache with shame—and, in the same breath, lights me with a burning, vicious anger.

Inside the room, Killian sighs. "Her father raised her to be auctioned off like a doll. You can hardly blame her for trying to fulfill the role he assigned her," he replies. His betrayal is a knife drawn clean across my throat, but I barely have time to bleed before his companion answers him.

"Yes, I'd forgotten—you've been spending quite a lot of time with her, haven't you?" Mandel asks coyly. "Looking to add that doll to your private collection?"

Killian coughs. "The opposite, in fact—I am trying to protect her," he says hurriedly. "If Estella truly is gone, then her sister is the late Lord Silas's only remaining viable heir. Sussex needs her."

Mandel falls silent after that, Killian's proclamation turning the atmosphere somber and bleak. Pressed against the wall, I feel the bite of his words, too. *Lord Silas's only remaining viable heir.* In the chaos of Essie's disappearance, I hadn't yet considered that—had barely spared a thought for who might come after my sister, when I'd barely started to comprehend the possibility of an *after* to begin with.

My skin grows hot, flushed. Only a few weeks ago, the idea of my becoming Manor Lord would have filled me with glee. Now guilt weighs me down, heavy as a chain around my neck. Surely no one would give me a crown stolen from my dead sister's brow?

Surely I would not take it?

Suddenly I have no desire to speak with Killian any longer. I push myself off from the wall, careful to move quietly lest I give away my position to the sentries inside. Cautiously I take a step forward, then another.

Crack.

I spit out a curse as my feet stumble over a fallen twig, snapping it in half. To my back, I hear the sentries' voices rise at the sound, and the urge to flee consumes me. Pulse pounding, I hitch up my skirts, breaking into a run as I hear the door fly open behind me.

"Merrick."

The use of my first name stops me short, just as I'm certain he knew it would. Embarrassment warming me, I turn reluctantly, schooling my expression into one imperious and ladylike—as if he is the interloper in this situation, and not I.

"I did not give you permission to call me that, *Mr.* Brandon."

Killian's features are half in shadow, his burnt-honey hair hanging about his face in sleep-mussed waves. Backlit by the stone walls of the barracks and dressed simply in a tunic and breeches, he looks like a hero pulled from the pages of a grand romance, like a painter's rendition of some pastoral ideal.

He approaches me cautiously, his hands upturned as if I am a deer, poised to bolt at his slightest movement. "I am addressing you as I would a friend," he says steadily. "Are we not friends yet?"

I hate the way my resolve wavers at his smile—crooked and sheepish in a way that's instantly disarming, as if he is inviting me to share a joke with him. In his eyes, though, I see the truth. Wrapped in the layers of warmth, there is something probing in his expression—as if his cheerfulness is a test, designed to produce a reaction. *He wants to know how much you heard.*

The realization anchors me. "Friends do not keep secrets from one another," I reply. "And it seems as though you have been hiding more than one from me."

I take a step toward him, holding his stare, and am pleased when this time, it is he who shrinks back. "I know that my sister thought she was being watched before my father's Memorial Ball," I say. "She kept a journal in the months leading up to my father's death—one that I presume was missed during the search of her room last night. Which is how I also know that you were helping her investigate the"—I cock my chin—"incidents, as I believe she termed them."

Killian is quiet for a long moment, tension dripping over us like cooling wax, hardening us both in our places. A muscle jumps in his cheek, as if he is waging some internal battle with himself—to let me in, or keep me shut out.

In the end, though, he only curses, soft and poisonous. "*Fuck.*"

Something about the grating despair in his voice, the weary grind of bone on bone, chills me. Letting out a long sigh, he grimaces, running a hand through his hair in frustration. There's a tremor in his fingers as he winds them through the strands, an uneasiness I haven't seen before.

"The Duchess didn't mention a journal," he says bitterly.

"The Duchess?" I struggle to keep my voice even, but indignation breaks through, my temper igniting in a smoky, jealous haze. "Cressida knows about this?"

"Only since last night," Killian answers. "I told her after your sister was discovered missing—after I heard about the note you found." His brows knit together, his scowl deepening. "I asked that she keep what I shared with her to herself, out of respect for your sister's wishes."

Around us, the branches sway in the wind, snatches of Killian's admission echoing back to me in the conspiratorial whisper of their leaves. *Only since last night . . . out of respect for your sister's wishes.* I regard him without speaking, my rage blazing higher every second. A dozen responses swirl away in my stomach, but they all feel too hot to speak aloud, as if they would burn coming up my throat.

"Merrick—Archdaughter—" Finally registering my fury, Killian starts to go on, only to drift off again as if he isn't sure how to proceed. His scars flinch with every flicker of emotion that crosses his face, pink skin pulling taut.

At last, he says, "Your sister was only trying to protect you."

"Protect *me*? She could not even protect herself." Frustration lurches within me, my emotions a chain about to slip from my grasp. I bite my lip, willing myself to hold on. *"Darling Manor will fall,"* I repeat heatedly. "You said you saw the note—had Essie received any others like it before last night? Who did she think was watching her?" My voice cracks. "What do they *want*?"

"No other notes, that I know of," Killian replies, his head dipping abashedly. "As for your latter questions, Archdaughter Estella had some ideas, but we were still looking into them all. I told her . . ." Running a hand through his already unkempt waves, he sighs. "Dammit. I told her to be more *careful*."

His admission frays, coming undone at the end. At it, my nerves tingle painfully under my skin. I am not sure which is more upsetting—the realization that my sister may have known she was in danger prior to her vanishing, or the fact that she chose a stranger to share her troubles with, rather than me.

"Tell me," I say to Killian flatly. "All of it."

And to his credit, the sentry obeys.

"I'm not sure how much you read in her journal, but from what your sister told me, the trouble started a couple months ago," he says. "At first, it was just a sensation—a feeling that something was watching her. That she wasn't alone." His mouth twists. "Initially, Archdaughter Estella tried to dismiss her fears as paranoia—a manifestation, if you will, of her worries about the breaches at the border. But then . . . it escalated."

His nostrils flare, and despite myself, cold trepidation slips through my veins. "She would hear noises in the woods when she was riding alone, as if someone were following alongside her," Killian continues. "Or, once, she told me, she came back to Norland after a patrol and found a dead bird on her bed, still warm. Her window was open—in all likelihood, the creature flew in on its own—but even so . . ." He wets his lips nervously. "It got to the point where she couldn't ignore the incidents any longer, and, as I'd only been in Sussex for a few weeks at this point and had no loyalty to anyone besides her, she chose me to help her seek out their source."

Falling silent, Killian shifts on his feet, his muscles flexing beneath his thin cotton shift. Observing him, I think back to another fragment of my sister's journal: *I have found that these new recruits, never having trained under Father, are more receptive to my orders . . . One, a young man from the Tudor line, has particularly impressed me.*

So far, at least, his story holds. "And?" I prompt him, impatient. "What did you find?"

"Not much. We didn't have much time—it was only a couple days before your father's passing that she came to me," he tells me. "We did notice, though, that whoever was harassing your sister seemed more focused on frightening her than physically harming her, which led us to wonder if there might be a political motivation behind their actions. Another member of your Manor trying to intimidate her out of accepting the title of Vessel, thereby opening the Lordship up for themself. Like your cousin and his wife—the Duke and Duchess." His voice drops when he utters my cousin's and his wife's titles, the falter so smooth it seems almost unconscious, like a hitch in his breath. "It was the natural assumption— who more likely to threaten your father's successor than one who desired to usurp her? And as Lord Silas's nephew, your cousin could make a case for his right to rule." Killian's lips twist, as if with a distasteful memory. "We dismissed that theory quickly enough, though, what with the issue of the marriage contract."

My interest piques. "Marriage contract?"

"The terms your father had the Duke agree to before his wedding to the Duchess?" Killian supplies. His tone is expectant, leading, as though waiting for me to catch on—to nod in understanding. When I say nothing, he clears his throat. "Your sister had been made aware—I guessed you'd been, too."

Ah. A flush rises to my cheeks, identical to the one I see reddening his own. "I gathered that the match was not one of love, if that's what you mean," I reply, trying to recover my ground.

"It wasn't only that," Killian answers. "Apparently, your cousin's potential ascension was a bargaining point during your father's early discussions with Elodie Faulk. The Faulk Manor wanted an alliance with yours, and a husband for Duchess Cressida, but not one that might impede the Duchess's own eventual rule. So the Duke signed his claim to Sussex away."

I raise my brows, taken aback. "He did?"

Killian shifts uncomfortably. Though he doesn't push the point of my ignorance further, it nags at me like a hangnail— another secret I've been left out of. "I gather he didn't have much of a choice in the matter," he admits. "Your sister mentioned gambling debts?"

He thinks I'll bow to him. My cousin's long-ago words stir in my mind; at once, I'm back inside Norland House, watching Tom slam the door on my father—his former benefactor, abruptly transformed into a foe. I'd assumed, since then, that Father had influenced Tom's engagement to Cressida, that my cousin's anger that night had been born of this manipulation. Yet all along, it hadn't only been the prospect of an arranged marriage that had triggered his fury—but the reality that in buying my cousin a bride, my father had sold something far dearer. His chance at the Lordship.

"Without a claim to your Manor, there would be no point in the Duke's threatening Archdaughter Estella." Killian interrupts my thoughts, pulling me back to the present. "Besides, your sister and I both agreed—Duke Thomas doesn't seem the type to be so vicious. His wife, perhaps, but him . . ."

I frown at him, trying not to hate his casual use of *we,* how it feels like a room I've been barred from entering. "You *both* agreed?" I challenge. "How is that possible? Had you even met Tom, at that point?"

To my surprise, the sentry, whose expression has turned contemplative, startles at my question—his eyes widen, as if he's been caught in a lie. "Ah—" He tugs at the collar of his shirt uncomfortably. "Not personally, but one of my elder brothers was schoolmates with the Duke when they were boys. *Before*—you know." He coughs. "He always spoke highly of your cousin, is all."

A vague aura of guilt hangs over him, like he's led me down a path he didn't mean to start on. *Before* . . . before he came to Norland, I assume. Inside me, suspicion narrows its feline eyes. Who is this person, truly? And what parts of his past is he so desperate to hide, that he would abandon his home for another?

Avoiding my gaze, Killian continues on, evidently desperate to change the subject. "It matters little, anyhow," he says. "Once we'd moved on from the Duke and Duchess, we considered other suspects. Most likely, we believed the culprit was someone with ties to Norland House—someone who would have been able to move about the grounds without attracting notice. Or at least a person with close enough ties to the staff that they'd be able to convince a servant to do their dirty work for them, like . . ."

He breaks off, his lips pressing into a line. That same guilt that bloomed beneath his features earlier is back, like a worm at the core of an apple, writhing in his eyes.

Oh. It hits like the strike of an iron—what he was about to say.

"Like me." The words stick in my throat, gummy and wet; I feel Killian's gaze rise to mine, but now it is me who can't look him in the face. Instead, I bite down on my lower lip, turn away. "Keep going," I demand curtly.

"Archdaughter . . . your sister never believed . . ." Killian shifts closer, as if to lay a comforting hand on my shoulder, then seems to think better of it. "Beyond that, there isn't much more to tell. Our investigation spanned only a few days; there was your father's death, for one, and then, the night after you arrived, the Archdaughter came to the barracks and told me to stop my search completely."

Confusion swirls through me, distracting me from the hurt that still pokes at my sternum. "She did?" I ask, looking up. "Why would she do that?"

Killian inclines his head, angling his chin toward me. "She claimed that she'd changed her mind—that she was sure the incidents were nothing more than a hoax, but to be candid, I think it was more that she wanted my focus elsewhere," he says slowly. "On guarding you, specifically. She emphasized to me that your protection was to be my priority."

"She . . ." Numbness spreads through my organs, sinks into muscle. *Impossible,* I want to protest. *Essie would never have sacri-*

ficed her own safety for mine—she hated *me. Resented me for leaving her alone, after Mother.*

Yet even as I form my rebuttals, I know they are untrue. After all, did she not urge me to leave Norland House as soon as I could, that morning in the gardens? Did she not push me away—out of anger, I'd thought initially. But perhaps she'd only been trying to keep me safe, keep me out of reach of the danger that was pursuing her.

"You must think me pathetic," I say softly, not caring when my voice wobbles. "Worrying over engagements, over men, while Essie was facing down a true monster just so I would not have to. Because I was too weak to."

Abruptly, Killian stiffens. "Don't do that."

His bluntness shocks me out of my self-pity for a moment. "What?"

"Blame yourself," he answers roughly. "Pretend like you're delicate. She didn't see you like that—like some creature in need of saving."

I stare at him, my emotions tumbling within me. Swallowing the tears that have risen up my throat, I ease my lips into a watery smile. "But Mr. Brandon, you yourself admitted what I am. A doll, I think you called me, did you not? Good only for auctioning off?"

Killian doesn't reply immediately. His hand flexes at his side, and for a second I'm overcome by the wild impression that he will reach for me—I feel the motion somehow, deep in my gut, like a premonition. Yet he remains still, letting the seconds tick by, the trees' cool shadows washing over him until finally, his lips part—

Just then, the door to the barracks slams open, a brash punctuation on the end of his unspoken sentence. Sentries' rough voices spill out—laughing, shouting. One calls out Killian's name, then goes silent as the group notices me.

I take a self-conscious step away from him, my thoughts swirling. I feel curiously as though I've been pulled back from the edge of a storm: frazzled, with the distinct sensation that I've lost out on—*something*. A sky waiting to open in my chest, its waters pouring forth.

"Go to them—it is fine." I nod toward the other sentries as I speak to Killian, gathering myself. "I shall see you again soon, anyhow."

He's still looking at me; for an unnamable reason, I'm hesitant to address him directly, to see what his eyes might hold if I peered into them. Then he blinks, as if freeing himself from an invisible force. "You shall?"

I smile weakly. "Oh yes," I tell him. "Are you forgetting your orders already? According to my sister, I am to be your top priority. And I have decided that finding her is mine."

CHAPTER SIXTEEN

The rest of the day passes like a dream; I blink, and hours disappear, lost to the black shadows behind my eyelids. Several times, I jerk to alertness only to find myself in a different room from the last one I remember, as if I am a marionette, being walked around my house by a force I cannot see.

Dinner that night is a grim affair, Essie's absence like a stern parent at the table, glaring us all into silence. I eat little, pushing bites of mushy potato around my plate and stealing glances at my cousin seated across from me. Knowing what I do now about the nature of his marriage makes Tom's figure seem more tragic: his laughing eyes turn pleading in my sight, the curl of his mouth a mournful frown. Despite Killian's insistence that my cousin couldn't have been the note writer, I still find myself searching for a sign to tell me otherwise—a crescent of blood under his fingernails, a straightness to his spine, as if he has been plumped up by victory.

More and more since my return to Norland, I've found myself

looking at my family, finding the stranger inside. *What have you done?* I want to ask Tom.

What would any of us do, if given the chance?

Finally, toward the end of our meal, Cressida cuts through the quiet. "I was told you made a visit to the sentries' quarters today, Merrick."

She peers at me from her position at the head of the table, both her dainty hands wrapped around a teacup. I lay down my fork, meeting her gaze. "Were you?" I answer in a dry tone. "Killian Brandon is quite the eager correspondent. My sister and I cannot take a step in this house without him reporting it to you, it seems."

Cressida sighs primly, as if already, I am trying her patience. "Mr. Brandon is not the person who told me," she replies. "Though, as I assume you may know, he did inform Tom and me last night of some troubling beliefs your sister had prior to her disappearance."

In his own seat, Tom pauses with a bite of food halfway to his mouth, caught. I can feel Cressida waiting on my response, but in lieu of giving one, I slump down in my chair and take my fork in hand again, stabbing sullenly at my dinner. Though I know it is childlike, I cannot make myself engage with her on the topic of my sister right now. Not when my own mind is threatening to buckle under the weight of what I learned from Killian—what Essie hid from me.

After a minute of quiet, Cressida gives in, exhaling noisily again. "I would advise you to take these fears of Estella's with a healthy dose of skepticism, dear," she says, sipping at her tea. "Your sister was under enormous pressure prior to your father's passing, and following it. Stress of that sort is wont to make a person excitable, but as tempting as it is, it will do us no good to lose our heads hunting down imaginary pursuers."

My annoyance snaps at her condescension. "And if these *imag-*

inary pursuers follow through on their note's promise, and come after me next?" I challenge, looking back up at her. "Shall I tell them not to bother—they are only fictional?"

Cressida rolls her eyes. "I have said it once already—as long as you remain at Norland House, you will be kept safe. We have dozens of guards here willing to lay down their lives for you, if it comes to that." She nods idly toward the doors of the dining room, where I know two sentries are standing watch as we eat, Ghostslayers in their hands. At the casualness of her gesture—the uncaring way she mentions our soldiers' potential deaths, like they are shattered plates we can replace—I feel a tug of shame, the conversation I overheard in the barracks this morning drifting back to me: *The Darlings don't give a damn about us, they've made that much clear.*

"I have written to my grandmother to alert her as to our situation," Cressida continues. My interest piqued, I shift my focus back to her. "She has led Norrin for going on thirty years now; there is not a person in the Smoke I would trust more to shepherd us through this trial. Once she replies, we will decide together how to inform the rest of the Council of Essie's absence." She arches a brow at me. "I know you find the politics surrounding our situation trivial, Merrick, but if you wish to see your sister crowned as Lord once she is found, rather than overthrown, I would encourage you to recognize the importance of our messaging here," she says, her expression stern. "Remember: there are Manorborn who would gladly take advantage of a power void in Sussex to expand their own territories, if they believed they could get away with it. Do not mistake my caution as inaction. Am I clear?"

Her gaze bores into me, but in response, I only nod. When dinner is finished, I push away my untouched plate and go to find Killian, a plan already knitting together in my mind.

* * *

Naturally, he is suspicious of it.

"Shoreham-by-Sea is not so very far from Norland, Arch-daughter," he says as we saddle up our horses an hour or so later, having dismissed the stable boys with a stern look. "You may be recognized."

I glance down at my outfit, borrowed from my reluctant lady's maid. I've clad myself in a plain wool dress, high in the neckline and tight on my arms, a fraying shawl wrapped round my shoulders. My feet I've slipped into a pair of worn leather boots, and my curls have been brushed into a severe bun. A pang of nostalgia shoots through me as I take in my appearance. I used to tease Essie for her drab wardrobe, how she would dress more conservatively than our own servants. Now I cannot decide if I look more like her or them.

I give Pegasus's flank a pat, shrugging off my insecurities before Killian can observe them. "There are a thousand blond girls in Sussex," I reply evenly. "And anyhow, commoners know Manor-born by their money, not their faces. I promise you, dressed like this, no one will spare me a second glance."

Beside me, Killian merely huffs, unconvinced. He, too, has dressed for tonight's expedition—shedding the stoic grays of his sentry uniform in favor of a simple linen shirt and cotton trousers. Arching a brow at him, I add, "Kyrie is not so very far from Sussex, either, Mr. Brandon. Who's to say you won't be the one recognized? Maybe one of the villagers can shed some light on your mysterious origins."

That earns me a scowl, and I turn away, satisfied.

"Remind me again why you're so firmly set on this idea?" he asks. His gaze is fixed on his horse, but I can sense him watching me from the corner of his eye, his attention needling at the back of my neck. "I'm not sure what knowledge there is to be gleaned about Archdaughter Estella at a local pub."

"I'm not looking for knowledge, I'm looking for gossip—and at a pub, that may be found in spades," I correct him sharply. "And it isn't only that. I've been thinking more about the note that was left on her bed: *Darling Manor will fall.*" I pause, cold stirring at the base of my stomach, where it's settled ever since I saw Essie's empty room, felt the icy breeze from her open window on my skin. "Whoever wrote it did so to frighten us, that much is evident," I go on. "If the person who took Essie wished to prevent her from becoming Manor Lord, it would make sense to threaten my father's remaining heirs as well—discourage anyone else from taking her place. But then I started to consider whether there might be anyone else who would have reason to harbor a grudge against my family, and I realized: Mr. Birks. He certainly seemed angry enough over his severance to threaten Essie, possibly more than that. And he made no secret of the fact that he detested our Manor for denying him whatever he thought he was owed."

Killian tugs on the strap of his saddle, testing the buckle. "A sound theory. Though I doubt your old valet abducted Archdaughter Estella, considering he's dead."

"Perhaps not him, then, but he had another man with him in Barton Woods, remember?" I shift to face Killian more directly. "Who knows how many people he might have recruited to his cause before he died? Maybe he told other commoners about his grudge—maybe some of them felt similarly."

"Mmm," Killian hums distractedly. "Perhaps."

Irritation flares within me at his answer. Though he's standing half in shadow, I could almost swear he's smirking at me—his lips are quirked up at the edges, as if he finds me amusing. Stepping back, I cross my arms over my chest. "Do you have a superior theory in mind, or do you just wish to continue standing there, brooding at me?" I snap.

A breath of laughter—Killian rubs his horse's neck reassuringly. "Excuse my brooding," he says, winding his fingers through its mane. "It was unintentional, I assure you. I simply enjoy hearing you think."

He looks back at me, his smile more evident now—bolder, almost as if he is daring me to return it. It flicks like a whip toward me, knotting in my chest, but before I can catch hold of it, it's slipping away again.

"I have nothing *superior* to offer, as you put it," he says, planting his foot in the stirrup of his saddle and hoisting himself up, onto his horse's back. "Let's go."

Taking his reins in hand, he gives his steed a light tap with his heels, urging it into motion. Shaking free of my daze, I hurriedly mount Pegasus, following briskly after him.

Past the end of Norland's grounds, the land is still and dozing, the twilight lulling it into an early slumber. If not for the presence of the cliffs in the distance, the hazy glow of the border lanterns cordoning off the mist, the scene would almost be peaceful. Instead, I feel the tug of the Graylands for the entirety of our journey. Imagine the twisted form of a Phantom lurking behind every swell of mist, their blank eyes following after me, a ravenous, silent herd.

It is a relief when the thatched roofs of Shoreham-by-Sea come into view. As is standard in the Smoke, a ring of burning torches surrounds the town, cruder than their proud cousins at the border, fashioned out of wooden staves with bundles of oil-soaked rags secured to their ends. On the other side of their blazing defenses, squat buildings cluster around a central gap—a square, I know from past visits, though I can't make it out—in which a bonfire roars, spitting angry sparks. With their leaning forms and simple, blocky windows, the houses remind me of a group of men, crowding near a fire to ward off the evening chill.

A claw of guilt strokes along my back as Killian and I pass

through an arched gap in the torches—the main entry gate—weaving our way into the village. On the sills of almost every residence we pass, a candle flickers away behind the window glass—smoky tallow, not the wax we burn at Norland. I can't smell them, but somehow this whole place stinks of fear, miasmic and humid in the air.

Yet these are our people, the ones Father always claimed it was our sacred duty to protect. How have we left them so afraid?

We tie up our horses outside the pub, a low-slung building with patches of moss growing atop its sloping thatched roof like spots of mold on a crust of bread. The name *The Watchman* is carved into a wooden sign hanging over its door, an etching of a hand grasping a burning lantern below it. Past its foggy windows, I can see the outlines of patrons moving about, can hear strains of their laughter—so out of place among all the fire and the dimness of the scene in the streets.

With Killian following after me, I push open the door and step inside.

A bell jingles above the threshold, sounding my entrance, and immediately, every eye in the establishment turns toward me. The pub looks to be at about half capacity, in the process of filling up for the night; single men hunch on barstools, while others cluster in groups around the roughly hewn tables. Still more flames dance in the stone fireplace at one end of the room, thrashing against their boundaries like a single flailing animal. They paint the now-silent patrons in shades of amber, the men's brows crumpled with almost identical suspicion.

To my back, Killian stoops toward me, his lips hovering just above my ear. "I did say you'd stick out," he murmurs, his manner slightly too self-congratulatory for my taste. "They aren't used to seeing ladies in here. But tell me again how there are a thousand blondes in Sussex."

I snap my chin in his direction—his eyes are bright, glittering with mirth. "You know," I reply waspishly. "It is curious—I thought I'd brought a guard along with me, but it seems my only companion is a jester."

"Oh no, don't go quiet now," I prod him when he falls back, silent. "Your insults are so very diverting. I shan't know what to do without them."

He shakes his head, the firelight playing off his scars, running like glistening beads of water along their seams. Despite the severity of our circumstances, I can't help but get the sense that this verbal sparring match excites him—that he's enjoying it, just a little bit.

Disturbingly, I find that I am, too.

"All right, then, Archdaughter," Killian says, perhaps noticing my discomfort. He spreads his hands, crossing to a vacant bar seat and sinking down into it. "We're here. What shall we do now?"

I take the stool next to him, fidgeting to make myself comfortable atop its hard, circular surface, as I ponder his answer. Truthfully, the plan I'd concocted back at Norland—visit a pub, see whether I can catch any rumors making their rounds about my sister or her whereabouts—seemed far easier when I wasn't facing a room of hulking locals. It itches at me, the way I'd assumed the villagers would just . . . speak to me when I arrived. That they would rush to fulfill the roles I'd assigned them, as they would with an Archdaughter, a Manorborn.

Their superior. Is that what I think of myself?

"I suppose we can talk," I say finally.

"Talk?" Killian repeats idly. He signals the bartender, who ambles obediently over, still pinning me with a dubious look. For a horrible second, I think he's placed me—either that, or he's about to ask me to kindly exit his establishment—but whatever reservations the man seems to possess about serving a woman disappear when Killian clacks a stack of coins on the bar top. Grumbling, the bartender whisks them away, replacing them with two tall mugs of ale a moment later.

I lift my drink to my lips, taking a hesitant sip. The taste is somehow tart and dull at once, like barley cut with a dagger, the alcohol settling warmly in my stomach. "Yes," I say to Killian, shrugging. "You said we were friends. Friends talk, do they not?" When he doesn't answer, I lean closer, resting one of my hands on the bar top. "Why don't you tell me about your family?"

His withdrawal is immediate, like pulling one's fingers back from a hot kettle. "Them, I'd prefer not to talk about."

But for some reason—perhaps because I myself am feeling vulnerable, perhaps because I want him to feel at odds with this place, too, to feel trapped inside himself as I do—this time, I am unable to respect his wishes. "Why not consider it from my perspective?" I press. "A mysterious stranger appears in my province, refuses to provide any information as to his background, his family, and soon afterward, an Archdaughter goes missing . . ." I take another sip of my ale, savoring the bitterness. "Some might think you have something to hide."

Killian's knuckles strain around the handle of his mug. "Some, meaning you?" he asks. All the laughter has gone from him; in its place, there is a soldier's wariness, a calculating frost to his gaze like he is assessing the danger I pose to him—the threat.

I meet his stare. "I think you are more than what you pretend. You posture as a sentry, yet you speak to me as an equal would— you can't help it. Whoever your parents are, you have a brashness about you that suggests a rank much higher in the peerage than that of a lowly Rouge."

Killian's features remain stony, unchanged, but along his jaw, a muscle jumps. An almost imperceptible wince; still, it gives me the confidence to push harder. "Does it have to do with your scars?"

Swiftly, he pivots away, peering down into his ale. I sense that my blow has landed as clearly as if there were a mark on his cheek. Hurt radiates from him, rancorous, swollen with betrayal.

He is your sentry, I reprimand myself, when regret twinges in my gut. *His feelings are of no importance to you.*

They shouldn't be. But as I repeat the words, I know they are a lie.

"You accuse me of hiding." Killian breaks our stalemate, his tone acerbic. He hasn't looked up from his drink; his back is curved, his elbows resting on the bar top as if supporting a great weight. "Have you considered, perhaps, that it is myself I am hiding from? That I am trying to forget?"

He sits still as he speaks, spooling his words out like a length of fishing line—slowly, slowly, so as not to startle. He is like Essie in that way, I think. Both of them hold themselves in, making cages of their own bodies as if they have looked inside themselves and discovered an ancient evil hiding there. Like they are forever glancing into mirrors and seeing a monster behind them, within them, a creature that only the pursuit of perfection can keep at bay.

Have you considered, perhaps, that it is myself I am hiding from?

Suddenly, I want to know, desperately, jealously, what Killian's monster is.

The scrape of the barstool to my right startles me out of my transfixion. I twist to see an auburn-haired man in his early-middle years settling down next to us, the buttons of his waistcoat straining over his protruding belly. He registers my gaze briefly, giving me a succinct nod before turning his attention back to the bartender, who is deep in conversation with a pair of timbermen at the other end of the bar.

I shoot a meaningful look at Killian, who has raised his head in interest at the man's appearance. He catches my eye, tilting his head to the right, then the left—*Maybe, maybe not.*

I choose the *maybe*.

"Excuse me, sir—please, pardon my interruption." I tap gently on the man's shoulder, smiling in what I hope is a disarming manner when he wheels around, nostrils flared in surprise. "Forgive me—I only wanted to ask whether you might be able to spare us a moment of your time. My husband and I are new to this province, you see, and have accepted a pair of positions at the estate of Norland House." Shifting toward Killian, I lay my hand atop his; he tenses beneath me but doesn't move away, which I consider victory enough.

"The steward seemed a sound man when he hired us on, but rather closed-lipped about the masters of the house. We were hoping to solicit a more . . . local opinion, shall we say. See what we're really in for." The man still looking doubtful, I lift my mug of ale meaningfully. "Of course, we would not make you answer on a dry throat."

That seems to soften him; the man huffs, slouches against the bar. "Norland House, eh?" he grumbles. "I'll tell you this much for free—you're better off leaving before you begin, when it comes to that family."

My skin prickles at the way he says *family*, spitting the word like a bit of rotten meat from his mouth. I signal for the bartender, Killian obediently flicking another coin onto the bar. "Why do you say that?" I ask as the money disappears into the bartender's palm, a drink shortly replacing it. I slide it smoothly over to the man beside us, who accepts it without thanks. "It is only that we have traveled quite a long way, and would be reluctant to turn back without very good reason. Are the Darlings cruel to their staff?"

He takes a long swallow of his ale before replying, as if judging the quality. "Not only to their staff," he answers ambiguously, but the thinly veiled disdain in his tone is enough for my breath to catch. "Not to say, mind you, that the other Manors are any better. I don't know where you hail from, but my brother-in-law is a merchant in Umberland, and the Lord there is as bad, if not worse." He scoffs, shaking his head derisively. "Selfish bastards. And the Darlings will only get worse with this new bitch"—catching himself, he ducks his head at me, his cheeks going ruddy—"pardon me, ma'am, *lady*—at their head. Silas considered our kind dogs, to be sure, but at least he had the decency to toss us a few scraps every once in a while."

Killian squeezes my hand, in reassurance or merely in reaction to the man's speech, I'm unsure. "What do you mean by that?" he asks calmly.

"His wife was one of us—a commoner, as they say," the man replies. "Artemis. Grew up in the old Holy Heart orphanage, right here in town." He takes another gulp of his drink, and I let out an appreciative murmur, as if the depth of his knowledge about my mother has impressed me. "There're a few folks around here who still speak about her as if she was the bleedin' Lightkeeper's angel herself, but that's another matter. Anyhow, Silas must've been soft for her, because he would send gifts over to Holy Heart every couple of months, even after she died. Food, clothes for the little ones, that sort of thing." He waves his hand dismissively, caught in the tide of his story now. "Last one came only a few weeks ago. The fool didn't bother to check that the place was still running before he had it delivered, though. Caretaker died over the summer—whatever he sent, ruffians've probably got to it by now."

He chuckles, as if the notion of my father's gift torn apart by thieves pleases him. I try to laugh along with him, but the sound is hollow—false. Father supporting a local orphanage is far short of a shocking secret to uncover, except for the fact that it *is* secret to me at all. *More charity.* I wonder if the final gift our companion mentioned was food taken from our shelves—food that should have been used to feed his staff. His daughters.

Killian's fingers press against mine, assessing. In response, I give him a minuscule shake of my head, withdrawing my hand and resting it in my lap.

"How funny," I say, flatter than I mean to. Letting my expression turn thoughtful, I tilt my head to the side, as if a thought has just crossed my mind. "Now that you mention it, my husband and I *did* correspond with a man formerly in Lord Silas's employ—a Mr. Birks," I say with a gasp. "He seems to have quite the grudge against his past master. Are you acquainted with him at all?"

I feel Killian tense beside me, but the man seems to swallow my performance whole, his attention on his ale. "Never heard of him, but a grudge isn't uncommon," he says, draining the last of his mug. "I'd wager half the men in this pub have lost a loved one to the Graylands because of the Manors." His hands tighten around his empty drink, his features darkening. "They claim to protect us from the Phantoms, yet leave us here on the front lines to fend for ourselves, then sweep in to clean up the mess after the bodies start falling. And it's been worse than ever, lately. Take what's happening up near Heath, for instance."

I swallow, my mask threatening to slip at the bald hostility in his tone, his fingers gripping the handle of his mug like it's a neck he'd like to snap. *My* neck. "Heath?" I echo hurriedly.

Perhaps sensing my weakness, the man lifts his shoulders as if in a challenge, casting a deliberate glance at the bottom of his now ale-less flagon. With a sigh, Killian beckons the bartender back over, silver flashing in his hand. I feel vaguely sorry for the amount of money he's been forced to spend on my behalf tonight; sentries receive only a small stipend each month beyond room and board. When we return to Norland, I promise myself, I'll be sure to reimburse him, though a part of me already guesses he'll refuse any attempts at repayment.

Then again, perhaps a few coins are nothing to him. I think

back to our conversation earlier, how I'd guessed his parents were higher in rank than he'd let on—at least a Marquess and Marchioness, I'd wager, possibly even a Red Duke and Duchess like Tom and Cressida. For all I know, he could be wealthier than me.

When our companion has received his new drink and drained nearly half of it, he starts again. "I've only heard rumors," he qualifies, wiping a golden sheen of moisture from his upper lip. "Word is that folks up there have seen men—strange ones—lurking about the border recently. Tampering with things, like. And this is the Manors' border we're talking about here, not makeshift defenses like we've got surrounding the town. The villagers wrote to Lord Silas a few weeks back, but he did nothing, of course, and it seems like his daughter aims to follow his lead."

Killian and I exchange glances, both of us alert. "Tampering with the border?" I prod cautiously. "Why would they risk that? Surely, no one in their right mind could *want* for the lanterns to fail."

The corpse in the breached house swims into my vision again—its staring eyes, the line of red along its throat, clean as a verdict.

Our companion hunches farther into himself, his elbows hemming in his ale. "Just telling you what I heard, ma'am. A local opinion, as you said." His answer has a jagged edge to it—his patience must be wearing thin.

I bow my head, schooling my lips into my finest simper. "And we are ever so grateful for it, sir. One last question, if we may." I inch closer to the man, allowing my fingertips to graze the meat of his arm. "My husband has heard . . . well, there's been talk of the girl you mentioned, the eldest Archdaughter, vanishing from her bed. Has any news of that kind reached you?"

He snaps his arm away from me, his recoil so aggressive that for a moment, I think he might curl his knuckles and bury them along my jaw. Instead, he studies my face, his gaze whetted as a blade, any alcoholic fuzz wiped away.

"That's a dangerous lie to tell," he growls, his eyes dragging over me. I have the sickening feeling that he's cutting away my disguise like the peel of an apple, searching for the core of truth at my center. "You sure you aren't already working for the Darlings?" he asks, his voice soft with the deadly restraint of a snake poised to strike. "They put you up to this?"

There's a clatter of wood on wood as next to me, Killian starts to stand, but I snag the sleeve of his coat before he can. "Not at all, sir," I say, careful to keep my demeanor friendly, light. "You are a married man—you're familiar with the ways of women. We can never resist a good morsel of gossip." Abandoning my seat myself, I pull Killian the rest of the way up along with me, keeping a tight hold of his arm. "Thank you again for your time," I finish, dipping into a curtsy.

Briskly, I turn us until we're facing the pub's entrance once more, giving Killian a reproachful nudge for his reaction. We've only made it a few steps when the scrape of a stool being pushed along the floor makes me freeze.

"Keep an eye on your wife there, boy," the man calls from behind us. On either side, other patrons are turning away from their conversation partners, their eyes flitting in our direction. None of them look friendly.

Thud. Thud. The man's footsteps are like the drop of a stone, like the menacing roll of thunder, promising more behind them. When he speaks next, his breath tickles the back of my neck, damp heat against my skin. "If an Archdaughter can disappear from her bedroom without any fuss," he whispers, "just imagine what could happen to a lowly peasant girl."

CHAPTER SEVENTEEN

I burst out of the pub like there's a fire nipping at my heels, my breath coming hard. There's an obstruction in my chest—a knot, a vine, it's alive and growing and it's climbing up my throat, choking me and I can't *breathe*—

"Merrick." Killian's hand finds my trembling one, but I bat it away, the prospect of his touch like drowning, somehow. Squeezing my eyes shut, I search for peace in the blackness, imagine myself taking hold of my emotions and physically reining them in. When I'm steadier, I lift my lids again and make my way to the post where we've tied up our horses.

The third time my fingers slip on the knot, I hear Killian let out a huff to my back. The subtle noise is enough to crack me—or maybe I am already holding my fist to the glass, waiting for an excuse to shatter. "If you're going to chastise me, please don't bother," I snap over my shoulder. Then, as another thought occurs to me, I drop the length of rein I'm fiddling with and turn.

"And why, whenever I'm upset, is it suddenly *Merrick* from you? Perhaps I've forgotten, but I don't believe I ever gave you leave to address me in that manner."

Killian drops back at my reprimand, his bicolored eyes flashing. "I wasn't going to chastise you," he says, his tone chilly. "It was a clever plan, even if it was wasted on a less-than-clever subject. And forgive me if I was overly familiar just now." He dips his head in what would be an apologetic manner, if not for the thin layer of sarcasm I detect overlaying the gesture, like a skin of fat atop a bucket of milk. "I will attempt to remember myself in the future."

He sidles past me, reaching for his own horse's reins. As always—as *always*, with him—his movements are cool, composed, like he is a lake at midwinter, all of his volatility locked away.

I want him rough-edged, for once. I want to see the boy he ran away from—who he's still running from, by his own account.

"Oh, Mr. Propriety now, are we?" I hiss, a thrill going through me at my own ugliness. "I'm sure you and my sister had a good laugh about me when I came home, didn't you? *What a mess poor Merrick is. No wonder her father passed her over for his Vessel*—is that what you said?" Without my commanding them, my arms lift toward his chest, poised as if to shove him.

Before I can push them forward, Killian's hands are flying up, clasping around my wrists. His grip is vise-like, tight without being painful, and certain in its strength. I go still under it, my sides heaving with exertion.

"If you are trying to break me," he says, his stare like forged iron, holding me fast, "you will not succeed."

He shifts, an infinitesimal movement, and I lean back in preparation for his release—only to have him abruptly pull me closer instead. A small, meek sound emits from my throat at the unexpected press of his frame meeting mine, my palms laid flat against his chest. I can feel the angles of his body beneath the fabric of his clothing, the flushed warmth, like live embers have been placed beneath his skin.

With excruciating delicacy, his mouth finds my hairline, just above my ear. "I have faced deadlier foes than you, *Archdaughter.*"

He drops my wrists and steps away, his eyes never leaving my face. My pulse is hurtling against my rib cage; I am like a stuck rabbit, unable to do anything aside from watch him watch me. His gaze is intense, as if I am a page about to turn, on the cusp of disappearing.

His throat bobs, and I feel the drop in the space below my stomach. Then he's turning away, grabbing his horse's reins again.

"We should be going, before someone realizes those two-mark coins I paid with are stamped with your Manor's seal," he says with infuriating calmness. When I don't answer in agreement, he arches a brow. "Unless you'd like to buy our friend in there another round?"

Glaring at him, I lurch into motion, the sense memory of his fingers a fevered circle of heat around my wrist.

"Stop."

To my left, Killian yanks sharply on his horse's reins, pulling it to a halt. We're nearing the edge of Shoreham-by-Sea; caught in the slivers of night that leak between the houses ahead of us, I can see a row of orange stars blazing away—the torches.

"Is something the matter, Archdaughter?" Killian's brow is furrowed in concern, his features bathed in shadow. In the dimness, his scars have been lost, the darkness like a painter's brush, hiding all his imperfections beneath a layer of silken black.

Atop my own stalled mount, I blush. "No, nothing. It's only . . ." My gaze drifts back to a ramshackle two-story building a little farther up the street we're on, its empty windows the only ones devoid of firelight in the line of squat houses preceding and following it. I hadn't meant to pause when I'd noticed it, much less call out, but then I'd seen the faded sign nailed above the front door, its block letters barely legible in the dark.

HOLY HEART OF THE BURNING KING'S HOME FOR ORPHANS.

Killian follows my eyes, his own widening with understanding as he takes in the orphanage, the sign. "My parents never took me to see it—where my mother grew up," I say haltingly, by way of explanation. I keep my attention fixed on the building up ahead of us—it's easier, somehow, to make this confession to its unfeeling façade, to pretend that the sentry beside me is just another static fixture of the town, rather than the boy from earlier who watched me like I was a storm about to break. Who has shared my sister's secrets with me and kept his own for himself, who leaves me feeling as though whether I give him mine or not, he already knows them all.

"Mother never liked us to interact with the commoners much when we were younger," I go on, to the orphanage. "I felt she was being cruel at the time, but now I think she worried that if she did otherwise, the people might remember that Essie and I were half her—half *them*. That they would lose all respect for us because of it, would doubt our capacity to rule." I bite down on the inside of my cheek, my throat stinging. "And yet all along, it was Father who was keeping us tied to this place," I murmur. "To her past."

Killian listens silently, his presence heavy, like the promise of rain in the air even though he remains unspeaking. After I finish, he remains still for a moment or two before breaking into movement again, giving his horse a swift kick. To my horror, it begins to trot in the direction of the orphanage rather than away from it, toward the path I know will take us out of town.

I urge Pegasus after him, panic buzzing in my veins. "What

are you doing?" I call in a harsh whisper. For some reason, I feel compelled to drop my voice the nearer we get to the building, as if it is a sleeping bear, poised to lash out at me if I startle it.

Killian throws me a crooked grin over his shoulder, swinging himself off his horse in a practiced, languid motion. "We're here, aren't we?" he replies, gesturing to the house, its door now looming directly in front of him. "Might as well go inside. Our friend at the Watchman did say it was abandoned, after all—it isn't as though we'd be disturbing anyone."

I part my lips, ready to protest—only to find that I don't really want to. Curiosity blooms within me like steam collecting under the lid of a pot, pushing upward. Over the past half year, I've watched my family fall, a row of playing cards tumbling one after the other. Is it so wrong, I think, to want to steal a little piece of them back from the grave?

With a begrudging toss of my head, I dismount Pegasus and go to stand by Killian at the orphanage's entrance.

The lock has long since been broken by vandals; the door opens easily when I turn the knob, creaking inward on rusting hinges. Beyond, inky shadows hang, mounding over the vague shapes of the furnishings within. I shoot Killian a questioning look, my mind catching on memories of the breached house we raided together: another open door, a swarm of monsters gathering behind it. Is that what we'll find here, too?

As if reading my thoughts, Killian offers me a small smile. Unlike the last one he gave me, there's no mischief in his expression now—only sympathy, compassion. *We don't have to,* the smile says. *But if you do, I will follow.*

Drawing a breath, I step across the threshold.

The space inside is large but cramped, the doorway depositing us directly into what appears to be a disused sitting room. It takes up most of the ground floor, a stairwell in the back left corner hinting at further rooms beyond. Worn armchairs, the stuffing spilling out of several of them, gather around a cold fireplace along the far wall; closer to the entrance, the floor has been cleared for play, remnants of the orphanage's past occupants visible in the tipped-over rocking horse on the faded rug, its stiff legs kicking aimlessly into the air, the corroding tin soldiers discarded next to it.

I suppress a shiver. Intermixed with decay, the evidence of youth is eerie, like a ripe apple hanging from a rotten bough. I turn away, casting my gaze over the rest of the sitting room, Killian lingering by my elbow.

As I shift to examine the patch of wall to my rear, my heart lurches at the sight of my mother's face peering back at me. Centered directly over the threshold, an oil painting of my parents presides over the house. They appear young, perhaps just a year or two older than in the marriage portrait Father had commissioned after their wedding. A bronze plaque winks in the murk below them, the room dim enough that I have to squint to read it. *Donated by Lord Silas Ignatius Darling and the Lady Artemis Darling, Seventeenth Manor Lord and Lady of the province of Sussex, in recognition of devoted service.*

My tongue feels swollen in my mouth. My mother may have tried to keep Essie and me from her humble origins, but it appears her roots have refused to relinquish her.

"He must have cared for her very much—your father."

I start, having nearly forgotten Killian in my observation of the portrait. He stands next to me, his expression solemn, thoughtful.

With some effort, I tear my gaze away from my parents. "For her, yes," I answer Killian, unable to keep a hint of bitterness from coloring my tone.

He glances at me sidelong. "And you and your sister, too."

The confidence with which he states it—as if it is a forgone conclusion, my father loving me, natural as the fall of snow, as the endless chase of day and night—twists my intestines. I rub at my arms through the sleeves of my dress, freezing despite the oppressive cling of the wool.

"After she died—Mother, that is—I approached him about the Nomination," I say, my vision wandering over the portrait of my parents, hooking on my father's strong jaw, the glossy, oiled-wood shade of his hair. So much like Tom—the resemblance is uncanny when viewed this way, with Father caught in his youth. "It was foolish, I am aware, but Father was so volatile in the weeks after she passed. Always speaking vaguely about the future of our Manor, his legacy, so on and so forth. I only wished to know . . . to know whether I had a chance." I pause, the recollection a needling pain at my side, like a pin shoved deep into the muscle. *"You will never be Manor Lord,* he told me when I asked. Just that, and nothing more, regardless of how much I begged him to explain his decision." I shake my head, biting at my lip. "It was as if he was possessed—like he was just a thumbprint in ash, an echo of the father I once knew. I left for New London shortly afterward."

"M— Archdaughter . . ." Killian's fingers flex at his side, straining—toward what? He balls them into a fist, letting out a shallow, frustrated grunt that scrapes like a dull razor over my flesh, then turns to face me. "What I said in the barracks this morning, the comment you overheard . . . I do not think you a doll," he says, his eyes probing mine. "I believe your father decided a very long time ago that your sister would be his weapon, and you his jewel. And I believe you have held yourself at fault for his choice for almost as long—a choice you were disallowed from playing any part in making."

Somehow, without my noticing it, he's closed the distance between us. He stares down at me, and his nearness is a physical thing—like a breeze rippling over me, touching me everywhere at once. "You are not a bad person, Archdaughter," he finishes. "You have simply been dealt a flawed hand."

The vine from outside the pub is back, circling my neck. If he takes one step more, it will coil tight, and I will be unable to speak. Forcibly, I tear my gaze away, then compel my body to follow, stumbling toward the back of the sitting room.

I stop when the toe of my boot collides with something—the corner of a solid wooden trunk shoved beneath a side window, the rest of the object obscured by shadow. Pulling my foot back, I bend down, grateful to the distraction for parting the fog in my mind.

"What's this?"

Killian trails after me. The air thins as he approaches, my head going full, clouded with a sweet haze like with perfume. I lean over the trunk, eager to put any measure of distance that I can between us.

Surely you cannot be that stupid, Merrick. I chastise myself. *He is your sentry—Killian may not even be his true* name. *You are not seriously considering . . .*

He sinks onto his knees, his shoulders aligned with mine, and my thoughts fade to nothing.

I cough to disrupt the quiet that has settled over us, turning my focus back to the trunk. Upon closer examination, I can see that this lock, too, has been broken, the latch hanging loose like a lolling tongue. I prod the piece of metal, the words of the man at the pub stirring in my memory: *Silas . . . would send gifts over to Holy Heart every couple of months, even after she died . . . Last one came only a few weeks ago . . . ruffians've probably got to it by now.*

"I think it's from my father," I hear myself mutter to Killian. "My relatives mentioned he became increasingly generous in the months after Mother. This would have been one of the last things he sent before he . . ."

—Essie's scream. Father, unhearing or uncaring, walking into the Graylands, the mist like a lover, rushing up to embrace him—

I blink, throwing open the lid of the trunk before the image can drag me under.

The inside is bare—it seems as though our companion earlier was correct about ne'er-do-wells having reached it before us. Rising up on my knees, I reach into the trunk and feel carefully along the bottom for any left-behind scrap of its former contents. The interior has been wiped clean, but near the back-right corner, my fingers graze over a pattern of shallow gouges in the wood. I go still. A carving?

Squinting, I lean closer. Etched into the base of the trunk is a crude marking: an icon the size of my two thumbs put together with a flat bottom topped by three jagged points, like a crown. Though I can't identify it immediately, something about the carving itches at my mind, familiar in a hazy way, like a place I recognize from a dream.

Have I seen it before?

"Mr. Brandon," I start. "Look—"

Thump. Killian and I freeze at the sound. It came from the floor above us—almost like the deliberate tread of a person's footfall. Trepidation raising a trail of goose bumps along my arms, I tilt my head up toward the ceiling, my breath catching at the small cloud of dust I see pluming from the rafters like an exhale.

Is someone in here with us?

"Rats," Killian says quickly. "Nothing mo—"

A series of thumps overpower the rest of his explanation, the unmistakable sound of a person moving across the floor. They echo over our heads, punctuated by sprays of dust like bullet fire, heading toward the left side of the building. *The stairwell.*

I reach for my Ghostslayer, only to remember with a spike of fear that I'd left it at Norland prior to our riding out, peasants having no need for a weapon primarily carried by sentries and Manorborn. Killian seems to have the same realization, because he pulls me to my feet, shoving me roughly toward the door.

"*Go,*" he hisses in the same moment that I hear the weary *creak* of the top step behind us, the owner of the footsteps drawing nearer. I don't wait to see whether they are human or Phantom; a drunk, nesting in an empty building, or something worse.

I take Killian's hand in mine, and I run.

CHAPTER EIGHTEEN

I don't speak to Killian again for several days after we make it back to Norland House—safely, despite the terror that followed me all the way home from Shoreham-by-Sea. All that we'd witnessed in town—the man's aggression at the pub, my parents' faces staring down at me from the wall of the orphanage, the sound of the feet on the stairs—mixed together into a nightmare tableau during my slumber, commoners warping into monsters and back.

Instead, four mornings later, I leave Norland in the violet hour, that ribbon of semidawn between darkness and light when the old day has died but morning has not yet come to cleanse the smell of its decay. Most of our estate is still slumbering when I depart. As I pass through the servants' quarters on my way to the inconspicuous back entrance, the sound of heavy breathing fills my ears, the soothing murmur of a flowing river.

Since Essie's disappearance, the house's energy has turned tempestuous. The servants scurry through the halls with their heads lowered as if shielding themselves from a downpour, their faces illuminating with lightning strikes of fear whenever I call out to them. As for my cousin and his wife, I encounter them most frequently in the fragments of their whispered arguments that slip out from beneath locked doors.

With Killian's agreement, I told Cressida and Tom nothing of our trip into town following our return, the little information we gathered paltry enough that I knew it wouldn't withstand the weight of my cousin-in-law's criticism. The Faulks acted before I could, anyway, their messenger appearing, exhausted and trembling on our doorstep, the evening after Killian's and my excursion, having ridden through the night and day in order to make it to us as quickly as possible. Elodie Faulk, it seemed, had received her granddaughter's letter.

And, as Cressida promised she would, she answered.

Additional troops came first, squads of Faulk sentries in saffron yellow arriving at Norland House shortly after the messenger did, all prepared to aid in the search for my sister. The rest of the Council was notified next. Then, yesterday, my sister's disappearance was broken to the public in a special edition of the *Toast*. The past twenty-four hours since its release have been a maelstrom of questions and answers, help provided and requested. Strangely and disturbingly, the spectacle of Essie's vanishing has succeeded where my cousin-in-law's previous social efforts failed: my family's popularity, in its death throes after the disastrous attack at the ball, has experienced a miraculous recovery. My normally stiff, introverted sister has become a martyr in her absence, the province unified in its thirst for Essie's safe return.

At the very least, no one is discussing the breaches anymore.

Back in the present, I slip into the stables quietly, looking like a wraith in my black wool cloak, my mane of flaxen curls tucked under the hood. Pegasus whinnies nervously as I approach her, calming only when I run my hand along her flank and murmur gentle reassurances in her ear. Darting my gaze around for any early-rising stable boys, I saddle her and lead her out into Norland's grounds.

The couple times I've attempted to seek out Killian over the past few days, he's been either on patrol or else sent to join one of the many search parties Cressida and the Faulks have organized. The hunt for my sister has been a convenient excuse for my distance from him, but I know that beyond it, there is another reason I haven't tried harder to contact him, one relating to the phantom press of his fingers on my wrists: how sometimes during the night I wake and still feel their touch. It disturbs me, the connection I can feel threatening to develop between us—the way, when my mind wanders now, it is him it drifts to. It feels safer to ignore it all together, and so I push it away.

Still, it's been impossible not to linger on what we learned together in Shoreham-by-Sea, even as I attempt to separate the memories from the boy I made them with. The more time passes, the more certain I become that the footsteps Killian and I heard in the orphanage were most likely those of a vagrant, taking advantage of the abandoned establishment—or else just the scurrying of rats, like Killian said, transformed to something sinister by our hysteria. Yet our visit to the Watchman, the man I'd spoken with in the pub . . . there, I feel, is a loose thread I may have the capacity to tie up.

I haven't forgotten our companion's mention of Heath, nor the rumors that he claimed have recently sprung from there: strangers, lurking near the borders. While I remain unsure what the goings-on in a far-flung, northern strip of our province could possibly have to do with my sister, I can't deny that the breaches have become something of a common denominator among all the odd occurrences in Sussex over the past few weeks. Perhaps, if I dig deep enough, I will find a reason for that.

It's a theory, but if I want to bring Essie back, I need more than that. I need a trail to follow.

And I am hopeful I can find one in Heath.

Ominous lead-colored clouds, their swollen bellies pregnant with rain, blot out the rising sun as I ride through Sussex. Ahead of me, the horizon stretches on in a thin, bare line, devoid of any sign of civilization. I passed through the last village before Heath almost an hour ago—the isolated hamlet of Blacksands, the entire town scarcely more than a smattering of whitewashed buildings—but since then, there's been nothing except field and forest, the *swish* of the wind through the brittle grass reminding me of gossiping women, bending their heads to murmur to one another as I go by.

Sweat crusting my upper lip with salt, I dig my heels into Pegasus's side, slowing her enough for me to catch my breath. Around me, the landscape is empty—nothing but lonely trees stripped naked of their summer finery and the barren earth. About a half mile or so in the distance, a thread of orange lights up the sky: the border.

I swear under my breath, frustration blistering within me as I'm finally forced to admit the unwelcome reality I've felt creeping up on me for the past twenty minutes or so: I'm lost. Too late, I curse myself for not accompanying Father on more of his patrols up north. Unlike the coastline near Norland House, I'm not as familiar with the landlocked, upper portion of our province, where our timber forests give way to endless plots of farmland and rolling hills. Essie had always been better at relating to the people in this area, with their clothing that forever smelled of hay and animal musk and their strong constitutions honed through years of backbreaking physical labor. By contrast, the few times Father did manage to drag me up here, I felt silly and vapid with my silk gloves and pink, rouged cheeks, like some idiotic princess descended from her pedestal—a sentiment I'm fairly certain our farmers shared.

I'd hoped when I rode out today that the memories of my prior few journeys would be enough to get me safely to Heath, but based on my complete lack of recognition now, I over-estimated my capabilities. My thighs and back ache from my time spent on horseback; with every movement, my muscles scream for the comfort of home.

Stupid, I chastise myself. The more I consider it, the more fool-ish my entire mission this morning seems. What did I think—that I would turn up in Heath alone and catch whoever's supposedly been putting out our lanterns red-handed? That they would lead me to my sister? Surely I couldn't have assumed it would be as simple as that.

Essie would have had a better plan. The fact itches at me like a flea bite. My sister knows Sussex like her own reflection in the mirror. If I were the one who had disappeared instead of her, I am cer-tain that she would have tracked me down within an hour of my absence. She would have noticed the minuscule shift in the land where my captors had carved out their hiding spot, the same way one notices a new mole on their cheek or a wrinkle creasing their forehead—imperfections that remain invisible to everyone else.

I swipe the heel of my hand over my brow, wiping away the perspiration that's gathered there just as overhead, the clouds burst, spilling torrents of rain down on the countryside. Spitting out another curse, I snap Pegasus's reins, spurring her hastily onward. Water blurs my vision and clings to my lips, filling my mouth with a mossy, earthen taste. I splutter, glancing fervently around for some sort of cover—anything to wait out the storm.

My heart stutters. *There.* To my left, near the steady line of border lanterns, is a boxy, shadowed shape, more obvious now for the way the rain parts around it. A house. Perhaps inside it,

I can find someone who's witnessed the disturbances the man in the Watchman spoke of—or, at the very least, shelter from the lashing gale.

I push Pegasus into a gallop, my soaked skirts clinging to my legs the faster we ride. As we near the building, the curtain of rain pulls back enough that the house's features come into focus: a single-story stone structure barely larger than a shack, its thatched roof sagging and rotted through in some places. The glass in one of the two lopsided windows is shattered, the building's interior a shadowed cavern beyond.

My heart sinks. The residence is derelict, any occupants either long dead or long gone. The only disturbances likely to be noted here are those of owls and foxes, darting through the night to snap up an unsuspecting field mouse.

The rain thrumming a steady beat against my skin, I lead Pegasus closer to the building, her hooves squelching unpleasantly against the sodden ground as we make our final approach. Dismounting, I walk over to the ramshackle structure, pulling Pegasus behind me. The grass cover is thin, the dirt beneath me rapidly turning to mud, clinging to my boots like prying hands. Abandonment hangs heavy on the building in front of me, its frame sagging with age, but still—I hesitate before I step any closer, memories of the orphanage still fresh in my mind. Perhaps I am not the only traveler roaming these parts this morning, in need of shelter from the storm.

Shivering, I draw my Ghostslayer from its holster at my side, grateful that I've had the foresight to bring it with me this time. The wind picks up, howling in my ear like a wolf's cry, as I make my way to the rotting front door and step through. Pegasus whinnies nervously as she follows me, ducking her head to avoid clipping it on the low doorframe.

Inside, the house is dark and utterly empty, the light reduced to watery gray rivulets that filter through gaps in the crumbling walls. Through the dimness painting the cramped room in thick gray swaths, I make out a writing desk and rotting chair, among other dusty furnishings.

Flexing my fingers around my weapon, I drop Pegasus's reins and move to the desk, unceremoniously pulling open its drawers and rooting through them. My efforts are rewarded when I find the half-burned stump of a candle pushed to the back of one, a tinder box tucked alongside it. A victorious smile playing on my lips, I set aside my gun for a moment to remove them, opening the tin box and taking the steel striker and flint in hand.

Crack.

I tense. My nerves, already frayed, snap like strings on a loom at the sound of something moving in the field beyond the house. Candle forgotten, I drop the instruments I'm holding. Outside, the sky is coal-dark despite the early hour, bloated storm clouds skidding across it like smoke pouring from a chimney. I don't see anyone fighting through the rain toward me, but still my thoughts speed and blur, fear numbing every impulse except those to *run, now, and never look back.*

It was an animal. Only an animal. I let the reassurances glide over me like oil.

Crack.

The noise comes again, and this time, there's a shape along with it.

Beyond the window, a flash of black darts past my eyes, one shadow slipping from another. Water sluices off the old glass in sheets, blurring my view, but even so I can make out the general shape of the figure: a man on horseback, the collar of his coat turned up to obscure his face from view.

My heart hurtles upward, pounding in my throat. Before Father died—before Essie disappeared—I might not have panicked at a stranger's appearance, might even have been grateful for it. Now terror blots out my logic. Acting on instinct, I leap for my Ghostslayer, which skids away from me. My elbow slams hard against the desk, causing an involuntary hiss of pain to slip from my lips. The noise is such that it should be lost beneath the rain, but on the other side of the glass, I watch in horror as the man's head snaps toward me—as a dark eye catches mine, widens in shock.

He calls out something—an indecipherable word—his voice muffled by the storm. I don't wait for him to repeat it. Instead, I snatch up my Ghostslayer and fire off a shot, the window shattering in a diamond-spray of glass. The bullet misses the man by over a meter, as I intended, but he rears back nonetheless, his shout swallowed by a clap of thunder. Spooked, his horse brays, thrashing against his hold.

Taking advantage of his momentary incapacitation, I dart toward the house's drooping entrance, my pulse pounding in my ears. *Just get out,* I tell myself as I grab Pegasus's reins, my hands shaking. *Get back to Norland, and you'll be safe.*

I reach the door, throw it open.

And collide directly with a body.

CHAPTER NINETEEN

The figure is hard, all angles and tense, compact muscle over bone. I lurch away from them, tripping over myself and tumbling to the floor, Pegasus whinnying anxiously above me. My Ghostslayer flies from my hand as I fall, landing with a clatter near the wall. Vision blurred with fear, I scrabble toward it, dirt streaking the skirt of my dress.

"—Archdaughter? *Merrick?*"

The call comes to me slowly, as if spoken through a body of water. At the sound of it, my panic recedes, drawing back like the tide. The voice belongs to a person; more than that, though it is familiar—known.

Pausing, I look up.

Ames Saint is standing in the doorway, his blond hair a dull gray-gold in the stormlight, his full lips turned down at the corners in a frown. His blue eyes are wide and worried, the frothy color of a churned-up lake. When they meet mine, something tugs inside me—anticipation and release, the tight pull of a bent willow bough.

"A—Archson Ames?" I ask, hoisting myself up on my elbows. My fingers dig into the packed-earth floor, soil wedging into the thin gaps beneath my nails. "What are you doing in Sussex?"

Ames moves closer, clasping my wrists and hoisting me gently upright. I flush instinctively at his touch, the intimate feel of his body against the soaked fabric of my dress as he leans in to steady me. I haven't seen him since the night of the ball, but now, memories of our earlier encounter rush over me—him leading me onto the dance floor, gazing down at me as the music crested around us. The crush of his form against mine when the Phantoms attacked.

Heat blooms in my stomach, red rosebuds.

"As it happens, I am on my way to Norland, to call on you," Ames answers, releasing me. "Or I was, before the weather put pause to my efforts. One of my men spotted this structure from afar and suggested it might be a fine place to wait out the storm." He smiles wryly. "Either fate has its eye on us, or there are so few houses in Sussex capable of withstanding a healthy rainfall that we have all been driven to the same one. Speaking of, actually—"

He strides back to the door, which has lolled closed, pushing it open and calling through. "All clear, boys. I've found us a friend."

With a sigh, he angles his chin in my direction. "Apologies for my chaperones, by the way. Since the incident at your ball, Mother has decided that I am too precious goods to risk a pastime as dangerous as riding on my own. Apparently, as her heir, I am an extension of her very being—and she has always placed a high value on self-preservation."

He holds the door open as he speaks, allowing a group of unsmiling men to pass through, all clad in identical wool coats paired with breeches and tall black boots. The uniforms are a similar style to those Killian and the other Darling sentries wear, except that these jackets are a light periwinkle instead of gray, with darker blue epaulets and gold stitching that matches the shining buttons down their fronts. *Saint sentries*—they have to be. But visiting me or no, what cause do they have to pass through this far-flung area of our territory?

Without moving from where I stand in the middle of the room, I peer around the sentries' figures, out at the landscape beyond. Already, the rain has begun to peter off, and through the veil of gray drizzle, I can just make out the horizon in the distance. Delayed recognition flares within me as I take in the way it bulges like a man's belly, lifting into the hillside. When I'd ridden off course on my way to Heath, I must have strayed nearer to the Sussex-Cardiff border than I realized. No wonder Ames and his men were riding this way.

"Well," I say, gathering myself, "if you were looking for me, it seems you have found me sooner than intended. Though I must apologize for my less-than-warm reception—in all manners of speaking. With Sussex in the state it is, I suppose I've been a little . . . jumpier than usual." I flush, trying to pick out the sentry I fired at from the group of stoic men and failing.

Giving up, I motion at Ames's sopping clothes. "You must be freezing."

Ames shakes his head, smiling. "I am fine—you forget I am still new to the countryside, and not yet fatigued by it as you are. I find all nature's moods endearing, even her foul ones." Tucking back a wet strand of hair, he motions at his sentries to stay put as he makes his way nearer to me, his brow creasing. "But Archdaughter," he says, his tone growing serious, "what are you doing out here all alone? Mother received word from Red Duchess Cressida Faulk-Darling about your sister—it is the reason for my visit, in fact. We were deeply shaken, all of us." His gaze flicks nervously around the ramshackle structure we're clustered in, his hand going for the gun I glimpse holstered at his hip. "Are you safe?" he asks tersely.

His concern is a mirror; through it, I view my own strangeness with a new clarity, how odd my presence here is—like I am a puzzle piece jammed into the wrong spot. My neck heats. Briefly, I consider telling him the true reason for my excursion, but his appearance has washed away my confidence. The man at the pub the other night had been reluctant enough to speak with me, and he'd believed I only *worked* for the Darlings. Even if I were to make it to Heath, what was the likelihood that any of its residents would be willing to engage in a discussion with the living embodiment of the Manor they hated? Perhaps they had information to share about the mysterious sightings at the border, or perhaps they didn't—either way, they'd likely divulge it to the town pariah over me.

Whether I wish to accept it or not, my visit to Shoreham-by-Sea has resulted in only two dead ends. Essie is as far away as ever; all that's changed is that now I know our people will be only too happy if she never comes back.

Shaking my head, I smooth down my frizzing hair, returning my gaze to Ames's. "I—I was on patrol," I say, and hope he cannot hear the lie in my speech. "With the search efforts for my sister ongoing, our sentries haven't been able to maintain their routes as usual, even with the Faulks' troops aiding ours. We've all been attempting to make up the gap." I gesture down at the ruined front of my dress. "I'm afraid the strain of it all has been challenging for me to bear, as you can clearly see. I must beg your forgiveness again for my rude greeting," I say with a hollow laugh. "As I said, I have not quite been myself these past few days."

Sympathy flutters across Ames's features. He has an open,

expressive face, one that displays his emotions clearly, like words on a page. The girls in New London would talk about this quality of his, too—how refreshing it was to converse with a man and see his enjoyment percolating upward like spring water. How he would bear his feelings without shame at gatherings, embracing them with an almost feminine delight.

"Of course," Ames says. Turning, he arches a brow at the Saint sentries, who obediently make themselves busy—some moving to rub Pegasus's flank, others muttering to one another in quiet tones. Though he doesn't step any nearer to me, their retreat makes the space between us feel narrower, as if we are surrounded by a wall of privacy.

"Archdaughter, I haven't been blessed with any siblings myself—and I am not arrogant enough to attempt to guess at your feelings in this moment, without them," Ames remarks. "But if I ever am fortunate enough to meet the disgusting fellow who took your sister"—his mouth twists—"I'd wring his neck once for whatever he's done to Archdaughter Estella, and another time for frightening you."

His speech is muted, soft enough that I know his sentries can't hear us. Still, I feel the fine hairs on the back of my neck lift at his words. Frowning, he reaches forward, and I stiffen instinctively—not with fear, but an anticipatory sort of paralysis, like watching a butterfly float near one's shoulder. Waiting for the moment of contact, of touch.

"You should have a doctor take a look at you—we wouldn't want any of those scratches scarring." The brush of Ames's fingers against my arm is searing, setting my emotions ablaze. I hiss when he grazes a scrape I didn't realize I had, and he pulls his hand back apologetically.

"Listen, Archdaughter," he starts again, "I do hope I'm not overstepping, but would you like to join my mother and me for breakfast at our estate? We have an excellent physician on call who can tend to you, and the Roost is only a couple hours' ride from here—we could have you home by the evening."

I am caught off guard by the plummy burst of temptation that spreads through me at his offer. Again, I recall the sure way he held me while we danced—how I felt, for a sliver of a moment, like I could fall without fear of not being caught—and desire unwinds in my stomach. Yet despite the urge to accept his invitation, I hesitate. "That's good of you, but I should probably make my way back home," I demur. "My relatives will be worried, you see . . ."

"I understand completely. Forgive me if the suggestion was too forward." Ames bows his head in apology, his gaze finding mine from beneath lowered lashes. "It's only that . . . well, in the name of honesty, Archdaughter, you've been on my mind quite a lot lately, since I saw you last—and not only because of your sister."

He takes a deliberate step forward, stopping himself just before the point where his nearness would become intimate, like he's testing to see where my limits lie. "I have?" I ask hesitantly.

His smile crooks upward on one side, as if my question amuses him. "It is strange," he answers, his tone hushed with the whispered urgency of a confession. "When those Phantoms appeared at Norland House, I felt something akin to a compulsion—the fierce need to defend you from them. I could not sleep for the rest of the night, wondering if you were being tended to as you ought to be. Whether you were protected."

His right hand has drifted in front of him slightly, his fingers—long and tapered, made for gentle activities like turning pages, for delicately cupping another's chin—a hairsbreadth away from mine. In response, my own hand flexes at my side. We are so close—all it would take is a tiny shift, a twitch of my wrist—

Then, in the midst of the impulse comes another thought:

the echo of a sentence, the impression of a pair of eyes locked on mine.

Don't do that.

And my own voice murmuring dreamily in response: *What?*

Pretend like you're delicate. Like you're a creature in need of saving.

The interruption surprises me—unbalanced by it, I stiffen, blinking away my shock. Noticing my discomfort, Ames backs up, a stilted half laugh rumbling softly in his throat. "Well. Perhaps we can discuss all that another time."

Turning on his heel, he starts back toward the front of the house, his sentries immediately abandoning their conversations to stand at attention. "Right then, Archdaughter," he calls behind himself. "Let's get you home."

Ames escorts me to Norland alone, having sent his sentries back across the border into Cardiff—against, I'm sure, the wishes of his mother, Ianthe Saint. We ride side by side, Pegasus trotting next to his own black mare, all evidence of the downpour that descended upon the countryside only an hour prior now erased except for a lingering dampness in the air. Beneath us, the ground is drenched and spongy, sinking under our horses' hooves as we ride.

"And how has the search been going, for your sister?"

My attention darts to Ames, riding on my left. He's staring straight ahead, only his profile visible.

My brow furrows. We've been silent for most of the journey so far, conversing in small bursts every ten minutes or so about light topics: the weather, friends we have in common. Though on the one hand, asking after Essie seems like the gentlemanly thing to do, something about the abrupt reintroduction of the topic makes me uneasy. I think back to Cressida's distrust of her fellow Manorborn at dinner, the evening Killian and I visited Shoreham-by-Sea. She'd refused to enlist the other Lords' help without first securing her own grandmother's support—had seemed just as frightened of their plotting as she was of whoever had left the note on Essie's pillow. Even more, perhaps.

Warily, I observe Ames, his shoulders rising and falling in time with his horse's lumbering steps. *I would caution you not to trust anyone who claims to have Estella's best intentions at heart, aside from yourself, Tom, and me.* Cressida's advice; though it pains me to admit it, maybe my cousin-in-law has a point.

"The Council has been incredibly generous with their aid," I respond, testing each word out in my head before speaking it aloud. "My relatives and I are grateful beyond measure for their support. Finding Essie is our only priority—so far, the last sighting we have on record of her is just after the ball, but beyond that . . ." I sigh, weariness fastening like weights around my wrists. "I'm afraid the trail, for the moment, at least, is cold."

Darling Manor will fall. My hands flex around Pegasus's reins, the message from Essie's room biting into me again. Whoever wrote that note is still out there—and after my failed attempt at investigation today, I'm no closer to finding them. But, I think with a shiver, that doesn't mean they aren't watching me.

The other night, I swore I saw a figure standing on the lawn just below my window . . . Essie's journal—I banish it from my mind.

Shifting in the saddle, I peer toward Ames. "Why do you ask?"

Ames shrugs. "Curiosity, primarily," he says breezily. "But it's been grating at me—how you said earlier that you haven't enough sentries to execute patrols, along with everything else. You and your family shouldn't have to worry yourselves with border security during a time like this." He exhales, as if the mere thought of my many responsibilities is tiring to him. "I told you I've been thinking of you recently—trying to conjure up some way I could be of use to you. I can't help but wonder . . ." He drifts off, twisting in his saddle to face my way.

I draw in an unsteady breath. Riding alongside one another as we are, I can make out every imperfect detail of his features: the divot above his right eyebrow that might be left over from some childhood injury, or might be a birthmark; the scatter of freckles across his tanned skin, an asymmetric constellation.

Ames's eyes dart to my mouth, then, with some effort, lift away again. Without realizing it, I've drawn Pegasus to a halt; we linger, unmoving, in the misty air, the land unfolding in lonely stretches around us.

"I know it is not my place to offer this," Ames resumes softly. "But my mother has plenty of sentries of her own—and we have not suffered a breach in well over a year. Our men are practically going mad with boredom." He swallows, the bob of his Adam's apple pebble-like against the long stretch of his throat. "Archdaughter—Merrick—I would be more than willing to see if she might be able to spare some troops to aid your cause. It would be my pleasure to do so, in fact."

I would caution you not to trust anyone . . . aside from yourself, Tom, and me.

Cressida's warning again, pressing dully at me. Yet when I go to answer Ames, I discover that my mouth has dried out. I feel flushed under his gaze, fevered. Never during my time in New London did I experience anything akin to this—this rush, this wanting. It is exhilarating and dizzying at once, like the paralyzing euphoria of standing at the edge of a cliff and looking down, seeing the world spread out before you.

"Why would you do that?" I finally manage, instead. "To lend my family your own men, and ask nothing in return—alliances have been forged and broken over less. You hardly know me."

"But I feel as though I do." Ames's response is immediate, his expression honed. "Merrick, you must understand—you have been a ghost in my mind, my whole life, and now that I have finally met you . . . it sounds nonsensical, I'm aware, but I feel as though I know you quite intimately." His hand loosens around his reins, bridges the distance between us to grasp mine. He holds me fast, his thumb grazing the ridge of my knuckles through my riding gloves.

"Let me help you, please," he says. "You do not have to carry this burden on your own."

His attention is still on me. This is a different way of looking than how Killian observed me outside the pub—all focus and hunger as if I were the second hand of a clock, ticking farther away with every beat. Ames watches me like he has time, like he knows I won't move another inch until he tells me to.

I can't look away.

Surely, when Cressida spoke of being careful around other Manors, she couldn't have anticipated this? Ames is not scouting my family out for a weakness he can exploit; on the contrary, he is sacrificing the security of his own province to help us. Because he cares about me—because he feels he knows me.

And do you know him? I shove the intrusive thought down, unsure of how to answer it. I can't deny that I am attracted to him— his beauty is such that *anyone* would be—or that it is a relief, after weeks of isolation, to feel as though I have an ally. A supporter. But do we truly *know* one another?

It matters not, another voice replies. He is handing me a lifeline, offering me more resources with which to find Essie when I was already on the cusp of running through my ideas. If I love my sister, how can I deny him?

"All right," I say. "Yes—thank you. I am sure my family and I would appreciate any aid your mother is able to spare."

Ames's face splits into a triumphant grin. As it does, a wind stirs around us, parting the curtain of drizzle. It is only when I glance ahead that I realize we've reached our destination. The grounds of Norland House sprawl in the distance, our estate sitting hunched in their center like a red devil, its many chimneys protruding, hornlike, from its roof.

"Ah," Ames says. "Here we are, then."

The sight of my home seems to have snapped him free of whatever undertow we were caught in—proper once more, he turns forward, nudges his horse into motion. I can't help but feel slightly spurned by his abrupt reversal in attitude; in contrast, my own body is trembling, my heart pounding arrhythmically in my chest.

What was *that?*

When we reach Norland's drive, Ames helps me off my horse and walks me to my estate's front door but politely declines my invitation to come inside. We exchange brief farewells and then he is leaving, pressing a delicate kiss to my hand that tingles against my glove long after his lips have left it.

I watch him as he rides away. When he is no more than a dot on the horizon, I turn and once again step back into Norland House.

CHAPTER TWENTY

The downpour that caught me in the countryside is followed by others. Ominous black clouds puddle over Norland House during the night, crowing with thunder, then linger through the next day. The rain is a knife, dull and gray; it severs our estate from the rest of our province as if daring us to challenge it. I don't, and each evening I fall asleep to the sounds of a wind lashing at my windows, beating its fists against the panes as if begging to be let in.

Two days after my run-in with Ames, my cousin-in-law finds me taking my breakfast in the dining room, halfheartedly picking a crumbling piece of amber-sweet honey cake while the sky continues to weep outside.

"Finish up, Merrick." Cressida sets a cup of watery-looking tea down in front of me, the steam tickling my nose. I resist the urge to push it away; I still haven't gotten used to the saccharine oversweetness of these new blends, rather than my habitual moorflower. "We have quite the agenda to fulfill today, and I refuse to let poor weather diminish our efforts."

I lay my fork next to my plate, eyeing her dubiously. Cressida is clad in a gingham frock, a bonnet tied neatly around her head with a white ribbon. If not for her delicate lace gloves and the shrewd light in her eyes, I could almost be convinced she was a wandering shepherdess, searching for her lost flock.

Shaking off my rain-induced stupor, I reach for the teacup. "What agenda?" I ask. As far as I've been made aware, the rain has put a damper on our search efforts, the sentries consumed with the task of nursing the lanterns through the dreary weather. In fact, I've barely seen Cressida or Tom since my failed trip to Heath at all. I woke early yesterday morning to the sight of their carriage rattling down Norland's drive outside my window, the tepid glow of the rising sun all but lost amid the rain. Cressida's lady's maid had been tight-lipped when I questioned her about their destination, and by the time they returned, it was nearing midnight, meaning I haven't had the chance to inform them about Ames's offer—or my acceptance of it—either. I know I need to, and soon, but for now my chest tightens at Cressida's words. *Have they found something?*

In response to my question, Cressida lets out an impatient huff, as if she finds me hopelessly dim-witted. "We have business to attend to in New London. I'll explain the rest along the way," she snips unhelpfully, her brown eyes sweeping over me. They narrow to slits when she takes in my plain wool dress, the fabric an unflattering shade of mustard. "I hope to the Three you aren't planning on wearing *that.*"

Her evident disdain makes me bristle. "Excuse me. I did not expect to be seen by good society before I've finished my tea."

"And that lack of forethought is likely why you left the capital without a ring last time." Cressida waves my retort away, already turning to exit the room. "Change, please," she calls over her shoulder. "Preferably into something halfway decent, lest I be forced to dismiss your maid for her disturbing lack of ability."

The carriage ride into New London feels tantalizingly like an escape. With each mile the coach rolls onward, I feel the weight in my chest lift a fraction more. Not even a month ago, I would have given anything to leave behind the season and its pressures; now, a selfish part of me wishes I could clamber back into my soft guest bed at the Eaveses' and sleep until the trauma of the past weeks has faded to an old bruise. Better yet, until it washes away entirely: my sister's disappearance, my father's death, slipping from my shoulders like a bad dream, one that would make the morning air taste all the sweeter when I finally awoke.

The sun is high above our heads, the rain a dreary memory to our backs when, like a needle stitching a seam together, the road in front of us narrows. Banks of iridescent fog roll in from either side of our coach, turning the dense woodland around us into an undulating sea of mist, cold and clammy-looking. Above the roof of the carriage, a promenade of burning lampposts droops over us, their iron boughs carving a narrow path through the haze.

Cloistered safely inside the coach, I lay my hand reassuringly over my Ghostslayer, nestled like a drowsy kitten in my lap. I've traveled this route before, but never has the passage before me felt as claustrophobic as it does now—the Graylands rippling like the muscles of two enormous ivory beasts, their flanks pressing up against me on either side. The fog's smell wafts in through the hairline crevice beneath the carriage door: a stinking, organic musk, like unwashed bodies, the dank aroma of rotting hay.

Breathing in long, steadying inhales through my nose, I focus on counting the stitches on the hem of my skirt and marking off the minutes as they pass.

Then, as abruptly as it appeared, the mists recede and we are through it, out into the open again. Ahead of us, what looks to be a blue-white forest rises from the horizon, skeletal trees stretching, enormously tall, toward the sky.

The flora flickers, surges, and illusion melts into truth. What appear to be trees are, in reality, flames—a wall of fire, imposing as a battalion of giants observing our approach. Their force is enough to burn the half-mile swath of land abutting them clean of fog, exposing the barren underbelly of the Graylands beneath. A wasteland of dead vegetation and unfertile, hard earth stretches out ahead of us, bleached bones scattered here and there like discarded scraps after a feast.

Settling back into her seat on the other side of the carriage, Cressida produces a lacy fan from the small satchel at her side and flips it open unhurriedly. "The savagery of this place," she murmurs, curling her lip. "It never fails to disgust me."

For once, I find myself agreeing with her. The sole passage into the capital, the Blood Road is both a testament to humanity's triumph over the Graylands and a solemn reminder of all we have lost to the mist's embrace. The saga of the city, built during my great-great-great-*great*-grandmother's reign, in the Ninetieth Year of the Turning, is one of the first tales every child of the Smoke learns: how alongside their sentries, the twelve Manor Lords rode into the Phantom-infested skeleton of Old London and set it ablaze, driving back the fog that had claimed it. How they raised a second city out of its ashes, a shining beacon of hope, grand enough for all the nation to see.

The Twice-Burned City, we call it. *The Phoenix City.*

New London.

At the end of the road we're on, the gate to the city itself thrusts into the air like a curving fishhook, full of ragged metal teeth. Flames billow, winglike, from either side of the structure; even from this distance, the heat they give off is all-pervasive, enveloping me like a set of thick sheets.

Once we pass through the entrance, we'll still have several miles to go before we reach New London proper—our resurrected city is located at the center of the cleared land, a pearl inside an oyster shell—but I know from my last stay that when the wind shifts just so, you can still feel the fire's savagery, even there. A hot breeze that turns the air rancid, that sits like cotton on your tongue.

When Essie and I were younger, our father would make this journey often—in addition to being a cultural hub, New London houses the Mortal Council's chambers, where the Manor Lords of the Smoke gather twice a year to debate, pass legislation, and generally snub one another. Is it them, I wonder, whom Cressida has come to see? Perhaps an emergency session has been called to discuss my sister—the thought, at least, gives me hope.

I ask as much, tugging on my sweat-sticky gloves. Across from me, Cressida sets her fan down in her lap, her lips pressing into a line.

"All in due time, Merrick, dear," she says primly. "We have much to accomplish in the capital, but first, there is another matter I should like to discuss with you."

From the same reticule from which she withdrew her fan, Cressida produces a letter—two plain, cream pages, one stacked atop the other, both inscribed with looping cursive script. I focus in on the handwriting immediately; it is unfamiliar, neater than the hurried scrawl of the threat I found in Essie's room. Still, something about Cressida's formal presentation of the papers makes my stomach flip. Her thin eyebrows are arched in expectation, as if she is waiting for me to recognize the letter—to react.

I meet her gaze evenly. "You wish me to read your mail?"

My sister-in-law lets out a tired laugh, the washed-out emotion somehow more unnerving than a reprimand would have been. "You always were clever," she says dryly. Her mouth purses, as if she's deciding how next to proceed.

"This is a report from a group of our sentries, delivered to Norland House last evening," Cressida continues after a moment, folding the sheets of paper again and placing them beside her. "Apparently, they encountered a regiment of Saint men attempting to cross the border from Cardiff into Sussex yesterday, fully armed. Our guards were alarmed, to say the least—but when questioned, the Saint soldiers claimed they had your permission to enter our territory. That it was part of some deal you'd arranged with Archson Ames Saint." Cressida settles back against the cushioned wall of the carriage, lifting her fan and tapping it idly against her palm. "Care to enlighten me as to the details of this arrangement?"

"I . . ." My response dries up under the searing force of her gaze, my palms itching with guilty white heat. It isn't that I've intentionally tried to keep my encounter with Ames a secret from my relatives these past two days—more that, with Cressida and Tom's absence, there hasn't seemed to be a proper time to bring it up. Yet now, as I'm forced to take in the reality of our sentries' letter in Cressida's hand, I can't help but wonder if their mysterious travels were the only reason for my delay; if, perhaps subconsciously, I haven't wanted to face the very judgmental look my cousin-in-law is currently directing my way.

Haven't wanted her to tell me that—yet again—I'd made a poor choice.

"I ran into Ames—Archson Ames—the other morning, while I was out on patrol," I offer pathetically. I decide not to mention my attempted journey to Heath, or the rumors about the strangers near the border that I'd been pursuing. Cressida's irritation is already evident enough—I'm fearful that any half-baked theories from me might just push her over the edge. "He'd been planning to call on me at Norland. I mentioned to him during the course of our conversation that our sentries have been stretched tighter than usual since Essie went missing, and he offered to help—it was as simple an exchange as that." I lift my shoulders, as if by doing so, I can shrug off Cressida's critical stare.

"Why shouldn't we accept the Saint Manor's aid?" I ask, indignant. "It isn't as if we've been turning down assistance from the other Lords—you wrote to Lord Elodie about Essie vanishing before our own people had been made aware of the situation."

Cressida clicks her tongue in wordless reproach. "Yes, I enlisted the support of my grandmother—a woman who has a vested interest in the continued prosperity of the Darling Manor—in locating Estella," she chastises me, her brown eyes flat bronze coins in the refracted firelight streaming through the carriage windows. "As for the rest of the Council—they have agreed to share any news of your sister's whereabouts that makes its way to their respective provinces, and to allow us time to sort out the matter of Silas's heir, but nothing more. Do you see Warchild sentries on Darling ground? Or Ibe guards?" She shakes her head reproachfully. "You are still young, Merrick—you have not yet learned that alliances are temperamental beasts, which, if not handled carefully, often end up wounding the very parties that bore them. The details of Tom's and my engagement took half a year to iron out. It was only by the Burning King's grace that we were able to reach a deal at all."

She sighs, her nails tapping a distracted rhythm against the ivory spine of her fan. "I am not certain you understand what you have given away here."

As it always does at the first hint of criticism, my temper

flares, anger bubbling in my veins like liquid fire. I fight against the venomous inclination within me to strike back at her, swallowing the insult that rises to my lips whole.

"Ames asked for nothing in return—" I start.

Cressida holds up a hand in warning. "But he may," she interjects tightly. "Or Ianthe might, and you would be obliged to give it to her. Your sister would have—"

There she breaks off, her posture stiffening as if she can catch the rest of her sentence before it escapes, force it back down into herself.

Her efforts fail; I hear her unvoiced words, nonetheless. *Your sister would have known better. Your sister would have been better.*

It is a difficult thought: that Essie's absence is superior to, less harmful than, my presence. Jealousy spears me first as I process it, then hatred at my own envy, then . . . emptiness. Nothing.

You are not a bad person . . . You have simply been dealt a flawed hand. Killian's voice—I am not sure whether I believe him. I am not sure whether I am a person at all. I feel blank, disgusted by my own emotions and at once removed from them, as if they belong to another creature entirely. A parasite that has filled the shell of my body and tossed the remnants away.

"Fine," I manage, my tone rough. "Then write to Lord Ianthe and tell her we have no need of her or her son's help. Say I had no right to ask it of them in the first place."

Cressida looks at me for a long moment. Her lips are parted slightly, her brow furrowed as if she is preparing to issue an apology—but then she shivers, and whatever emotion had grasped her slips away. Collecting herself, she gives a stern shake of her head.

"I cannot do that," she says. "I am but your cousin's wife—not a blood member of the Darling Manor. No . . ." She inhales, her chest rising, and her gaze seems to intensify—boring deeper into mine. "That kind of authority resides in a Manor's Vessel alone, Merrick. And from today onward, that person is you."

You will never be Manor Lord, Merrick.

My father's words clash against Cressida's, one blade swung high to meet another. Across from me, my cousin-in-law's eyes are depthless, cedar fathoms. It is impossible to parse them—impossible to tell whether what she has just uttered is true.

It can't be. The morning after Father's Memorial Ball, Cressida told me we would have a couple weeks of leniency, at least, before anyone would expect us to Nominate an heir to replace my sister. It's scarcely been *one.* Surely, my relatives have not given up on finding Essie already? Surely, I am not—I cannot be . . .

Feeling suddenly lightheaded, I hear myself ask, "What?"

"Tom and I drove to New London yesterday to alert the Council." Cressida responds evenly, nodding to herself as if her statement is nothing out of the ordinary. So *that's* where they were traveling so early yesterday morning: to the very same destination I'm now headed, oblivious as a pig being taken to slaughter. I wait for the familiar red wash of ire to sweep through me at her admission, but none comes—only a tingling numbness, like ants marching over my skin.

"I am sorry we did not inform you earlier—the meeting was arranged rather quickly, and we felt it would be placing an undue burden on you, were we to throw you into the fray with no warning," Cressida continues. "Though, of course, the decision came as no surprise to the majority of the Councilors," she goes on with a decisive bob of her head. "You *are* Silas's nearest eligible heir, after all. The Nomination Hearing has been set for ten days' time—we felt any further delay would give the commoners too much of a chance to start fussing."

At last, she stops, and it is as though a wall has crumbled within me. Like I am a dark room into which light has suddenly been poured. Me, Father's Vessel. Me, Lord of Sussex. Cressida's words settle in: not a fantasy after all, or a delusion, but something solid. Real.

On one level, the revelation is tantalizing, sugared berries mounded in a bowl. Part of me wants nothing more than to claim them—to crush them on my tongue and suck their juice, taste their sweetness.

But, a meek voice whispers, *if you are Vessel, what about . . .*

"And what of Essie? You said we needn't select a new Vessel for weeks. What's changed?" I ask aloud, and only then does my joy recede, clotting guilt sweeping in to replace it. Has any of this—my attempts to find my sister—been about keeping her safe at all? Or has it only ever been a façade, an elaborate performance so that on the day I finally steal her throne, no one can reproach me for it?

Have I only ever wanted to *win*?

Cressida's expression has thawed at my question. Her long lashes flutter—not with her usual cold indifference, I realize with a stab of anxiety, but in distress, as if she's trying to blink away tears. "Merrick . . ." she starts, and in the quiver of her voice I hear it: pity.

My heart hardens, curls like a dead bird against my ribs.

"No," I say. "No, please don't—"

Cressida's mouth twitches at my rejection, almost as if I've offended her, but she doesn't relent. "Merrick," she repeats again, stiffly, "there has been a new development in the search for your sister."

Her back straightens, like she is tensing against an invisible blow. "A timberman reported a discovery to one of our sentries the evening before last—something he and his fellow men had stumbled upon while working in Barton Woods." She pauses, her skin graying. "It was a nightgown—one of Estella's, her lady's maid confirmed it. And it was . . ." Her speech falters, drops low. "It was covered in blood."

She sighs, smoothing out a wrinkle in her skirt. "You are an intelligent girl, Merrick. I will let you form your own conclusion from there."

Silence descends over the carriage like the swing of a gavel. Eyes stinging, I turn away, as if by avoiding my cousin-in-law's gaze I can put enough space between myself and her words that I will no longer hear them resounding in my mind. *A timberman reported a discovery . . . covered in blood.*

The nights I have spent lying awake, poring over every detail of the hours following the attack at the ball as if I can sniff out Essie's abductor from the folds of my memory—they cloud around me now, a bleak haze. Is it possible, somehow, that none of it mattered? None of my ridiculous theories, my childish quests with Killian.

All this time, all the stones I've turned over . . . has Essie been dead, before I flipped the first one? And if she is—if I am now Vessel—does that mean I'm next?

Darling Manor will fall. My mother, then my father, and now my sister have left me. And while I know Tom is still here—still by my side—I am, in many ways, the last Darling left.

I am, I realize, completely alone.

"They're wrong." My throat is sore, my voice a croak. "The maid—the timberman. They're lying—they must be."

"I wish that were the case. But we, both of us, know that they are not." Cressida's reply is sympathetic, but steady. "Merrick . . ." Her mouth tightens, a flicker of remorse crossing her features. "You think me callous," she murmurs, glancing away. "You have always done so, since I wed your cousin. Yet . . ." Her eyes travel back to mine, mist over. "To be Manorborn—to be what we are—is to lose, dearest. Love, happiness . . . those pleasures are too sweet for us, too simple. In the face of power, they wither easily, like sour grapes beneath the sun."

Her knuckles tighten around her fan. "I believed differently once," she goes on faintly. "I was like you, assuming I could hold the flower of our gift, keep myself from the thorns." She shakes her head. "They found me; they found your sister. Now they have found you, too."

"So, what then?" I challenge, unmoved. "I should forget Essie? Should stop loving her, just because she is . . . she may be . . ."

I bite my lip, unable to go on.

Cressida reaches across the middle of the carriage, gently taking my chin in hand. Her skin is creased along her brow, her eyes shadowed and deep beneath the brim of her bonnet.

"Not at all. We will not cease searching for your sister's killer, just because she is gone. But you must give Estella the same grace that she gave you, Merrick, when you left her for New London," she says solemnly. "You must learn to let her go."

CHAPTER TWENTY-ONE

We disembark in the neighborhood of Blindchapel, a stretch of exclusive shops and lavish homes situated near the center of the capital, along the muddied bank of the Thames. As I descend the steps of our carriage, I swivel my gaze from side to side, taking in the expansive, well-swept streets in front of me, the townhouses that perch like gilded vultures along their edges. Before the mist came, I've been told, this area of the city housed Old London's parliament, served as the beating heart of its long-ago empire.

Now it has been overtaken by the Manors. Like fast-spreading weeds, the Smoke's ruling families have rooted themselves atop the carcass of their predecessors as if they can soak up whatever's left of the ancient rulers' legacy through the soil. I recognize several houses situated farther up the road we're on: Number 11, the austere, gray-trimmed dwelling of Sanguin Layton Savager and his wife, and Number 15, its somewhat more cheerful neighbor, where I attended Vera Cachemar's end-of-summer ball only last month.

Next to me, Cressida sniffs, adjusting her bonnet. "Come along, Merrick. We have an appointment to make."

I obey, allowing myself to be pulled into the tide of the city. My cousin-in-law has still to inform me as to the reason for our visit—the remainder of our ride into New London was passed in a silence so oppressive I got the sense it would have stolen into my lungs like smoke and smothered me, had I dared open my mouth—but considering the neighborhood, my earlier suspicions about a visit with the Council may prove correct after all. Has Cressida called for another emergency session to further discuss the news about my sister? I imagine the eleven remaining Manor Lords robed in their crimson Councilor regalia, crowns of yellowing antlers fastened around their brows like laurels as they stood in their chambers yesterday, imagine them listening on as Tom and Cressida named me Vessel without my knowledge, and something in me twists—a broken shard of bone.

Merrick Darling, Lord of Sussex. What I would have given for a sliver of a chance at that title weeks ago; what I would give for it to be taken from me now.

As I trail behind Cressida, I scan the street ahead for a glimpse of the dual towers that crown the Council's chambers, formerly belonging to a centuries-old church before the city's death and resurrection. It always seemed fitting to me that my ancestors chose to take up residence in an ancient house of worship rather than repurpose Old London's burned-out parliament. The latter, after all, had been made with mortals in mind; the former, for the divine.

Which of the two categories the Manors most closely aligned themselves with has never been in question.

Yet when I do catch a peek of the looming structure, its buttresses like exposed ribs jutting from its side, Cressida turns away from the Council's chambers rather than toward them, heading toward the west of Blindchapel, where the neighborhood melts into that of Rosing Cross, the fashion district. Curiosity pricks at me, but my normal instinct to question her is diluted, barely more than a nudge at the corners of my mind. What does it matter, anyway, where we are going? Whatever our destination, my sister will not be there.

A vision swells behind my eyes like a lake bursting its banks: Essie, running from a shadowy captor, her nightgown a white flash against the black maw of the dark. A rose-bloom of red across her chest as her pursuer brings her down, blood mixing with the earth, staining it maroon.

Impossible, I want to protest. *She can't be gone—she* can't *be.*

But if what Cressida told me in the carriage is true, what else could she be?

A breeze snakes past me as I walk, my nose wrinkling as a whiff of something caustic and charred reaches it, like burning flesh. Logically, I know the unpleasant aroma originates from the border fires along the Blood Road, but during my recent stay in the capital, I heard other rumors regarding the smell's origin, too. Legends whispered in candlelit drawing rooms, of how even after almost a century, remnants of Old London still lingered in our grand city, a miasmic reminder of the night our ancestors burned it until it was nothing but ash.

I shiver. Sometimes, New London feels like a miracle. Other times, it feels like a grave.

Eventually, Cressida stops in front of a compact, well-tended shop, a sign with the looping words *Madame Villette's* hanging out front. I raise my brows at the name. Lucille Villette has meticulously cultivated her reputation as New London's premier modiste over the past decade, and her prices have risen along with her demand. I've known Manorborn who have struggled to meet her hefty fees—though in almost all cases, they accepted the private shame of debt than risk the public humiliation of living on a *budget*.

I eye Cressida suspiciously as we step inside the building. Even the Faulks, with their deep coffers, do not frequent the Madame's shop without worthy cause. What could my cousin-in-law possibly be shopping for that would justify purchasing a Villette creation?

"Ah, Duchess Faulk-Darling, welcome."

Upon our entrance, Madame Villette herself sweeps toward us from the back of the shop, her supple curves draped in folds of amethyst satin. Well into middle age, the dressmaker is still a vision with her high cheekbones and berry-red lips, her eyes dark and intelligent. Dropping into a deep curtsy, she flicks her gaze up toward me.

"And I see you've brought Archdaughter Merrick with you. My lady, it is a privilege to meet you." The dressmaker bows her head respectfully before straightening. "My deepest condolences on your loss."

I stiffen on instinct, my neck prickling as if brushed by a cold draft, but my cousin-in-law only smiles. She takes Madame Villette's hand gracefully, giving it a squeeze of gratitude. "We are delighted to see you as well, of course, Madame," Cressida says. She exchanges a conspiratorial glance with the other woman, dropping her voice a half octave as she goes on. "Now, your letter said the gown I'd commissioned was nearly ready?"

"It is indeed." The dressmaker nods. Her eyes dart toward mine again; this time, they are curious, skittering away almost immediately when I meet them as if afraid of divulging a secret. "But, forgive me, Duchess, I thought—"

"Excellent," Cressida interjects smoothly. "We shall need alterations done, of course. Please, bring it out."

I glance at her, thrown by her brusque interruption. My cousin-in-law's expression is steely, the warmth she'd shown the Madame only a second ago having evaporated like dew at high noon. Pressing her lips together, Madame Villette dips her head in an obedient nod, then disappears into a back room, leaving Cressida and me alone except for a few naked mannequins positioned around the space like idling eavesdroppers.

"My poor grandmother is still paying off the wedding dress we commissioned from the Madame last year," Cressida scoffs after a moment, breaking the tense quiet that's stretched between us. "The woman is a leech, but she knows her silhouettes, at least." Absently, she reaches out and tucks a stray ringlet of hair behind my ear, offering me a soft grin. "The Council will expect nothing short of perfection at the Nomination Hearing, my dear. If we wish to impress them, you must look the part."

My spine goes rigid. So *this,* at last, is the nature of our errand, the occasion that warrants a Villette-sized expenditure. "The gown you mentioned," I say. "It is for me, then?"

Cressida's fingers flinch against my cheek, her nails biting briefly into my skin. When she steps away from me, her expression is tight. "It is for the Darling Vessel," she says, her voice smooth and oily as sealskin.

She turns her chin away from me so I cannot see her face, but her response is explanation enough. This dress—though I may be the one receiving it, it was not made for me. No, like the Nomination itself, it was intended for someone else—someone who is no longer present to claim it.

Essie's gown. Essie's title. How many more pieces of my sister will I take?

I part my lips, another question ready on my tongue, only to be interrupted by a high, musical tinkling from the shop's entrance. Like a single creature, Cressida and I swivel at once to look in the direction of the entrance, where additional patrons are stepping into the shop.

There are two of them: a man and a woman, the latter's gloved hand looped through the former's elbow. The first of the pair is younger, tall and lean, his head covered by a gray Regent-style top hat that's pulled low across his brow. He tilts his chin up as he crosses the threshold and I make out a flash of blond hair peeking from beneath the brim of his hat, the pearlescent cut of his grin.

My pulse stutters, the space around me compressing like the room is drawing a breath. *Ames.* If possible, the Saint Vessel looks even better in the glare of midday than he did painted by the wan storm light two days ago. For a fevered second after I've processed his presence, I think he's come to see me—that he's been turning over our recent encounter as much as I have these past few nights. Lying in my bed, conjuring up his whispered words just so I could run my tongue over them again.

You have been a ghost in my mind, my whole life . . . I feel as though I know you quite intimately.

Then his companion steps over the threshold, and reality breaks over me. The woman holding on to Ames is diminutive, the top of her head barely clearing Ames's shoulders. Her thinning gray hair is pulled into a neat bun above the purple velvet collar of her pelisse; set deep into a softly lined face, a pair of pale green eyes observe me curiously.

Next to Ames's obvious beauty, the woman should appear weak, lackluster—yet when I follow the tug of power I feel pulling at my middle, it leads me back to her. There is a certain quality to the way she moves, with a lethargic elegance like dripping honey—something confident enough in its value to take its time— that tells me exactly who she is. What title she bears.

Cressida reacts first, her skirts pooling around her as she drops into a deep curtsy, one hand placed reverently on her chest. "Manor Lord Ianthe. It is an honor, Your Eminence."

Hastily, I sink into an identical curtsy, craning my neck toward the floor like a swan. From beneath lowered lashes, I watch as Ianthe Saint's lips curl into a modest smile at the sound of her name, crow's feet puckering the corners of her eyes.

"If it isn't Duchess Cressida Faulk-Darling," she says. Her voice is unexpectedly meek, the soft warble of an herbivore. Despite the fact that she can't be far past forty, she's carrying a mahogany cane carved with winding orchids—resemblant of the ones I know can be found in the Saint Manor's crest—which clicks against the floor as she approaches. I can feel the moment her attention shifts to me, like a finger tracing the line of my profile.

"And who do we have here but Archdaughter Merrick," she murmurs. "Hello, dear."

I go still as Lord Ianthe closes the distance between us and crooks her thumb under my chin, turning my head left, then right, in an assessing manner not dissimilar to the way I have seen our stable hands examine new foals for defects. In my peripheral vision, I catch Cressida's jaw tensing at the Manor Lord's inspection, but she makes no move to interrupt the other woman.

When she's finished, Lord Ianthe pushes my gaze upward to meet hers with a gentle flex of her wrist. Her eyes are large and unblinking, focused as an academic's, her irises the color of pond weed. They are the eyes of a woman who picked apart a dying Manor and from its scraps constructed an empire.

Or at least, that is how my father always described Ianthe, his tone equal parts wariness and begrudging respect. As he told it, Ames's mother was never intended for the Saint Lordship—the younger of two siblings, she was born weak and grew up ugly, traits which diminished her worth as a leader and potential bride, respectively. Among the Manorborn of my father's generation, Ianthe was the ugly duckling in the noble set he ran with: un-pretty, frustratingly unsubmissive, and generally unaccommodating toward anyone who attempted to alter the aforementioned pieces of her. Though no one dared say it to her face, the consensus was that she would amount to nothing more than an old maid, clinging to the coattails of her older brother—her parents' favorite and chosen Vessel—wasting away in their family's grand estate until the end of her days.

That was before her brother died. Before she was Nominated in his stead and, over the years, grew the relatively small province of Norrin into the agricultural behemoth it is today.

My thighs burn, Lord Ianthe's thumb still pressing into the underside of my chin, like a hook preventing me from dropping my curtsy. Then, with a low hum of approval, she gestures for me to rise. I do, my limbs shaky as a fawn's, fighting the urge to wipe away the beads of cold sweat that have erupted along my upper lip.

"Ames, you must apologize to the Archdaughter. Your description of her was terribly lacking." Lord Ianthe extends her index finger, beckoning her son over. Lowering her voice, she adds to me with a wink, "My son told me you'd grown into a lovely young woman, but he failed to accurately convey the beauty you've truly become. You are the spitting image of your mother."

"I—thank you, Your Eminence," I say, flushing at the unexpected praise.

Taking her son's arm, Lord Ianthe makes a shooing motion with her cane, as if shoving my thanks away. Positioned next to Ames as she is, the scars of her childhood illness are evident—she is bird-boned, delicate in comparison to his natural fitness, her cheeks gaunt as if with perpetual hunger.

"I was ever so relieved when Ames informed me that he'd run into you the other day, Archdaughter," Lord Ianthe says, giving her son's biceps an appreciative squeeze. "A beautiful girl such as yourself cannot be too careful when traveling in the countryside, you know—especially in times such as those we now find ourselves in." She chuckles, a parched rasp. "Despite what we ladies may wish, a handsome knight will not always be nearby to save us."

"Save who?" Cressida says. "Forgive me, Lord Ianthe, but the *countryside*, as you put it, is Merrick's home—she is familiar with every inch of Sussex, and more than capable of defending herself from any dangers lurking within it. It is your son, in fact, who was traveling through unfamiliar lands."

Cressida's voice is the prow of a ship, breaking through the rough waters of my mind. She presses her palm flat against my lower back as she talks, her unspoken message clear: *collect yourself.* I straighten in response.

"My mother has always had a flair for the dramatic. I rescued the Archdaughter from a spot of bad weather, and nothing more," Ames answers my cousin-in-law. His gaze finds mine over his mother's shoulder, the warmth in it loosening some of the tension knotted in my chest.

"Do not diminish your own good deeds, Ames. We have spoken about this."

Lord Ianthe's command snaps through the shop, biting and curt. Her nails pinch tighter into the meat of her son's arm, her mouth twisting into a stern frown. I can't repress a concerned inhale when I see him flinch beneath his mother's grip, a muscle jumping along his jaw.

Registering my reaction, the Manor Lord darts her eyes to me—and then, like a bowstring whipping back into place, she is loosening again, her features serene once more.

Beside her, Ames stares at the ground.

"As I was saying, I was somewhat dismayed to hear that the Archdaughter was unaccompanied when my son came across her, what with the tragic news you shared with the Council yesterday, Duchess," Lord Ianthe goes on breezily, as if her son's interruption never occurred at all. "Why, if it were my Manor that had just lost a daughter, I would take greater care to guard my remaining one."

She sighs, resting heavily on her cane. "But I suppose that is why you have requested our aid, isn't it?"

My blood flushes with ice. Ames's mother is studying me as if I am a hare on the other end of her rifle—no, worse, as if I am a particularly shiny jewel she'd like to string round her neck. What was it she said, just a minute ago? *My son told me you'd grown into a lovely young woman.* Why do I get the sense now that her comment had not been the compliment I'd initially taken it as, but an assessment? The cool, appreciative nod of a collector before they take their prize in hand, tuck it away behind glass.

Cressida was right, back in the carriage—I should never have accepted Ames's offer. How could I be so naïve, to swallow down his kindness and not consider the cost?

As if she is reading my thoughts, my cousin-in-law's hand flexes against the base of my spine. "Is that what you *suppose*?" she parries in a level tone.

Lord Ianthe's attention drags with painstaking deliberateness across my cheek, keen as a switchblade before finally flitting to Cressida. She draws in a breath as if preparing to reply, only to be cut off by the jingle of the front door as it opens to admit a new gaggle of customers. The group enters in a rush of taffeta and lace, the lively babble of their conversation dying instantly upon contact with Ames's mother's glare, as she whirls around to face them.

"It is convenient, our running into you two here," the Manor

Lord says, turning back to us with a joviality that feels like a stretched grin, jerky and false. "My son's encounter with the Archdaughter reminded me that it has been far too long since we all dined together—and I should like to catch up with Duke Tom as well."

Reaching forward, the Manor Lord takes Cressida's gloved hand in hers. "What do you say, Duchess—shall we continue this conversation over dinner?" She smiles; her teeth are small and pointed, yellow at the roots. "Unless you'd like to discuss it more here."

Delicately, Cressida extracts herself from the Manor Lord's hold. "We will be grateful to accept any invitation the Saint Manor chooses to extend to us, of course," she replies politely, and I feel as though I have led her into a trap.

Pleased, Lord Ianthe stamps her cane against the ground. "Wonderful. I'll have our footman send over the details this evening. And, ah—there you are, Villette. I have a request for you."

With a departing wave, she brushes past us to where the dressmaker has at last emerged from the back room, a veritable river of red lace streaming from her arms. *The gown.* I'd almost forgotten about it, but now renewed apprehension presses like a balled fist against my sternum.

"It seems as though fate is not quite through with us yet, Archdaughter." Ames's breath is hot, curling against the shell of my ear. I snap to attention. He's paused by my side on his way to follow his mother, his words hushed enough that I know they're intended only for me. Briefly, he catches my wrist, the press of his thumb against my veins somehow more intimate than his lips would be. "Until we meet again," he murmurs.

Then he's moving, sparing me a final backward glance as he goes.

CHAPTER TWENTY-TWO

The invitation arrives a couple days later, printed in blue ink upon a white card:

HER EMINENCE LORD IANTHE SAINT

REQUESTS YOUR COMPANY

AT

BERKSHIRE ESTATE ("THE ROOST"), CARDIFF,

TOMORROW AT EIGHT O'CLOCK IN THE EVENING.

DINNER WILL BE SERVED.

Preparation consumes most of the next afternoon. Maids are summoned and dismissed, usually carrying at least one gown in their arms; hair is curled and set, and in the bedrooms, lips are painted in the orange half-light of a dozen candles, the curtains drawn over the windows to mimic evening's glow. For the first time since Essie's disappearance, Norland House feels alive again, its dim halls somehow brighter, as if it, too, is attempting to bring a little color back into its cheeks.

Cressida demanded we coordinate our wardrobe before departing—another ploy by her to present ourselves as a united front—so when she, Tom, and I finally do set out for Cardiff, it is in varying shades of purple. My lilac dress is simple in structure, with thin lacy straps over my shoulders and more of the same sewn along the edge of my skirts, like a froth of waves. The effect, when I caught a glimpse of the outfit in my looking glass before departing, was transcendent, turning me from a girl into something sugared and ephemeral, as if I would melt on the tongue of anyone who brought me to their lips.

Yet instead of pleasure, apprehension settled over me as I watched myself in the mirror, as my stays were yanked tight and my nose powdered. Though my ensemble resembles that of a young lady, the fabric weighs heavy as armor on my shoulders for the entire ride to the Roost, pressing claustrophobically against my chest as if with a fierce protectiveness.

As if in truth, I am preparing for war.

"Ianthe Saint is a gamemaster—all Manor Lords are," Cressida had advised me earlier, while my maids wove ribbons in shades of heliotrope and wisteria through my hair and arranged my unruly curls into a glossy, plaited updo. She was sitting in an armchair tucked in the corner of my room, her own dark locks loose and wild around her shoulders. "Taking power is crass and primitive in their eyes; they prefer to win it through strategy, and even that is not as desirable to them as you laying down and handing yourself over willingly. Ianthe has scented weakness in you—now she is trying to see if you will break."

She stood then, crossed behind me, and laid her hands on my shoulders. In the wavering candlelight, her eyes were black, depthless. "You will not," she said simply.

By the time we pass into Cardiff, I am itching with anxiety. We divided ourselves into two carriages for the drive; Tom and Cressida are in the one following behind me, while my vehicle rides up front, empty except for me and Killian sitting across from me, his Ghostslayer in his lap. Technically, he is here to act as our line of defense in the event of another breach, but part of me is simply grateful for his companionship, the way it keeps me from being alone.

Most of me, though, is made all the more restless by him. We've still barely spoken since the night we ventured into Shoreham-by-Sea, and now his presence feels like I am being confronted by my own failure. Aside from the bloodied nightgown in Barton Woods, there have been no new developments in the search for my sister. And while Cressida and Tom have reassured me that they will not rest until Essie's body—living or otherwise—is recovered, and her captor brought to justice, their efforts have felt less urgent these past few days, every action tempered with a grim sort of resignation. As if in their minds, a verdict has already been delivered: my sister is dead, and whether my Manor survives her loss rests on me.

For my part, I've allowed Cressida to shepherd me through preparations for my upcoming Nomination Hearing—have stood obediently still through dress fittings and dutifully memorized the names and drink preferences of each of the other eleven Manor Lords and their families. Yet through every lecture, I've been plagued by a sense of restlessness, as if I am early to a party, waiting for the true host to arrive and relieve me of my duties.

Try as I might, I can't make myself believe that Essie is gone. Wouldn't I have felt it, if she were? Have sensed the subtle ways the world shifted to accommodate her death, the same way a farmer smells a storm in the air?

And then, too, there is the reality of the threat from her bedroom: *Darling Manor will fall.* I haven't forgotten it—can never forget it. If Essie truly has been killed, how long do I have before her murderer turns their attention to me?

What do they want? I still don't know; worse, I have no idea how to find out.

I think we may reach the Saint estate without a single word spoken between Killian and me, but finally, as we near our destination, he sighs, slouching back against his seat. He quirks a brow at me, his expression provocatory. "What?"

I drop the fold of fabric I've been fiddling with, returning his gaze with my own imperious stare. "What, what?" I ask. "I could ask you the same question."

He folds his arms, undeterred. "Something is evidently bothering you, Archdaughter," he challenges. "I am giving you the opportunity to share it with me, but if you prefer to freeze to death in this carriage, we can continue in this manner as well." He inclines his head. "You'll find I have quite the cold tolerance."

It is a struggle not to redden under his stare. The ease with which he's read me is disconcerting; I dislike it, the notion of my own transparency, as if I am a book splayed out before him. Angling my chin toward the carriage window, I avert my gaze, like by doing so I can close a window that has been left open, shut him out of me. "My sister has been killed, Brandon, at the hands of a person whose identity I may never know," I say, purposefully snide. "Should I be more cheerful?"

At first, I think my tactic has worked—Killian's mouth slackens, the cocksure expression slipping from his face like water draining from a leaky pail. But just as I ready myself for his apology, he pivots, shifting forward and resting his elbows on his knees.

"No, it is not that," he says thoughtfully, rubbing a contemplative hand over his jaw. "There is something more."

A fire sparks in his eyes, his concern crystallizing into an emotion sharp-edged and cutting. "Is it the Saints?" he asks tightly, his shoulders tensing beneath his jacket. "Ames—has he treated you poorly?"

Ah. I bite down on my lower lip as memories of my encounters with Ames stir within me, a hot palm pressed against my stomach.

You have been a ghost in my mind, my whole life . . .

. . . I feel as though I know you quite intimately.

Guilt and desire mix in my gut. Ames and I have done nothing untoward—but even if we had, the Saint Vessel is precisely the sort of match I ran to New London in search of: titled, with a future grand enough to support my weight without sagging. So why does the idea of telling Killian about him make me wilt?

"Ames Saint is a gentleman and has treated me as such," I say, keeping my eyes fixed on the rolling countryside beyond the window. "He is the picture of what a young Manorborn man should be, in fact—kind, chivalrous, not to mention exceedingly handsome. I am sure there are many young ladies who would willingly forfeit their inheritance for the chance to dine with him tonight."

"I did not ask about the preferences of other young ladies."

The temperature of the carriage seems to crawl upward at Killian's response, as if in its wooden underbelly a great fire has been stoked. Unable to resist, I snap my gaze back to him—only to find him settling back in his seat, glancing away. "But fine," he says softly, after a moment. "So long as he has been kind to you."

It isn't a question, but I sense his curiosity nonetheless—and something beyond it, too. A hint of disdain, well-disguised, but present, nonetheless.

"He has," I reply slowly, my own interest peaking at the glimmer of his. "Do you have reason to believe he wouldn't be?"

There: a flash of something rotten rises to the surface of his expression, like the dark shadow of a fish stirring in the shallows of a lake. It is only there for a second before he shrugs it away, his face settling back into an inscrutable mask. "You are an Archdaughter. My opinion is of little consequence to someone like you."

I shake my head, unrelenting. "But Ames—you dislike him. Or dislike my association with him, at least. I could hear it clearly when you spoke just now."

Killian's forehead creases. "I distrust him," he counters carefully. "It is not the same. I—" Swiftly, he breaks off, the rest of his sentence withering away, unspoken. "It is not my place to speak on any of this," he says in a clipped tone, final as the drop of a stair.

His withdrawal strikes a nerve within me. "*Distrust* him?" I snap, leaning closer. "What is there to distrust? Ames has only ever been forthcoming with me—unlike you, I might point out."

At my accusation, Killian goes rigid, his eyes flaring like stoked coals. "If you truly wish to know, he seems overly concerned with the goings-on at Norland, in my opinion," he replies hotly, his composed demeanor cracking—just a bit, but still enough to send a thrill down my spine. "The other sentries say he called on Arch-daughter Estella more than once, while you were away."

"Yes, Essie told me about his visits, though there was nothing sinister about them," I fire back, surprised to find my own temper warming, rising to clash with his. "He was merely being diplomatic."

I force my shoulders, which have hunched defensively near my chin, to relax, drawing a steadying breath. "Let us speak candidly," I say, sitting back and locking my gaze with his. "The issue isn't Ames's trustworthiness at all, is it, *Killian*?"

There's a sick pleasure in it—watching him startle at my use of his first name, observing the way his lips part as if with a shocked breath. It is satisfying, for once, to knock him off his axis, to unsteady him the way he seems to be constantly doing to me.

He doesn't have a chance to respond to my jab. Before he can say another word, the carriage rolls to a halt, the driver shouting from his perch up front that we've reached our destination. The news of our arrival seems to snip us clean of the spell we've been caught in; for a second, I'd almost forgotten we were headed anywhere at all, that the evening did not end with the polished walls of this coach.

Gripping Killian's arm for support, I step out of our vehicle and onto solid ground, taking in my first up-close glimpse of the Roost.

The house before us is palatial in its proportions, sprawled out over the flat, manicured land that surrounds it rather than raised up tall as Norland House is. Ionic columns flank the ground floor; above them, rows of symmetrical windows shine golden with interior light, conjuring up images of roaring fires and well-heated rooms, a place without drafts or creaks—without any of the dozens of ailments that fester like mold in the bones of my family's estate.

A parade of graceful, elongated shapes are carved into the pair of columns that frame the entryway, wrapping around them like twin strands of ivy. Though I can't see their details from here, I know they are birds. A flock of stone ospreys, more specifically—in honor of the animals that grace the Saint crest, and the architectural feature responsible for the estate's nickname.

To my back, Cressida and Tom are disembarking from their carriage as well, Cressida coming to stand by my side. Her gown is a darker shade than mine, a vibrant plum that makes her skin glow like satin. "You remember all that we discussed?" she asks tonelessly. When I nod, her shoulders relax. "Good."

She snaps her head to the side. "Mr. Brandon," Cressida orders Killian, who is lingering behind us. "You'll wait here for us. If you're needed inside, we shall send for you."

Obediently, Killian nods, his eyes fixed stubbornly on my

cousin-in-law. Leaving him behind, the three of us process toward the Roost. Tom has barely raised his fist to knock when the double doors swing soundlessly open, a ferret-faced butler standing mutely behind them.

Unspeaking, the man beckons us inside. His silence prompts in me an uncanny sense of foreboding: the sinking certainty that we have been expected here for a very long time. As if all the times I walked to the top of Sussex's hills as a child and stared at this place, it was watching me, too. Waiting for the moment I'd finally pass through its doors.

Shivering, I follow the servant through the entry hall, awe briefly overshadowing my anxiety as I take in the high ceilings painted with elaborate frescoes and smooth marble floors. After a few more turns, we enter into a grand dining room. Candelabras mounted on the walls spill tangerine light across the floor, glazing the space in honeyed hues. In the center of the room, an elaborate brass chandelier throws the dining table beneath it into even brighter relief, flickering firelight ghosting over the pale faces of the diners seated below.

Situated at the head of the table, Lord Ianthe rises smoothly, her small frame dwarfed by the enormity of the room around her. The disparity should make her appear insignificant, but instead the grandeur suits her as it would a child king. "Ah, the Darlings! You've arrived at last. How delighted we are to see you, dear friends."

On her right, Ames stands as well, bowing his head in echoes of his mother's greeting. As he lifts his chin, he catches my eye, throwing me a roguish wink that makes me feel flushed to my core. I smile in response, then glance away when I see Cressida watching me, her brow furrowed with an emotion I can't place.

Gesturing us forward with one hand, Lord Ianthe snaps her fingers with the other. At the sound, a trio of black-clad figures strips away from the room's shadowed corners and rush toward the dining table, beetle-like. I flinch before realizing they're servants, dressed crisply in starched navy uniforms, their hair hidden beneath the powdered white shells of their wigs. They each pause by a chair, helping Tom, Cressida, and me into our respective seats before retreating again.

I follow them with my gaze as they go. Now that I'm looking, I see similar silhouettes hovering in every nook and cranny of the dining room, a horde of watching eyes and neatly folded, long-fingered hands.

Shivers of revulsion trickle down my spine. I knew that Cardiff has prospered under Lord Ianthe's rule, but I wasn't expecting this level of opulence. Witnessing it feels unsettling, like turning over a leaf and finding a spider lurking beneath—an unexpected threat.

Cressida's words come back to me: *Ianthe Saint is a gamemaster.* The title fits; I feel, with a sinking certainty, that my Manor has just lost the upper hand.

Clearing her throat, Lord Ianthe gives another wave of her hand and additional waitstaff emerge, peeling themselves from their hiding places one after the other like a string of paper dolls. In perfect synchronization, they pluck identical gilded teapots from a sideboard and ferry them over to us, pouring steaming tea into the dainty cups placed in front of us.

My mouth dry, I pick up my drink and sip on it, the herbal bite of the moorflower too strong for my already fraying nerves. Hurriedly, I set it down, the earthy aroma cloying in my nostrils.

"I should like to begin our evening with a toast." Lord Ianthe raises her cup with a soft *tink* as she turns toward me and grins. Red liquid swirls within it, stark against the white porcelain.

"To the newest Vessel of the Darling Manor," Lord Ianthe continues. "I regret that I was unable to suitably congratulate you at Villette's the other day, Archdaughter, but I hope you will allow me to remedy my mistake now. Your father would be most proud, I am sure."

It is a struggle not to squirm under her gaze. Nervously, I take another swallow of tea. Aftertaste clings to the back of my tongue, curdled perfume.

"I am only doing my duty, Your Eminence," I reply. "No compliments are necessary."

Evidently displeased by my response, Cressida clears her throat primly. "You must forgive my cousin—she is still adjusting to her new role," she says to Lord Ianthe. "It has been quite painful for her, losing her sister so abruptly."

My teacup quivers in my hand, my fingers suddenly unsteady. Quickly I set it down, before Ames or his mother can notice my trembling.

Essie is dead, I recite to myself. *She's gone, and she isn't coming back.* What my head understands to be the truth, my heart refuses to accept. I wonder if I ever will, if instead I will live my entire life staring out of windows, waiting for Essie to return to me.

"Of course." Lord Ianthe nods sympathetically, her brow pinching in the center. "The recent findings have been most . . . upsetting." Her head tilts, her eyes narrowing as if inspecting me closely. "Let us hope you are able to *adjust,* as the Duchess puts it, in spite of them, Archdaughter Merrick."

"We are confident that Merrick will be just the ruler Sussex needs to guide the province through this tumultuous period," Cressida answers. Her posture is relaxed, her hand resting casually atop her husband's, but I hear the warning in her tone, like the flash of a knife from within someone's jacket.

Lord Ianthe seems to pick up on it, as well. "Indeed," she says, shifting back in her enormous chair, steepling her hands under her chin. "And what better way to usher in a new season than with a new alliance? As I said when we crossed paths in the capital, my dear girl, it would be the Saint Manor's honor to assist your family in its time of need. No repayment necessary—we are neighbors, after all."

Her teeth wink in the candlelight, stained crimson by her tea, and I'm abruptly struck again by how small she is. It is as if her body has not grown past its girlhood—as if she has aged within the chrysalis of her youth.

"You are too generous, Lord Ianthe." I bow my head, speaking each word carefully, just as Cressida and I rehearsed back at Norland. "And I appreciate your son's offer of aid more than I can say. Yet I am afraid we cannot take advantage of your kindness in this manner. If Sussex is to prosper once more, it must learn to stand on its own two feet."

My palms are slick with sweat; surreptitiously, I lower them to my lap, wipe them on my skirt. At my response, Lord Ianthe's expression hardens, her features closing like a clamshell snapping shut.

"Is that so?" she replies. Her voice has dropped low; there is a restraint to it, like the rumble of the sky just before it bursts open with rain. She glances toward Ames, an emotion flickering between them, but it flutters away before I can catch it.

"Well, then." In a burst of motion, the Manor Lord shifts forward in her chair again, clapping her hands together decisively, "I will be eagerly awaiting your Nomination Hearing, in that case. I must say, the Nomination rites can get rather tedious once you've performed them as many times as I—but your candidacy, Archdaughter, will spark quite the debate."

She lifts a hand, twirling her index finger lazily in a wordless command. At her signal, the host of servants rushes forth from the shadows once more, silver trays held aloft. They swirl around us, depositing dishes and straightening silverware, then fade away again, the only sound of their departure the soft brush of their steps against the thick burgundy rug.

Lord Ianthe picks up her fork, thrusting it toward the rest of us like a spear. "Eat," she urges, "enjoy it while you can." Her gaze turns to me. "If you do join me on the Council, dear, you will soon find that the privileges afforded to us Manorborn taste much sweeter when you are not also the one bearing their weight."

The remainder of dinner passes with all the rigid formality of a school lesson, dragging on for an eternity until finally the cake plates are cleared and the final teacup drained, and Cressida, Tom, and I are at last ushered out of the Roost by the same closed-lipped butler who welcomed us only a few hours prior. The front door has just swung shut behind us, our carriages waiting loyally up ahead, ready to ferry us away, when I reach to pin up a stray curl that's brushing the nape of my neck and freeze.

"My comb," I gasp, feeling the back of my head for the pearl-toothed ornament that had previously been affixed there and grasping only a handful of blond hair instead. I bite my lip, directing a pleading look at Cressida and Tom, who have come to a begrudging halt next to me. "It must have come loose during dinner—I didn't notice."

Cressida *tsks*. "Leave it. No jewelry is worth subjecting oneself to that torture again."

Tom nods in agreement, already stepping forward, but I stay where I am. "My mother gifted it to me."

My cousin and his wife exchange looks—his sympathetic, hers irked. In the end, though, Cressida relents, sighing reluctantly through her nose.

"Fine," she says, waving me back toward the entrance. "Be quick about it."

With a rushed thank-you, I hurry back inside and past the frazzled butler, who calls after me. I throw the man a placating smile over my shoulder but don't stop, quickening my pace when he starts in my direction. Gathering my skirt in my arms, the purple fabric pooling in my hold like a bundle of picked lavender, I retrace the path to the dining room, darting through the entry hall, into the main corridor—

"—not one but *two* chances fate has handed you, and yet here you have managed to fumble them both."

I stop, catching my breath at the sound of a voice—chastising, even waspish, as if it carries a sting. Up ahead, the door to the dining room is open. Lord Ianthe and Ames linger over the threshold, him slouching against the doorframe, her standing erect and resolute in front of him, her shoulders curled censoriously. Light from the chandelier inside spills over them, petaling their features with gold.

As I watch, Ames shakes his head. Though I am too far down the hallway to make out his expression, his movements are strained despite his relaxed posture, as if his dispassion is only a mask, held loosely over his face. "You rush to conclusions, Mother. Nothing has been lost. We still may—"

His chin whips violently to the right, a noise like snapping reins bounding along the corridor toward me. I do not realize, initially, what has happened—not until I see Ianthe's raised hand, her arm rigid, punishing as a blade. See Ames clutching his cheek, hunching over himself as if he's trying not to cry out.

She hit him. She—

"Your Eminence! Your Eminence, the guests have returned."

The butler bursts into the hallway behind me, then slows to a waddle, bracing his hands against his thighs as he wheezes. Irritation wells in me, rapidly turning to fear as Ames and Lord Ianthe both shift to look my way.

"Archdaughter," Lord Ianthe says, stepping forward. She tilts her head to the side, examining me pensively. "I believed you'd left us."

The heels of her slippers click menacingly over the stone floor as she draws nearer, her expression intrigued but unflustered. Though she must know I witnessed her argument with Ames, just now—the punishing force of her blow—she makes no move to acknowledge the action or apologize for it. Instead, her pale green eyes drill into mine, as if daring me to challenge her.

"Actually, Mother." Ames strides forward, clasping a hand over his mother's shoulder with an affection that curdles me, after seeing what I have seen. The echo of Lord Ianthe's slap seems to hang in the air, thickening the atmosphere like milk gone sour. "I'd forgotten—I'd promised to take Archdaughter Merrick to view our gardens before she departed, if you would permit it," Ames says, nodding at me. "Thank you, Archdaughter, for holding me to my offer."

"I . . ." My reply lodges in my throat, my pulse skipping at his unexpected address—and his blatant lie. Aside from his initial winked greeting, Ames paid me little attention during the course of our meal—though not unfriendly, I had the distinct impression that he'd hardly registered my presence, his gaze vacant, trapped in some other world. It reminded me of the abrupt way his mood had shifted the morning he'd escorted me back to Norland, one moment longing, the next distant, all as sudden as turning a corner.

Now, though, his blue eyes are on me, warm and inviting as if they'd never left.

"Did you?" Lord Ianthe's response is contemplative, as if beneath the question she is posing, there is another answer she wishes to discern as well. Her brow furrows and I ready for her refusal, but then Ames coughs, his eyebrow twitching upward. It's a minor shift, hardly noticeable; somehow, though, I sense the message in it, like a private plea between them.

With a hum that reverberates down the length of the hall, Lord Ianthe nods her approval to Ames. "Well, I'll not have any son of mine breaking his promises. Go ahead, darling—some fresh air will do you young people good, so long as the Archdaughter is fine with the arrangement."

Her neck swivels in my direction, the test in her words apparent. "I—it sounds lovely," I stammer to Ames. "I should be delighted to accompany you."

Ames grins. Navigating carefully around his mother, he approaches me, extending his arm. I take it, following him back up the corridor, past Lord Ianthe and the dining room entrance, toward the heart of the house. The scent of his cologne catches in my nostrils, leafy and charred, like an expensive cigar.

With sure, easy steps, he leads me into one side hallway and then another, his profile illuminated by the soft glow emanating from the lit sconces along the walls. The flames cup his chin and jaw like tender hands, and I think, briefly and irrationally, that the effect suits him—that he is one of those people made for dusk, when his fierce beauty is dulled just enough that it is almost possible to believe you can hold it without being cut.

The silence itches at me, clinging and uncomfortable; after a minute, I cast it off. "Ames," I start. "I only came back for my comb—you don't need to—"

"Shh." He cuts me off, a finger rising surreptitiously to his lips. I fall quiet as he inclines his head, nodding toward a point farther along the corridor we're passing through—where, I see with a start, a Saint sentry is stationed, the man's blank profile painted white by the moonlight spilling through the picture windows. "They are loyal to her, not me," Ames murmurs softly. "Be wary of what you say."

His tone is low, barely above a whisper; still, as if he can hear us, the sentry's chin turns our way at Ames's comment. The man's eyes lock onto mine, glittering darkly like a pair of black pearls.

Swallowing, I give Ames a nod.

We don't speak after that. Finally, we exit the Roost entirely, passing through a pair of double doors—whisked open by two servants—and onto a paved terrace jutting out from the back of the estate. Here, the air is cooler than it was inside, crisp and pleasant as a fresh set of sheets. Breathing it in makes me feel looser, the tension retreating from my arms and back, letting me move freely once more.

Ames drops his arm, breaking our touch, and lets out a whooshing exhale. "Sorry about that," he murmurs, twisting to face me—at ease now. "I didn't mean to corner you into consoling me—you're free to go back to your relatives anytime you like. I'll show you the way. But what you saw back there—what you heard . . ." Consciously or unconsciously—I am not sure—his fingers drift toward his cheek, which is flushed red from the impact of his mother's palm. "My mother has a bit of a temper, I'm afraid," he says apologetically. "And like many powerful people, she dislikes it when her pawns reject her control."

Her pawns. I wonder if it is himself Ames was speaking of just now, or me. Now that the shock of her striking him has faded a bit, Lord Ianthe's words come back to me: *two chances fate has handed you, and yet here you have managed to fumble them both.*

Slowly, I walk forward, leaning on the colonnaded railing surrounding the terrace. Beyond it, the gardens spill out, silver-tipped by the stars. In the dimness, their beauty is transformed, monochromatic and strange but undiminished: a field of satin flowers, swaying gently in the night breeze.

"Does it happen often?" I say, casting the words away from Ames so they drift above the grounds. "Her . . . temper, as you put it . . . flaring up in that manner?"

Ames sighs, coming to stand next to me. He tips his head back, his nostrils flaring to inhale the fragrant, floral scent of the gardens.

"Only when someone has displeased her. So, more than often, one might say," he responds after a moment, with a wry smile that falls flat, sliding quickly from his lips. "I am not sure what all you overheard—primarily, she is upset with me for failing to sway you toward an alliance. After my father died, when I returned to the Roost, she gave me a . . . mission, let's call it." His shoulders stiffen, disgust trailing over his features. "She wished me to get close to you Darling girls—you, and your sister. Your father never warmed to her, back when he was alive, so she supposed she'd try to worm her way into his good graces through you."

His knuckles tighten over the balcony railing. "Ianthe Saint and her gods-damned mind games."

His resentment is deep: a frigid, bottomless well. I glance over at him, perturbed, and find him already looking at me. The sapphire blue of his irises has gone dark, inscrutable as the sea.

Then he blinks, and his anger cracks like spring ice, fading into the darkness. "Forgive my language, Archdaughter," he says with a bashful dip of his head. "I only mean to say, I know what it's like to find oneself trapped beneath my mother's magnifying lens. It aggravated me to see you subjected to the same torment at dinner earlier, when you've done nothing to deserve it."

I knit my brows, shifting instinctively away from him. "And what of how you've treated me?" I reply, my sympathy for him giving way to a spike of indignation as I take in his statement, the nature of his *mission,* as he termed it. "These last few weeks, the . . ."

Heat creeps up my neck as I tumble into the past, how closely he held me when we danced at the ball, the night Essie disappeared. The hours I spent reliving the event afterward, lying in my bed in the dark, retracing the path his fingers had mapped over my arms. "The conversations we've had," I finally stammer, reorienting myself. "The help you've offered me. Was all of it just an effort to appease *her*?"

"Merrick, no." Ames's denial comes swiftly and without hesitation, his expression stricken. When I shoot him a reproachful look, though, his certainty seems to dim, a shadow of guilt visible in the nervous way he gnaws at his lip. "All right, I'll admit that with Es—with your sister, perhaps it was," he admits, tossing his hair. "I called on her a couple times while you were in New London, but I think she scented my motives right away." His mouth lifts in a bashful half smile. "She was too clever for me by a long shot. With you, though . . ." Sliding atop the stone railing, Ames's hand reaches for mine. I pull away from his touch, wary, lifting my chin toward him.

He meets my gaze head-on, unashamed. Even in my unease, his attention is enthralling, brazen and deliberate in a way that makes me feel stripped bare. "I told you when I found you in that storm—ever since our first meeting, I've felt as though I know you," he says in a hushed tone that makes all the hairs on my arms stand up. "You did not say if you feel the same. Do you?"

"I . . ." There is an unfamiliar sensation pressing against my diaphragm, like a river swelling past its banks. How has he managed to turn the conversation back toward me—so smoothly, slipping the blade from my grasp without my even realizing it has been taken? My skin is buzzing, stinging as if rubbed with salt.

"I am not sure," I manage to respond, somehow. "At times I feel as though I cannot read you at all."

Ames's stare is total, swallowing me whole. "And at others?" he whispers.

"Then, yes. I have sensed a . . . connection, I suppose you could say." I blush. "A similarity of our dispositions."

"Merrick." He speaks my name gently, like a caress—like a

confession made to me alone. Hesitantly, he reaches for my hand again, and this time I let him take it. His lips are an inch from mine, close enough that I can feel the warm brush of his breath when he speaks.

"I understand why you turned down my offer earlier," he says. "Why you won't take our sentries, even if you need them."

I lean back, unbalanced by the change in subject. "You do?"

He nods fervently. "Mother always said that to accept one thing is to release another—usually, power," he explains. "Between Manors, even neighboring ones, there can never truly be friendship. Only alliances. *Deals.*"

His fingers tighten around me, drawing me in. "Let me be your friend, Merrick. Marry me."

It is the absolute last thing I expect him to say. I choke out a laugh. "You don't mean that."

"I do." Ames's response is immediate, swelling with cold certainty. His gaze is steady as he speaks, the sure, unmoving blue of a promise. "What my mother said tonight, about your Nomination causing debate—as unpleasant as she is, she is not wrong," Ames goes on urgently. "Your situation is precarious, at best. Trouble at the border is one thing, but your candidacy is also rushed, a patch over the wound of your sister's death. It will be easy for the Council to argue that your claim to the Lordship is a weak one."

A patch over the wound. I flinch at that, its harsh bite—and its truth. Cressida may assure me otherwise as many times as she wishes, but in the sour pit of my stomach I remember the lesson my father taught me almost half a year ago: that the Darling throne was carved for my sister, and not me. Wanting does not change that; being given the Nomination does not change that. Nothing can.

At best, I am a legitimized thief. Why would the Council support me? Why would anyone?

"I do not say any of this to upset you." Ames must see the crush of self-pity in my features, because he presses his thumb comfortingly into the heel of my palm, pulling me back to reality. "Listen, Merrick," he soothes, "society was not kind to my mother when she was young, and its cruelty made her cruel in turn. But she is also shrewd, and ever since my father passed, I have spent the last year studying her."

With his free hand, he rubs at his jaw, as if working loose an idea. "If Mother believes that she can convince the other Lords to do the same, she will vote against you at the Nomination Hearing, and encourage them to instead install someone more malleable—someone she can influence," Ames says. "Yet if you were my fiancée—if we were to be wed—your interests and mine would become one. It is the same principle that governed your cousin's union: two healthy Manors strengthen each other, like roots feeding the same tree. My mother could not maim you without also injuring me—and thereby, herself."

Delicately—so delicately—Ames brushes at a loose curl, tucking it behind my ear. "Our families have failed us both in their own ways, but united, we could defy any doubt they—or anyone else—raise against us," he murmurs. "We could lead Sussex and Cardiff into a new era, one where the only roles we'd have to play would be the ones we crafted for ourselves. We could find your sister's killer, could carve out every inch of our provinces until we brought them to justice, if that's what it takes. All you have to do is say yes."

No.

Essie's voice resounds in my mind, pure and pealing as a bell. The sister I was raised with, I am positive, would never take what Ames is offering me—would not even be tempted by the idea of it. She would say that our province was our burden, to bear and raise alone. That she'd prefer to lose her claim to Sussex entirely

249

than share it with another, watch them stake their name in her land.

But the sister I was raised with is gone.

A heat blossoms inside me, a recklessness.

"What do you want, Merrick? Safety? Love? I can give you that." Ames's whisper is satin and stone, making my every nerve hum with energy. One of his fingers idly traces the curve of my lower lip, back and forth. "I can give you more."

I don't know who moves first, only that we come together. My arms snake around his neck as he lifts me, my body birdlike and weightless in his arms. Bending down, he presses his mouth against mine. He tastes like lavender and wind, like the steep ecstasy of Sussex's seaside cliffs, joy almost tipping into danger, and when I kiss him it feels like a fever, a foreign sort of warmth. His hands find mine and then he's gripping them, guiding my bare fingers into his hair. I wind one hand through the sweat-sticky strands at the base of his neck and let the other trail down his back, feeling the way his muscles shift as he adjusts his hold on me, bringing me closer still—

I break away, my mind fractured glass. "All—all right," I rasp. My body feels scraped raw, aching as if bruised. I resist the urge to do a quick inventory of my limbs, ensure that none have fallen away.

Ames opens his mouth, then closes it again. "All right?" he repeats, a bit breathlessly.

I draw a long inhale, then nod. "Yes," I agree. "I'll do it. I'll marry you."

He watches me, biting his lip. I raise my palm to his chest—to push him away or draw him closer, I'm not sure—but then the breeze picks up, blowing indigo clouds across the moon, and darkness wraps us in its ebony wings and we say no more.

CHAPTER TWENTY-THREE

We remain on the terrace for another ten minutes, or perhaps it is an hour—time moves strangely around us after that first kiss, bending like a river, puddling, stilling in the seconds when his skin meets mine. It is clear, by the delicate, intentional way he holds me, the practiced grace with which he whispers low words in my ear, that he has done this before, but even so, I cannot bring myself to care. Being with him, touching him, feels like a swallow of wine: an escape, as if the press of his fingers has released some weight from me, removed the anxious strain of the worries that I have lashed around my shoulders these past weeks.

It is addictive, this feeling.

We separate only when my prickling awareness of Cressida and Tom, waiting in front of the house for me, becomes too distracting to bear. Though he offers, I reject Ames's attempts to walk me out, allowing him to see me only to the entry hall. Yet when we reach it, I pause, the grand front doors like a sheer expanse of rock, somehow—impassable.

Sensing my hesitation, Ames plucks playfully at my elbow. "What is it?" he asks, gazing down at me. "Scared to give them the news? Relatives do hate it when one does one's own match-making for them. I'm sure the Duchess was dying to fix you up with a cousin of hers." Grinning slyly, he loops an arm around my middle, drawing me closer and nuzzling at my ear. "Marrying a Saint—how wicked."

His breath is warm, tickling me like a blast of oven-heated air, and it makes me redden—the intimacy of the gesture, and of his words. *Marrying a Saint.* Have I truly agreed to such a thing? What will Cressida say?

What will Killian?

Let us speak candidly. The issue isn't Ames's trustworthiness at all, is it? In my mind, my own voice rises like a specter, sneering and cruel. My stomach flipping queasily, I push the memory aside. "It's nothing," I say to Ames. "I'm considering how to phrase every-thing, is all."

He leans his torso away, still retaining his hold on me, and for a flash of a second, I wonder if he will see it: the lie in my eyes, the seed of doubt. But he only smirks, reaching forward to wind a ringlet of my hair around his knuckle. "I'll come see you soon," he says, ducking to give me a lingering farewell kiss. "Think of me often, will you?"

And then, with a wink, he is leaving me, striding back into the deep golden bowels of his estate. I watch him for a while, waiting to see whether he'll go on—or if, perhaps, he'll look back, come running to rescue me from the challenge of facing my relatives at all. Take my burdens away for good, the way it felt like he had when he kissed me.

But he does no such thing, and I walk out alone.

Outside, Cressida is pacing the width of the drive, the gravel crunching beneath her heeled slippers, while Tom and Killian linger anxiously behind her. Killian's gaze finds me first; I watch as the worry leaves his eyes when he registers me, his expression opening like a door swung wide. He gives a shout, and Cressida's and Tom's heads rise in unison to follow the sound, their stares quickly landing on my figure.

"Merrick." Cressida's address has none of the warmth that I glimpsed in Killian's expression, only a wintry disdain, as if I have failed her expectations and met them at once. She steps forward, and I move to meet her, making my way down the front stone steps. "Where in the Lightkeeper's name have you *been*?"

I tuck a loose curl behind my ear, at once conscious of how mussed I must look—my hair pulled half free of its updo where Ames wound his fingers through it, my dress wrinkled. Suddenly, I am intensely grateful for the lack of daylight, the night sky a raven cloak around me, obscuring my flaws from view. "I ran into Ames."

Cressida pauses, momentarily caught off guard by the brusqueness of my excuse. "Oh—all right, then," she says before steadying herself and continuing in a sharper tone, "I hope he apologized for his mother's beastliness. That woman . . ."

"He asked me to marry him."

It is as if my words cast a kind of curse: in the same breath, all three of them go still, caught in the current of what I've said. Even in the dimness, the shock on their expressions is clear—stark and bold as a lightning strike—but though Cressida is nearest to me, it's Killian to whom my attention is drawn. His lips are slightly parted, his skin pale beneath his scars, and as I watch, his brow furrows, creasing with the barest trace of emotion. Not noticeable if you weren't looking for it; barely there at all, like an impression in clay.

It feels like a blade driven into my stomach.

Cressida breaks free of her stupor first. "Excuse me?"

Her voice is dangerously soft, the gentle coil of a cat just before it leaps at you. I turn my attention back to her, grateful for the excuse to pull myself away from Killian. "He said he understood why we wouldn't accept his offer of aid," I tell Cressida evenly. "That he knew we couldn't afford to be indebted to another Manor, even if we needed his men. And then he asked me to marry him." I swallow, the memory of Ames's offer—of his kiss—pinkening my cheeks like rouge. "He told me . . . that if we were wed, we could exchange resources freely. Help one another, as Lord Elodie has helped us. And that Lord Ianthe would have no choice but to support me, her son's fiancée at the Nomination Hearing, lest she weaken her own Manor."

"And what did you say?"

Killian's voice cuts through the darkness, raising the hairs on my arm. In front of me, Cressida whips her head around to face him, the slice of the indignant frown I catch on her features letting me know she isn't pleased he's spoken out of turn, but Killian doesn't meet her gaze. Instead, he's watching me steadily, his blue eye almost silver in the starlight, his expression set with a focused—almost greedy—intensity. As if he wants to crack me open, pluck my answer from my chest.

I level my stare with his as I answer him. "I said yes."

Between Killian and Cressida, Tom utters a loud curse, springing into motion at last. "Divine Three be damned, Merrick," he growls, shaking his head. I glance over at him in time to see his mouth curl in a grimace, his right hand fisting by her side. "What were you thinking?"

"No—Tom, wait a moment." Cressida holds up a palm, stopping her husband short. Concentration ridging her brow, she twists back my way. "Ames said Ianthe would support your Nomination at the Hearing, if you were to marry?" she asks carefully. "That she would be in favor of this—this union?"

Her demeanor has shifted during the course of our conversation, I notice. Her initial distress at my announcement is gradually draining away, being replaced by a shrewd sort of curiosity. Encouraged, I nod.

My cousin-in-law breaks into a smile, the glint of her white teeth against the night taking me aback. "Well, then." She tilts her head to the side, assessing me with new approval. "I daresay, you may have made yourself quite the match."

Snapping her fingers, she beckons to her husband. "Congratulate your cousin, Tom," she instructs. "We'll need to ensure the *Toast* hears about this immediately, of course. Perhaps even offer them an exclusive if they allow us approval over their profile—they adore feeling special." Businesslike now, she turns and begins to make her way back down the drive, where our carriages are still waiting. When she's gone a few steps, she looks back at me over her shoulder, her expression more cheerful than I've ever seen it. It makes a stone slide into my gut. "This is excellent news, dear, excellent," she says. "The longer I consider it, the more I believe it truly is. The Council will not be able to deny you now. Who wishes to say no to a bride?"

The ride back home is agonizing, silence sitting like a third companion between Killian and me throughout the painful hours of our return journey. The dark countryside rolls by us in great ebony waves, the horizon rising and falling in the distance until at last the blackness parts, a familiar shape looming large outside my carriage window. Norland. We've made it back to Sussex.

Beyond the window glass, our estate waits like a fretful mother, eager to greet us. Farther down the drive behind Killian and me, I can hear the steady crunch of gravel as Cressida and Tom's carriage rolls up, slows to a halt.

Across from me, Killian clears his throat. "Good night, Arch-daughter. A privilege spending time with you, as always."

His words are a lobbed stone—by the time they reach me, he is already gone, throwing the carriage door open and descending the fold-out wooden step to the ground. Gravel grinds under the heels of his boots as he turns back to aid me in my exit, proffering his arm to me stiffly.

Hesitantly, I take it. His muscles are wooden under my fingers, ungiving as I lean against him. Briefly, his gaze flicks to mine—it is vacant, the marble gape of a statue.

"Mr. Brandon," I start, unsure of what will come after, yet unable to leave him without offering some sort of . . . explanation? Absolution? "Killian, I—"

I break off, my attention snagging on a flicker of motion past the bulk of our estate, near the start of the woodland. There, where the manicured flora of the gardens frays into wilderness, a shape is outlined against the ragged edge of the tree line, white and ethereal in the moonlight. A shiver goes through me at the sight of it, an insect-scuttle of trepidation down my spine. *Another Phantom?*

Across the grounds, the figure slows, as if my attention is a fishhook, caught on its collar. Aside from its tangled swath of midnight hair, its whole body is that same blue-white, like the cold heat at the very center of a flame, like the heart of winter, like a spill of fresh milk. It is clad in what from this distance looks to be a dress of some kind—torn ivory tendrils of fabric wisp spectrally over the grass as it glides forward, muddy stains darkening at least the bottom five inches of the garment's hem.

The figure turns—its neck whipping to the side with a ferocity that makes me gasp—revealing a sharp, bladed profile, the pink smudge of a mouth. A pair of eyes, traversing the distance between us. Locking onto mine.

Not a Phantom. The realization is a knife twist in my gut, certain as a pang of hunger, as seeing myself in a mirror: I know this girl. Have felt the infant-squeeze of her child hand in mine when we were small, my earliest and most steadfast ally. Have smelled the crack of her heart like blood on the wind as I walked away from her years later, my final and most sorrowful enemy.

This girl is a ghost. This girl is dead.

And yet somehow, she's here, a stark white vision among the trees. She's back.

My sister.

PART THREE

Resurrections

Metamorphosis is painful for the creature that
is changing. For one form, it is the end.

> **EXCERPTED FROM** *ON PHANTOMS: A HUMANE*
> *STUDY OF OUR BEASTLY COUSINS,* **BY JEDIDIAH**
> **ADAMS**

And with the spilling of my blood, may the blood
of my people be spared. And with the death
of my old self, may I be raised eternal in my Manor . . .
now sting me, knife, and see how I shall live!

> **LORD ACACIA BLESSED DARLING, 11TH**
> **MANOR LORD OF SUSSEX, ON THE EVE OF**
> **HER NOMINATION HEARING**

CHAPTER TWENTY-FOUR

The New London Toast

Sunday, October 5, Year 211 of the Turning

A MIRACLE AT THE MANOR: After vanishing from her bed following her father's Memorial Ball, Archdaughter Estella Darling has returned unharmed to Norland House, this paper was notified in a special dispatch. An anonymous source close to the Darling family has exclusively revealed to the *Toast* that following her homecoming, the Archdaughter chronicled a daring escape from captors who had been holding her deep within Barton Woods. Though the identities of these criminals, and the reasons for their abduction, remain a mystery, the Archdaughter purportedly revealed to her relations that she believed she was being kept alive at the request of another, unknown party, who her captors implied wished to meet with her in the days before her ultimate escape.

Vessel of the late Lord Silas Darling, Archdaughter Estella is currently recovering at her family estate, where she is under the care of her relatives, including the Red Duke and Duchess of Sussex, Thomas Darling and Cressida Faulk-Darling, and her sister, the Archdaughter Merrick Darling. As of the publication of this paper, her abductors remain at large.

CONTINUED INSIDE:

~Estella's lady's maid tells all: why the Archdaughter may have suspected she was in danger prior to her disappearance.

~Sibling rivalries: Archdaughter Merrick in tears over losing the Lordship!

SCENES FROM THE SMOKE: The latest in the lives of the Manorborn

~Multiple sources confirm that Manor Lord Reginald Ibe and his wife, the Manor Lady Della Ibe, have been living separately for the past fortnight, following Lady Della's discovery of a monthslong affair between the Lord and an unknown woman, rumored to be one of the Ibes' own chambermaids.

~After a whirlwind courtship, Sir Fitzgerald Vannett and Miss Amelia Crowe have wed in a private ceremony at the Vannett Manor seat of Blackbriar. The happy couple is expected to travel to

Southhook for an extended holiday before returning to Heatherton.

~Archdaughter Merrick Darling and Archson Ames Saint, of the Darling and Saint Manors, respectively, are engaged, several reports claim. No official betrothal announcement has yet been made.

That first night following Essie's reappearance, I kept searching for the seams of an illusion. I would glance at her and then skeptically back over the landscape outside her bedroom window to see if it had changed in the minute since I last looked, whether the horizon had shifted like in a dream. But the trees beyond the glass remained rooted firmly in their places, and so did she, solid and true as if she had never left.

About the men who took her, she knows almost nothing—not their identities, nor the reason for their assault. The few details she was able to provide to Cressida, Tom, and me when we questioned her—crowded by the fire in my father's library the night of her return, wrapping blanket after blanket around her bony shoulders—were vague. Her attackers, she told us, ambushed her the night of Father's ball, pulling her from sleep roughly, with the muzzle of a pistol pressed to her forehead. If she screamed, they warned her, they would shoot her, then creep down the hallway and find me.

They took her deep into Barton Woods, pausing only once, when they forced her to change out of her muddied nightgown, slashing her arm and rubbing the fabric with her blood—a ploy, she thinks, to ensure that any attempts to search for her quickly met a quite literal dead end. She does not know the exact location of where she was kept, only that it was damp and earthen, possibly an abandoned root cellar, and that the few times her captors spoke to her—always masked, with scraps of cloth wrapped round their noses and mouths—they mentioned a master. Someone they were holding her on behalf of, who wished for her to be kept alive until their meeting.

She escaped before she had the chance to thank them for that kindness.

Beyond that is blankness. When I'd tried to press her further—to ask about the threat on her pillow, whether she had any idea of who might have penned it, or what it meant—Cressida cut in swiftly, insisting that my sister was too weak for additional inter-rogation. Once she'd had time to rest, my cousin-in-law said, we could revisit such subjects, but until then, Essie needed peace. Quiet.

The next day is consumed by a steady parade of physicians progressing in and out of Essie's quarters, where she's been se-questered by Cressida until she's proven well enough to move about freely. With their constant, hovering presence eating up all the space in the room, I don't get the opportunity to speak to my sister at length again until her second full day back at Norland, the same morning the *Toast* breaks the story on her reappearance—and my engagement. The shock of Ames's pro-posal has been dulled by the larger upset caused by Essie's re-turn, so that apart from a few rushed congratulations from my relatives, I have barely had the ability to dwell on the promise I made to the Saint Vessel at all. Aside from a bouquet of roses de-livered to me by a Saint footman the morning after our dinner at the Roost, I haven't heard from him, either, nor has he made any effort to announce our engagement officially, beyond a few rumors. His distance makes me wonder whether he is regretting his offer. Whether he still finds me as enthralling, as admirable, now that it is no longer I who will wear my Manor's crown.

I shiver as I approach the door to Essie's room. The air has turned chillier over the past couple nights—frost slinking in on stealthy feet and then settling, the temperature plunging in a sudden snap like a snow-heavy branch—and I feel the cold bite of the floorboards even through the silken soles of my slippers. Aside from myself, Essie, and the staff, Norland house is empty this morning, Tom and Cressida having gone into town just after dawn to attend to a few last-minute details relating to the upcoming Nomination Hearing. With the time it takes to travel there and back, I know they won't return for a few hours, at least—meaning for now, my sister and I are alone.

It is an opportunity I refuse to waste.

I flex my fist tighter, listening for the reassuring crinkle of the note within. Cressida has yet to lift her ban on discussing Essie's disappearance with her, and though I understand that my sister needs to heal, I haven't been able to stop myself from dwelling on her abduction—and, more pressingly, how little we still know about it. The men in the woods . . . the mysterious figure they worked for, who wanted to speak with Essie . . . it throbs against my skull like a head cold, the fact that they're still out there. That with every second we do not catch them, they could be regrouping, like roaches gathering behind a crack in a wall, waiting for the moment they can swarm forth again. They let Essie escape once; if they come for us a second time, I have a horrible feeling they will not repeat their mistake.

Darling Manor will fall.

Besides Essie's memories, the threat from her room is the sole clue that could lead us to their identities. Perhaps if I show it to her, I can spark something—a realization she hadn't known she was holding back. It's a thin chance, I know this; for now, though, it's also the only one I have.

Rubbing at my arms to warm myself, I knock hesitantly on Essie's door and call a greeting, half expecting silence—for my sister to deny me entry, as she did when it was I who'd come home, and not she.

But her voice rings out immediately, clear and cheery, if a bit weak.

"Merrick. Come in."

I obey, opening the door and closing it after me as I slip inside. In the cheery wakefulness of the morning, it is difficult to reconcile the bright, open space before me with the sinister den the room appeared to be the night of my father's ball. Sunlight pours through the open windows, frothy and luminous, the pale color of ale; the floors are well-swept, and my sister's book collection is newly straightened along the back of her desk, the jewel-tone spines glinting with a reptilian sheen like snakeskin.

Essie, too, has undergone a transformation. She observes me from her bed, half sitting up with her sheets tucked tightly around her middle, her ebony hair in a loose plait over one shoulder. Though evidence of her recent trials may be seen in the collection of shallow scrapes and gashes along her arms and chest, and her cheeks have a gauntness about them, derived from weeks of malnourishment, her skin is glowing—practically radiant, with a rosy tint to it like the red flush of a summer strawberry. She smiles at me as I enter the room, a full grin, unrestrained by the constant anxiety that seemed to haunt her in the days leading up to my father's ball.

It is strange, but if I didn't know better, I'd almost say she looks healthier now than when she vanished. The miracle of her survival must have heartened her, filled her with the sense of invincibility our sentries get when they face down a monster and return unscathed.

Crossing to her, I sink into the wooden chair that's been positioned by her bedside for the physicians' use and take her hand, tucking the threat into the pocket of my dress, where it rests against the fabric like a stone. Her fingers twine willingly with mine, warm, her grip unexpectedly strong. "How are you feeling?" I ask, leaning to brush a stray lock of black hair from her forehead.

Laughing, Essie swats me away. "Perfectly fine," she answers, her teeth winking like pearls in her smile. "You're like a hovering mama—all of you," she chides playfully. "I've told Cressida, if there's anything that might kill me, it'll be you lot's worrying."

I frown, chastened, and loosen my hold on her reluctantly. "I thought I would never see you again."

She sobers at that, the mirth fading from her face. I immediately feel like a villain for stealing it from her—for slipping my fears like a noose around her neck, one more weight for her to bear. "I know," Essie says softly. "So did I. But I'm here."

She squeezes my hand, and a fierce rush of appreciation gusts through me anew at the reminder of her presence. "Thank you for everything you did to try to find me, Merrick, while I was gone," Essie continues, gratitude roughening her tone. Then, guilt passing like a breeze over her features, she gnaws at her cheek, looking away. "I never should have kept secrets from you," she says, picking at a thread along the hem of her sheets. "I was just so frightened—and through some twisted logic, I was convinced that if I shared my anxieties with you, I'd be bringing you into it, in a way. Making it all real."

"It's all right," I say, turning her chin gently back toward me so she can see the truth in my expression. "Killian explained it to me."

I want to cup her jaw—to gather her to my chest like a field mouse, a creature I can tuck between my palms and protect from harm—but I force myself to sit back, releasing her. "You truly know nothing of what they wanted—the men who took you?" I ask instead, hesitantly. "Nothing about their allegiances? Who they were working for?"

Essie's shoulders droop at my inquiry, as if a heavy cloak has been slung over them. Sighing, she gives a slow, weary shake of her head. "I wish I could give a different answer, but no," she replies. "They asked nothing of me for the entirety of the time I spent with them. No demands, no requests for a ransom of any sort. They didn't so much as lay a finger on me, aside from the cut on my arm they gave me in Barton Woods." She bites her lip, her expression clouding over. "I . . . I got the sense that their master, whoever that may be, wanted me in good condition when he came for me," she admits, and my skin erupts into prickles. "It was by pure luck that I escaped. The men would rotate shifts, guarding me—there were two of them, in total—and one was a drinker. The night I got away, he'd fallen asleep on his stool, and his bottle of ale had fallen to the ground and shattered. I was able to reach a piece of broken glass and use it to cut the ropes they'd tied me with." She pauses briefly, her voice quivering as she goes on. "The whole time, I kept waiting for him to wake up and realize what I was doing. To kill me."

Another stab of self-loathing punctures me at her words—how close she'd come to death while I remained here, safe. My hand drifting to my side, I trace the outline of the note in my pocket, readying myself to reach for it, when a knock at the door interrupts my efforts.

I turn, expecting one of the number of physicians I've encountered in our halls over the past couple days—only to startle when I discover they're nowhere to be found. In their place, framed in the doorway, bronzed and blond like an extension of the morning itself, is Ames Saint.

And he's staring at Essie as though he's seen a ghost.

CHAPTER TWENTY-FIVE

"Archdaughter."

Ames doesn't differentiate between the two of us in his address, but his focus is so singular—tethered to my sister like a mooring line to a ship—that there is no question to whom he is speaking. His expression has an awestruck quality to it: a dazed, ensorcelled disbelief that comes with witnessing an act of the divine, or the work of the devil.

"So it's true, then," Ames says, his voice barely above a murmur. "You've come back."

There's a rawness to his tone that unsettles me, a lack of formality—of any boundaries at all—that feels different from any way he has spoken to me before. My stomach lurches with something like envy. I know Ames and my sister are familiar, but this level of emotion . . . it seems well past the realm of acquaintanceship.

I cough, if only to remind myself that I am here as well, that I have not disappeared simply because Ames is not looking at me. "Ames?" I ask. "What are you doing here?"

At last, Ames's eyes flick my way, widen as if registering my presence for the first time. Like stripping off a coat, he seems to extricate himself from whatever trance has taken hold of him, dipping into a bow of greeting. "Archdaughter Merrick—my apologies," he says hurriedly, rising. "Your butler showed me in. He told me I might find you here."

A beat of silence passes, cut short by a stilted chuckle from Ames as he realizes he's left my question unanswered. His barked laughter is dry, forced—absent of the suaveness I have come to expect from him. I hazard a look at Essie, but she's tucked wordlessly among her pillows, her mouth dipping in perplexity.

"Forgive me," Ames says to me, pulling my attention back to him. "I've come to see you, of course, and—and to congratulate your family on your sister's safe return." His gaze drifts back to Essie, but there's a restraint in it now; he only observes her sidelong, as if anything more direct would burn him. "Your reappearance is nothing short of a miracle, Archdaughter Estella," he says, ducking his head in another half bow.

Essie gives an appreciative, if somewhat baffled, smile at his comment. "Thank you, sir," she says, patting my hand, which is still lying beneath hers. "And congratulations to you, Archson, on the happy news of your engagement. You are a very lucky man indeed."

Ames grins—but am I imagining it, or is his expression strained? "That I am," he answers with a wink in my direction. Donning his top hat, which he's been clutching protectively in front of him like a torch in the Graylands, he sighs decisively. "Well, I must be going," he says, raising a conspiratorial brow at Essie. "Archdaughter, perhaps together we can tempt your lovely sister to show me out?"

He's leaving already? Essie seems as thrown by Ames's abrupt departure as I do, but she shifts obligingly away from me, swatting at the air as if encouraging me to go. Muttering a *thank you* under my breath, I rise from my chair, nodding amiably at Ames before following him into the corridor.

The second the door clicks closed behind us, I wheel on him, my muscles already tensed.

"Ames, what is the matter?" I hiss, stepping nearer to him—close enough that he has to tilt his head down to follow my movements. I want to be able to study him, to catch any tics in his behavior and pin them down like moths on a bit of cork for my examination. "Back there, you seemed"—I fumble for an appropriate term, landing only on—"agitated, I suppose."

"The matter?" Ames laughs, cool and elegant like ice clinking in a glass. "Nothing, of course—I am not sure what you mean." Leaning against the doorframe, he reaches for me, drawing me toward him and cradling my waist with one arm. "I am only glad to see you."

His free hand trails down the length of my dress, pressing down just above my hip. His touch is lazy, seductive in its exploration, and at it, my thoughts fuzz, latent desire unspooling within me. The sense memory of him leaps to the surface of my skin, heated trails where he touched me, my lips chapped with his kiss—

I break away from him, and instantly, my mind clears. "Don't pretend," I snap, crossing my arms defensively over my chest like a barrier between us. "Something disturbed you, just now—it was obvious. Are you . . ." My resolve wavers, but I grit my teeth, forcing myself to push out the anxiety that's lodged itself like a pebble in my throat. "Do you wish to rescind your proposal, now that my sister has returned?" I ask. "Since there is no need for me to replace her as Vessel any longer?"

Ames's lips part softly, his expression turning tender at my question. "Merrick, no," he says, catching my hand and stroking the heel of my palm with his thumb. "I am *delighted* to be your fiancé. How could you think me so fickle?"

His eyes lower to mine. I can see the sincerity in them, can almost feel it wash tangibly over my skin, deep and sweet like well water, and despite myself, my suspicions abate a fraction at his assurances. But then I recall the way he looked at Essie moments ago—like she was heaven and hell at once, like she was his sister returned from her deathbed, and not mine—and my hackles rise again. I yank my arm back, a scowl carving lines into my forehead.

At my withdrawal, Ames's nostrils flare, his eyes briefly alighting with something akin to indignation. His fingers ball into a reproachful fist at his side, and I stiffen unconsciously, in preparation for—*what?* Do I truly believe he would strike me, as his mother did him? My body's reaction to him sets me on edge, like watching a cat yowl at a bare patch of room, spitting at an unseen intruder.

Then Ames exhales, and all the tension seems to rush from him as the breath leaves his nostrils. "Fine," he admits, rubbing exhaustedly at the bridge of his nose. "It is true that Mother is . . . less than pleased by the recent developments regarding your sister. Now that I have put the idea of my marrying the Darling Vessel into her head, it seems, it is a difficult notion for her to shake out." His jaw tenses, his features darkening. "But despite whatever she may choose to believe, she does not control me."

The rancor in his voice sends a quiver of apprehension through me: bitter and distilled as an old rivalry, as grave dirt. I make to step away, but before I can, Ames is brightening, the loathing fading from his face as rapidly as it appeared.

"Listen," he says in a friendlier tone, "I really must be going. Mother doesn't know I'm here—she gave me explicit instructions not to visit you, in fact. But . . ." He leans forward, brushing a loose curl hanging near my temple with a gentleness that makes me shudder. "I needed to see you."

He glances up and down the corridor, searching for observers. When he confirms that we are alone, he tugs lightly on the lock of hair he's gripping, not drawing me forcibly toward him so much as inviting me in, and this time, I am unable to resist him. He kisses me, long and affectionate, and I return it, parting my lips for him.

A subdued *ahem* makes me flutter my eyes open, breaking Ames and me apart. The air between us buzzes like a plucked string as I pull away and twist to address our interloper, already blushing.

The reprimand I'm preparing dies in my throat when I see them. Instead of the servant I was anticipating, Killian stands a few meters to my left, his gaze studiously fixed on the door beyond me. His face is expressionless, the intentional blankness of a slate wiped clean, but I can sense his disdain like the kiss of lightning, electrifying the atmosphere. And something else beyond it, too—hurt. He has a defensiveness about him, his careful lack of emotion somehow reminding me of a hand pressed over a wound.

"Mr. Brandon." The words break from me, my flush spreading, overtaking my entire body. "Archson Ames was just—"

"Just leaving, actually," Ames breaks in casually. He doesn't seem disturbed by Killian's appearance; if anything, his smirk tells me there's at least a part of him that enjoys being caught, knowledge that makes my shame only deepen. He turns back and traces the curve of my ear idly, chuckling at the shiver I know he can feel pass through me, then drops his arm to his side. "We'll sort this out, Merrick, I swear it," he tells me, thumbing my chin in farewell. "I'll write you soon. Until then . . ." He pauses, his eyes cutting to Killian. Stepping closer to me, he lowers his voice and adds, "Your sister hasn't said anything disparaging, has she? About our engagement?"

He utters his question softly enough that only I can hear, and the hairs on my arms stand at attention. His demeanor is relaxed, but it's the levity that bothers me—like he's trying to slide something past me, play coy while he picks my pocket. "Of course not," I reply tersely. "Why would she?"

Ames smiles crookedly. "Because that might explain why you've been looking at me as though I may bite you," he says, teasing. He turns on his heel, his mouth quirking higher at my flushed cheeks. "I'll see you soon, dear."

He nods briskly to Killian, a condescending duck of his head, then strides away down the hall. I watch him go, my emotions jumbled within me like they are tiles he has shaken in a bag and then handed back to me to sort into order. On the one hand, our conversation has proven, at least, that he does not wish to break the pact we made—but when coupled with his earlier reaction to Essie, his assurances seem more like a paradox. Regardless of the excuses he gave, I do not believe that it is only his mother's unsupportiveness that has upset him. No, the source of his distress in Essie's bedroom was as obvious as a knife wound in his chest, and my sister was the one holding the blade. The only question that remains is, what is it about her that unnerved him so?

I think back to our conversation on the Roost's terrace, the words I'd spoken to him then. *At times I feel as though I cannot read you at all.* It is curious how much of a stranger Ames still is to me. Even now, when we are set to enter into a relationship of the most familiar kind—the most intimate—I cannot name his breakfast order, much less predict his behavior, recite his likes and dislikes. Not how it is with . . .

"Killian." Collecting myself, I shift to face him, my skin still warm with embarrassment. "I'm sorry—I didn't realize . . ." I hesitate, every excuse that rises to my mind feeling inadequate, feeble. Finally, I settle lamely on "I thought he and I were alone."

Killian doesn't react, his eyes assessing me for a drawn-out moment—searching for something in my own, though I don't know what. "It's fine," he says at last, his voice clipped. "Congratulations again on your engagement, Archdaughter. As you said, Archson Ames is the picture of what a young Manorborn man should be."

He bows shallowly, the motion so graceful that it almost hides the stinging ridge of sarcasm in his tone. "I was sent to check up on Archdaughter Estella, but I'll come back later."

I step toward him, suddenly filled with the pressing urgency to take him by the hand, to explain myself to him. As if my betrothal to Ames is a theory I can convince him of, as if he only needs to *understand*. Before I have the chance to, though, he's walking away, disappearing down the hall. My stomach sinks as he goes, my desire to call after him tempered only by my fear that if I did so, he would not turn back. That I have lost him for good.

Hiking up my skirts, I turn instead and head back into Essie's room.

My sister waits alertly for me inside, her eagerness to confer with me all the clearer for her efforts to hide it. Her face is a meticulous mask of ambivalence, her hands clutching loosely at her bedsheets as if she is every bit the recovering, fragile invalid Cressida keeps insisting she is, but behind it all, there's an intentness to her demeanor that she can't hide. Glancing back at the door, I wonder if she was listening in on Ames and me while we were speaking—then I balk at the image of Killian's flat eyes that flashes through my head, pricking me like a needle.

"Everything all right?" Essie's smile is strained, a shallow imitation of the one she wore when she greeted me before. "No lovers' quarrels yet, I should hope."

I shake my head, making my way back to her bedside, the need to question her about the note in my pocket usurped, for now, by this new strangeness. "No. And yes—everything is fine. It is only that . . ." Retaking my seat, I drift off, pushing Killian from my mind and running through Ames's and my interaction again. "Essie," I ask, leaning closer to her. "Did you find his behavior odd, just now?"

Essie curls farther into her pillows, the white cushions framing her face like plush wings. "Whose?" she replies, as if there is not only one *he* I could be speaking of—one person whose actions could fall under the category of *odd*. "Archson Ames's?" She licks her lips, her tongue darting over her teeth. "It was quite . . . *sudden,* his bursting in here, to be sure, but I am sure he was only looking forward to seeing you. He seems quite enamored with you, Merrick."

She arcs a brow, grinning, as if she's expecting me to giggle and blush, to weave her a story of my escapades with Ames. Yet I only frown, sinking lower in my wooden chair.

"But that's the thing—it wasn't me he seemed enamored with," I say, catching her eyes. Though she meets my gaze, hers is furtive, as if she's retreating into herself. "In fact, I believe he forgot all about me, initially," I go on, emboldened by her avoidance. "He was entirely preoccupied with—well, with you."

Essie scoffs. "Merrick, don't be silly. I told you when you first arrived, I hardly know him."

"And yet the last question Ames asked me before departing was whether you had said anything disparaging about him to me," I press, and am rewarded when her fingers flex atop her sheets, her nails digging into the fabric. "Why would he ask that about an acquaintance, Essie?"

She glances down, then up, her movements rushed with the desperate urgency of a child trying to hide a broken vase behind their back. My pulse quickens at her evasiveness, then speeds faster when she looks back at me, her expression resigned. "I . . ."

She trails off, hesitating, and for a moment I want to clap my hands over my ears before she can say any more—to walk back in time and follow Ames down the hall, out into the sunshine. To let him strip my anxieties away and paint me a future, one I could bed down in like a promise.

I sense, with a horrible, bleak certainty like a premonition, that whatever words come from my sister's mouth next will make me unable to do any of that for a long while.

"I thought . . . I hoped he might have told you himself." Essie continues, then stops, searching my expression for some kind of acknowledgment, perhaps—a sign that the language she is speaking is familiar to me.

It is not. Instead, numbness is tingling at the tips of my fingers, along my lips—all the places where Ames touched me. Where I touched him.

"Told me *what*?" I ask, my voice cracking.

Essie doesn't reply immediately, but in her gaze, I catch it: a melancholy depth like the black bottom of a lake, like a mourner's wan smile. *Pity.* It blooms under her features like a poisonous vine, and its presence tells me everything I need to know.

I swallow. "You were involved?" I guess. My voice is high and brittle, like the squeal of a kettle. *It is impossible.* A desperate whisper presses against my mind. *I would have seen it—would have smelled her on him when we . . .*

When we—

Blessedly, my sister shakes her head. "No," she says, and then my heart frosts over as she continues, "though that was his wish. He . . ." She hesitates, her head dropping to rest in her hands. "Merrick," she murmurs, "I do not wish to speak of this. I—"

I cut her off, my tone like iron. "Go on."

She lifts herself up enough to peek up at me through spreading fingers. I'm not sure what she sees in my eyes, but it seems to sober her; she sits straight, addressing me head-on, though her bottom lip quivers slightly as she speaks. "I was lonely," she starts, "completely isolated, and so was he—" Abruptly, she stops herself again, biting down on her cheek with a ferocity that would make me wince, were all of me not stone, resolute and unfeeling. As it is, I only stare at her, wait for her to gather herself.

"It matters little," Essie says softly. "Suffice to say we were each in need of a companion, and after his first visit to Norland, we fell into a correspondence of sorts. I believed it to be friendly"—her voice swells, her eyes widening as if trying to show me the truth embedded in the gray of her irises—"I swear to you, Merrick, I did—but after a while the tone of his letters began to change. He became obsessed with the idea of us marrying—you should have seen the notes he wrote me. Pages and pages of him raving about his supposed love for me, when I knew very well he would never have spared me a thought had we been in New London—that he was only tired of being alone." Her mouth crimps shut, her expression fogging over, dividing us, and at the notion of what lies behind that veil—memories I'll never share, arguments that carried more weight in their every syllable than all the meaningless banter passed between Ames and me—rage stirs in my core.

"Anyway, it all came to a head when he proposed, and I rejected him," Essie summarizes. "This was perhaps a month before Father died."

She turns away, gazing toward her window and the grounds beyond. "Ames did not take it well," she remarks, and succinct as her comment is, the darkness with which she utters it makes me flinch. "He said I'd regret my decision—and maybe I would have, but then Father passed so soon after, and there was you, and the Nomination Hearing . . ." She exhales. "I was too ashamed to tell you, when you asked me about my relationship to him after you came home," she admits, glancing at me fleetingly. "I justified it to myself by thinking it would not matter, whether I kept our entanglement a secret or not. By the time I realized how wrong I was, it was already too late."

At last, she stops. I barely notice; I am floating somewhere above us both, my world fuzzing like the shadows at the edge of a candle flame. I drift back through Ames's and my relationship, returning all the way to its initial seeding—his first visit to Norland, before Essie had even disappeared. A memory unsnarls, my sister's hollow voice amplified as if spoken into a glass jar:

Ah, Archson Ames. How nice to see you again.

And the blank expression that had accompanied her greeting, as if her words were props—wooden things, unsubtle in their falseness. Hadn't I thought her abrupt, that day? Hadn't I wondered about that word, *again*, what it meant?

Ames did not take it well . . .

I jerk myself free of the panic before it can crush me. Later, when I am alone, I will let myself feel the bruises I know are spreading inside me, staining my organs with their sunset hues, but not here, not yet. Not while Essie can see.

Painfully, I drift back down to the earth. "And what of my engagement?" I demand. "Belated or not, did you not think the fact that he was—likely still is—in love with you would have no bearings on my decision to *bind myself to him for the rest of my life*?"

My body is shaking with anger—my temper slipped free of its leash. I stand, smoothing down my skirt with unsteady hands as if the action will help me regain a fraction of control over myself, only to go still when Essie reaches forward, brushing my palm with her fingertips.

"I'm sorry," she says.

I look down at her. The apology is mild, humble, and though I don't want it to, its simplicity dulls my anger. "You are completely right to criticize me," my sister says, carefully pulling her arm back. "When I heard you and Ames were to be married, I wanted to go to you, but I—I did not trust my own motivations." She keeps her gaze locked on mine, shining and earnest. "I am sure that all he kept from you, he did so only out of a desire not to injure your impression of him. He seems to care for you very much." Essie's throat bobs. "Cressida told me about the roses."

The roses. I picture them, half dead in their vase by my bedside, hunchbacked and pungent, and nausea rises up my gullet. The day he visited Norland, Ames had brought flowers with him, too—a bundle of wildflowers, summer-vibrant in my hands. He'd given them to me, but had they been intended for my sister all along?

At once, the remainder of my fury departs, swift as a flame guttering out. Without its burn to warm me, I feel only exhaustion—a bone-deep tiredness, ashy and formless as a plain of snow. Whoever Ames intended his offering for, it does not matter; either way, he has set my sister and me against one another, passed himself like a trophy back and forth between us without a thought for the damage he'd leave when he withdrew. If there is a villain to be found in this story, it is undoubtedly him.

Tucked in bed, Essie leans forward, frowning abruptly at the floor. "What's that?"

Caught off guard by her shift in demeanor, I follow her gaze, inhaling when I see a slip of white resting atop the floorboards: the note from my pocket, now fluttered to the ground. It must have fallen loose when I stood a few moments ago. Collecting myself, I stoop and pick it up. The paper has a worn feel against my fingers, its edges rubbed raw from the many times I've worried at them over the past weeks—as if by doing so, I could soak up their meaning like a smudge of ink, wish my sister home.

"Oh," I say to Essie as I examine the note in my palm. It takes a minute to reorient myself around it; my mind feels sluggish in the wake of everything she's just confessed to me, my thoughts garbled as if they've been dragged through mud. "It's . . . it's what I came to see you about, actually," I tell her. "The threat we found the night you disappeared. *Darling Manor will fall*—I mentioned it the night you came home, remember?" I hold the note out to her, trying not to stiffen when she takes it, the brush of her skin on mine like grazing an open wound. "I know Cressida said not to bother you with this type of thing until you'd had the chance to rest, but I thought it might be useful to see if you recognized it."

Carefully, Essie flattens the note in her palm, running two fingers across it like she's feeling the ridges and dips where a pen carved words into the paper. I hold my breath, waiting for her to dismiss the threat—to tell me no, she hasn't seen it before—but as I watch, the confusion creasing her forehead begins to change, bemusement giving way to alarm like a breeze stirring up sand. She brings a hand to her mouth and presses it against her lips, her gray eyes wide.

I swallow. "Do you? Recognize it, that is?"

Slowly, as if she is moving through a body of water, she looks up. Her gaze latches silently onto mine, and there is fear in it, but something beyond that, too—a dark knowledge that cuts at me like a bad fortune.

Blood crashes against my eardrums, a red wave, as abruptly, my sister rises from her bed, stumbling toward her wardrobe—the same one I found her journal in, ages ago—still clutching the note as she goes. Her shins are two ivory matchsticks without the blankets to hide them from view; gathering myself, I start after her.

"Essie!"

"Shh." She whirls on me, her eyes wild. "Just give me a moment. There's a false panel at the bottom—I hid them there."

I frown at her explanation but reluctantly pause my approach as she throws open the wardrobe's doors and kneels on the floor, the skirts of her dresses brushing against her nose. Batting them aside, she presses down on the wardrobe's wooden bottom, my heart leaping when I see a section in the back left corner rising up at her touch. Reaching into the shadowed space beneath, she lifts something out: a stack of ivory letter paper, neatly tied with a pink ribbon. With shaking hands, she turns back toward me, sliding the top letter from the bundle and passing it over.

Giving her one last befuddled look, I begin to read.

Dearest Estella,

Mother agrees that you are a fool and a tart for rejecting me as cruelly as you have, after all the attentions I have paid you. Through wicked trickery, you made me believe myself in love with you, and being an honest man, I did not see the devil behind your mask until I was well caught in the flames.

It is only due to the good values Mother has instilled in me that I am writing to you now, to offer you a final chance to right the wrongs you have made. Marry me, or face the consequences of your choice—for there will, I assure you, be consequences. Your Manor has grown sleepy and fat under your father's rule, overly self-assured of its own strength. Yet I have in mind several ways to wake it up.

I lower the note, sour bile biting at the back of my throat. It is one thing to hear of Ames's obsession; quite another to see the evidence of it on a page: the twisted, sharp claws of his love. How did I ever miss it, I wonder, when he kissed me? How did I not sense him searching for another figure beneath mine—the outline of my sister?

Passing the letter back to her, I blink away the burn from my eyes. "Essie . . . this is horrible," I say. "But I don't understand—why show it to me now? The handwriting here is distinctly different from that on the threat."

My sister shakes her head stubbornly. "Not the handwriting," she counters. "Look."

I follow her finger, which is stabbing at a small marking in the top right corner of the letter: the Saint seal, I realize, a blooming orchid etched onto the paper in stark black ink, no bigger than the size of my thumbnail.

"Their official stamp," Essie says dully. "Ames uses it on all his letters."

Still unsure of her meaning, I nod at her, observing wordlessly as she unfurls the threat still tucked in her other hand, placing it directly atop the larger letter. My pulse quickens as her fingernail sweeps across the paper, directing my attention not to the words written on it but a stray scribble of ink along the top. The swooping black lines I'd registered when I first found the note in her bedroom and then immediately dismissed as nothing more than the work of a faulty quill.

Looking up at me through lowered lashes, Essie delicately slides the threat across the page beneath it, lining the edge of the smaller note up with the stamp at the top of the letter.

I gasp. The marking on the threat matches perfectly—not a flaw at all, I see now, but part of a grander design: the curving, leaflike petals of an orchid.

My stare rises to meet my sister's, my heart squeezing violently in my chest, and finally—*finally*—I understand.

Darling Manor will fall.

We've found him.

CHAPTER TWENTY-SIX

The Saint estate juts from the surrounding fields, as much a feature of the landscape as the grassy earth beneath my feet, the soaring hills that swell against the horizon in the distance. This close, its bulk is mountainous, ancient and immovable—exactly like the Manorborn who have made their home within it.

I gather myself, facing down the stately yellow house in front of me as if it is a beast at the end of my arrow tip. To my back, a horse whinnies, the carriage I commandeered to ferry me across the Sussex border waiting obediently behind me. I hardly remember my ride to Cardiff; rather, it is as if I simply stepped from Essie's bedroom to here, a province away. Armed with nothing but my Ghostslayer, strapped against my thigh beneath my dress, and the knowledge of what I've come to do.

Essie urged me to wait. To bide our time until Tom and Cressida returned from their errands, and we could show them the letter from Ames—and the stamp on it—ourselves. It was too dangerous, she'd said, to attempt to confront Ames on my own, without any sort of backup. It was only my temper getting the best of me once more.

I knew she was right—*is* right. And yet, for hours now—ever since the moment my sister matched up the orchid seal on Ames's letter with the partial marking on the note from her bedroom, the lines lying perfectly atop one another like a kiss—wrath has been twisting within me, coiling and uncoiling like a length of rope.

Ames is the author of the threat. Ames is the one who took my sister. It should be enough, knowing the truth, but it isn't. I need to hear him admit it himself, after he has fed me so many lies—I need his confession, spoken and irrefutable and real. Otherwise, I fear, he may still get away.

Lifting my skirts, I make my way up the drive to the Roost's front entrance, flinching a little less this time when the towering double doors swing open upon my arrival. The same butler who greeted Tom, Cressida, and me at the start of our dinner waits behind the threshold, his beady eyes widening when he sees me.

"My lady." He bows, his tone reedy, nervous. "One moment, please. I will go fetch Archson Ames."

He ushers me into the entry hall before scurrying away, his footsteps clipped and harsh against the polished floor. As soon as he's out of sight, I reach for my Ghostslayer, rubbing its handle like a good-luck charm under the plain cotton of my dress. Though I hadn't honored Essie's pleas to delay my visit here, I wasn't reckless enough to leave Norland without any defenses in place—but will my dashed-off note to Killian, asking him to gather a group of men he trusted and lead them to the Saint estate, be enough to secure my safety? What if he's misunderstood my request? What if it hasn't reached him at all?

Alone, I inhale deeply, my palms moistening at the thought of confronting Ames. *What will I say? What will he say?* In some ways, his absence is far more terrifying than his presence—I feel him everywhere, every second that ticks by pregnant with the possibility of his arrival.

To distract myself, I look around the entry hall—at the fullness of the Roost's glamour, revealed in its totality in the day. Tall windows pour light into the space, gilding all the furnishing with a sleek, wet-looking shine, as if they have been rubbed with oil. Dust glints in the air like a scatter of snow, drifting soundlessly downward. Despite its enormity, the estate is entirely silent, the atmosphere reverent and somewhat stuffy in a way that reminds me of a vast library, or a house of worship.

"—orders were clear—"

Spectral fingers hook into my dress, cradling my waist, at the sound of Ames's voice drifting from farther inside the house. Memories of his touch pursue me, the ghost of his breath like pipe ash, staining my jawline, the swoop of skin between my shoulder and neck. Without my willing them, my feet begin to move in the direction of his voice, anticipation sticking like a bone in the back of my throat.

It will be all right. Killian is already on his way, surely—he will be here soon, and besides that, you have allies. Ames won't dare lift a finger against you while he knows the full weight of the Faulk Manor will swing back toward him, should you come to harm.

But what if he will? What if he does?

I walk through the entry hall and into the long gallery that serves as the ground floor's main passageway, sun spilling like golden nectar through the regimented line of windows and draping itself over the line of portraits that decorate the opposite wall. Among the paintings, I spot a young Ames, cherubic and blue-eyed, nestled between his mother and a handsome, cheerful-looking man I take to be his father.

I pause, look closer. Though the painter has added a dab

of pink to child-Ames's cheeks, there's a pained quality to his expression—his small mouth is pursed, his body is angled as if squirming away from his mother's hold. Beside him, Ianthe sits proud and tall, her features blunt even in the portrait's gentle pastel palette.

"—Mother's instructions were specifically to pull all forces near the border back. As I've already said, our objectives there have been accomplished—it isn't worth the risk of another sighting—"

In a flurry of motion and color, Ames appears at the end of the gallery. He's changed since his appearance at Norland House this morning and is now dressed in a navy waistcoat paired with crisp ivory breeches. A squat Saint sentry trails after him, the man's thick eyebrows furrowed in consternation—likely trying to keep up with Ames's commands.

"Merrick?" When he sees me, Ames stops short, his posture stiffening. "What are you doing here?"

There's a note of alarm in his tone, spiking and defensive, that unnerves me. *Does he know, somehow? Why I've come?* I cut my gaze to the sentry still lingering behind his shoulder, mute and watchful, and then back to him again, suddenly feeling as though I've intruded on something. "Apologies," I say by way of greeting, dipping into a curtsy. "One of your staff received me. I was waiting in the entry hall, but I heard your voice and . . ." I hesitate, glancing at the sentry once more before continuing. "Has there been a breach in Cardiff recently?"

"A breach?" Ames exhales, a breathy, forced laugh. "No—why do you ask?"

I step back instinctively as he walks a few paces forward. "You mentioned a sighting just now," I reply cautiously. "Has a Phantom been spotted nearby? I hope I am not interrupting anything urgent."

My explanation seems to relax Ames; his strides loosen, his

demeanor brightening like a flame flickering to life. "Ah—no, no," he says. "Well, there was one, but it was . . . dealt with. Forgive me." Advancing leisurely toward me, he smiles. "To what do I owe your visit?"

Though I know it is only my imagination, I swear the sentry behind him leans forward at his question, as if eager for my answer. "I . . . I was wondering if I might be able to speak with you for a moment," I start again, attempting to curve my lips into an endearing smile. "Privately."

"Of course," Ames replies with a dismissive wave to his companion. The anxious knot within me unspools a fraction as the other man disappears, scuttling back around the corner and deeper into the estate without a word. The last thing I need is for this conversation to garner an audience.

"Come to call on me so soon, then?" Ames asks when he reaches me. "Not that I am unhappy to see you, but it has only been a few hours since we spoke last. Why, if I didn't know better, Archdaughter, I'd say you must be quite smitten with me."

He's grinning, bladed and wry, but I remember those same lips pressing against mine in the corridor outside Essie's room, and the knife lodged in my side gives a savage twist. The smell of him is overwhelming as he moves to take my hand, somehow more powerful than it was during our last encounter—perfuming the air like incense.

It is instinctive to draw away, like moving out of a predator's reach. "There is no need to play games with me," I say, my heart pounding. *Do it, Merrick. Confront him—get him to admit his crimes, else this entire trip go to waste.* "I know what you've done."

Ames's fingers, still stretching toward mine, waver. "What?" he asks. His question is pitched low, spoken with the hard edge of a dare. From our close position, I cannot make out his face—my eyes are level with his chest, and my pulse is pounding too rapidly for me to consider raising them higher—but even so, his alertness is tangible as the quiver of approaching lightning, buzzing along the ridges of my teeth, zipping down my spine. He chuckles once, the sound rumbling softly in his throat. "They were only patrols, Merrick."

His answer throws me. "Patrols?" I blurt, looking up at him. Already I can feel my control of the conversation slipping like a fish from my hands—I need to get us back on topic. "I was not speaking of any patrols—why did you not tell me you were acquainted with my sister before her disappearance?"

Ames pauses, an implacable emotion dipping his mouth for a moment before he collects himself again. "I barely knew Archdaughter Estella—your sister," he says tersely. Gone now is his welcoming manner; instead, he speaks with a chilly restraint that makes my nerves quake. "As I've already explained to you, she rejected my overtures of friendship when I offered them, months ago. I would hardly call that an acquaintanceship."

He walks another pace forward, his hand finding my chin, tilting it upward. "Why would you ask such a thing?" he continues, his eyes roving over my face as if mapping it out. He smirks, a mocking crook of his lips. "Don't tell me you're jealous, darling."

The feel of his touch repulses me, but I don't break away from his hold. "Oh no," I reply, gazing deeply into his eyes. "I am not jealous in the slightest—only curious. What *would* you call your relationship with Essie, then? You did court her, after all, did you not? Propose to her?"

At my accusations, the color leaches from Ames's face. "For the Bloodletter's sake, keep your voice down, Merrick," he growls. He moves still closer, swallowing the distance between us just as I snap my head to the side, tearing free of his grip. Desperately,

I hoist up my skirt and reach for the gun strapped beneath, stumbling backward, but I've barely gotten my fingers around the handle when he catches my wrist.

Shock unfurls across his expression as he takes in the weapon. His teeth gritted, he twists my wrist viciously, and the Ghostslayer slips from my grasp. I hiss in response, pain flaring through me, and buck to try to shake him off, but it's no use—he rushes nearer, pressing his entire weight against me so that I have no choice but to fall farther back. My heart stops when my spine meets the smooth flank of the wall, the raised bump of a portrait frame jabbing into my shoulder blade. *Nowhere left to run.*

Ames pants unevenly against my neck as he restrains me: one hand locking my right wrist firmly to the wall, the other flattened just above my left shoulder, caging me in. He grunts as I writhe beneath him; then, to my horror, his breaths steady, dissolve into laughter.

"You would bring a gun into the home of your betrothed, then?" he asks, shifting still closer to me—his thighs pinning mine, his chest rising and falling with each of my labored inhales. The heat of him is unbearable, like a lantern pressed to my flesh, searing into every inch of me. I go rigid as I feel his mouth graze the side of my head, lowering to murmur in my ear.

"What were you planning on doing, Merrick? Shooting me?" he says with another rough chuckle. "Do you know how many sentries would have been on you, had you done so much as fiddled with the trigger?"

Cool air rushes into my lungs as he backs away—I wheeze it in hungrily, steadying myself in time to see him send my Ghostslayer flying along the corridor with a lazy kick. It comes to rest, unfired, at the base of a polished mahogany stand about halfway down the hall, the vase of fresh flowers balanced atop the table's surface wobbling at the impact. Adrenaline surging like an unvoiced scream within me, I gauge the distance between myself and my weapon; it is traversable, barely over twenty meters, give or take. If I sprinted, I could . . .

As if reading my thoughts, Ames scoffs, stepping farther to the side of the corridor. "Go on, go after it," he taunts, sweeping his arms wide as if waving me onward. "Seal your own death, just as your father did his."

Fists clenched, I look again between him and my Ghostslayer, afternoon sunlight glinting invitingly off the muzzle. The urge to run for it is beyond tempting—like a compulsion seizing hold of me—but though I despise myself for it, the logical part of myself knows that there is truth in Ames's words. If I fire at him now, with no forces of my own to support me, I will be buried beneath Ames's men, any questions about the nature of my passing drowned beneath their collective testimony that the first shot was mine.

Avoiding his gaze, I let my shoulders slump, the motion like a white flag held above my head. A dull reflex tells me I should be frightened—should cower at the realization that I am completely at his mercy—but when I reach for my terror, only anger comes to greet me. A powerful fury that seems to emanate from my very bones.

From his place near the wall, Ames watches me gleefully, his usual debonair mask knocked aside to make way for a victorious sneer. "That's right," he says, his pleasure at my resignation like a spill of dirty water, slicking over me. "You know," he goes on, inclining his head. "Mother was right about you Darling girls. She said you and your sister are like wild horses—you kick up a storm, but truly, all you want is someone to break you."

I meet his gaze, seething. "And is that what you did to Essie?" I ask. "Break her?"

He sighs, tossing his hair, the sun glittering against the strands like light off a golden crown. "Essie, Essie, Essie," he chides. I get the sense he's enjoying himself, now that he's confident he's back in control. Toying with me like a man who's caught a fox in his trap, secure in the notion it won't bite back at him. "It's a pity she got to you first, you know," Ames remarks with a wounded frown. "Tell me, how did she cast me in the tale she spun for you? I must be the villain—otherwise, you would not despise me so.

"I don't blame you for believing her," he muses when I remain silent. "She's a good storyteller, that one." With a shrug, he stretches to rub at the back of his neck. "Certainly had me fooled."

The way he says it—as if he feels sorry for me, as if it is I who have had the wool pulled over my eyes, and not him—shatters my resolve. "She didn't fool you, you idiot," I snip curtly. "She just didn't love you."

"Oho." Ames's eyebrows shoot upward; he clutches at his chest as if struck, then breaks into a grin. "There's that cheek. It suits you, dear."

He takes a step in my direction, his smile broadening when I shrink reflexively back against the wall. Once again, I'm overwhelmed by the sensation that he's playing with me, rattling my cage and delighting when I spook; what's more, that he'll continue to do so until he grows bored, or one of us breaks.

If I want to survive this, I cannot allow that person to be me.

"Is that why you kidnapped her?" I challenge, forcing myself to stand straight. "Because she denied you her hand, when you wished for it?"

Ames's regal stance falters at my accusation; for a moment, I feel his power wobble like a plate balanced on the edge of a table, his mastery over the hall diminish.

"Why I . . ." He shakes his head, a definitive cut to the right. "You're talking nonsense. I didn't *kidnap* your sister—the very notion is insane."

"You were not the person who left the note on her pillow, then, the night of her disappearance? *Darling Manor will fall*?" I counter, my gaze darting to my Ghostslayer as I speak, still resting by the decorative table down the hall. With how he's shifted, Ames has partially blocked my path to the weapon—but the way he's positioned himself, with his back to the gun, leads me to believe his focus might not be entirely on it, either. If I can just keep him distracted until Killian's arrival, there's a possibility, however slim, that I can escape unscathed, and with evidence of Ames's crimes to boot.

My hopes leap up from where they've settled at my feet. *I haven't lost yet.*

"It will do you no good to deny it." I plunge onward, praying my questions are enough to hold his attention. "Essie kept your letters, Ames—the ones you wrote her, before my father died? You must have been very much taken with her, to correspond as much as you did." I click my tongue, emboldened by the dread that's stirring in his expression. "Unlucky for you, we were able to match the stamp from your love notes to a partial mark on the threat. I'm sure you thought you'd cut your seal out completely when you left it, but my sister has a sharp eye."

Ames snarls, feral and ragged. He stalks forward, bracing his arms on either side of me before I can move away. Like a quenched thirst, my brazenness disappears in an instant, my hopes of rescue fading under his razing stare, his shoulders hunched by his chin, his lips curled back to expose gleaming teeth. "This is ridiculous," he growls. "I—"

"Cressida knows." The lie appears like the yellow bloom of a torch in the fog, and I grasp it with both hands, a lifeline amid the gloom of my despair. "I showed her the letters before I left Norland House—and the stamp on the note, as well. She is likely alerting the Council as we speak." I swallow, my thumping pulse calming as Ames seizes at my words. His fingers flex against the wall, his muscles tensing—my end like a jammed bullet, held off for another precious second. He observes me with silent fury, his gaze calculating.

"Whether you admit it or not matters little," I go on, meeting his stare. *Confident*—that's how I need to appear to him. Like I have an ace in my pocket. Like I am telling the truth. "As I said, we have your letters, and they are confession enough. What was it you wrote to Essie? *Your Manor has grown sleepy, but I can think of a few ways to wake it up*—or something like that?" I *tsk* reproachfully. "Silly of you, really, to be so loose with your tongue."

"Fuck's *sake*." Like a shorn rope, Ames's body goes slack, his hands slamming against the wall in frustration. The noise rings in my ears like a warning: *that was nearly you.*

"You think *that's* what I meant?" he spits, backing away. My story seems to have knocked him firmly from his pedestal; he is jittery as a man on the run, his defenses shakier than I dared hope they would be. "I wasn't threatening to *abduct* her, you idiot—I was only talking about the—"

He freezes in the same breath that I do, the weight of his slip striking us both at once. *I was only talking about the . . .* The back of my neck prickles with trepidation, the feeling that I am barely missing something, like walking into a room and catching the tail end of a conversation—the subject hovering just out of reach. "Don't stop now," I say steadily. "The what, Ames?"

He doesn't answer, his eyes flickering right, then left, as if he's searching for an escape. He is hiding something, of that much I am now certain—it is obvious as if he were clasping his hands behind his back—but *what*?

A snatch of speech echoes suddenly in my mind, rattling like a spoon in a tin cup: *They were only patrols, Merrick.* Ames's earlier response, when I told him I knew what he'd done—so odd that I'd dismissed it entirely, then. But perhaps I shouldn't have. My pulse races, adrenaline speeding my thoughts onward like a river. What was it he'd been saying to his sentry when I interrupted them?

Mother's instructions were specifically to pull all forces near the border back . . . it isn't worth the risk of another sighting—

Cardiff's border, I'd assumed. A Phantom sighting. Only, the more I consider it, the less sense that explanation makes. If the Saints were having trouble at their border, why would they pull their troops away? Wouldn't the natural response be to station more men near their lanterns, like my family did when we had—

"The breaches." I breathe aloud. It's a long shot—a lobbed stone, arcing away into the darkness—but then Ames flinches, his expression faltering like a hand passed over a candle, causing the light to jump, and it is admission enough.

Abruptly, I am thrown into the past, into another house in another province, this one slithering with mist, with hopelessness thick as the tang of blood in the air. And corpses—three of them, two dismembered, a feast for the Phantoms that had beaten Killian and me to their bodies, but the final one, the man . . .

The epiphany turns over within me, a painting flipped to reveal a blaze of color. Perhaps it has been there for a while, waiting for me to acknowledge it, to face it toward me and confront the truth I'd long denied. Hadn't I said it from the beginning, after all? That kind of kill, meted out with such efficiency . . . it never could have been one of the beasts who dealt the blow that felled that man.

No, that kill was the work of a different kind of monster.

"You caused the breach in our territory—you killed that family," I say, stepping toward him. Strangely, my discovery has lessened my fear of him; after the way he lorded himself over me only minutes ago, Ames's pale face makes me feel almost immortal, like he is insignificant, an insect I could grind under my heel. "Did you cause all of them?" I press.

Even as I ask it, a voice reverberates through my thoughts: the patron Killian and I questioned in the Watchman, the night we visited Shoreham-by-Sea, speaking about a spate of rumors from the north of our province. *Word is that folks up there have seen men— strange ones—lurking about . . . Tampering with things, like.*

I'd traveled to Heath because of his comment, had made it my mission to track down the strangers he mentioned. I thought I hadn't found any—but hadn't I?

A shadowed blur outside a window, turned hazy by the rain. A Saint crest, glittering on Darling land.

Why had I believed Ames so easily that day, when he said he'd been traveling through Sussex in order to see me? Because he was beautiful? Because he made me feel as though I were, too?

Something settles over me: a screaming chill, like the darkest part of a winter night. All those attacks—all those dead lanterns, gone out with no explanation. There *had* been one, after all. And he is standing directly in front of me.

"Merrick, please—let's not jump to conclusions, now." Ames stumbles back as I advance on him, my temper burning high enough to make up for my lack of weapon. "It was never our intention to hurt anyone—Mother made that very clear. That family . . . we didn't realize there was a dwelling so close to the border until we saw their smoke signal. Couldn't risk being identified, but that a child was present"—he wrinkles his nose in distaste—"it was an ugly turn of events.

"You must believe me, Merrick," he urges, his tone pleading. "I had no choice—I have never had a choice, not with *her.*"

Step after step he retreats and I follow, as if we are dancing again, each of us focused wholly on the other. "You have no idea what it was like, growing up under her rule," Ames continues, a slight tremor in his tone. "She calls herself a mother, but in reality, she has always been a queen, demanding nothing less than her subjects' absolute loyalty. And like a queen, she is intent on conquering—especially the lands of those who doubted her when she first rose to the Lordship."

Ames pauses to catch his breath, a tendon bulging along his neck. "I told you what she asked of me when I returned to Cardiff after my father's death. I thought she would train me to succeed her. Instead, she tried to sell me off like some prize pig." His voice falters, his speech turning rough. "She offered me to your father—a groom for either of his girls, in exchange for an alliance—but he refused. He said his daughters could do better than a union with us small, provincial Saints." A growl rumbles in his throat. "But Mother was determined to expand her influence, so I was tasked with winning Estella's heart, driving her so mad with love for me that she would accept my proposal on her own. Even after your sister rejected me, Mother refused to relent. Said we only needed to humble your Manor, show Essie how desperately she truly needed our aid. The breaches were nothing more than a tool to accomplish that goal—I never would have pursued such a measure, had she not forced my hand." He swallows. "Once we were wed, it would have been natural for Mother to become more involved in Sussex's affairs, until the line where her reign ended and your family's began dissipated altogether."

At last, he falls quiet, and I shiver, thinking of Lord Ianthe's wan green eyes, summoning forth a servant with a single glance. Though I feel no sympathy for Ames, I can't help but wonder what it might be like to be under their command. At the mercy of her subtle power, like a scalpel in the hand of a physician, splaying its victims open for her to observe.

Shaking myself out of the vision, I turn my attention back to him. "But the breaches weren't enough, were they?" I press. "No matter how many attacks you launched, Essie still wouldn't take you back. So naturally, you had to remove her altogether. Maybe you couldn't bring yourself to kill her right then—maybe you did love her, in some way—but so long as she was Vessel, you'd never get a chance at a union." I rush on, the logic seamlessly knitting itself together before me, all the way to its conclusion. "No," I finish, "you needed a new heir—one you could scare with threatening notes and a stolen Archdaughter, and then swoop in to save. You needed me."

Ames is silent for a long moment, unmoving, his expression inscrutable. Then he hums. There is a finality to the noise, as if he has come to a decision.

"You are clever, I'll give you that," he sighs. "It's a pity no one else will have the privilege of hearing your theories. Thanks to you, I shall be forced to remain Mother's marionette, dancing when she desires me to."

He turns and lunges for my Ghostslayer just as, from back toward the front of the estate, the pounding of footsteps splits the air. I whirl around, my pulse racing as behind me, a group of figures pours into the hallway—Saint sentries?

The man at the front of the pack lifts his head, the afternoon sun edging the scars on his face in gold—

He's here. He made it, after all. My chest squeezes, tightening with a gasp, and in that second, as I turn back and watch the despair cracking over Ames's features, I know: I've won.

CHAPTER TWENTY-SEVEN

The way Killian tells it, on our journey home to Sussex, I'd barely left Norland House when Cressida and Tom arrived back at the estate, Essie eschewing her bed rest in favor of immediately tracking down our relatives and informing them of my destination. My sister, he says, confessed everything—her correspondence with Ames, his anger when she'd refused his hand—sharing the letters she'd shown me as proof. It had taken only a single glance at the orchid stamp in the corner and the incomplete but identical mark on the threat next to it for my cousin and his wife to rally our sentries and send them after me.

In return, I give him what I've learned: that Ames and his mother manufactured the breaches at our border to try to weaken Essie's resolve until she was desperate enough for an ally to accept Ames's proposal. And that, when she hadn't budged, they'd removed her by force, then turned their attentions to me in her stead.

I should, I think, feel satisfied. I've gotten what I came for—proof of Ames's guilt—and then some. But for some reason, all throughout the drive to Norland, I keep returning to the look I glimpsed on Ames's face as Killian and his men ferried me away. He'd looked more than defeated, staring blankly after me, then. He'd looked dead.

Night already has Norland in its inky grasp by the time I make it back home. Hours later, I wake to blackness, the receding, furry shape of the dream that broke my slumber already scampering away from me. I reach for it, catching its fading outline—

A princeling, perfect and golden, the sun behind his head and a girl in his arms. She is dark-haired and pale, his wraith, his shadow, squirming in his hold as he leans closer and lowers his lips to hers. My sleep-self recognizes her; I turn away, embarrassed by the display of affection. It is then that I hear her scream.

The vision breaks just as I look back, toward my sister. I do not need to see its end to know that she is gone.

Brow damp with sweat, I push away my sticky covers and flail in the murk for my nightstand—and the candle and tinder box I'd used to light it before I crawled into bed. *Ames and Essie, Essie and Ames.* The image of the pair of them, twisted together like dusk and dawn, lingers in my mind like a specter, her terrified shriek a piercing descant overhanging my thoughts. I need to see my sister—I need *light*—

My hand collides painfully with the heavy bronze candlestick, sending it tumbling to the floor with a *thump* that rattles my bones. I groan in frustration, press my palms to my chest; my lungs feel as though they've been filled with hot oil, burning me from the inside out.

A pounding at my door startles me. "Archdaughter." The voice is worried, muffled by the wood; I cannot identify it through the gauzy cling of my panic. "Is everything all right?"

I blink, my vision gradually adjusting to the darkness. My bedroom crawls into view: the heap of my comforter, now slid from my bed and piled on the ground, the liquid drape of the curtains pulled across my window.

"What?" I call back irritably. "Who is it?"

A pause. "It is only me, Archdaughter," the voice says again, after a moment. There is a fringe of restraint to the person's speech, an intentional caution as if they are carefully placing every vowel.

I recognize them now.

"Killian." I slump back against my pillows, relief mixing with embarrassment. "What are you doing here?"

"I am on duty." The sentry's reply is simple, though I detect a hint of wariness still lingering in his tone, as if in the hallway he's shifting on his feet, parsing the gloom for an intruder. He clears his throat. "I heard a noise."

Essie and Ames. The white absence in his arms where she had been only a second before, her moving body like a wink—a black fan of hair against lighter skin, there and gone in an instant. Her scream.

It was a nightmare. Only that, and nothing more.

I shake myself free of the illusion, returning to my bedroom again. "Am I to be forbidden from making noises now?" I snip irritably. It is a petty, pointless jab—obviously taunting—but I don't care. Killian's voice, his presence, is a guard wall, keeping back the rush of emotion I can feel lurching at the base of my stomach like a sea swell. If he leaves, I fear I will tumble into the waves, be crushed in their angry froth.

Beyond my door, I hear the soft huff of a sigh. "If you want a clever response to that, you'll have to wait till morning," Killian answers dryly. "My reserve is generally depleted by midnight." Another hesitancy—this one jagged and abrupt-feeling, as if he was about to say something else, only to decide against it at the last second. "Apologies for bothering you. Good night—"

"I had a nightmare. About Ames."

The words are out before I can stop them, clipping the end of Killian's farewell. Tucking my knees beneath myself, I lean forward in my nest of sheets, awaiting his reply. The total spread of the night around me, like a velvet cloak laid across the room, and the solid boundary of the door between us have lent a confessional quality to the air. It wafts away any humiliation I might otherwise feel at my disclosure, leaving only the breathless, desperate need for companionship—for absolution.

Yet when Killian does speak again, it is terse and stiff as a freshly pressed shirt. "I'm sorry to hear that, Archdaughter," he says. "If you like, I can fetch someone—your cousin, maybe, or the Duchess. I am sure they would be more than happy to discuss your dream with you."

"I do not wish to discuss it with Tom." My response is pleading, embarrassingly whiny. "I want to talk to you, as we have in the past. Not as Archdaughter and sentry, but as equals." I swallow, my speech hitching. "As friends."

"But we are *not* equals, Merrick," Killian replies immediately. The fierceness in his rebuttal—the sudden release of his composure—lashes through the space between us, stinging me like the kiss of a whip. "Forgive me," he says, after a pause, his apology muffled through the wood. "I'm glad I was able to reach you in time, today. Yet . . . I'm afraid I've allowed myself to cross too many boundaries these past weeks, under the guise of assisting you." There's a lull in his speech; I imagine him tensing, the angles of his jaw becoming more pronounced. "I forgot my standing," he finishes at last. "You were correct when you told me that I can't . . . can't help but revert back to old habits, around you. I allowed myself too much freedom—and for that, I am sorry."

He breaks off, exhaling roughly. There is an emotion in the sound, like a kind of frustration, and it pulls at a memory: his expression when he'd caught Ames and me in the hallway, less than a day ago, somehow. I'd wanted to stop him then, wanted to take him by the elbow and explain it all, as if laying out my motivations for marrying Ames would lessen the unnamable guilt that clotted, knotlike, in my stomach every time his eyes grazed mine.

I hadn't, though. I had excuses; then again, I always had excuses. Always had a reason to run away, the sins I left behind me invisible, practically nonexistent, until I turned back to look at them.

I can sense the flush stirring in my cheeks even though I can't see it, like passing one's palm over the lid of a pot and feeling the trapped steam beneath. "You acted only at my command," I whisper. "I wanted an ally, and you were too kind to deny me what I wished. If there is anyone to blame for that, it is me."

Killian isn't present to meet my eyes, but still, I cast my gaze toward the shadowed outline of my bare feet as if doing so will shield me from my own vulnerability. "I know you owe me nothing—you have done too much for me already. But please, for an hour, could we just pretend? You cannot see me—I could be anyone. A village girl you came across at the market, perhaps. Please." My voice is thick as I repeat it for the third time.

A stretch of silence. Outside, the corridor seems impossibly still—the quiet like a veil, smothering all else. Has Killian left? The thought is painful, dragging its nails down my chest in a furious swipe. My vision blurs, burns.

"You had a nightmare about Ames."

I glance up, my pulse racing. Killian's response is resigned, barely above a murmur—but there. *He* is there.

"Yes," I say hurriedly—if I take too long, he might change his mind, might leave me alone again. "I can't stop thinking about

303

our conversation at the Roost. He admitted the truth about his and my sister's relationship—he even confessed his involvement in the breaches. But when I first accused him of abducting Essie, he seemed . . . I don't know. Surprised." I pick at my pillow, allowing the reservations that have been nagging at me all evening spill forth. "It just struck me as odd."

"Perhaps he's simply a good liar," Killian replies evenly. "Besides, he admitted it all at the end, didn't he?" He sounds nearer now, as if he's leaning against the door, contemplating. I straighten.

"I suppose. He said I was clever. And that it was a pity no one else would get to hear my theories." I gnaw at my lip. "It is of no matter, anyway. Like you said, he's a good liar. I'm not sure why I keep questioning myself."

Neither of us speaks for a minute, the night breeze blowing a gentle melody against my windowpanes. I can feel the conversation drawing to a close, its tail slipping through my fingers—another second, perhaps two, and it will be gone, just another shadow in the blackness.

"I'm afraid I'm still jealous of her. Essie," I say, and with a lurch, our connection rears to life again. Letting my eyelids flutter shut, I continue, in a tone so hushed I wonder whether it will reach him: "That I envy her, for being Father's Vessel. For coming back and reclaiming her title so soon after it was passed to me."

"And does that matter so very much?" Killian's remark comes faster than I anticipated, hitting me like cold steel, the flat of a blade. "Being Vessel—becoming a Manor Lord—is it truly worth a life like your father's?" he continues. "Or Ames's, for that matter? Decades spent in the constant fear of challenges to your reign, always scrabbling for more power, more land, more influence?"

My skin prickles, the lightless air suddenly denser, collecting like dust on my shoulders. "And the alternative is so much better?" I fire back, curling my hands in my lap to keep them from trembling. "You forget that unlike you, I am not a man, Killian. If I am not Lord, there is no option for me besides marriage—almost certainly to a widower twice my age, who'd make Ames look like a gem in comparison. I cannot just . . . walk away from my past and start anew, as you have."

A creak of a floorboard, somehow defiant—out in the hallway, Killian is turning, the dark obsidian of his shadow beneath the door shifting as he moves. "You forget that my life did not begin at Norland House," he says tightly. He must be facing my room now, speaking directly into the wood. "There are parts of my history—parts of *me*—with which you are still unfamiliar."

I roll my eyes to the ceiling. "Oh, yes, I forgot—your as-yet-untold tragic backstory." I huff. "*Do* enlighten me, Mr. Brandon. What sin are you covering up that is so horrible I could never stand to look at you again?"

"That is not my name."

His tone is level, emotionless, yet it shocks me all the same. "What?"

He sighs again, and this time it is filled with regret. "My surname is not Brandon—that was my mother's maiden name," he admits. "It is Moran."

My stomach sinks to my feet. "As in . . ."

"Red Duke Logan Moran of Kyrie, yes, he is my father," Killian confirms. I don't miss the acidity in his voice—the way he says *father* like the word is a slice of lemon on his tongue. "I'm the youngest of the family."

The revelation is the sudden sweep of dawn, illuminating all around it. "*You're* Kelly Moran?" I say, incredulous. "But he's—I've always heard it said that he was . . ." I trail off, blushing, uncertain as to how to continue.

"A great beauty?" Killian finishes, with a wry cynicism that makes my insides clench with mortification. "I was often told that, too. Until I wasn't."

His shadow twists again. There is a rough scraping noise from the hallway, followed by another groan of protest from the floorboards—it takes a moment for me to realize that he's sitting, his back pressed against the door.

"My parents had four sons before my mother died," Killian starts. He sounds more tired than he did a moment ago, as if the story is a stone grinding against him, wearing him down. "My father's mother was Lord Albion's sister, far enough removed from the Lordship that my siblings and I were not prime candidates for the Nomination, but still—a Dukedom is a considerable title to inherit." The door trembles as he adjusts his position. I picture him running a hand through his hair—the waves painted a cool blue-black in the night. "Like your father, my own did not name a successor while my brothers and I were growing up, but unlike Lord Silas, he expected us to fight for the honor." He pauses. "Or perhaps I am wrong—perhaps our childhoods were similar in that way, too."

He stops, presumably lost in thought. A stabbing pain like the sting of broken glass jabs into my side at his words; unsettled, I push the emotion away.

"Anyway," Killian continues, "as I said, I am my father's youngest son, with three elder brothers above me. By the time I was born, they had already been warring over the title for years. I was a spare sibling, with nothing to do besides spend my family's money, hunt, and wait around in case one of my brothers died and I was needed to take their place. They're the ones who coined my nickname, you know—*Little Kelly*, they'd call me, never Killian. I hated that it stuck." His speech sours. "I should have been content to stay out of the fray, but I resented my lot. I wanted more."

An uncanny sort of recognition settles in my gut, like meeting a stranger on the street and seeing a bit of yourself thrown back at you in the shape of their nose, the curl of their hair. An heir born to all the trappings of power, yet with none of its weight to ground them. A child whose love of their sibling rotted to envy, poisoning the blood between them like waste flowing into a stream.

I know a girl like that. I was a girl like that.

"I started picking fights with my brothers," Killian goes on, oblivious to my discomfort. "I became immersed in their rivalry quite quickly from that point onward, like stepping into a bath. Because I was so junior to the rest of my siblings, they'd never seen me as a threat, and had commonly disclosed their insecurities to me when I was young." He clears his throat, the sound grating. "I used their fears against them—to embarrass them in front of one another and my father. I wanted them to look weak."

The sick feeling inside me intensifies, sitting like rancid meat in my stomach. I struggle to remain silent as Killian releases an exhale, his intonation shifting, becoming hesitant, almost reluctant. "A little under a year ago, my brother Declan and I were on patrol near the border of Norrin," Killian tells me. "There was a breach—one of the lanterns had gone out, and a few Phantoms made it through the gap. Declan goaded me, telling me if I was so fit to succeed Father, I could take them myself."

There is a roaring in my ears, and a swift dizzying sensation, like the earth is sinking around me. "Killian, no," I whisper.

He doesn't falter, only the slight hitch in his breath letting me know he's heard me. "I was rash and hotheaded; I accepted his challenge," he says tightly. "I slew the first Phantom easily, but there were three more with it, and they overwhelmed me." He takes a beat; the room seems to pulse with it. "You have witnessed the result."

As if summoned, an image leaps forth—I picture the scars that wind their way over his skin like a spray of ivy. Injuries from a

Phantom attack, I'd assumed when I'd first met him. I suppose I was not wrong, but this—his full explanation—withers me.

"Declan came when he heard my screams," Killian finishes at last. "I suppose he knew it would be far crueler to take away my vanity than to take my life."

I clutch my sheets, my knuckles white. Beyond the door, I can hear the rustle of Killian's movements; I want, desperately, to go over to him, to throw open the boundary between us and embrace him, but when I try to rise I find myself paralyzed.

"And did your father punish him?" I ask instead. "Your brother?"

"On the contrary," Killian answers flatly without a flicker of emotion. "He made Declan his heir.

"Afterward, my family wanted to send me to stay with a cousin of mine until the scandal died down, but I refused." Killian keeps speaking, but his words seem to part around me like a forded brook, barely registering in my mind. "I could tell that my disfigurement made my relatives uncomfortable, and my pride was too great to accept charity from the few of them that might have extended it. So instead I went south. I served as a sentry to Lord Florabelle and the Carringtons in Southhook for a while, and then, when your sister put out the call for additional forces, I came here. To Norland House." He taps his fingers against the floor, a dull patter like rain. "I always wondered if your sister recognized me. We met, once, as children—Lord Silas took her to some party my father was throwing at our estate. But if she knew the surname I gave her was a lie, she never mentioned it."

"Killian." I say his name because I don't know what else to say; it leaves a tang in my mouth, like spoiled milk. Finally able to move, I push myself from up my bed, padding over to the door—but as I reach for the knob, Killian speaks again.

"Please, don't," he says, so close now, like a ghost in my ear—

only an inch of wood separating us. More quietly, he adds, "I do not think I could bear it if you comforted me."

Behind my ribs, my heart stutters, stills. Thoughts fuzzing, I drop my hand to my side.

"I tell you this only so you understand that whatever emotions you feel toward your sister, I would never condemn you for them," he says. "Power . . . the Manors flash it like a coin, make you crave it, but it is a lie. The only gifts my father's title ever bought me were resentment, hatred, and pain." He hesitates. "I wish only for you to be free, in this and all things."

His words—the sincerity with which he utters them—break something within me. Unbidden, tears flood my vision, rolling down my cheeks, and stain my skin with salt. I wipe at my face with my palms, embarrassed, but every motion seems only to shatter me further. I'm not sure if I'm crying for him or for my sister, or perhaps for all of us at once, for what we have lost and what we have taken from others.

Without allowing myself time to reconsider, I lower myself to my knees, splaying my hands against the dusty floor. My pulse pounds as I slide my fingers underneath the door, into the narrow space Killian's shadow is currently pouring through. The hall air kisses my fingertips, chillier than inside my room.

"Merrick." I can hear the house settle around him as he shifts, can feel the floorboards quiver under his weight.

"Merrick," he repeats, and in that instant I think that no one has ever held my name as beautifully as he has: so delicately it might have been his own. Then the floorboards creak again and he's reaching forward, interlocking his fingers with mine. His skin is dry and rough, like sandpaper, and the touch of him eases loose something inside me. It feels like an admission, like anticipation, like the held breath before a *yes*.

I want more.

"Merrick," he says a third time, steadier now, his grip on me tightening in a way that makes my stomach clench pleasantly. "I cannot offer you a Lordship or a grand estate. But if you ever wished to rid yourself of all of this—I would go with you, if you asked me. If you left, I would follow you wherever you went—to the Far Reaches, if you desired."

I close my eyes, embracing the emptiness I find there. The places where our fingers meet are buzzing points of connection, and I yearn to cross the threshold between us entirely, to see him staring back at me through the dark. To accept his offer and flee with him, like my father did, running somewhere my past cannot touch.

Instead, I raise my free hand to the door, rest it against the smooth wood as if it is his cheek, as if I can grasp him. "I know," I say.

We exist in quiet for a moment. When my thighs ache and my knees groan from kneeling, I lie down, keeping my arm outstretched, and so does he. I catch the wink of his eye through the crack beneath the door and it is startling, the vibrant blue a lit spill held up to the gloom.

The hours wash over us, the night waning, time running onward, until at last my lids grow heavy and I fall asleep.

CHAPTER TWENTY-EIGHT

Ames and his mother's trial is set for the winter solstice—the next time the Mortal Council gathers in New London, a few months from now. Though to call it a trial at all is generous. True, my Manor has brought charges—abduction of a Manorborn, along with trespassing and border interference—charges that were seconded by the Faulk Manor, meeting the minimum threshold required for a formal inquisition. And it is true, also, that with what Ames confessed to me regarding his family's role in the breaches, coupled with the partial Saint stamp on the threat from Essie's room, there is ample evidence with which to convict them. A judgment that, if made, would see their Manor dissolved for good, its lands folded into its neighboring territories.

Yet already I have heard Cressida's and Tom's whispers about our fellow Manors—Lords who, they say, have seen the Saints' actions as a proof of weakness in our own line, rather than a failing on Ames's and Ianthe's parts. Each time a new rumor arises, I think of Cressida's reaction after Essie first vanished—how harshly I'd criticized her for prioritizing politics over my sister's safety. *Though the other Manor Lords may be our allies in name, they are not our friends,* she'd said to me then. Now I'm starting to see what she meant.

Power, I am learning, dulls the lines of good and evil until they are nothing but a blur. Power *is* good; it *is* evil. It only depends on whose hands it falls into: yours, or someone else's, whether you are reaching for it or trying to tear it down.

And one can never have enough.

For now, at least, the Saints have been put on a probation of sorts—confined to their province until the proceedings are resolved, with Lord Ianthe barred from attending the upcoming Nomination Hearing. In the meantime, I try to take solace in the understanding that in the most important way, we have won. Essie is safe, and the person who took her identified. Why, then, do I still feel so unsettled, as if I am trapped in an illusion of my own, entangled in the translucent strands of a mystery I insist to myself is solved?

On our own part, my family has yet to formally acknowledge the transfer of power that has occurred since Essie's return. Rather, the matter of my sister taking back the title of Vessel has simply been assumed, so natural it goes without saying. Like the slide between summer and fall, no one bothers to question the shift—it just *is*. To ask why would be strange, even nonsensical.

So I don't. I play the role of supportive sister diligently, sitting by Essie's bedside in the early days when she is too weak to walk more than a few meters, and then, as her strength returns, accompanying her for strolls around the grounds, her hand clasped in mine. It is victory enough, I tell myself, that the Saints have been unmasked.

* * *

Two days before the Nomination Hearing, I am lounging in the drawing room, plucking idly at the bone-white keys of the pianoforte before me, when the sound of footsteps disturbs me. I snap my head up, not realizing I'm searching for a pair of mismatched eyes until two brown ones greet me, disappointingly consistent in their coloring. *Cressida.* Giving her a nod of greeting, I turn my attention back to my instrument, attempting to arrange my scattered notes into something resembling a melody.

My thoughts, though, remain on Killian. It's gotten so that his absence presses just as firmly on me as his presence does, recently; like a misplaced hairpin, I am constantly, frustratingly aware of his lack, forever reaching absent-mindedly for him and grasping nothing. The itch is made worse by the knowledge that I could find him, if I wanted to—could march to the sentries' quarters and demand to speak with him, could crack my bedroom door open at night and catch him as he passed by the other side. And yet every time I am tempted to do so, another part of myself stops me.

He is too good to deny me if I call for him, of that much, I am sure. But while I am no longer engaged to Ames, what else had changed between us, really? He told me he would leave with me before, and instead, I chose Norland—just as Father raised me to do. And after Essie's Nomination is confirmed, I will travel back to New London and become the bride Father raised me to be, too, securing a good match that strengthens my Manor, regardless of how much it drains me.

Pretending otherwise is too painful and would be too cruel to Killian. It is better, I insist to myself, to let him go—to give him the freedom he said he wished for me.

All of this, I ponder as I stab a discordant song on the piano. I assume that Cressida has long since drifted away, continuing on through the drawing room toward whatever destination she's headed to—which is why, when she lays her hand on my shoulder, I jump.

My cousin-in-law frowns, stepping away at my reaction. "Did you not hear me?" she asks, her tone clipped with impatience. "I called your name three times, at least."

I shift on the cushioned piano bench to face her, chastened. She's dressed for the indoors, in a plain yellow dress, and is carrying a packet of papers at her side, bound together with string. I can't make out their contents, but they look to be of varying age and size—some yellowed, others crisp. "I—I'm sorry," I say, pushing any lingering thoughts of Killian from my mind. "I suppose I was distracted."

Cressida huffs. "Well, not by your musical ability, that's for certain." She casts a withering look at the piano, as if its mangled warble has personally offended her, before turning back to me. When her gaze skims over my face a second time, her expression thaws, her irritation chased away by a suppler emotion.

"I've just come to let you know, your sister has given the staff permission to commence with clearing out your father's quarters," she says flatly—directly—but her eyes jump away from mine, as if she can't quite manage to hold my stare. "Space must be made for guests who will need to stay overnight after the Nomination Hearing concludes, lest the Lords be forced to bunk in the sentries' barracks."

"Oh. Of course—that's understandable." I trace the floral pattern of my chintz dress with my index finger, looking down at my skirt. I'm not sure why Cressida's pronouncement upsets me—since Father's death, my mourning has been cut through with resentment, my grief sour and bilious, if one could term it grief at all—but her words land like a jab to my gut all the same. The removal of his physical belongings feels final in a different sort of way than the Memorial Ball. Once his things are taken away, once there is nothing tying him to this earth but my memories, how can I prove that he ever existed at all? He will become no more than a bedtime story, a tale I clutch close to myself at night when I am cold and cannot sleep.

Cressida seems to understand this, because she sighs, her features sagging farther. "I assumed the news might be difficult for you to hear," she says. "The servants will begin their work this evening—I requested that they delay a few hours, to give you and Estella time to retrieve any personal artifacts you'd like to keep for yourselves. In the meantime, here—" She hands me the packet she's carrying, the paper weighty against my palms, heavier than I was expecting. "These are from his desk. If there is anything relevant, retain it for your records; all else, feel free to throw out. I tried only to include what looked recent."

She gives my shoulder another squeeze, more gingerly this time. Then, with a sympathetic smile, she departs, sweeping gracefully back out of the room.

I remain seated for another minute, staring blankly at the collection of pages I'm holding, running my thumb over their edges, curled like flower petals. After a moment, I sigh, tugging loose the string binding them together and setting the stack down on the bench beside me. Mostly, I see as I sift through them, they are bits of old correspondence—notices about this year's timber harvest and propositions to increase taxes, missives from other Manors, a few reports from sentries alerting Father to disruptions at the border. On many of the letters, his handwriting fills the paper, preserved like a fossil, and the sight makes the ache in my heart throb harder. Setting one note aside, I flip to another: a half-empty sheet on which a list of names and numbers has been arranged in a neat column, like a log of some kind.

I frown. At the top of the page is a symbol, hastily drawn and centered like a title.

It's a crown. And more than that, it is familiar.

Rubbing the corner of the paper, I think back to the empty trunk I found the night Killian and I visited Shoreham-by-Sea, the one with the strange sigil—the crown—carved into it. I'd wondered, then, what the marking meant, had noted it and forgotten all about it in my rush to flee the orphanage with Killian shortly after. Seeing its twin, though, pulls the memory back to the surface. Did Father use this symbol to denote goods he intended to give away?

Hunching closer to the paper, I skim the names below the marking.

1 case to Holy Heart Orphanage, Shoreham-by-Sea.

1 case to Greene's Home for Widows, Chatham Crossing.

2 cases to the Church of the Lightkeeper, Framwick.

On and on the list continues, one case here, another couple there. All the establishments listed, I notice, are charitable organizations—churches, orphanages, and the like. Including the name I recognize: Holy Heart Orphanage.

Well, I think as I sit back, here is one minor mystery solved, at least. The trunk's missing contents must indeed have been charity of some kind—likely one of the many shipments of food that Father sent out prior to his death. His attempts to *clean house*, as Tom put it, just after I'd arrived at Norland. I skim the list again. The amount tracks—there are upward of a dozen towns in this log.

I shake my head. I suppose it should provide me with some measure of peace, the notion that my father wished to help our population in the weeks leading up to his passing. But it doesn't feel right. I can't get past the feeling that it wasn't the commoners Father cared about at all; more that he just wanted to tear down as much of our Manor as possible while he was alive.

Darling Manor will fall. In some ways, he made sure of that, far before Ames did.

I set the paper down. The amount of correspondence left to sort through is already giving me a headache, and besides, it is pointless to continue on with the rest of it without Essie. What if I deem something unimportant that she wishes to keep? Gathering the stack and tucking it under my arm, I rise, resolving to make my way to her bedroom and enlist her in my efforts.

When I arrive, though, her room is quiet, the door swinging easily open on its hinges when I push it. "Essie?" I call hesitantly, peering inside. My heart clutches as I take in her empty bed, the bedsheets crumpled casually at its foot; the cup of tea resting on the nightstand, steam still issuing from its surface in smoky wisps. *She's gone.* The fear leaps forward with rapid speed, crawling into the forefront of my mind from the shadowy recesses where I have shoved it ever since Essie's return. *Ames has got her—she's been taken again—*

Inhaling, I will my nerves to settle. Ames has been caught, and in all likelihood, my sister is just fetching a few biscuits to go with her tea. I'll wait for her here, I decide, and if she doesn't return in ten minutes or so, *then* I may consider sounding the alarm.

Crossing to her nightstand, I move the teacup to the side and lay the stack of papers down next to it, cursing myself when one mops up a bit of brownish spillage from the brew within—Cressida has yet to lift her ban on moorflower, insisting our remaining reserves be saved for the Hearing. Wiping away the rest of the drip with my thumb, I settle myself on the chair by Essie's bedside and wait.

Tick. tick. The seconds pass with excruciating slowness, as if my solitary presence has made time drag its feet, unworried about impressing a crowd. From my chair, I glance around the room, my gaze drifting from Essie's cold fireplace, a few embers still burning among the ash, to her desk, to her—

Wardrobe. My skin itches; I force myself to look away, but now that I've seen it, I can't stop thinking about the letters Essie stored in there. The love notes from Ames. Though I would never admit it aloud, there is a jealous part of me that feels a surge of envy at the thought of the two of them together—even knowing how wrong it is, even knowing all that I do about Ames and his crimes. A shallow part that still hates how easily I fell for his act.

Without fully understanding why, I feel myself rise, cross to her wardrobe, and pull the doors open. I don't let myself think through my motives as I kneel down, find the loose board in the back, and remove it, lifting the ribbon-bound papers out. I just want to see them—I just want to—

The slither of paper on wood makes me pause. At the edge of the shadowed space where the board has been removed, the white border of another sheet of paper, separate from the stack, is sticking out like a cat's tongue, likely dislodged by my jostling. *Did it fall out?* Curious, I pinch it by the corner, pulling it free.

Others come with it—three additional pages sliding into sight as I tug on the first one. Frowning, I gather them all, splaying them out on the floor in front of me.

What I see stops me short.

The rightmost letter bears Ames's handwriting, though not much of it. The sheet is mostly blank except for a dashed line along the bottom middle—*meet me by the stables*—that in any other time might stoke my anger all its own. Now, though, I barely spare the message a second of thought before turning my attention to the upper portion of the letter, where a sizable rectangle near the top right corner has been ripped away. The corner where, I know from the rest of Ames's letter, the Saint seal is usually stamped.

Swallowing hard, I measure the missing bit of page with my hand. My stomach sinks when I confirm: it is approximately the same size as the threat I found on my sister's bed, the night she disappeared.

A blade punctures my heart. It is the rest of the papers, though, that drive it in.

Unlike the last, these show no signs of Ames's writing—or any familiar script at all. Instead, tens of messages are drawn out in variations of a single hand, some sloppier than others, as if the writer was trying to perfect their script.

All the messages—every last one—say the exact same thing.

Darling Manor will fall.

Something cold and sharp-tipped slides down my throat, the frozen stab of a needle. Suddenly, I feel quite unable to breathe. My eyesight blurs, black dots swarming from the corners like flies, making me dizzy . . .

And then, from behind me, comes the creak of the door.

I stand, turn, Ames's ripped letter still in my grip. She is waiting there like a dark swan, like a grim fortune, like silty dregs at the bottom of a teacup, foretelling death.

"Merrick," my sister says evenly. "I wasn't expecting to see you here."

CHAPTER TWENTY-NINE

She steps farther into the room, the door closing with a *snick* behind her. The clean sound is like the fall of a blade; it feels final, somehow, as if the rest of Norland has retreated, leaving only this room, only us.

"What do you have there?" she asks, her question genial, intrigued rather than alarmed. By the way her eyes flash, polished silver, I can tell she already knows. Still, I clutch the half-torn paper close to my chest, curling my knuckles protectively around it.

"Ah." Her voice drops to a velvet whisper, the flat-bellied slide of a snake through a field. "That's what I was afraid of."

She *tsk*s, advancing toward me with her arm outstretched. The hem of her sage dress skims over the floor as she moves, a subtle hiss trailing in her wake. "Careless of me to leave loose ends, really. No one warns you what a preoccupying business mourning is. Important things just . . . slip one's mind."

I stumble back a step, nearly tripping over my feet in my haste to put space between us. "Stay away from me."

Obligingly, Essie pauses, her brow crumpling as if with hurt. "Merrick, don't be silly," she says with a trilling laugh. "What do you think I'm going to do to you? Kill you?"

My pulse spikes, my nerves buzzing with the instinct to flee. Instead, I take another measured step away from her, careful to keep my tone even. "You framed Ames. You wrote the threat yourself—not him. Why?"

"Why?" Essie laughs in disbelief. "Because Father forced me to!" Her lips twist like a wrung cloth. "Or the man I believed to be my father, at least," she spits. "He was going to destroy us if I didn't do something to stop him. Ames was only a casualty—what matters is that I was *protecting* you, Merrick, if you'd only let me explain—"

"What do you mean, the man you believed to be your father?" I halt my retreat, my feet suddenly rooted to the floor, but Essie only flicks my question away as if it bores her.

"In all seriousness, Merrick, let's be through with this. Give it here." She beckons me forward expectantly, tapping her fingers against the heel of her hand, her mood shifting from resentful to demanding as easily as stepping out of a dress. When I don't move, she sighs impatiently. "Do you really want to undo all your excellent work?" she chides. "You followed my trail so splendidly—I'd hoped you'd find the journal, of course, but just think of how quickly you sniffed out Ames! Who, I am certain you will agree, was no innocent bystander in all of this." She shakes her head, her expression turning contemptuous. "I warned Silas that Ianthe was growing greedy, but did he listen? Of course not. The Saints would have eaten us alive if we hadn't dealt with them, and now look at them—laid low, just as they deserve." I watch, caught in a stupor, as she breaks into a smile, her eyes winking merrily at me. "See what a wonderful team we make?" she says, her tone now saccharine, sticking to my skin. "I always believed you had potential, Merrick. All you needed was a guiding hand."

She shifts as if about to resume her approach, and the movement snaps me free of my trance. "What do you mean," I growl, edging toward the windows, "you believed Silas to be your father?"

Essie gives a peevish roll of her eyes. "Please—this repetition is getting tiring now. Besides, can't you put it together? You've done so well with everything else. You even found the orphanage, for the Three's sake."

Foreboding rolls under my skin, billowing through me like a snapped cloth. "How do you know about the orphanage?" I ask. "Did Killian tell you?" The backs of my calves bump against the windowsill, forcing me to a halt, and it is as if the nudge breaks free a memory. *Footsteps on the second level, pattering toward the stairs.* I inhale, daggered and cutting. "The noises we heard . . ."

Essie smirks, clapping shallowly as if congratulating me on my revelation. "Yes," she replies breezily, "I had matters to attend to there. I nearly died of fright when you and Brandon interrupted me." Her smirk lifts higher, her eyes narrowing. "What a funny little match you've made for yourself, by the way," she says. My neck prickles with embarrassment, a flash of heat like a gust of stove air warming me as she goes on. "You *have* realized who his family is, haven't you? I should hope you aren't dense enough to be fooled by an uncreative surname."

I don't answer. My escape cut off by the windows, I glance around for an alternate exit, finding only the bedroom door. I'll have to make a break for it, then, and hope that Essie's strength hasn't returned enough to fight me off. My muscles tense, my breaths coming faster in preparation to run.

"Wait—Merrick, please, wait." Essie's cry stops me, my attention flicking involuntarily back to her. In an instant, her haughty confidence has disappeared; her hand is held out in front of her, a nonverbal extension of her plea; her lip trembles like a scared child's.

It tears the illusion I've cast over her—the façade of a villain—in two. Suddenly, all I see is my sister again, the girl who came to my room at midnight because she couldn't trust anyone else, the girl who, for years, tended my wounds and smoothed my hair.

The girl I left.

"Please don't leave," Essie says, her voice nearly a whimper. "Why don't we make a deal? If you stay here, I'll explain everything to you, just as Silas told me—and then, if you still think me evil, I'll stand aside and let you go." She takes a hesitant step closer, near enough that I can see the tremble in her shoulders, the panic that shakes through every part of her. "We are sisters, Merrick," she begs. "Will you not hear me out?"

I wrap my fingers around the windowsill, my nails digging into the wooden sash like it is a sword I can take by the hilt and slash a boundary between us. Once more, I look toward the door, heavy and solid, waiting for me to open it.

Then—because I am pathetic, because she is the only family I have left—I turn back to my sister, letting my head dip in a nod.

Essie's relief is visible, like a bolt of fabric going slack. "Thank you," she breathes. Inhaling, she draws herself taller, brushing down her dress—gathering herself to speak.

"It began as I have already told you," she says evenly. "After Mama's death, Silas—Father—became a recluse, barely leaving his room. But what I withheld from you is that a few days before he died, he called me in for a . . . discussion." She stiffens, the memory hardening on her like scales of armor. "In the journal I left for you, I made it sound as though it was Father who abandoned his duties—and it is true that at the beginning, he did struggle to carry the dual load of his grief and his responsibilities. But in reality, I came to him with the proposal of my taking on more of the day-to-day border maintenance, a month or so after you left us. I was frustrated that he hadn't yet named me Vessel, and believed if he could see how well I ran the province, he'd finally understand I was ready. But . . . I made a mistake." She hesitates. "It was one I didn't realize I *was* making, at the time, but the consequences were less than ideal, I'll admit. When Father found out what had happened, he was furious. He told me exactly what I knew he'd told you, months prior—that I would never be Manor Lord."

My nails carve deeper into the sill, slivers of wood biting into my skin as if in protest. "What?" I reply briskly. "Why would he deny both of us the title?"

"I haven't finished." Essie crosses her arms, her tone chastening. "He said I could never rule, because I am not Manorborn—not immune to the mist." She shoots me a look that I barely register, so held am I by the leaden pull of her admission, the way it drags me down with it. "After he and Mama wed, she was unable to become pregnant for years—long enough that they believed the miracle would never come to pass. They could not have an heir naturally, they supposed, so they . . . they took one, from the same orphanage Father had plucked Mama from back when they first met. They took me and raised me as their own."

She breaks off, her voice strained, her stare parsing mine as if she is trying to peer into my mind, peel my reaction from me like a card she can predict. Yet at her admission, an uncanny quiet has descended over me, complete as a winter night. Her words linger in the air, almost a part of the atmosphere, as if they have drifted in on a breeze: *They took me and raised me as their own.*

I shiver. All the times I teased her when we were children—her with her dark hair and gray eyes, so dour-faced next to my mother and me, like our shadow personified . . . is it possible she was never one of us at all? A stranger, slipped like a cuckoo into our nest?

She never belonged to you. She is not your sister.

Finally, the shock settles into me with a vicious rattle. "But that's impossible," I burst out. "I've seen you go into the Graylands, Essie—Father took you on twice as many hunts as he ever did me. If you were not Manorborn, you'd be a Phantom a dozen times over by now."

In response, my sister gives another sad shake of her head. "Yes, well—that goes back to the unfortunate mistake I made. And the plan of Father's, related to it."

Her mouth turns down in a scowl. I grasp at her words like a bit of driftwood, using them to haul myself up out of the waves. *Focus on this, now—forget about what she just told you. That will come later. For now, only this, here.* "What plan?" I hear myself ask.

Essie raises a brow. "I'm afraid I can't share it with you, Merrick," she answers primly, and the unexpectedness of her reply is enough to bring me back to myself, at least for the moment. She clucks her tongue against the roof of her mouth, a wordless reprimand. "What he was plotting . . . it needed to die with him, or our entire line—all that our ancestors have built, that we've worked for—would have perished instead," she continues ominously. "Suffice to say that he didn't intend for either of us to succeed him as Lord. He was prepared to drive a stake through the heart of our Manor himself, in fact, and yet he expected me to *understand.*" Her fists clench at her sides, her knuckles bulging. "To support his cause, if you can believe it. I—"

Like clipping a stem, she stops short, her lips pressing into a line. The master of herself, even now. "No matter," she says, a brusque dismissal. "We argued, and by that evening, I knew what I had to do." She nods, composed and unapologetic. "So I spent a couple days preparing, and then I wrote him a note saying I wanted to make amends. The morning after that, we walked out together, early, to Mama's grave."

All at once, it hits me—the meaning hiding, unspoken, in her words. *What he was plotting . . . it needed to die with him.*

"You killed him. You pushed him into the fog." The proclamation seems to come from another person; I am motionless, bound to my body by thin strings.

"I laid him to rest near his wife, the woman he loved most in the world," Essie snaps, my comment riling her. "I did him more of a kindness than he *ever* did us."

She flutters her eyes closed, her chest rising, then falling again. When she's calm, her lids blink open again, slate irises once more looking into mine. "Passing his death off as self-inflicted was simple. More challenging was crafting my own reason for vanishing. There were several loose threads I needed to tie up—pieces of Father's plot I had to ensure were put to bed—but I'd already proclaimed myself his heir by that point, his Vessel. I couldn't just go tearing off around the province, not when preparations for my own Hearing were already beginning." Essie hums, the noise calculative in a way that makes goose bumps erupt on my arms. "No, I needed to disappear, and fortunately, Ames presented himself as the ideal candidate for my imagined abduction.

"I hadn't told a soul about our involvement, naturally; had hidden away those idiotic letters he sent before one of the staff spotted them and took it upon themselves to start a rumor. *Marry me, or face the consequences of your choice*—really." She chuckles, as if she finds his attempts at intimidation feeble, amusing. "But then, I realized—what if he wasn't just a petty boy, spitting poison to make himself feel bigger? What if his threats were followed by action—an Archdaughter vanishing from her bed?" she asks, not waiting for a response before continuing. "It would be killing two birds with one stone, so to speak—my so-called disappearance would give me the time I required to take care of Father's remaining business, and Ames would get his due for crossing me. The pieces of the story were all there; I just needed someone to tell them to. And then you came home."

Her focus intensifies, pride stealing into her expression. "I wrote the journal to set you on the right path—point you to Killian, who I'd already made sure to plant a story about my 'incidents' with—but you, Merrick, you did better than I ever could have anticipated. Putting together the truth behind the breaches—getting Ames to confess to his role in the attacks—frankly, you've astounded me. I knew staging my own reappearance would be a risk, but with the case you've compiled against the Saints . . ." She gazes at me, her expression grateful, verging on awestruck, like I am something come out of the clouds. Something divine. My toes curl inside my slippers, a finger of ice trailing down my spine.

"Ames can deny stealing me away all he wants, and no one—not even his mother's staunchest allies—will believe him," Essie goes on, drawing nearer to me. "I am forever indebted to you, Merrick."

I barely feel it as she closes the distance between us and takes my free hand, her touch a faint buzz at the edges of my consciousness. Though I want to break away, there is a deliberateness to the gesture that warns me not to, as if to reject her would be to fail a test—one that carries penalties that I am not prepared to face.

Wetting my lips, which have gone dry while she's been speaking, I challenge her. "So what comes next, now that you've saved us all from Father's supposed plan? We pretend that you never laid a hand on him?" It is a struggle to keep the reproachful tenor out of my voice as I continue. "That you and I share the same blood?"

Essie grins, jubilant and victorious. "Now our reign begins.

Don't you see?" she effuses. "In just a couple days, I'll become Lord of the Darling Manor, and when I do, I'll ensure you never have to beg for the companionship of a man like Fitz Vannett again." She clutches me tighter, her nails daggering into me. "You can have whatever you want—whoever you want," she tells me eagerly. "You can have Killian Moran, if you wish it. I will provide you a dowry such that you could wed a peasant off the streets, and you would still be one of the richest women in Sussex."

I shove away the image of Killian that rises in my vision, the sapphire wink of his eye beneath the door. *If you left, I would follow you wherever you went.* What would it feel like, to take him up on his offer? To know that I could do so without sacrificing an income, or safety—that no matter where we ran, we would have the money to make our path smooth?

The prospect is too tempting to dwell on; if I do, I am sure that I will cave, so instead, I turn my attention back to my sister. "And what makes you so certain I won't tell Cressida about this as soon as I leave you?" I ask. "That I'll keep your secret?"

Essie's smile remains undiminished, though it gleams a little less strongly at my question. "Dear, tell her what?" she says, tilting her head to the side curiously. "That you found a torn note from Ames? A few sheets with some scribble on them?" She releases another half-sighed laugh, and my stomach plunges to my feet. "There is certainly nothing suspicious in any of that. As for what I've confessed to you, here . . . it is your word against mine. I am confident that I would prevail, but even if by some twist of fate, you did . . ." She releases me, stepping back so that we stand facing each other, a few inches apart. Positioned parallel like this, she could be my double, her pale face and black hair the charcoal rendition of my own.

"I would be executed, Merrick," she continues bluntly, and I wince. "Slain." She bites out the word, her features hardening in emphasis. "Not to mention, our Manor would never be the same afterward. You might gain the Lordship, but our reputation would be beyond tarnished—it would only be a matter of time before the other Manors took it upon themselves to rid themselves of our stain." She hesitates, allowing her words to seep into the space like water into the dirt, letting the air become heavy with them. "What I did, I did in part to protect you," she goes on, after another few seconds. "Can you meet my eyes and tell me now, you truly wish me dead?"

She speaks softly, rage and defiance and sorrow all knitting together within me at her question. I urge myself to answer her—to say something, anything—but in the end, all I do is look down, the drop of my stare an admission enough.

Essie exhales, pleased. "I didn't think so," she murmurs. I startle when she lays a palm on my cheek, the heel of her hand cupping my chin. "You are a good sister. Better than I deserve, but—we have a lifetime ahead of us for me to make it up to you." She pats me once, like a dog; then, before I can react, she swiftly reaches down and plucks the torn letter from my fingers.

"For safekeeping," she says, folding the paper into a square and stowing it in the bodice of her dress. She darts forward, planting a chaste kiss on my forehead. The brush of her lips withers me, drying as salt. "Thank you, dear," she coos, leaning away. "I love you so very much."

She leaves me after that, me and her empty room—and her goodbye, spinning around and around again in my mind, a dancer raised on tiptoe.

I love you so very much.

CHAPTER THIRTY

Despite the stuffy name, Nomination Hearings are less trial than party—a sort of coronation and reception ball rolled into a single hedonistic evening. Traditionally, the night begins with a public dance, hosted by the Nominating Manor and open to all residents of their province; then, at midnight, the Mortal Council retreats with the Nominee into a private chamber, where they deliberate the prospective heir's merits until dawn. The finale to the entire affair occurs just before sunrise, when the triumphant Nominee emerges again, swathed in their Manor's regalia with the rest of the Mortal Council parading after them like a flock of geese, and completes the ceremonial Spilling of the First Blood for all to see.

Once the life source of the new Lord has been poured into the earth of their province, their title is official, and the Manor is theirs.

I flex my gloved hand as I make my way to Norland's main ballroom, studying the sleek silk covering me like a second skin—

the pure, pale blue of fresh water, an exact match to my dress. The gown from Madame Villette—the one that, for a few brief days, had been tailored to fit me—has now hastily been altered back for my sister's use. I imagine the crimson fabric peeling back to reveal vulnerable pink flesh below, the action like scaling a fish, and wonder if the land will sense its new leader in the iron tang of my sister's blood. If the people will chafe under her unfamiliar grasp, or if they will lean into it gratefully, sheep flocking to a benevolent shepherd, all thoughts of their past rulers put aside.

I laid him to rest near his wife . . . I did him more of a kindness than he ever did us.

The heel of my slipper twists beneath me as I recall Essie's words, my steps faltering. It's been like this each time my mind has drifted to my sister in the two days since her confession—my body suddenly turns to that of a prey animal, ready to bolt. As they dressed me earlier, my maids tutted over the newly sallow tint of my skin, the purple crescents under my eyes. Evidence of days spent looking over my shoulder, of nights interrupted by a dozen trips to my bedroom door, just to check the lock one last time.

There is still so much I do not know: what my father was planning, for one, the scheme that Essie was so afraid of that she preferred to kill him rather than allow it to succeed. Or, just as baffling—how, if she is truly not Manorborn, she has been able to go into the Graylands all these years without becoming a Phantom.

Her speech lances through my thoughts again. *They took me and raised me as their own.*

Thus far, I haven't uttered a word to anyone about what passed between Essie and me in her room that day. Not that I haven't considered doing so—I've spun out so many potential ways of phrasing it to Tom and Cressida that they've tangled like a web inside my head—but conspiring with myself is a private sin, a wound inflicted on me and me alone. Unable to hurt others.

I would be executed, Merrick.

Slain.

"No," I murmur out loud, my gut clenching in rejection of my sister's words. Whether she is mine by blood or not, I cannot be the one to hurt Essie again. I think back to last summer, the warm air wafting over me, damp and sweet as cows' breath as I left Norland for New London. If I had not abandoned her then—if she had not had to face Father alone—who knows how differently the past months would have turned out? Maybe we could have discussed Father's admission together; maybe no one would have had to die at all.

Maybe this is my fault. And if it is, how can I force Essie to suffer the consequences, simply because she is tethered to the end of a chain that I began?

"Presenting Archdaughter Merrick Darling, daughter of the late Manor Lord Silas Darling and Manor Lady Artemis Darling, stewards of Sussex."

So lost to my inner turmoil am I that I don't notice I've arrived at the entrance to the ballroom until a servant is calling my name, a pair of double doors being whisked open for me. I step through on instinct, and the room before me shudders to life.

I am at the top of a landing, from either side of which two staircases spiral down toward the floor below like a pair of tongues. The ballroom is a great ocean stretched out before me, packed with a jostling crowd of people. All of them are turned my way, their parted lips like an open-mouthed school of fish.

The sight of them all—expectant and desirous—fills me with revulsion, the same as holding up a candle and being confronted with dozens of beady gazes, pests lurking unseen in the dark. Who *are* these strangers? My pulse quickens as I take in their shadowed eyes, all the hidden thoughts they hold secret, like moths clasped in a child's hands. All their wantings.

Is my sister somewhere among them? I doubt so; generally, the Nominee does not make their public appearance at a Hearing until after the Mortal Council's debate has finished, emerging from their glittering chrysalis no longer merely a Vessel but a full-formed Lord. Most likely, she's in my father's library—where the actual "Hearing" portion of the night will take place—preparing to present her case to them. Still, I can't keep myself from searching for her hawk-eyed gaze among the partygoers, clever and testing, waiting for me to fall.

Now our reign begins. Don't you see? . . . You can have whatever you want—whoever you want.

Nausea does a lazy flip within me. When tonight is through, I will have everything I craved when I fled to New London: freedom, power, enough money to marry for love, or not marry at all, if that is what I prefer. And yet Essie's promises sit sour on my tongue despite their sweetness. How can I enjoy any of what my sister is offering, knowing the lives that were taken in order to make it all possible? The blood that she has spilled?

My father's blood. A retch builds in the back of my throat, cresting higher—I shall vomit, right here in front of the entirety of our province, and then they will all see that something is wrong—

One guest breaks rank with the rest, climbing the staircase to my right with a buoyant grin on his handsome face—Tom, coming to escort me to the floor. When he reaches me, I take his proffered arm, digging my fingers into his bicep for support as he leads me down the steps. The partygoers are applauding politely now, but the nearer I get to them, the more their smiles seem like leers, their cheerful calls of praise discordant and jarring, like a pack of animals howling for their prey.

I distract myself by focusing on my surroundings. Norland is displayed in its full glory tonight, shining with a grandeur I have not seen in ages. Like a village girl in a fairy tale, the house has had its grime scrubbed away to reveal the hidden beauty beneath. The normally dusty wooden floors have been polished until they gleam, and above me, the trio of chandeliers have been swept free of their cobwebs, blazing with the light of a hundred candles.

The crowd parts as Tom and I reach the ground, then closes around us again, drawing us into its gullet. I recognize some of the faces that surround me as fellow Manorborn, but the vast majority of the guests are unfamiliar to me. Many are clad simply, in plain dresses and trousers that stand out like sores against the elaborate frocks around them. Commoners, no doubt. Their stares are the hardest of all, flint and steel, pressing like edged daggers against me.

Tom leads me through a series of introductions, each more stilted than the next, before I'm finally able to excuse myself and break away. In search of a refreshment—my thoughts are cutting as glass, and I long for the fuzz of alcohol to dull them—I push my way toward the far side of the ballroom, where I can see a line of servants standing with drink trays.

"Allow me, Archdaughter."

At the sound of a voice by my ear, I glance to my right. A man is standing a few feet away, in a close-fitting suit jacket with a forest green waistcoat beneath, one arm stretched forward to offer me a pale yellow glass of champagne, the other holding his own identical drink, condensation beading like dew down the side. His dark-honey hair is styled in loose waves; scars cut through the clean canvas of his face, one dragging down the proud column of his throat and vanishing into the knotted silk of his emerald cravat.

"Oh." I'm not sure if the noise is one of surprise or pleasure—or more likely, a little of both. I turn to face Killian more fully; he is observing me with an inscrutable expression. He looks different out of his sentry uniform—not better, necessarily, but looser, as if his past garments have all been sized a fraction too tightly, and only now is he able to breathe. "Brandon. I—"

"I'm here as Killian Moran tonight, actually," he interjects, an abashed smirk playing over his features, like the admission embarrasses him, but only just. He nods toward the crowd, surging against one another like a great school of fish. "Great-Uncle Albion is in attendance this evening, and I figured he would prefer that I not approach him dressed in the garb of a rival Manor."

I frown, following his gaze. "Approach him?" I ask mildly, accepting the proffered glass from his hand. "What for?"

Killian flushes, tugging self-consciously at the glossy knot of his cravat. Being in his presence again after so many days apart sends a trickle of warmth through me, dulling the abrasive pound of my guilt. Memories of our late-night encounter unspool slow and decadent in my abdomen, like silk ribbons strewn across a vanity.

"Serving you and your sister has been a privilege," he starts unsteadily, redness creeping farther up his neck. Something about the nervous energy he's exuding is magnetic, making me want to draw closer, rub a calming hand over his brow. I remember waking near dawn to the sound of his fading footsteps the morning after I rode to the Roost, my fingers still curled beneath my bedroom door. If not for the candlestick lying sideways on the ground—if not for the echo of Killian's voice in my head, the story he told me so clear, so impossible to manufacture—I'd almost have believed our entire conversation was nothing but a fever dream, born of my own anxieties.

A flood of sensations—anticipation, bashfulness—wash through my veins. We'd barely touched that night—just a brush of our fingers, nothing more—yet it had all felt so intense, the desire that had risen up within me different from anything I'd experienced before, even the hot longing when Ames kissed me. With Killian, the emotion had been . . . thicker, somehow. Richer, like honey, sticking to me for days afterward, coating me in amber.

I'm ripped from my reminiscing as he continues. "But . . . the other night, you were right to deny me." He grips the stem of his drink harder, his jaw tightening. "I cannot keep running away from my family. I must face them—face myself, or the self I left in Kyrie, at least." His smile returns, melancholy now. "Perhaps then I can finally improve him."

I blink at him, unable or unwilling to comprehend his statement. "You're leaving?" I'm humiliated by the whining cadence of my voice, even more so by the tears I can feel springing to my eyes, burning in my nasal cavity. My reaction is pathetic, but piled atop everything else, the prospect of his departure is one too many bits of silver on a scale, sending the entire system out of balance. A bleak vision of the future unrolls like a premonition before me: Killian will be the first to go after Essie's Nomination is complete, and then following him, Tom and Cressida, their work finished, and then only my sister and I will remain, chasing each other like cat and mouse around Norland . . .

Seeing my distress, Killian steps closer, gracefully extracting my drink from my shaking hand. "Merrick, I—forgive me," he apologizes, his features alight with worry. "I did not mean to upset you. Here, why don't we . . ."

Drifting off, he ushers me out of the ballroom through one of the pair of glass doors set into the exterior wall, leading me to the stone veranda outside. Unlike the one abutting the Roost, our estate's terrace is hunched and crumbling, ivy twining over the colonnaded railing like leafy green eavesdroppers, listening in on us.

Descending the stairs, Killian leads me through Norland's grounds, not stopping until we reach a tidy copse of apple trees tucked near the back of the gardens. Any attempts at decorum long abandoned, I collapse on a bench set between two of the trees and rub at my eyes, crying freely.

"Merrick." Killian's hands find my knees; when I look up, he is staring at me anxiously, kneeling in the grass, the purpling evening a frame around him. We lock eyes, and something zips between us, a fizz of lightning. It stoppers my sobs, dampening my emotions enough that I can swallow them down.

"I'm all right." I bite my lip, self-consciousness at my display rapidly overtaking my panic. "I'm sorry; I'm not sure what came over me. I'm just grateful to you, I suppose—for everything you've done for me. I don't know how I'll ever repay you for your kindness."

He inclines his chin, the suggestion of a nod. "You must know," he says in a hushed tone. "It was my pleasure. All of it."

I am struck by the tenderness in his expression—the way he seems to drink me in, as if I am forever becoming new before his sight. Before I can respond, he coughs, glances away.

"I should not say this," he says, still holding my knees. His head is bowed so that his features are hidden, swathed in indigo, his hair dappled with pearlescent moonlight. "You've given your answer already, I know. But I—I am not as strong as you believe me to be," he murmurs. "I cannot . . ."

He blows out an exhale, his gaze rising again to meet mine. His stare is wicked, devouring me whole, his pupils dilated and depthless. "I will not mince words. If you have felt even a fraction of what I have these past weeks, then, please—come with me to Kyrie," he says roughly. "My pride is gone, Merrick; I will beg you if I must. I . . . I am afraid of what it will do to me, leaving you. I am afraid I will fail."

He rises halfway, his hands creeping higher up my legs, grazing my thighs through my skirts. His embrace is unexpectedly

337

gentle; I assumed his touch would be rough, coarse and stumbling like a boy's fumbled caress. Instead, Killian holds me as though he's done it before. Like the physicality of me is familiar to him, easy in the way that reaching for a loved one feels like coming home.

I tip my head down, studying him. His lips are slightly parted, and there's a wildness in his expression that I've never seen before; a boundlessness, as if I could reach up and wipe away all his edges. Without breaking my gaze, he cautiously lifts one hand to cup my cheek. His thumb trails along the line of my jaw toward my mouth, a question evident in the gentle motion.

"Merrick," he repeats, "I—"

"Killian . . ." My voice cracks as I say his name, but regardless, Killian releases me at once, standing and stepping abruptly back. At his retreat, a lurch of desire heaves in my stomach and the rest of me bucks in protest, tamping the reaction down and away. My skull pounds as if with a hangover.

"I can't go with you," I say, my tears returning, muddling my voice as if I'm speaking through water. My skin is on fire, the dim evening too bright somehow, the kiss of the air against my neck overly intense. "I do not mean to lead you on, or hurt you, but Essie—I—she told me . . ."

I break off, burying my face in my hands. I hear the crunch of leaves as Killian comes to sit next to me. He settles near enough that I can sense his presence, a reassuring weight to my side, but doesn't touch me.

"What is it?" he asks urgently. "What did your sister tell you?"

And like a gate thrown wide, it tumbles out of me—looking for Essie in her room, finding the notes in her wardrobe. Our resulting confrontation, how despite myself, I couldn't turn her in, couldn't do anything except bow my head like a servant to their master. When the last of it is out, the whole of my misdeeds hovering, miasmic, in the atmosphere, I gather myself and risk a glance in Killian's direction. Throughout the entire time I've been speaking, he's remained silent, and now he sits focused on the trees ahead of him, his features shuttered and unreadable.

"An orphan . . ." he finally repeats. There's a quiver of shock in his tone, but otherwise, his speech is level, calm, and at the sound of it, appreciation floods through me like a released breath. He rests his elbows on his legs, his brow creasing in concentration. "She must be mistaken. How could she have survived the mist this long, if she is not Manorborn? I've seen her go into the Graylands myself—it is impossible."

I lift my shoulders in a shrug, shifting nearer to him. "I asked her the same. All she said was that Father had a plan of some sort—she wouldn't tell me what it was, but I assume it has to do with her immunity." Another surge of self-loathing, more potent than the first, threatens to overtake me as I recall our conversation, and my resulting silence. It seems more sinister now that I admit it aloud—like I haven't been trying to protect Essie so much as secure my own fortunes—and I cringe, angling myself toward the trunk of the nearest apple tree as if I can clamber into it, hide myself away. "You must hate me," I say miserably.

"No." Killian's reply is firm, bordering on affronted. He bridges the distance between us, taking me by the arm and turning me gingerly back toward him. "Merrick, look at me," he orders, his voice low, sincere. "I don't hate you. You have only been trying to help your sister—it is a noble quality."

My mouth wobbles at his earnestness, his sympathy—always so close at hand, like an overflowing well. "My false sister, you mean, who killed my true father, and will never be punished for it," I reply with a shake of my head. "And Ames . . . he could hang for the crime we've pinned on him, Killian. Kidnapping an Archdaughter?" A stone lodges in my windpipe at the image of

Ames's pretty face, slack and broken, his body swinging from the gallows. "What he's done is horrible, to be sure, but does he truly deserve to *die*?"

Killian's nose wrinkles. "Ames will be fine," he says; then, more forcefully, "He *will*. These trials are just another type of political game—the Saints will get off with a slap on the wrist, at the worst." He glances sidelong at me. "As much as I dislike it, you know it is true."

I hold his gaze for a moment before looking away, scuffing the toe of my slipper into the dirt. "I suppose it doesn't matter, anyway," I say. "If it weren't him being judged, it would be her. I . . ."

"Merrick!"

I go rigid at the far-off sound of my name, raising my head to search for its source. In the distance, buttery light spills from Norland House, and I relax as I take in an illuminated form moving on the terrace, clad in a vivid yellow dress I recognize. The figure is pacing the length of the stone pavilion hurriedly as if searching for something—or, more accurately, someone.

"Cressida," I say aloud, turning back toward Killian. "She'll be wanting me back—I'm sure the Hearing has started."

Killian's mouth parts as if he's considering protesting. After a second, though, he nods and rises silently, offering me his hand once he's standing. I take it, but delay getting up myself, tugging gently on his fingers. "Wait—let's go around the side," I say, motioning with my chin toward the left wing of Norland House, which is dimly lit, positioned farther off from the centrally located festivities. "There's an entrance through the kitchens we can use. I just . . . need a few more minutes to collect myself."

Killian's eyes soften at my request, his hand flexing against mine. "Of course," he says quietly. "Whatever you need."

I ignore the way my heart drops at his words as I stand up.

Even once I'm steady, it is difficult to let go of him—the buzz of his touch is a grounding force, holding my anxieties at bay.

His stare finds mine, that now-familiar tension blooming between us again. Drawing an inhale, I squeeze him harder, then pull away.

Wordlessly, we make our way toward the side of the house, the hum of the chatter of the crowd inside rising in volume as we get closer. The door to the kitchens is propped open, and unlike the rest of the estate, I see that no tidying has been done here. Empty crates and strips of burlap lie in haphazard piles along with vegetable scraps and damp-looking crusts of bread—debris from the party preparations, no doubt.

I hold my breath as we pass a particularly fragrant heap, casting my gaze over its moldering contents. My steps falter as my attention catches on a single broken crate, its wooden boards splintering— and, more specifically, on the symbol I see burned into one.

"Killian." At my call, he pauses, twisting to look back over his shoulder. Beckoning him closer, I point at the marking. "Do you see that?"

A blackened sigil of a crown mars the brown wood, the charcoal lines clear enough that they're visible even against the night. The shape is identical to the one I glimpsed at the bottom of the trunk in Holy Heart orphanage—and the twin mark I'd found in my father's records, the one I'd assumed he'd used to indicate goods bound for charity. I step closer to the trash heap, squinting at the marking. Why would a crate containing donations be tossed out here, mixed with kitchen waste?

Coming to stand next to me, Killian frowns in the direction of the debris. "What is it?" he asks. "That crate? Looks like it held moorflower leaves at one point." He angles his chin my way. "Is there something the matter with it?"

I snap my head toward him, thrown by his unexpected response. "Moorflower leaves?" I question. "As in tea? Why would you assume that?"

Killian's forehead creases in confusion. "I recognize the symbol there—that crown," he says slowly, drawing the words out as if he's just as perplexed by my answer as I am by his. "We use the same one to mark moorflower shipments in Kyrie; my father made me oversee our household deliveries a couple times, when I was younger. Said it was important to know how much went into keeping our family fed." His brows inch higher. "Why do you ask?"

His confidence makes me doubt myself. Have I mistaken the etching on the wood for the one I saw in Holy Heart? It *is* dark out, but then again, I can picture the latter image so clearly—and there is no doubt it matches the one I glimpsed in his correspondence. "I . . . no." I shrink back, embarrassed. "I suppose I'm wrong. It's odd, though—I swear I saw an identical marking in the trunk we ran across in Shoreham-by-Sea. In the orphanage, you know." I look over at Killian, relieved when I see his expression light up with understanding. "I assumed it was meant to signify that the shipment was meant for charity, but . . . it seems strange, doesn't it, that my Father would send a crate of moorflower leaves, and nothing else, to an orphanage? They're expensive, to be sure, but a trivial luxury—it isn't as though you can feed children off them." I drift off, gathering my thoughts. "Does moorflower have any health benefits that you know of?"

Killian frowns, his features sharpening in concentration. "Not that I'm aware, no," he responds a second later. "I've been drinking it since I was a boy—all Manorborn do."

He peers at the crate for a long moment before turning back toward me. "The orphanage . . ." he says, and my heart speeds when I see a new spark flaring in his eyes: an idea. "Didn't you say your sister was there that night, too?"

The realization makes me inhale. "You're right—she told me she had business to take care of there. I'd forgotten about that." I feel back in my memory for the outlines of our conversation, but the details are blurry, dulled by the shock of her larger confession. "Do you think it was related to the trunk?"

"Hmm." Killian doesn't reply, only hums, low in his throat—but I can sense an answer in him, lodged like a stone.

I give him a pointed look. "Go on."

He releases a breath. "It's likely nothing. Speaking of moorflower just reminded me . . ." He shakes his head, focusing his attention on me. "In Kyrie, my great-uncle had a practice of allotting his sentries a cup of moorflower tea with their supper every night," he starts with a shrug. "A reward, so to speak, for a job done well—I believe most Manor Lords do the same. The men here told me that your father used to, as well, but when your sister took over his duties, she did away with the evening tea—said it was needless waste, and the Manor needed to conserve its resources. Her decision angered the sentries quite a bit. I believe a couple even complained to your father about it, but he passed less than a week later, so the matter was left unresolved."

Ducking his head, he rubs at the back of his neck. "Like I said—pointless," he says with an apologetic half laugh. "I shouldn't have brought it up."

In my mind's eye, something glints—a piece of Essie's and my conversation that I'd pushed aside, now dragged back into the light by his words. *I made a mistake . . . When Father found out what had happened, he was furious.* Killian's story . . . it seems like a minor slight, revoked tea privileges, but is it possible there's something more to it? A second meaning lingering just out of sight, like an object sitting beyond the scope of a mirror—there and yet left out of its reflection?

"No, I'm glad you did," I tell him, jerking myself back into the present. "Killian . . . the plan my sister spoke of," I say carefully. "Whatever my father was plotting, the only reason Essie found out about it is because he was angry with her. That's how it all began—she said she'd made a mistake, the importance of which she didn't realize at the time, and he called her in to speak with her." I hazard a look at him, find his stare already on me. "It sounds ridiculous, but could the mistake have been related to the tea?"

I hold my breath, part of me afraid that he'll dismiss me altogether. But instead, Killian nods, his face contemplative. "Perhaps," he answers. "Like I said, the sentries were displeased with her decision to deny them moorflower. It would follow that your father wished to keep his men happy, but how such a minor mistake could relate to this so-called plan of Lord Silas's—something your sister stated she was willing to kill to prevent from getting out . . . I can't imagine."

I follow his gaze, observing the marking silently. Then, after a minute, I turn, tilting my head back to take in the soaring bulk of Norland above me, its windows glowing with the burn of a hundred candles. Somewhere within it, the Mortal Council is likely debating my sister's Nomination, preparing to declare her the next Lord of Sussex.

The heir to the man she put in the ground. And up until now, I've let her get away with it.

I twist back toward Killian. "I can't, either," I say. "So why don't we ask her ourselves?"

CHAPTER THIRTY-ONE

The bickering voices of the Mortal Council break over me like a wave as I push open the heavy doors of my father's library—polished wood that's been carved with trellises of climbing roses, the svelte forms of foxes peeking out from around blooms—Killian trailing just behind my shoulder. Beyond me, the room glows gold, the mahogany surfaces gilded with a soft amber cast like the dull half-light of memory. Walls of glittering tomes amplify the effect, catching the illumination and stretching it over their leather skin so that in stepping over the threshold, it seems as though we have left the night behind entirely and arrived into a blushing dawn.

Like the rest of Norland, the library has been transformed for the Hearing—a new creature wearing its predecessor's skin. Interspersed throughout the room, fire leaps in the bellies of bowl-shaped bronze holders, fragrant smoke emitting from the caches of incense that hang above the dancing flames. Where a clutch of worn armchairs used to rest, twelve obsidian thrones now line the back wall of the room, their blocky forms like rotten teeth curved in a sinister grin. Ten of them are occupied by figures in crimson robes that seem to ripple in the flickering light, the fabric rich and glossy as fresh blood. Two of the chairs are empty.

My eyes dart to the first vacant throne—the Saint Manor seat, its former occupant now confined to her house, awaiting a much less friendly trial than this one—before drifting back to the second chair. My father's chair.

Or at least it was, once.

In the center of the library, Essie stands facing away from Killian and me. Her trailing black waves have been twisted into a riot of spiraling curls and piled expertly atop her head, a silver comb in the shape of a fox snapping from within the ebony mass. Below them, the elegant ivory swoop of her neck extends, her gown covering her shoulders, but dipping low enough to expose a crescent of her back: her shoulder blades, jutting from her skin like ax heads.

And then, of course, there is the dress itself—the same one Cressida had Madame Villette fit for me, not so very long ago. My sister is clad in a layered gown, a ruby satin garment overlayed with a diaphanous overgown of darker crimson lace, rosebuds meticulously stitched onto the delicate fabric. Taken together, she resembles nothing so much as a silk-tipped sword with her rigid posture and elegant ensemble—a lady and a king all at once.

I'm still lingering at the fringes of the room, watching her, when the Councilor seated in the center-right chair—Manor Lord Hyacinth Ballantine, her olive complexion and wry hazel eyes, common Ballantine traits, leaving no question as to her identity—breaks from the rollicking debate long enough to snap her gaze over my sister's shoulder, to where Killian and I stand in the shadow of the entrance. My thoughts unravel like a fraying thread as the Manor Lord rises, her robes billowing in a cloud around her, the silver circlet of intertwined ivy leaves around her forehead glinting intimidatingly in the light. Beneath the beatific veneer, her expression is hard. Curious.

"A moment, my Lords," she calls, the chatter dying at her command like the waters of a lake smoothing over. "It seems the candidate has a challenger."

Murmurs ripple through the rest of the Council, the stirring of their forms like a many-limbed beast as their attention catches on me, then Killian. With their shadows pulled longer by the firelight, their red robes and silver circlets, they appear almost godlike; their stares are constricting, a snare tightening around me. The pressure intensifies as my sister turns, too, as her gray eyes find mine. Unlike the others, Essie's movements are smooth with a liquid elegance, a snake readying to strike.

"Merrick," she coos as she takes me in. "What a surprise. I must admit, I didn't think you had it in you."

I bristle, repulsed. Before I can gather my thoughts, Essie is clearing her throat, twisting back to face the Council. "My Lords, please, allow me to apologize for my sister's interruption," she says coolly. "I believe she got rather too comfortable with wearing the title of Vessel while I was away. Now, if we may continue with the proceedings . . ."

"I haven't come for the title." At last, my words come. I step forward, lift my chin in challenge. "Excuse my intrusion, my Lords. I would not disrupt these proceedings, but I cannot allow you to continue while knowing that you are being deceived." I inhale, readying myself to continue. "You see, my sister has been lying to you all."

A second round of whispers, louder than the first. The petite Councilwoman in the farthest left chair—Manor Lord Florabelle Carrington—scoffs, peering down her bladed nose at Essie and me. "Lying?" she repeats shortly. "Whatever about?"

"Whether the stable boy fancies her or her sister more, no doubt." Lord Percival Warchild, only a few years older than Essie and I, slouches on his throne, a laconic smirk spreading across his full lips. "We have no time for children's rivalries, girl," he says, waving a lazy hand at me. Rings glint on his fingertips, gems fat as berries. "Be on your way."

A few of the other Councilors—including Albion Tudor, whom I noticed observing Killian earlier, his vulpine features impossible to parse—chuckle at Lord Percival's remark. The remainder shift in their seats, their demeanors curious and slightly annoyed, but on the whole untroubled. A few seats away from Lord Florabelle, Lord Reginald Ibe stifles a belch.

Their indolence makes anger press against my ribs. *These* are our leaders—the esteemed Lords tasked with guarding all the Smoke? They remind me of a group of summer picnickers, sun-dazed and tipsy, lazily observing my sister and me like we are no more than a nuisance, a pair of flies circling above their heads.

Meanwhile, a rashlike flush has crept into the apples of Essie's cheeks, darkening them to an overripe pink. She's half-turned back toward me, any traces of amusement now absent from her expression. I can sense her readying herself for a fight; her gaze sharpens, a blade unsheathed.

"Yes, Merrick," Essie says. "You should know better than to bring such slander into this chamber without proof to support it. Of which I am certain you have none, since your claim is indisputably false." Her voice is low, but not so faint that I can't make it out. Her gray eyes linger on mine, a warning in them.

Can you meet my eyes and tell me now, you truly wish me dead? I shiver, the memory of her words seeping into me like marsh water.

"Oh, dear sister," I reply aloud. "But I do."

Steeling myself, I force my legs forward, closer to the Council—

though I'm careful to remain out of Essie's reach. "Please, my Lords, I beg of you to hear me," I implore, clasping my hands to my chest. "My father did not Nominate my sister as his Vessel—in fact, he made it explicitly clear to her that he never wished her to rule."

For the first time, I glimpse a trace of fear like a dark worm writhing in Essie's eyes, and my voice catches. If I continue with my speech, I realize, no matter the outcome of this night, I will lose my sister. Never again will she allow me to hold her hand as I sit by her bedside, or open the door to me when I come knocking—never will I be able to rely on her coolheaded wisdom to counter my brash temper. I will be, effectually, totally alone.

But then again, whether I voice it or not, in a way my family has been dead for a long time. My sister is not my sister; we have been but paper flowers growing from a barren branch, unaware of our own falseness, sustaining ourselves on the illusion of our grandeur.

"Prior to his passing, my father made my sister aware of a plan of his. A plan that, by my sister's own confession to me, she disapproved of." Swallowing, I force myself to hold Essie's stare. "The mistake you made, Essie—it has to do with moorflower, doesn't it?" I bluff. "Father had been sending crates of tea leaves out to the commoners, and to make up for the loss, you restricted our remaining stock. But when Father found out, he was furious. The tea was far more important to him, to his plan, than you realized." I flush a bright red as in my periphery, Lord Florabelle leans forward, intensely aware of the holes in my story but unable to stop now that I've begun. "You'd made a fatal error by denying it to the sentries, one so damning it prompted him to reveal everything else to you," I go on, to my sister. "He told you the truth—that you would never be Manor Lord—and for that, you killed him."

In front of me, Essie's cheeks have gone white. A deadly quiet has fallen over the room, the silence broken only by a pair of footsteps rushing past in the hallway outside. They grow louder as they near the library doors, then fade away.

My sister is the first to react—the wrath on her face is blatant, so potent it burns like acid against my skin. She opens her mouth—to rebuke me, no doubt—but before she can, there's a discontented grunt from the Council behind her.

"Wait just a moment—Lord Silas told his daughters about the tea?" Lord Percival leans forward in his throne, his knuckles curling around the gleaming jet armrests. He's scowling, but astonishingly, it isn't me his ire is directed toward—he swings his head from side to side, like an accusing finger pointing at his fellow Lords. "You lot said I was sworn to secrecy!"

Tearing my eyes from Essie, I frown. I've just revealed that my sister killed my father, and yet the first thing any member of the Council remarks on is *tea*? I ready myself to speak again, but before I can, the Manor Lord next to him—Manor Lord Clare Ireland of Queensbridle, I think—adjusts his spectacles, peering blearily through the lenses at his neighbor. "You are, fool," he drawls. "Their awareness must be a new development—though I must admit, I find it less concerning than the notion that Silas was distributing moorflower leaves to commoners. Do we know whether any of them were made aware of the plant's protective abilities?" He *tsk*s. "The very *last* thing we need is scores of villagers blathering about a tea that makes one immune to the Graylands. Can you imagine the hysteria?"

I go still. A tea that makes one . . . *what*? Instinctively, I glance at Essie, but my sister only glares at me with wordless fury, none of the astonishment I feel evident on her face. Almost as if she is not surprised by Lord Clare's words at all. As if she has heard them before, has already taken them in.

But that is impossible. What he is *saying* is impossible.

"Agreed, Clare." Manor Lord Lavinia Cachemar—one of my father's most resolute allies—sighs in her seat, rubbing a weary hand across her brow. "Silas must have gone soft in the wake of Artemis's death," she says, directing a glare at her companions from beneath her fingers. "I warned you all when they wed, he was overly fond of her. No such union would have been allowed in our predecessors' time, I said—but I was overridden by the rest of you, with your *modern* notions of love." She stabs at her armrest with a pointed nail. "It is imperative we halt the information spread here, and fast. You there—" She leans forward, her stony gaze pinning me. "Silas's youngest, yes—who all did he tell about the tea prior to his death? We'll need a comprehensive list—thank the Bloodletter he died before he could do too much damage."

"Don't ask her—she doesn't know anything, it's the sister we need—"

"—peasant-loving imbecile, I always knew his brother would have made the better Lord—"

"—Ianthe should have finished with the whole lot of them—"

The other Manor Lords explode into argument, but I barely hear any of it. I look back toward Killian and see the same panic dawning on his face that I feel welling within me, a fear like a sunrise, illuminating everything around it. *A tea that makes one immune to the Graylands* . . . surely I must have misunderstood Manor Lord Clare's remark, just now. He can't possibly mean— there can't be . . .

But even as I think through it, the picture shimmers into my view, and finally I understand.

Why my sister, supposedly adopted from a commoner orphanage and with no Manorborn blood of her own flowing through her veins, has yet to be corrupted by the mist. Why she remains human, rather than a Phantom.

Why my father was supposedly furious when he discovered

that Essie had stopped giving our sentries their nightly moor-flower tea—a mistake that, as she put it, she hadn't understood the severity of until he explained it to her. Hadn't realized that by denying our men a drink, she was threatening more than her relationship with them—she was putting their very immunity at risk.

Even why Mr. Birks, our former butler, sought me out after the turning began to work its way through him. Why he insisted that my father owed him something, a promise he had yet to fulfill by the time of his death.

What he was plotting . . . it needed to die with him, or our entire line— all that our ancestors have built, that we've worked for—would have perished instead. My sister's words—they are clear to me now; I see their truth like my own face in a mirror. What is the root of our Manor, if not our exceptionality, after all? Our ability to walk where others cannot, to travel into the white and back out and rule in the stead of those who are unable to do so.

What else would destroy us, more than the removal of that blessing? Of our gift?

Can it be true? That my father knew there was a way for all people, not only the Manorborn, to resist the Graylands' curse— and that to keep her power, my sister killed him for it?

My skin is clammy, my pulse howling in my ears. Was our immunity ever real, or has it always been a lie? Are the ancestors I've spent my life looking up to . . . nothing more than impostors?

"You idiot." My sister's reprimand is a razor, slicing cleanly into me. She steps forward, her hands fisted at her sides. "Do you think yourself noble? Are you pleased—"

The scream is the first in a chorus, a howling descant. It shudders against the door, arcing through the library—quivering, shrieking—before crashing to the ground in a climax like a breaking wave, a shock of cold water against your face. A second, equally piercing, follows it—and then, a third.

My blood freezes at the sound, inches through my veins like floes of ice. From underneath the library doors, wisps of a white, smoky substance appear, like ghostly fingers extending toward us. The ivory tendrils snake across the floor, separating and then weaving back together like river water parting around a rock. The sight is beautiful, in a way—the gentle beckon of a woman, luring you closer.

It is also not smoke.

Mist? My mind moves sluggishly, a slow moonrise. *Impossible.* How could it have gotten here, so far past our defenses?

As if on cue, the doors burst open, a man clad in a gray uniform with red epaulets—a sentry, I realize—darting through. Past him, my chest constricts when I see that the hallway has vanished, swallowed up by a thick bank of white. It extends from floor to ceiling, smothering as a fall of fresh snow, separating us from the rest of the house like a palm laid over our eyes.

No. On instinct, I take a step back, my thoughts running like a yolk from a cracked egg.

"M-my Lords." In front of us, the sentry stops to catch his breath, clutching at his knees. I hear the scrape of stone against wood as the Lords in question rise from their thrones behind me, some pushing them back in their surprise. "You must leave now—all of you," the sentry continues, panting. "The Graylands— they've breached the house."

"How?" My sister speaks over the resulting tide of muttering voices, moving past me in the direction of the doors. Despite the scene unfolding before us, her face is calm and composed, her rage at me now locked away. "That's not possible—you must be mistaken."

The sentry raises his head to address her, his shoulders still heaving with the effort of his breaths. "Saint sentries, Archdaughter," he says. "A group of them near the cliffside lanterns, enough to easily overwhelm the guard we had posted there. One of our men spotted them from the house and went to raise the alarm, but it was too late." He pauses, and do I imagine it, or do his eyes dart to me for a moment before flicking back to my sister? "Archson Ames was with them."

Ames. A strange dizziness overtakes me at the sound of his name, as if my head, my limbs, have all gone fuzzy. But, I want to protest to the sentry, Killian and I were outside less than half an hour ago—how could we have missed a Saint attack, if it came?

Because you were looking the wrong way, comes the immediate reply. Killian and I were ensconced in the orchard, part of the grounds that extend from the back of the estate and eventually turn into forest. The front of Norland, though, faces cliffside, where a line of lanterns blazes to ward off the fog coming in from the sea.

The library faces the cliffs. Barely aware of my own movements, I cross to the windows lining the back of the room, picking one at random and throwing the drapes open.

Milky white presses up against the windowpanes, pulsing gently like the sides of an enormous cat, rubbing itself lazily against the house. A horrible droning noise, like the screech of crickets, issues from the fog. Terror sets into me, pure and ancient—a howl of an emotion—as, while I watch, the mist in front of me parts, a single human hand reaching through the haze to slap against the glass.

Bam. Bam. The hand pounds at the window insistently, as if demanding to be let in, its long, ragged nails clicking on the panes as it does.

Letting the drapes fall back in place, I step away, fear a throbbing knot in my throat. Phantoms are coming. Phantoms are *here.*

"Lightkeeper, save us." Lord Lavinia speaks first, her features pale as if they have been cut from marble. Her words are punctuated by another cry from the corridor—this time succeeded by a bone-jarring thump, like a body being dragged to the floor. At the sound, the sentry rushes out of the library, raising his Ghost-slayer as he disappears into the fog. I wince as two shots ring out, then a scream.

His? Or a Phantom's?

Either way, if I don't do something soon, the monsters like the one I glimpsed at the window will be coming for us.

The world turns to honey, every second stretched to an impossible length as I turn in a circle, searching for a miracle; an escape route, a hidden passage I can use to whisk us all away from this. Better yet, to undo time altogether—to kill *this* before it ever arrives.

I don't find one, but my gaze does catch on something else.

Barreling past my sister, I rush to my left, where the nearest ceremonial bronze holder stands with its blazing bowl of fire. The heat is a searing brand pressing into my cheek, the metal cumbersome and heavy. I lean against it, heaving with my entire body weight.

The holder shivers. Wobbles on its stemmed base; then, with an earsplitting crash, tips over and falls to the ground.

Like a hungry dog, the flames previously contained within it leap out, racing across the wooden floorboards. When they arrive at the closest bookshelf, they hesitate only for a moment before climbing the structure easily, licking the edges of the tomes stacked within.

One by one, like a row of candlesticks, they catch.

And I jerk back to look as around me, my father's library begins to burn.

CHAPTER THIRTY-TWO

O urs is a nation drowned in mist, reborn of fire. Yet we are named for smoke.

As a child, I often struggled to comprehend it—why my fore-fathers selected such an unimpressive, even bland, feature of our land to memorialize in so grand a way. Against the orange fever of our lamps, against the white melancholy of the fog, who would think to look for the thread of gray winding over the horizon? Who would pause to consider the snow-dusting of ash draped over the site of a burning like a burial shroud, rather than the bones that lay beneath?

Now I understand. After the hot knife of fire, smoke is the proof of loss, a reminder that rebirth is always precipitated first by death. It is charcoal memory, staining your fingertips black. It snakes by your ear and whispers of the violence of resurrec-tion.

We are the Smoke because we are the second, forever existing in the shadow of those who came before. Those people and places we burned, so that we could rise from their dying embers.

And I have just sent another to its grave.

Norland House screams as the flames bite into it, and in its agonized cry I hear the sting of betrayal. It rumbles like a great beast; trapped within it, I am insignificant and minuscule. A parasite who has slain my host.

Like a rush of wind, the fire slithers outward, leaping from one bookcase to the next until I am circled by a halo of flames. The library is gilded in their light, the garish hue of a ripe orange; their heat beats down on me, the cumulation of every summer day I have ever known, of the red warmth of a stovetop and the thick woolen sensation of a bonfire burning too high.

Back by the line of thrones, smoke washes over the Manor Lords as they stumble over themselves and one another in their attempts to distance themselves from the blaze. I feel as though I could push them over with a blink of my eyelashes, so frail do they seem to me now. So *weak*.

"Run!" I yell at them. "The fire will hold the Phantoms back, but not for long. If you wish to live, go now!"

Roused by my cry, they scramble to obey me, moving in a mass lurch of limbs. Shoving past Essie, Killian, and me, they flee, pouring through the doors into the hallway beyond and vanishing into the fog. Some of the Councilors lift handkerchiefs or elbows to cover their noses and mouths; most, though, simply plunge onward without protection, their eyes large as those of startled does.

"Merrick—" Killian reaches for me, the brush of his hand jarring, as if my skin has been rubbed raw. His voice is strained, a warning evident in the urgent way he speaks my name: *We do not have much time.*

I nod in understanding, turning to my sister. Essie is standing frozen beside me, watching the fog spider closer to her with the terrorized expression of a rabbit facing down a fox.

Gingerly, I take her by the biceps, staying firm when she flinches. "Essie, we need to go," I tell her. "Here, Mr. Brandon will help you. Killian—" I motion to him, directing him to grab hold of my sister's other arm.

The second his fingers close over her, she rouses, coming to life as if waking from a deep sleep. "Get away from me," she hisses, tearing free of my and Killian's grasp. Breathing hard, she clutches herself as if we've burned her, moving clumsily away from the library entrance and the mist flooding through it.

Killian and I exchange harried looks. Gesturing for him to remain where he is, I take a careful step toward my sister, my hands held placatingly in front of me. "Essie, please—"

From the hall, another shriek rips through the haze—not the desperate wail of a human this time, but buzzing and resonant, the predatory yowl of a creature caught in the throes of blood-lust. Ice cracks through my chest; instinctively, I spin in the direction of the cry, then let out a shout of my own as a weight slams into me, dropping me to the ground.

"Merrick!" Killian leaps for me just as I process my sister's blurred form sprinting around us both, slipping out the door. *She pushed me.* The realization is an arrow through my chest, piercing me as Killian pulls me up, sets me on my feet again. She heard the Phantom and shoved me toward it like bait to secure her own escape.

"Are you all right?" Killian pats me down, examining me for injury, but I can barely focus on him over the crowding heat of the fire. The blaze is a dense forest, pressing ever closer, flakes of ash and charred bits of paper fluttering past my eyes like falling leaves. Its presence is all-pervasive, like a hand clasped over my mouth, scorching my esophagus.

I push him aside, tucking away the sting of my sister's betrayal. "Yes," I say firmly. "Let's go."

One step. To my back, a bookcase groans, plunges to the ground with the force of a felled tree. The crackle of leather book covers reminds me of human skin splitting open.

A couple paces more, and then we're through, out into the hallway. The fire has started to spread here, too, gnawing at the edge of the carpet, its force burning the area of the corridor we're in, for now at least, free of mist. As far as I can see in either direction, the area is abandoned. Though it's difficult to tell, the banks of fog seem thicker at one end of the hallway—toward the front of the house, which the Graylands must have already swallowed—so I start in the opposite direction, jerking my chin over my shoulder to ensure that Killian is following me.

Another swell of white confronts us as soon as we round the corner, fog leaking from the walls like smoke. I stumble back, colliding with Killian as up ahead of us, two shadowed forms emerge, mist stripping from their bodies like sweat.

Phantoms. I sway unsteadily on my feet. Only a few meters in front of me, a pair of beasts lurk in torn black suits, as if they've been ambushed on their way back from a ball. Their arms hang at their sides, hands ending in ragged, uncut nails that poke their way through tattered satin gloves. Sunk into their gray faces, sightless eyes dart left, then right, blank white moons.

One of the creatures sniffs the air. Thin, blistered lips part, and the beast lets out a squeal like a stuck pig, as if it senses its quarry nearby.

My jaw goes slack and fishlike with terror. Acting on impulse, I shove Killian back, retreating the way we came. As I do, the second Phantom stumbles blindly forward, its mouth contorted in a howl, its flesh weeping dual aromas of sweat and blood. From elsewhere in the house, resounding screams answer it—mourners' groans, maybe, or the calls of a pack readying for a hunt. They vibrate through the air, lilting and discordant and growing ever louder, ever closer.

How many of them are there? How many more will follow?

My next actions come like breaths, reflexive, impossible to stop. Steeling myself, I plunge rashly toward the Phantoms, ducking under their extended arms and coming up on their other side. Just as I'd hoped they would, the beasts pivot at my nearness, turning their attention away from Killian and toward me.

"Merrick!" His cry hits me in the throat, desperate and furious—but too late.

"Run!" I call back to him, and then I'm moving again, sprinting down the corridor. Roaring, the Phantoms stumble after me, bodies cleaving easily through the mist.

I race on, white haze burning my nostrils, filling my lungs until I cough. Though I don't dare glance back, I can hear the Phantoms' pounding footfalls echoing behind me; each one sounds like the beat of a funeral drum, as if I am marching to my own death.

Then: a few meters ahead of me, my gaze catches on a break in the fog. Branching off from the hallway I'm currently hurtling down is another, narrower passage—easy to overlook and relatively free of mist. Without pausing to consider, I duck down it, pressing my back against the wall, the chemical tang of adrenaline dripping down my throat.

For a moment, it is just me and the claustrophobic darkness, the mammalian sound of my breathing, like a horse's gentle pant. My pulse speeds as the Phantoms approach, then slows as they plunge past my hiding place, continuing their tear down the corridor.

The high-pitched whine of panic in my ear abates, fading to a hum. I'm allowing myself an exhale when the shadows painting the passageway I'm in shift and Ames Saint dashes out from between them, tackling me to the ground.

I collide, grunting, with the floor. A burst of agony obscures my vision, turning Ames to a silhouette above me, but I know his touch by now; his fingers drag over me with a gravity all their own, like stones in my pockets, pulling me down. He hisses in my ear and it is rotten fruit, it is sour chocolate, it is every luxury brought to the point of decay.

"Found you," he says, his voice torn and grating, his lips wet against my neck. "I hate these lovers' spats we keep finding ourselves in, dear. What do you say we kiss and make up?"

Beads of perspiration drip from Ames's forehead and onto my shoulder, leaving salty trails on my skin as I wriggle beneath him. Roughly, he flips me over, holding my face so I'm forced to look him in the eye.

"Do you like my little party trick?" he asks, gesturing at the mist that floods the hallway beyond us, colorless antennae of fog already reaching across the floorboards toward me. "I hate to ruin your evening, but it seems a fair price to pay, doesn't it, after what you did to me? You know, I'm not Mother's Vessel anymore—she stripped the title from me after you came to the Roost, to punish me for my failure. And to think, you Darlings got so worked up about a few measly breaches—a few peasants dying." He laughs, his breath sour where it tickles my nostrils. "I was being *merciful*. All along, I could have done *so much worse*."

He squeezes my cheeks harder, a violent caress, pinning me to the ground with his body weight. "You . . . you . . ." I cough, my throat dry, my tongue leaden in my mouth. "You've doomed us both."

Ames grins, a blade all its own. His left hand darts away and then something cold and hard is pressing against my throat. A gun—his gun. "Maybe that's true," he says, "but I think it's best to make certain in your case, no?"

He drives the muzzle harder against my skin and pain blooms, my heartbeat a trapped bird fluttering against the weapon's tip. My fear leaps through me, turning me wild.

I squeeze my eyes shut just as Ames's weight lifts off me, a sickening crack splitting the air like a snapped bone. Body shaking, I sit up. To my right, a second figure has Ames pinned to the ground, blood dripping from a fresh gash in his temple. Ames moans under the new man's hold, a sad, kittenish whimper.

"Killian." I call his name to the darkness as much as to him, but Killian hears, snaps his head toward me. His eyes soften when they meet mine, relief darkening his brown one and flaring light into its blue twin. His lips part, a response ready on them.

Then Ames thrashes beneath him, landing a punch to Killian's shoulder. The confidence slips from Killian's face as they tumble, each wrestling the other for control. In the dimness, I see Ames find his pistol again, ready himself to strike.

I cry out, but my shout is lost beneath the resounding boom of a gunshot. My vision blurs, fuzzes; when it clears again, Killian is standing, and Ames is splayed on the floor, his jaw hanging open and his face angled in my direction. Blood trickles from the side of his mouth, a spindly red river; his eyes are wide and unblinking, a vacant, empty gaze.

He's dead.

I wait for some emotion to grab hold of me—remorse, maybe, or guilt—but all I feel is a hollow ache in my stomach. Rising unsteadily, I move to his side and swipe a palm over his eyelids, closing them. His skin is still warm, flushed with the pink tint of youth, the illusion so convincing that I almost expect him to stir beneath me—to gasp awake like a fairy-tale prince, brought back to life by a kiss.

A wet substance soaks through my shoe, licking my foot. I stand, revulsion rolling through me when I see a slick of crimson already puddling around Ames's body, glossy as spilled wine. The sight of it—the hot feel of it on my foot—punctures the dreamy façade; one blink, and he is no longer a prince, no longer a boy at all.

He is only a corpse.

Unprompted, his words come back to me: *I could have done* so much worse. In a way, I know there is a measure of truth to his statement—know that what he did, he did for his mother, for his Manor. But then I think of the man and his family in the breached house all that time ago, think of the ruby line across his neck, and my heart hardens over again.

How many of our citizens have died, I wonder, because of similar Manorborn games? How many more will, if Essie has her way? If the Council does?

Looking up, I find Killian's gaze. He's breathing hard, Ames's Ghostslayer still clenched in his hand.

As if remembering himself, he helps me up, ushering me hurriedly down the narrow hall and into an empty room, blessedly clear—for the moment, at least—of both mist and smoke. It takes a moment for me to orient myself, but when I do, I see we've stumbled into what my mother used to call the Magenta Room—a compact drawing-room-like space and the sole area of the house that my father declared exclusively hers, after they wed. She used to host friends of hers in here when Essie and I were children; I remember rising on my tiptoes to peek in through the keyhole, catching a glimpse of tittering women and walls papered with vibrant cerise roses—the feature for which the room was named.

Killian shuts the door after us, barricading us in the room. Because of the way I'm positioned, just past the threshold, he has to reach around me to do so, my body pressed between him and the wood.

My belly clenches as he tucks Ames's gun in the waistband of his breeches, his gaze sweeping over me. "Did he hurt you?" he asks, his hand rising to lightly brush my throat, tender from where the pistol's muzzle dug into me. His touch is like a static shock, dulling my awareness to anything beyond the place where his skin meets mine.

Gritting my teeth, I glance away. "No," I assure Killian. "Nothing beyond a few scrapes. I'll be fine." I start to push past him, only to sway backward as a sudden wave of wooziness crashes into me, my legs threatening to buckle beneath me like twigs. The adrenaline that's carried me through the night thus far has finally withdrawn, leaving my muscles shaky and exhausted, my head full.

"Merrick . . ." Killian moves closer, gripping my shoulders through the sleeves of my dress. His finger catches in a rip in the fabric, a minuscule tear I haven't yet noticed, like a tiny gaping mouth. I go rigid as, like water circling closer to a drain, the pad of his fingertip grazes the frayed edges of the cloth, connecting with the patch of exposed flesh beneath.

A shiver whispers over my skin—ever so slight, but I know he feels it. Our stares meet naturally, as if we are complicit in something—as if we both have been caught red-handed and are waiting to see if the other will tell. Beyond the door, I can hear the faint echoes of screams—smell the charred promise of fire, eating its way nearer—but this close to him, the chaos outside Norland seems curiously distant. Like the rest of the house and this room exist on two sheets of paper, pressed together yet distinct, separate.

I am the first to break the stalemate.

"Thank you," I say, my throat dry. "For coming back for me."

His huff of laughter catches me off guard, humming in his chest. His gaze hasn't left mine, and it's oddly intimate, this manner of watching one another. Even the smallest shift in his emotions is laid bare to me, like a dog rolled on its back. "Please," he answers, the word falling from his tongue with a droll bluntness, "now, of all times, do you still insist on propriety? You know I had no choice in the matter."

Desire blazes in the pit of my stomach, his touch, his words, opening something, an empty space below my abdomen. The effort of holding myself back from him is staggering, like leaning over a staircase, fighting against the pull of the drop below. "I—I don't want that for you," I reply, my voice hushed. "Caring for me—returning to find me—because you have to. I want you to have a choice."

He shifts toward me—half an inch, perhaps more. "Is that all you want?"

I'm silent, still, rooting myself in his touch. Slowly—like a fern unfurling, like the crawl of the seasons—I open my palm and wind my fingers through his. Tug him closer. It feels natural, my thirst for him, like a yearning for light.

His lips brush mine so softly that at first, I can't be sure I haven't imagined it. But then his arms are around my waist and he's pulling me gently against him and I know, with certainty, that the question between us was always going to be answered in this way. A sigh escapes me as I angle my face toward his, deepening the kiss.

The scent of him—rain and salt—fills my nostrils. I can feel his fear in the way he holds me, can sense his hesitation even as he traces the curve of my neck, thumbs a lock of my hair. He's not quite sure if this is a good idea.

I'm not, either.

My hands push beneath his jacket, wrap themselves in the fabric of his waistcoat. Gingerly, like I am a dandelion cupped in his palms—like the slightest wind will break me apart, send me scattering—Killian pushes me more firmly against the door, his torso flush with mine. He hovers over me, filling my vision, his form infinite and elemental: he is heat and light and all warm things, a collection of sensations pressing against me. His mouth is wet and cold, finding mine again and again, and when his fingers touch my skin I feel like I am blurring past my own boundaries, like a storm at its peak.

A gasp slips past my teeth, then roughens as from the main corridor a far-off shriek sounds—the cry of a Phantom. At the sound of it, Killian's weight lifts off me, the dim interior air filling the space between us. His arms braced on either side of my head, he pants, his breaths tickling my nose and his eyes bright and wild, the blue one a glinting jewel.

Shaking his hair from his face, he pushes away from the door and steps back, swallowing. "We need to go," he tells me matter-of-factly, only the sandpaper quality of his voice giving away his unsteadiness. "Come here—I'll carry you out if you're too weak to walk. The sentries are gathering the guests on the front lawn—they've set up a lantern barricade there. It won't last long, but it should keep the mist back while we load carriages."

He moves to lift me, but I push him away, still blushing faintly at the heat of his skin. "Essie," I say, gathering myself. "And Cressida and Tom—do you know if they've made it out?"

His subtle flinch, like a stutter in his expression, tells me everything I need to know. "I . . . I've been making runs in and out, looking for you," he replies unconvincingly. "I didn't see them the last time I was on the lawn, but that hardly means anything—I'm sure they're out there."

Cautiously this time, he re-extends his hand—but I'm already turning toward the door, ignoring the screams of protest from my exhausted body, my smoke-filled lungs. "You focus on my cousin and Cressida," I tell him over my shoulder. "I'll find Essie. We can't just leave her here."

Killian's features darken. "Merrick, the fire is devouring Norland even faster than the fog," he protests. "If one doesn't get to you, the other will. And your sister—back there—she *sacrificed* you, like you were an animal. Less than that, even." His jaw flexes. "You owe her nothing."

"Neither did you owe me anything, but you risked your life to search for me, still," I reply. "It is as you said—in this, I . . . I do not have a choice." I step nearer to him, his warmth a soft, familiar blanket around me. Tilt my head back to meet his stare. "Killian, you once told me you desired my freedom. Allow me to be free in this."

Killian's reaction is immediate: he recoils, as if I've pressed my finger on a still-tender bruise. Anger slips across his features, then regret, resignation. All of them linger for only a second before drifting onward like bits of debris caught in a current, leaving only blankness behind.

When he sighs, hesitant and begrudging, I know I've won. Before I can react, he leans down, brushes a gentle kiss against my lips. It leaves a fluttering impression behind when he pulls away, like a moth's wings beating against my mouth.

"Live tonight," he says, and his voice is a murmur, a secret, whispered against my ear, "and whatever you think I have done for you, I shall consider your debt repaid."

He steps away, his words sinking into me like a seal pressed into hot wax. Something pounds in my chest—a second heartbeat, fragile as spring ice—as he moves to open the door, and suddenly I want him to touch me again, to promise me that this won't be the last time I see him. As if reading my thoughts, he lingers for a beat, his gaze tracing my outline against the darkness.

Then, as I asked him to, he twists the knob, and he runs.

Norland House is dying.

Like a burrowing insect, the fire has eaten away its insides first, stripping the rooms of their grand furnishings, bubbling the wallpaper and bursting the crystal chandeliers. Where the mist has been driven away, corpses line the halls, Phantom and human alike. Their bodies are blackened with soot, their faces so disfigured it is nearly impossible to tell which are monsters and which are not.

Of course, I have met several monsters myself over the course of this night, and none of them bore the features of a Phantom.

Now the blaze has turned its attention to Norland's skeleton. The creak of collapsing timber echoes above my head, entire sections of the estate's floor giving way to gaping holes, the splintered wood surrounding them like jagged teeth.

Dry air scorches my lungs as I heave in another inhale, my windpipe a desert, parched and cracking. Halting briefly to catch my breath, I lean against a doorframe—one of the few the fire hasn't touched.

I searched for Essie on the ground floor, to no avail. By the time I finished scouring the first level of our estate, the flames had overtaken it completely, rising like walls across every exit and making escape impossible. With nowhere else to turn, I've been driven to the second floor. The wooden floorboards are hot under my feet, burning the soles of my slippers as I limp forward, no real destination in mind.

Haze clouds my mind, muddling my senses. Smoke or mist, I do not know; either way, it will take me. There is no third level of our estate for me to ascend to after the fire pounces on this one. Nowhere else I can run.

No one coming to save me.

Did Essie escape? The question pounds at me urgently. Despite all she's done, the notion of her death still makes me feel like withering every time I consider it. So long as she survives, I think, I can justify this ending for myself, perhaps even find some bleak poetry in it. I tried to take Norland from her; now it will take me.

A cool breeze strokes the planes of my face. I turn, blinking the fog from my eyes. To my right stands an empty guest room, as yet unclaimed by fire or mist. A small balcony extends from it, its glass doors propped open to let in fresh air.

Hope budding behind my breast, I pass through the room and walk outside, half-drunk on the dizzying plumes of smoke I've inhaled. Above me, the sky is black and endless, the moon an eye turned unfeelingly on me. It is difficult to believe that were this any other Nomination Hearing, in a few short hours the Council would be escorting their newly proclaimed Lord onto our grounds, to draw a blade across their palm and drip their blood over the earth. The wheel of our province would begin to turn once more, cycling through leaders and seasons, but held forever in order by the axis at its center: our Manor.

Below me, Norland's gardens have been overlaid by mist as pure and glistening as a first snow. Coal-colored smoke streams from the house's broken windows, the air bitter with the taste of soot. Darling blood will be spilled here today, but there will be no resurrection to follow it. Rather, our line will join our estate in the ash.

The creak of a loose floorboard disturbs me, pricking the hairs on the back of my neck. Movement in the room behind me—someone is there, I'm almost sure of it. I can detect their careful steps, their slow approach toward me.

"Observing your empire, are you?"

The temperature plunges, an icy knife lodging in my chest. My muscles like iron, I turn around.

Standing between the thrown-open doors to the balcony is my sister. Essie's elegant gown has been reduced to little more than a collection of barely-held-together tatters, hanging from her slim body like pauper's rags. Scorch marks dot her long gloves, some still glowing with lit embers as if someone has smoked a cigar and used her body as their ashtray. But it is her face that disturbs me the most. Essie watches me with undisguised hatred in her eyes, her skin sallow and waxen, indistinguishable from that of the corpses I passed in the halls.

"Essie." I move back reflexively, only to run into the balcony railing. The metal presses into my back, my pulse rabbiting in my ears.

Essie steps forward, across the threshold. "You know, Father loved this house like his child—or should I say more than his children?" she says, gesturing behind herself to the ruined carcass of our estate. "He would hate to see what you've done to it. What you've done to me, too, though I doubt he would care so much about that."

She hisses, cringing as a breeze gusts past us, irritating a patch of raw, red skin on her arm. Along with the wind, noises catch in my ear: muffled shouts, the far-off sound of a horse's whinny. Immediately, I feel myself loosen. The sentries' barricade—I'm on the wrong side of the house to see it, but it must be holding.

I face down my sister, drawing my shoulders back in a manner more confident than I feel. "Come with me," I tell her. "The sentries are evacuating guests—if we reach them, we can still escape, Essie." I hold out an arm, inviting her to take it. "We can survive this."

But Essie only laughs, advancing closer. She smells like charred wood, acrid and sour. "Oh, my little sister, how naïve you are," she mocks. "Haven't seen enough yet to understand—whether I live tonight or not, there is no future for me. Nor you—not after what you've done."

Her mouth strains in a grimace. "Why couldn't you just be *grateful,* Merrick—just thank me for saving our family, our way of life?" she growls, her words thick with resentment, like clotting mud. "If Father had told the commoners the truth about the moorflower tea, do you think they'd have thanked him? Have praised him for his selflessness?" She shakes her head, a warped chuckle slipping between her teeth. "No, they'd have driven us all to our graves by now—and in much less kind a manner than I did, I'll wager. And yet you just *couldn't* . . . let it . . . be."

Quick as a leaping cat, she darts forward, pinning me to the balcony railing. I cry out as the rail digs into my flesh, agony momentarily turning my vision white. One of Essie's hands presses hard against my shoulder; the other wraps viselike around my throat.

"How long?" I cough, desperate to keep her talking. "How long has there been a cure?"

That laugh again, torn and mangled. "There has always been a cure, you imbecile," Essie sneers, her eyes blazing with disdain. "Maybe not right at the beginning, but for over a century, at least. As long as the Manorborn have been intermarrying, diluting their own bloodlines with inferior lineages, there have been defects—those who did not inherit their parents' gifts." Her fingers tighten their grip over my neck, my airflow cutting to a trickle. "Do you truly think the Manors would have given up their own when that began to happen?" she continues, her words sickly-sweet. "No, they spread rumors about sentries turning to discourage poor breeding, even allowed a few to do so on occasion—cautionary tales, to scare families into good behavior. But for everyone else . . ." Her voice drops to a reverent whisper. "There is the moorflower."

I swallow, feeling my throat move against her hand like a stone in her palm. "And only the Lords know of it?" I ask, recalling the argument in my father's library.

Essie nods, bitterness coloring her expression. "It is neater that way," she says. "The sentries are dosed routinely—a precautionary measure, as I believe you puzzled out—but for everyone else, the tea is just . . . tea. An exclusive blend, of course—hard to source and generally only available to the Manorborn—but still, something almost all of us drink every day. Without it, who knows whether the Manors' immunity would hold, or whether, for many of its members, their gift would have withered away by now." She smirks, a mirthless curve of her mouth, like a sickle. "Better to stay ignorant, if you ask me."

To my great relief, she seems to lose herself in her story for a moment, her grip around my neck lightening. Breaths rush into my lungs, clearing my head. "Silas, of course, was overly generous," she spits. "Overly . . . careless. Letting me take over sentry duties, and not telling me the necessity of their nightly cup!" Her lips curl. "He was furious when he learned that our men had started turning, but really, he only had himself to blame. And the sentries . . . they couldn't wait to go running to him with complaints about me. Not a single loyal man in the lot of them." She scoffs. "After he died—after I named myself Vessel—I considered giving them back their precious tea, but . . . I suppose I wanted to punish them for a little longer."

My stomach twists with disgust as I watch her smile stretch wider. "I know it was cruel of me," she says, the satisfaction in her voice evident. "Yet . . . didn't I deserve a bit of revenge, after what they'd done to me? After all this entire family has done to me?"

I open my mouth, another question ready, but Essie's confession seems to snap whatever measure of restraint was holding her back. She steps closer until her chest is flush with mine, her grasp on me tightening again.

"It is better that it ends this way," she snarls, spittle flying from her bloody lips. "With what we know, the Council would never let us rule—we are too much of a risk. Better, then, that we die together, as Archdaughters, than live disgraced." Her fingers flex, my pulse a bird beneath them.

I choke against her hand, gasping for air and finding none. The world turns fuzzy, swims in incomplete patterns. I focus on the sensations of Essie's fingers against my windpipe, her spoiled breath panting against my cheeks. Grunting, she clenches my throat harder, making me gag.

"Essie," I gasp, around her squeezing grip. "Behind you—a Phantom—"

She rears back, shock twisting her features. "Wh—"

Her voice rises to a garbled shriek as I swing my free arm toward her face, raking my nails down her cheek and neck. Howling, she releases me, clutching at her scraped flesh. With her other hand, she flails for the balcony railing, her legs buckling beneath her.

Time slows, overtakes me like a tide pulling me under. I watch from outside myself as her chin snaps to the side, her eyes locking with mine. I lose myself in the gray of her irises—always so calm in our youth, a lake at winter. Now frothing with terror.

Then there is a snap like a cord splitting, and I am back in my body again as my sister tumbles over the rail and falls, plunging like a sparrow with her wings cut, toward the earth. The fog is a cloud, parting around her; I brace for the sound of an impact, but it never comes. Instead, the Graylands smooth over the place where her body vanished and silence resumes, the stagnant, heavy quiet of death.

I collapse in a heap on the balcony floor, alone, as Norland House burns around me.

EPILOGUE

TWO WEEKS LATER

Cloud Abbey, the Faulk Manor seat, sits on the crest of a hill, presiding over the land below with the regal elegance of a queen. From my bedroom window on the west side of the estate, I can watch the sun as it sets, see how as it edges toward the horizon, its waning light casts the house in a bronzed glow like a torch held aloft. To the nearby towns, the estate must appear immovable: a fixed point, as much a part of Norrin as the streams that cut through it, as the seashore they flow to, forever standing guard against the waters beyond.

The Manors have dressed themselves in the garb of gods, have feigned immortality. But I have seen my own fall now; I know they are fallible. That they can die.

A fortnight I have been here, tucked in a guest room in Cressida's family home, caught somewhere between a refugee and a guest. Thanks to the work of Killian and the other Darling sentries, the vast majority of the guests who attended the Nomination Hearing—including all ten present Manor Lords—escaped

Norland House unharmed. But though the fire I set was enough to keep the Graylands at bay, it came at the cost of our estate. Norland, the house my forefathers claimed as their own, the seat from which every Darling born in the last century has reigned, is no more, and neither is my title.

I should have been buried alongside them both—would have been, if Killian had not managed to fight his way back through the inferno, arriving at the second-floor balcony shortly after I'd sent my own sister to her grave. He saved my life, but it was not enough to keep our Manor from falling—on that count, at least, my sister was correct. It took only two days after the event that the newspapers have now dubbed "the Shrouding" for the Mortal Council to declare that the Darling line had proved itself incapable of fulfilling its sworn duties, deciding in a near-unanimous vote to dissolve Sussex and divide its lands between our neighboring Manors. Only Elodie Faulk dissented.

So far, the Faulks have been hospitable enough—feeding me, lending me clothes from the wardrobes of Cressida's five sisters, swatting away the visitors that buzz around the perimeters of Cloud Abbey like flies—but though I have not found it yet, I am certain even their charity has a limit. That soon I will cross it and then . . . what? There is no more Norland House to flee to, no more suitors to offer me their hand. There is only my discovery, the one the Manors are doing everything in their power to keep me from spreading. Even Cressida's grandmother, whose kindness is the only reason I am not out on the street like a beggar, refuses to engage with me on the topic of the tea. My sole attempt to address it, the first day I arrived at Cloud Abbey, resulted only in her chilly insistence that I was confused. And, as she made clear to me, there was no room in the Faulk household for confusion.

I debated, then, simply bringing news of the moorflower to the people—letting it spread among them, grow like weeds beneath the Manors' feet. But with no proof, with my own reputation in tatters . . . my claims sounded feeble even to me sometimes. So I said nothing.

Two weeks after Norland's fall, I'm lounging in the Faulks' drawing room, stabbing at an embroidery hoop, when Cressida comes to visit me. She's dressed for travel, dark velvet gloves reaching to both of her elbows, her ruffled bonnet still tied under her chin; whether she's coming or going, though, I can't tell.

"I'm glad to see you're keeping yourself occupied," she says, observing me from the threshold as I work the needle in and out of the fabric. I'm unsure if the arch in her thin brow is one of sarcasm or sympathy as she moves forward, stepping into the room. "A mind in mourning suffers when left idle—at least, that is what I've found."

My eyes lift from my task to flick over her ensemble—all black lace and elegance, the estranged twin of the outfit she wore after my father died—and guilt floods through me like hot blood. Essie's ghost has haunted me since the night of the Nomination Hearing, the image of her face as she fell overlaying the blackness behind my eyelids when I lie down to sleep. In my memory, she is pale and surprised, in disbelief of my betrayal even as she plunged toward the ground.

Sometimes I feel as though I will never be clean again. Like all I am is the bad fruit pruned from my family's tree, good for nothing except to be tossed away.

"I came to speak with you, Merrick." Cressida takes another step toward me, drawing me back to the present. "Forgive me that I have not been able to spend much time with you these past weeks. It has been"—she dips her head—"overwhelming, to say the least."

I lift my shoulders in a shrug, her apology prickling uncomfortably at me. "As you said," I reply, averting my gaze. "We have all been in mourning."

"Yes, well," Cressida continues, shifting the topic. "One of your sentries paid me a visit the other day, while I was in New London. Killian Brandon, or Moran, rather—do you remember him? He had some fascinating things to say about the attack at the Nomination Hearing—and your sister's role in it, if you can believe that."

My skin heats, as if lit embers have been stoked beneath my flesh. *Killian.* I haven't seen him since the Nomination Hearing— I'd heard, vaguely, that his father had called him back to Kyrie— but he's become a familiar presence in my slumber, his words slipping into the space between sleep and reality, lingering like afterthoughts as I wake. *Live tonight, and whatever you think I have done for you, I shall consider your debt repaid.*

Cressida's bait gives way to a hook, a sharp spike of interest through the heart. She has me. "You spoke with Killian?" I ask. "What did he tell you?"

"The truth," she replies simply. She glances sidelong at me, her cheekbones like blades. "About your sister—who she was, and the truth she attempted to bury. That the Manors have helped her bury."

I turn back to my work, my fingers trembling against the thin spine of my needle. In the weeks since the Hearing, I've tucked Essie's actions deep within me, left them to fester like a mildew—a damp stain unfelt and unseen by anyone other than myself. Like if I held them for her, it would undo the death blow I dealt.

"It matters not," I say, laying my embroidery hoop aside to face my cousin-in-law more directly. "The Manors have made it clear to me that Essie's secrets are best left in the ground. And even if I attempted to unearth them, they would only discredit me—it would be pointless."

Cressida hums, her skepticism evident. "That may be the case," she replies. "Killian, however, seems to believe otherwise."

Closing the distance between us, she produces a letter from the folds of her dress and passes it over to me. The envelope is the color of pine needles, heavy and expensive, an unbroken seal a blot of crimson blood in its center. Glancing at Cressida for approval, I break the wax, sliding my finger along the envelope's lip. The paper within feels like cream when I take hold of it, smooth and cool.

I lift the letter to my eyes and begin to read.

Merrick,

Your father had more friends before his death than you realize. Warden Savager of Cael has agreed to support our cause—and more beyond him, too. They know what you have started, and they wish to help you finish it.

We have not yet reached the end. We stand only at the beginning.

With admiration,
Killian

P.S.—I have changed the terms of your debt. Your living is no longer enough—I must see you again.

ACKNOWLEDGMENTS

No book is written alone; mine, even less than most. *The Monstrous Kind* would not exist without the tireless efforts of the below group of people. The time, belief, and support they have given me, and this novel, are far beyond that which I deserve, and it is an honor to have the opportunity to acknowledge them in these pages.

First, and foremost, thanks to Krista Marino, who means more to me than she knows. Krista, you saw Merrick's story in my messy, stitched-together first draft eons before I was able to, and it is because of you that I was finally able to find the tools to set her free. You have taught me to be a better writer and a better editor; most importantly, however, you are a wonderful person, and one whom I count myself lucky to know. Cheers to many more Alamo nights in our future, and thank you for starting *Housewives* so we could talk about it. I promise, I will now begin *Vanderpump* in return.

I cannot speak of editorial feedback without also thanking Arianne Lewin, my faithful partner in the trenches for—I think—almost a year as we worked to turn this "book" into a Book. Ari, thank you for kindly saying no to all my bad ideas, and patiently staying on the phone with me until I unearthed a good one. You helped me find the heart of this narrative when I thought I had lost it, and for that, I cannot express my gratitude enough.

Next: without her agent to console her, a writer is just a sad girl crying over *Gilmore Girls* reruns. Thank you to Sarah Landis, my hero (but truly, Sarah—you are my hero) for listening to me, advising me, and caring for my book like no other. Your wisdom could fill a hundred novels this length, and if you told me to jump off a cliff, I would say it sounded like a great career direction and get going.

Thank you to my Delacorte Press cohort—Beverly, Wendy, Kelsey, Hannah, Bria, Ali, and Rebecca—for supporting me in taking this step, and in all others. Thank you especially to Ali for reading the very first version of this story and for brightening my weekdays with your own work, and to Beverly for her endless guidance and leadership. It is a blessing that I get to do this with you all by my side.

A hundred thousand thanks, too, to my larger RHCB family: Tamar Schwartz, an exceptionally kind human and the best managing editor on the planet; Colleen Fellingham, who is always able to see what I cannot; Ken Crossland for making this interior beautiful; Liz Dresner and Trisha Previte for the cover of my dreams (as well as martini chats); Barbara Marcus, Judith Haut, Gillian Levinson, Nicole Yeager, Kortney Hartz, Erica Henegen, Sarah Pierre, Kris Kam and the entirety of the RHCB publicity and marketing departments, Joe English and the stellar RHCB sales team, and so many more. Thank you to every person who took the time to write to me with a kind word about this book—it means the world to me. As well, a very hearty thank-you to Molly Powell and Hodderscape for bringing *The Monstrous Kind* to international shores and caring for it so excellently, and to Hannah Vaughn, Joe Veltre, and the team at Gersh for guiding me through the equally foreign land of Hollywood.

Thank you to Amélie Wen Zhao, Erin A. Craig, Ava Reid, Allison Saft, Sophie Kim, Emily Thiede, Gabi Burton, and A.M. Strickland, for taking the time to read and support my work, and for sharing your own with the world.

Now, to those who have been with me since the beginning: thank you to Cathy Berner, who taught me how to love books, and who loved mine even when I doubted. Thank you, too, to my writing partner, Isabel Banta, for standing by my side from the first draft to the last, for the hours of *Love Island*, the laughter, the feedback, and, above all, the friendship. My birthday twin, it is a gift to have met you.

To Mallory Abrenica, my first and forever best friend; my Georgetown Girls, Avery Beam and Meredith Rasmussen, with whom I would drink Long Island Iced Teas and karaoke any night of the week; and Merlyn Miller, who makes New York feel like my home—I love you all deeply. To my FYSAs—thank you for letting me join your flock, for poker nights and all-you-can-eat sushi, for trips upstate, for making me laugh and, quite simply, making me happy. I try to cherish the good things in my life; the friendship I have with you all is one of the best of them. Last but not least, to all my friends, far and near, who have given me their time when I needed it, who have believed in me, challenged me, and sharpened me: there are too many of you to name, but please know, you have made me a better person, and a vastly more interesting one. I hope this book is worth your wait.

These final few mentions are the hardest. It is impossible to put into words all that my family has given to me, and for me. Mom and Dad, thank you for always pushing me to step beyond my own boundaries, whether that be moving to New York or writing a novel, and for teaching me how to be brave. I am so proud to be your daughter. Andriana—thank you for being one of my very best friends as well as my sister, and for never giving up on me. And, Milo, I am so grateful for your endless creativity and humor, which inspires me every time we speak. I love you all, and promise that no characters in this book are inspired by any of you.

O: George Saunders once said, "Love just *is*, and you happened to be in the path of it." Thank you for being in my path—for your patience, understanding, and your complete comprehension of me. Because of you, I know that life can be kind. *Seni seviyorum.*

To conclude—thank you to Jane, who is separated from me by multiple centuries, but whose work nonetheless found me when I needed it. Telling stories is how we speak to the dead; I hope, if you were here to read this novel, you would enjoy my interpretation of yours.

ABOUT THE AUTHOR

Lydia Gregovic is an author and editor of young adult fiction whose identity is rooted in the Texas Gulf and along the coastline of Montenegro. She currently lives in New York with her complete collection of the works of Jane Austen and several half-dead plants. *The Monstrous Kind* is her first novel. You can find her at lydiagregovicwrites.com.